The author of over 50 novels, Anna Jacobs grew up in Lancashire and emigrated to Australia, but still visits the UK regularly to see her family and do research, something she loves. She is addicted to writing and she figures she'll have to live to be 120 at least to tell all the stories that keep popping up in her imagination and nagging her to write them down. She's also addicted to her own hero, to whom she's been happily married for many years. In 2006 one of her novels, *Pride of Lancashire*, won an award for the Australian Romantic Novel of the Year.

THE TRADER'S DREAM

Bram Deagan dreams of bringing his family from Ireland to join him in Australia, where he now runs a successful trading business. But when a typhus epidemic strikes Ireland, it leaves the Deagan family decimated, and it is up to Maura Deagan to look after her orphaned nieces and nephew. Forced to abandon her own ambitions, Maura recognises that their only hope is to join Bram in far-away Australia, so they set sail via the newly opened Suez Canal. It is only when a storm throws her and fellow passenger Hugh Beaufort together that Maura realises this journey may also give her a chance to pursue a dream she set aside long ago — to have a family of her own. That is, until someone from Hugh's past threatens to jeopardise everything . . .

ANNA JACOBS

THE TRADER'S DREAM

Complete and Unabridged

CHARNWOOD
Leicester

First published in Great Britain in 2012 by
Hodder & Stoughton
An Hachette UK company
London

First Charnwood Edition
published 2015
by arrangement with
Hachette UK
London

A catalogue record for this book is available
from the British Library.

ISBN 978–1–4448–2385–1

Published by
F. A. Thorpe (Publishing)
Anstey, Leicestershire

Set by Words & Graphics Ltd.
Anstey, Leicestershire
Printed and bound in Great Britain by
T. J. International Ltd., Padstow, Cornwall

This book is printed on acid-free paper

This book is dedicated to the memory of
Allan Frewin, whose warmth and humour
are sorely missed by his family
and many friends.

Thanks once again to Eric Hare,
my nautical mentor,
whose input is invaluable.

Prologue

Western Australia: 1869

Bram Deagan watched his assistant check that the Bazaar had been tidied up properly at the end of the day. He couldn't help marvelling sometimes that this spacious store was his. Two years ago he'd come to Australia with a little money and a few goods, risking everything to set up as a trader, bringing in goods from Singapore.

His gamble had paid off so quickly, he felt breathless sometimes. He was selling some goods himself and allowing other people to rent stalls in his Bazaar or let him sell their goods for a percentage. What upset him was the thought of his brothers and sisters living in poverty in Ireland, those who were married as well as those still at home. He knew only too well how hard their life was.

He turned as Isabella came into the Bazaar. Forgetting about business, he moved towards her, holding out one hand. Oh, he was a lucky fellow, he was so! He'd found himself a wife in Singapore, and now he had a baby son and an adopted daughter.

Isabella took his hand and they stood there smiling fondly at one another like a pair of young lovers, instead of a happily married couple of thirty-two.

'Are you too tired to take a stroll with me in

1

the last of the evening sunshine?' she asked. 'Sally will look after the baby.'

'Never too tired to spend time with you, my love.' He nodded as his assistant came to stand nearby. 'Go home now, lad. You've worked hard today and deserve your rest. I'll finish locking up and let the night watchman in later.'

As Bram and his wife strolled along the street, he took a deep breath and put his hopes into words. 'Our Bazaar is doing so well, Isabella. I can hardly believe it. I just wish . . . Well, you know I have another dream and . . . '

She finished it for him. 'You want to bring your family out to Australia and help make better lives for them.'

'Some of my family. Not my parents.' His father had tried to coerce his sister Ismay into marrying a man she hated, even condoning rape to force her into it. Just thinking of what his father had done made Bram feel sick with disgust.

Isabella's voice was soothing. 'No, of course not, my darling. But Ismay's happily married to Adam now, so everything has turned out for the best. And since Dougal and Adam have bought another ship together, well, things are going to be even better, aren't they, with more regular shipments of goods?'

He nodded. No use dwelling on the past. 'Do you think my other brothers and sisters will want to come to Australia? Would you mind if I suggested it to them and got permission to sponsor them?'

She laughed. 'Fancy asking me if they'll want

to come, when I've never even met them. And no, of course I don't mind you bringing them out here.'

'Ah, you're a wonderful woman. I do love you.' They stopped walking to smile at each other again. If they weren't in the street, he'd give her a hug. Ah, he gave her a quick hug anyway.

A little flustered by this public display of affection, she pulled away. 'Stop that! How many of them do you think might come, Bram?'

'The more the better. I doubt they'll all come.' He grinned. 'And even if they do, I won't expect them to live with us.'

She frowned. 'I hope they don't all come at once. We're not rich.'

'We're rich by their standards. And that's partly thanks to you. Your silks are selling so well. You're a very good businesswoman, and thank goodness I have you to do the accounts.'

'I love silk and Xiu Mei sends me some beautiful lengths.'

'It was a lucky day for me when you went to work for Mr Lee in Singapore.'

'I was lucky too. The Lees are lovely people. I'm glad we're still dealing with them. Just one thing, Bram. We'll need to buy a new house before any of your family arrive. We've been thinking about it for a while. Time to act.'

He loved her so much, he'd buy her the moon if he could. 'We'll do it soon.'

'I know you don't want to move. We've been very happy in our little cottage.'

'We have. The new house won't be the same, however grand it is.'

'Nothing ever stays the same, Bram. But given your position in Fremantle trading circles, you do need a better house.'

'I'm not a member of the elite. Bateman, Marmion and the Samson brothers nod to me in passing, but I don't even want to be as rich as them. I'd have to neglect my family to manage businesses that big and I won't do it.'

'It's a wise man who knows when he's happy.'

'You're happy too, aren't you?'

'You know I am.'

'So, I'll write to Ireland and ask Kieran Largan, the landowner, to put my offer to all my brothers and sisters. Then maybe he will help any of them who want to come, as he did my sister Ismay.'

'I'd have thought you'd write to your family directly.'

'Most of them aren't much good with the reading and writing, and anyway, I can't send a letter to the house, because my father would probably throw it away unopened. I don't even know where my married brothers are living now.' He paused and smiled dreamily. 'I don't think *all* my brothers and sisters will come here, though I wish they would. Just imagine it, the nine of us together in Australia — even the little ones, like Padraig, Ryan and baby Noreen. No, that won't happen, more's the pity. But some will come here, surely?'

He started walking again, with her arm in his, saying softly, 'I can dream of that, can't I? Dream of having some of my family living near me?'

1

In Lancashire, Maura Deagan, senior housemaid at Brent Hall, cast a quick look over the drawing room, nodding approval. The new maid was a hard worker and had learned her job quickly, thank goodness.

Maura turned as she heard footsteps, nodding to the butler who joined her in the doorway. She always tried to slouch when standing next to him, because she was three inches taller than him, taller than most of the indoor servants, the only tall person in her family that she knew of.

'You have a knack for finding good maids, Deagan, and for training them too.'

'I do my best, Mr Pearson.'

'The mistress wishes to see you. She's with the housekeeper.'

'I'll go at once. Thank you for letting me know.'

She found Mrs Brent sitting with Mrs Jerrold, who was on very good terms with the mistress. Both of them smiled warmly at Maura.

'Do sit down,' Mrs Brent said, with one of her fluttery waves of the hand.

Maura knew better than to take an easy chair in the presence of her mistress, so sat bolt upright on the edge of a spindly chair.

'Miss Walton has written to give notice. Her mother is no better, so she will have to move back home permanently to care for her.'

Maura tensed, not wishing ill to Miss Walton, but hoping this meant what she thought.

'I'd like to offer you the position of Assistant Housekeeper in her place, Deagan.' The mistress cocked one eyebrow and waited.

Maura couldn't help beaming at her. 'I'd be delighted to accept, ma'am, and I promise you I shall do my best to give satisfaction.'

The housekeeper nodded approval. 'That's good. I'm certain you'll do a good job, Miss Deagan.'

Maura nodded. Addressing her as 'Miss' showed that she'd risen in the servants' world. She would eat her meals with the senior staff after this.

'Now . . . you'll need to move into the Assistant Housekeeper's bedroom, so if you can pack Miss Walton's things for us, we'll send them to her.'

'I'll see to that today, ma'am.'

The housekeeper made a gesture of dismissal, so Maura stood up and left the room quietly. But she was unable to resist twirling round for joy once she'd left the family's part of the house.

'You got the job, then?'

She turned to see the butler smiling at her. 'Yes, I did, Mr Pearson.'

'You'll be housekeeper here or elsewhere before you're through, *Miss Deagan*.' He smiled and walked on.

She certainly hoped so. It was her dearest ambition and she was working very hard to achieve it. Not that she minded hard work. She went to examine the bedroom that would be hers from now on. *Miss Deagan's room. A place of* her very own. She'd done it, climbed up another rung of the ladder.

She'd come to Brent Hall as a junior housemaid after her husband died, and had known within days that she'd found a safe place at last. You shouldn't be relieved at someone's death, but she had been. Vincent had been her family's choice and they'd nagged and browbeaten her into accepting him.

But he'd been even duller to live with than she'd expected, though at least he'd never ill-treated her, as some men did. That was probably because he was too lazy to bother thumping her, just as he'd been too lazy to bother her much in bed, which was probably why he hadn't fathered a child.

That last thought was part sadness, part relief. If she'd been left with a child, she'd not have been able to take advantage of the opportunity to make a new life for herself. She'd come to Lancashire before she told her family what she was doing. The doctor's wife had found her a place as maid at Brent Hall. It was a good distance from Shilmara and the north-western part of Ireland, far enough that they couldn't stop her doing what she wanted.

She'd sent money to her parents when she first came here, mainly for her mother's sake, but after they'd died a few years ago she'd refused to send anything to her brothers. Sean and Eamon especially would have wasted it on drink.

She kept sending letters every year, though. It seemed wrong to lose touch completely with your family.

Well, reminiscing wouldn't get the work done. She ordered Miss Walton's trunk brought down from the attics, and had packed it within the hour. Then she brought in the maid of all work to clean out the room thoroughly, just on principle. This time she didn't have to ask anyone for clean sheets, because managing the bed linen was now one of her tasks.

By nightfall, she had her own possessions in place. She didn't have much: a few books, a couple of good ornaments she'd bought second-hand during her annual week's holiday, which she'd spent in Manchester last year, having a fancy to experience city life. There was also a Bible.

Father Patrick hadn't approved of anyone in Shilmara besides him reading the Bible, so of course when she was given one at Brent Hall, as all the servants were, she'd started to read it gradually, in between reading any other book she could get her hands on. The words in the Bible were so beautiful she had to go slowly and sometimes ask Mr Pearson or Mrs Jerrold what they meant.

She didn't hesitate to do that, because she wanted to improve herself. She'd listened carefully to how the master and his family spoke as well, and now felt she had only a hint of an Irish accent.

In the evening the housekeeper came up to check that everything was all right, bringing her an old spirit burner and matching kettle, somewhat dented. The family had no more use for it, but Maura was delighted because she'd be able to make herself a pot of tea whenever she wished.

If she stayed here at Brent Hall for the rest of her life, she'd be more than satisfied. It was a large house, with twenty indoor servants. The family had lots of visitors, who brought their own servants, so there was always something going on and new people to chat to after work. Maura did so hate to be bored and idle.

Perhaps she'd look around for a position as housekeeper somewhere else in a few years' time. Who knew where that might take her?

But she'd never, ever marry again, even to fulfil her old dream of having children of her own. She looked in the mirror on that thought. She was thirty-five, with threads of grey in her dark hair at the temples, getting past the age of child-bearing anyway.

You couldn't have everything in this world. Some people had almost nothing. She should be content with the comfortable life she'd made for herself. And she was . . . most of the time.

* * *

Since it was the first fine day for a while, Kieran Largan decided to get some fresh air and sunshine. In Ireland you could only rely on two things about the weather: it would soon change and rain was never far away. Still, the rain made the place beautifully green and lush as long as you raised your eyes above the mud.

He rode round his own acres first, gazing up at the hills on the other side of the lough. The water was sparkling in the sunshine today and a light breeze was riffling the surface. He turned his gaze to the fields closer at hand, where his horses and cows were grazing peacefully. All was as it should be in his little kingdom.

Skirting the woods, he let his mare pick her way delicately along the path that led to the village.

The three cottages he'd built in the past year were a sight to gladden any landowner's heart: neat and tidy, weatherproof, with gardens full of summer flowers and vegetables. He'd made sure they were offered only to good tenants who would look after them. And he'd also insisted they kept their own bodies and clothes clean, as well as the cottages. He didn't want the new places infested with lice and fleas.

He wished he could afford to build better homes for the rest of his people, but thanks to his father's bad management, he had to be careful with his money.

Reluctantly Kieran made his way into the village itself. He'd promised his wife Julia that he would speak to Father Patrick. Again. The priest didn't believe in educating girls and was making a nuisance of himself at the little school which Julia paid for with her own money.

Before Kieran inherited the estate, the girls had fulfilled their educational obligations by learning to chant the alphabet, read simple words, count up to a hundred and do plain sewing for an orphanage run by some nuns — when the girls bothered to turn up, which wasn't nearly as often as they were marked present.

And his father had not only allowed this, but encouraged it.

No chance of letting the boys and girls share a school in Shilmara, even now, because Father Patrick would throw a fit and forbid it in church.

Unfortunately, the man couldn't let well alone with the girls and regularly erupted into the school to check on what was going on. And the priest would often accost Kieran to complain about the schoolmistress, or the lessons, or anything else he could find to pick on. What a sour-tempered fellow he was! Not a good example of a modern priest.

Kieran had had a word with the bishop's secretary only the previous month about getting someone younger assigned to the parish, but they said they couldn't move Father Patrick, because the old man had been there for forty years.

Speak of the devil. He braced himself as Father Patrick stumped out of the church and stood waiting for him, arms akimbo.

'You'll do me the favour of having a word with that young besom of a schoolmistress, if you please, Mr Largan.'

'Oh? Why?'

'She's teaching those girls compound arithmetic now, as if simple sums aren't enough. She'll addle their brains, so she will, and then what sort of wives and mothers will they make? And she doesn't have them saying their prayers often enough. They'll grow up into heathens like her.'

'Miss Drew isn't a heathen; she's just not a Catholic.'

'And what is that but a heathen?'

'We've had this argument before.' Kieran suddenly grew so angry about the priest's interference that he added sharply, 'I came here today to ask you to stay out of the girls' school from now on, Father. Let Miss Drew get on with her work. She's a very capable woman and my wife is supervising what she does.'

The old priest stared at him incredulously, then seemed to swell up, anger turning his face a reddish purple colour. 'If *I* can't go into that school, then neither will those poor little girls,' he roared. 'Their parents will listen to me and keep them away from contamination.'

'The law says all children must attend school. There's been no attempt to ensure there was a proper school for girls in all the years you've been parish priest, so I think you have nothing to complain about if my wife takes charge of their needs.'

The priest opened his mouth as if to let out another bellowing complaint, then clutched his chest, his eyes rolling up. The world seemed to stop moving for a moment and Kieran could only stare aghast as Father Patrick fell like a log and lay there, his belly jutting up, one arm outflung.

Suddenly jerking into action, Kieran yelled for help, dismounting to kneel by the still figure. But he could see at a glance that the priest was beyond help, as ugly in death as he had been in life. He reached out to close the staring eyes.

12

The villagers crowded round, exclaiming and pushing.

'Stay back.' He chose two men and told them to carry the body back to the tiny presbytery, where the housekeeper, Kathleen Flynn, was standing at the door, waiting for the man she'd served for over thirty years.

It was the first time anyone had ever seen her weeping.

Unfortunately, the body was so heavy, they had to ask another man to help them. Whoever had gone hungry in this poverty-stricken village during the bad times, it hadn't been Father Patrick.

⋆　⋆　⋆

A week after they buried the priest, the sickness appeared in the village. At first no one thought anything of it, beyond a brief sadness when a couple of children and old Bridie Malone fell ill and died, because children and old people were always at risk.

But then others fell ill, people of all ages, many of whom had seemed to be in good health. Some of them died too.

Terrified of whatever it was passing to his own wife and small children, Kieran brought in the doctor from Enniskillen to ask his advice.

The doctor examined the sick people and came up to the house, standing outside and asking that Kieran come and speak to him there.

'Keep your distance, Mr Largan!'

'What on earth is it?'

The doctor spread his arms in a helpless gesture. 'Typhus, I'm afraid.'

Kieran's heart sank. 'How has that come about? Do you know how it starts?'

'We do have some idea. Medical knowledge is always improving. It's passed through lice, usually. Body lice and less often, head lice. Dirty houses and people let it sneak in and then they in turn spread it to others.'

'I see.' Kieran remembered his obligation as host. 'Can we offer you some refreshments before you go? We can bring something out here, if you prefer it.'

'No, thank you. There have been several similar calls, so I fear we're in for an epidemic of typhus in the district. I'll be checking myself for lice each day before I join my own family. Such a bore but at least I have the facilities set up to do that in my stables. Do you have somewhere to check and delouse people?'

'Yes, in a room off the laundry. But it's only needed usually for new servants. My wife makes sure our house servants keep themselves clean. I'm keeping an eye on the tenants of my new cottages, but I can't do much about the other cottages or the people in the village, especially those with absentee landlords.'

'Pity, that. But if you can take some extra precautions, you'll be doing yourself and the village a favour. I fear this is likely to be a bad outbreak. Buy the poorest people some clean clothes, if necessary, and make sure they wash them and their own persons and change their clothes regularly. There are plenty of garments

14

for sale secondhand at the market in Enniskillen. Ask the new priest for help. People will always listen to a priest.'

'They haven't sent us one yet.' He'd had to bring in a priest from the next village to say the last rites for those who died and that man had been reluctant, making sure to keep his distance from people.

'Well, let's hope your new priest arrives soon, Mr Largan. You'll need all the help you can get. In the meantime, you've young children of your own, so you'd better keep your family and servants clear of the village for several weeks, until there have been no more cases reported for two or three weeks. And afterwards you'll have to find some way of cleaning up the whole place permanently if it's not to happen again. Maybe you should consider building a washhouse and a bathhouse too, in the village.'

'Good idea.' It wouldn't cost a fortune. He'd manage it somehow.

The doctor looked at Kieran sympathetically. 'It's hard to be faced with this, I know. You're a good landlord and doing your best for your people after years of neglect.'

'Well, at least you seem clear about what we should do. That'll help.'

'I've lived through it before. We had serious outbreaks of typhus in Ireland after the potato famines of the forties, and it still crops up from time to time. Watch out particularly for people with running noses, a cough, vomiting or a high fever. Some get a rash of red spots on the trunk, arms and legs.'

Fear settled in Kieran's heart as he watched the doctor's man drive his master away in the smart little gig. If anything happened to his family, he didn't know how he'd face it.

He decided to write to the bishop again, asking urgently for a new parish priest to help deal with this, emphasising that there was no one now to give the final rites and bury people decently.

★ ★ ★

Three days later Father Hilary O'Neill arrived in the village in a cart loaded with trunks and odd items of personal furniture. He smoothed his black cassock as he stared round, feeling the weight of responsibility for his first parish settle on his shoulders.

As he'd been told, the presbytery was easy to find because it had a cross on the roof and stood next to the church. Both were small, but were neat enough structures, built of the local stone. The church had a couple of small stained glass windows which would brighten it up, he was sure. He did love a stained glass window with the sun shining through it.

He walked up to the front door of his new home and hesitated, not sure whether to knock or just go inside. He didn't want to startle the housekeeper.

The matter was solved for him by the door being opened by a thin, elderly woman with a pinched mouth.

'I'm the new parish priest: Father Hilary.'

She didn't attempt to smile, but crossed herself. 'Heaven help you, then. 'Tis a bad time for you to arrive, Father. You haven't touched anyone yet, have you?'

He looked at her in surprise at this final comment.

'There's typhus in the village and the doctor says it comes from lice. You'll find no lice in this house, but there are all too many elsewhere, so I don't want you bringing them in.' Her scornful sniff said what she thought of the people in the village. 'I'm Kathleen Flynn, *Miss*, housekeeper here.'

The house was immaculate, but Kathleen peppered her tour with so many instructions about what he should and should not do that by the time it was over, Hilary was already certain he couldn't live with the woman.

'Remember not to go near anyone till the epidemic is over,' she repeated as she finished showing him round.

'If someone needs me, of course I'll go to them.'

She stared at him in horror. 'But you might bring the typhus back with you!'

'I'm sure I can wash myself each day and check the seams of my clothing.'

She shook her head and walked away, muttering.

★ ★ ★

Later that day a man rode up to the presbytery. Kathleen appeared in the priest's study without

17

knocking. ''Tis Mr Kieran, the landowner. He won't be coming into the house, not till the epidemic is over.'

Hilary watched the man for a moment longer from the window, noting how easily he sat in the saddle as he waited for someone to come out to him. He was quite young, though older than Hilary, and had a kindly expression, not an arrogant one, thank goodness.

'What are you keeping him waiting for?' the housekeeper said in her shrill voice.

Hilary went outside and introduced himself.

'I'm sorry for not dismounting to shake your hand, Father. I will help you in any way I can, though.'

'I understand,' Hilary said. 'Is there somewhere in the village to nurse the sick? In case a lot of people succumb?'

'Not really. The only buildings of any size are the church and the two schools, and the schools aren't very big at all, just one room each.'

'Then we must take people into the church, if necessary.'

'If you need money, ask me. And once this is over, I'll make sure we clean things up properly, I promise you. I hope I'll have your help and support with that?'

Father Hilary nodded. 'Oh yes, you will for sure. I can keep an eye on the village for the time being, with your permission. If things get bad, I'll send for some of the nuns I've worked with who look after the poor. They're wonderful with the sick. I've never succumbed to anything before, so shall put my trust in the Lord that

18

he'll continue to protect me. And you can be sure that if I come to the big house, I'll wash myself first and change my clothes.'

The man on the horse smiled at him suddenly, a very sweet smile. 'I think you're the breath of fresh air we need for this parish, Father Hilary. May I wish you a very warm welcome, in spite of these sad times.'

Which was a good start to the day, Hilary thought, as he watched Mr Kieran's horse trot away.

* * *

That evening Kathleen presented Hilary with a burned offering of a meal, slamming it down on the table with a scowl. He pushed the plate aside. 'Can you do no better than that?'

'I've been busy. It takes a lot of work to keep a house clean in times like this, if others won't take care.'

'And we'll be even busier if the epidemic continues. I can't eat this. I presume you have some bread and cheese? If not, I must go and beg one of my richer parishioners for food.'

She continued to glare at him. 'There's bread and jam.'

'That'll do for tonight.' He glanced at her sour face and decided he didn't want to live with her. He always did have trouble turning the other cheek to people who upset him. But it would look bad to dismiss her, so he tried a bit of cunning. 'I shall need your help from tomorrow setting up a soup kitchen for the poor. We must

19

all lend a hand while the typhus is in the village.'

'*What?*' She made a throaty noise of revulsion. 'No! I'll not do it. I'm not going near them till it's over.'

'I must insist.'

'In that case, I'll have to give notice. I'm too old to change my ways and I've no wish to risk catching my death from those feckless folk.'

'They're all God's creatures. We can't turn away from their needs.'

She sniffed. 'I'll be leaving tomorrow. I've a brother who will take me in till I find another place. I'm owed some wages. Father Patrick died suddenly.'

'Let me know how much.'

He didn't protest about the amount she named, which he was sure was larger than the reality. He took the money from a cash-box he'd found in the desk, a box with more money in it than he'd expected in such a poor parish. Well, he could put it to good use once he was sure it belonged to the parish and not Father Patrick himself.

He wasn't sure how he'd find another housekeeper, but the Lord would surely provide.

★ ★ ★

The butler stopped Maura on her way to luncheon in the servants' hall. 'There's a letter for you, Miss Deagan. Well, I think it's for you. Wasn't Phelan your married name?'

'Yes. But I reverted to my maiden name after my husband died, as I told Mrs Jerrold when I

20

started here.' She looked at the envelope he was holding out, feeling apprehension run through her. Letters from Shilmara were written by the parish priest on behalf of her brothers, usually to give her bad news. The first one after she'd come to Brent Hall had been to say that her parents had died. Father Patrick had added the hope that she wouldn't change the arrangements for sending money to help her family, since times were hard.

She'd been too late to attend the funeral, so had merely written back to her brother Sean saying she was sorry their parents had died, but she wasn't going to send any more money. She needed to save as much as she could for her own old age. She didn't want to be dependent on anyone again, not ever.

There had been no replies from any of her brothers. Which didn't surprise her. They hadn't had much education. Her nephew Bram could write, but he was in Australia. Two of her other brothers had emigrated to America a while back, followed by their children and families. The priest had written to tell her about that each time. So many people were leaving Ireland. Cruel, it was.

She took the envelope from the butler reluctantly, studying the writing on the envelope. It was very neat, nothing like Father Patrick's untidy scrawl, and she didn't recognise it. On the back it said Fr Hilary O'Neill, Shilmara. Had they a new priest in the village, then? She hoped so.

'You think it might be bad news?' Mr Pearson asked gently.

21

'It's the only reason anyone from Shilmara would write to me.'

'Perhaps you'd like some privacy in which to open it, Miss Deagan?'

She was tempted to say she'd open it later, but she'd never considered herself a coward before and wasn't going to start now. 'Thank you, yes. I'll go up to my room for a few minutes, if that's all right. I'll just let Mrs Jerrold know.'

'I can tell her for you. I have to consult her about something.'

Maura walked slowly up to the rear attics where the women servants were housed. It was quiet at this time of day. Her room had been cleaned and her bed made. That daily service still delighted her, visible proof of how she'd risen in the world.

The small room with its dormer window was bright with sunshine. She took the letter to the table near the window, stretching out one hand to catch the warmth of the sun's rays. She came here to read in the evenings sometimes, but at that time of day she needed a lamp.

She sat turning the envelope round and round in her hands, not wanting to open it, then clicked her tongue in exasperation. 'Oh, don't be such a coward, Maura!' She ran her finger along the top of the envelope to open it, spreading out the single sheet it contained.

Dear Mrs Phelan,

I'm the new priest in Shilmara and I'm writing on behalf of your family with sad news. There has been an epidemic of typhus in the village and many have died.

I'm sorry to tell you that your brother Eamon and his wife, and all but one of their five children, have succumbed to the contagion, which has taken some families and spared others.

The survivor is a little girl of nine, your niece Brenna. She's being cared for by Mr Largan at the big house, together with other orphaned children, but we need to make more permanent arrangements for her.

Since others in your family have either left the country or cannot find the money to feed another mouth, you seem to be Brenna's only close relative left. I'm hoping that you'll take on this task of raising her. If not, she'll have to be sent to an orphanage.

Mr Largan says he'll help you in any way he can and will pay the cost of your fare to Shilmara, whether you're coming to make arrangements for an orphanage or to stay here.

Yours in God,
Hilary O'Neill

Maura stared at the letter in horror, then reread it slowly. But the message stayed the same.

She couldn't believe so many of her family had died at once. Her brother Eamon had been a strong man. And four of the children dead too . . . ah, that was sad. Tears filled her eyes as she stared down at the letter.

There was no getting out of it: she'd have to go back to Shilmara, something she'd vowed never to do. She couldn't leave her niece to go into an orphanage.

But oh, she didn't want to go back!

2

Kieran heard the church bell tolling and looked across the luncheon table at his wife. 'Another one. Padraig Deagan this time.'

Julia's shoulders sagged and tears came into her eyes. 'Oh, that poor boy! How many more must die? Life in the village is going to change drastically after this.'

He covered her hand with his for a moment. 'We must do our best for them afterwards, turn the village into a cleaner, better — and safer — place for us all.'

There was the sound of a horse clopping slowly past the front of the house, an animal that always sounded tired. 'There's the post arriving. Are you expecting anything?'

'Not particularly, though it's always nice to have letters from my family.'

Five minutes later, the butler brought in a silver tray with several letters on it and presented it to his master. 'Kevin Gill is taking a cup of tea in the kitchen, sir, in case you wish to send any replies back with him.'

Kieran examined the first envelope, which he was sure had been deliberately placed on top by his butler. 'This is from Australia. Bram Deagan's handwriting.' He shuffled through the rest then passed them to his wife. 'Nothing from my brother Conn again and the next ship won't reach England for a while. What's he doing with himself lately that he can't put pen to paper?'

She took the letters, glanced briefly at the handwriting on each but didn't open them. 'I'll stay till you've read the one from Bram. It may be something you need my help with, as it was when we made it possible for his sister to leave for Australia last year.'

Kieran used the silver paper knife, which was always brought with the mail, to slit the envelope open. After scanning the letter, he let out a soft 'Oh!' then reread it before passing it to her.

Julia read it more slowly, then looked up at him sadly. 'He doesn't even know about his brothers emigrating to America, let alone the deaths.'

'They said they'd write to tell him, but clearly they haven't done so yet, so I'll have to do it for them. There hasn't been time for my letter about the deaths of his parents to have reached Australia. It's probably not even got as far as Gibraltar yet. Sean and his wife went so quickly, it surprised everyone. And now Bram's lost his younger brother Padraig as well. And he won't know where the other brothers are, not even the one in England. He'll be devastated.'

'We must hope the two who went to America manage to find good jobs and then can pay you back the money you lent them for their passages,' she said rather sharply. 'You're all too generous with your tenants.'

'We have so much compared to them. It'll take time for the Deagan boys to have anything to spare in America, if they ever do, so I don't mind if they don't repay me. In any case, it was money

26

particularly well spent because leaving may well have saved their lives.'

'You're a lovely man, Kieran Largan.' Her voice was soft and the smile she sent his way was full of love. 'Do you think Bram's Auntie Maura will have received the letter from Father Hilary yet? He wrote to tell her that her niece Brenna had been orphaned and needed her, and now there are two more children in the family left orphaned as well. What are we going to do about Ryan and Noreen?'

Kieran shrugged. 'Maura should have got Father Hilary's letter by now, but if she comes straight back to Ireland, my letter about her brother Sean will probably cross her en route, which means we'll have to tell her the news when she arrives.'

'It's asking a lot for a single woman to take on responsibility for two nieces and a nephew, don't you think? How will she support them? She won't be able to continue in service.'

'We can help her a bit at first.' He laid one hand gently on her arm. 'We must, Julia. We have rooms here and the food won't cost us much.'

'Maybe she'll refuse to take the children. She has no reason to love her family. They nagged her into marrying Vincent Phelan and from what I've heard he was a lazy fool.'

'If she doesn't agree to raise them, I suppose the children will have to go into an orphanage.'

Julia looked at him. 'I know that you want to care for your tenants, Kieran, but there will be too many orphans after this outbreak. With the

27

best will in the world, we can't afford to take care of them all, not while we're still struggling to pull the estate into better shape.'

'I suppose not. But we can look after them till they find somewhere decent to go. That we can do, at least. I'll not turn any people from Shilmara out to tramp the roads.'

He reached for Bram's letter again, reread it and tapped it with his forefinger. 'Maybe what he's suggesting will help Maura.'

Her face brightened. 'Of course. That's it. She can take Noreen and Ryan to their brother in Australia! She and Brenna can go too. Bram wants his family to join him.'

'But will Maura want to go?'

'I don't think she'll have much choice with three children to care for.'

★ ★ ★

Maura realised with a start that she'd been sitting in her bedroom for some time and should have been back at work. She slipped the letter into her apron pocket.

When she went downstairs, nothing had changed and she felt it ought to have. Staff were going about their duties, all was in perfect order — except for her life, which had just been turned topsy-turvy. She'd better go and see the housekeeper and ask for leave to deal with this.

Mrs Jerrold's door was half open, which signified she was available if anyone needed her. She looked up as Maura hesitated in the doorway. 'Do come in.'

28

'Would you mind if we closed the door?'

The housekeeper nodded and gestured to a seat, waiting till Maura had taken it. 'Mr Pearson said you'd received news from home.'

'I have, yes. Bad news, it is too.' She held out the letter. 'Read it for yourself.'

When she handed the letter back, Mrs Jerrold said, 'You'll need to go back to Ireland to sort things out, of course.'

'I suppose so. I'd hoped never to return to Shilmara.'

'Were you that unhappy there?'

'Yes. The old landowner at Shilmara was a dreadful man, who tyrannised his tenants, and my father was a bully who pushed me into marrying a fool. My eldest brother Sean tried to do exactly the same to one of my nieces just a few years later, but Ismay ran away. She had more courage than I did.'

'I'm sorry you have to go back, but you can't deny you now have responsibility for a little girl who's been left alone in the world.'

'I know I have to arrange something for Brenna.' She looked at the housekeeper. 'But once I've done that, I intend to return.'

'You're not thinking of looking after her yourself, then?'

'I'm happy here. I won't leave the child in need, but I've given up my dreams of a better life for my family once, and I won't do it again. As soon as she's old enough, I'll find her a place in service.'

'Very well. You'd better leave by the first train.' Mrs Jerrold rang the bell on her desk and asked the maid who answered it to fetch the master's Bradshaw.

The railway guide was over a thousand pages long, but it was easy enough for the two women to work out that if Maura left within the hour, she could catch the local train to Manchester and go on from there to Liverpool, from where she'd take the night ferry to Ireland.

It was happening so quickly Maura felt a sudden wave of terror as she left the housekeeper's room. But the thought of Brenna steadied her. The child needed help and though she'd never met her, Brenna was her niece. Maura sometimes felt very alone in the world. How much worse must that be for a child of nine?

She hurried up to her bedroom to pack, sighing as she took a last look round. She had loved having her own room, relished the ordered life at Brent Hall and enjoyed the companionship of the other staff.

And why was she thinking of it in the past?

'I'll be coming back,' she whispered. 'I'm *not* giving up my life for my family again. *I'm not.*'

★   ★   ★

In Wiltshire, Hugh Beaufort gazed down at his little daughter in despair. Adèle was lying in bed, her face pale and her breathing laborious. She was wasting away before his eyes, often ill, and yet she never complained.

He looked at the doctor pleadingly. 'Is there nothing else you can do to help her?'

30

'It's in God's hands now, Mr Beaufort, I'm afraid. In God's hands.'

Then God was unkind, Hugh thought, to make a child of eight suffer so. But he didn't say that aloud because the doctor would be shocked, and heaven knew there had been enough to shock people round here since the child's mother ran away five years ago.

The doctor cleared his throat to get Hugh's attention. 'If she survives the night, you'll have some hope.'

'Till the next attack.'

'If she recovers from this one, the best thing I can suggest is taking her to live in a warmer climate permanently.'

'That would help?'

'Sometimes it helps. We never know who will benefit. Some do; some don't. But we both know she can't go on like this. She's had to fight for her life during each of the past two winters. It's late summer now and for the first time, she's fallen seriously ill before the winter. Her body is worn out, Mr Beaufort. It can't cope with another cold season, however well you heat the rooms.'

'Where do you suggest we go? Italy is in political turmoil from what I hear, and so is France.'

'I did hear of someone going to Egypt.'

'I don't think a country as alien to our way of life as Egypt would make either of us happy.'

'What about Australia, then?'

'Australia.' He frowned as he stared at his daughter. He'd once dreamed of visiting

31

Australia, but not for this reason. 'Hmm. I'll look into it.' If Adèle survived the night.

Hugh wasn't a religious man, but as the long hours of darkness passed, he kept watch over his child and prayed as he'd never prayed in his whole life before. If she pulled through, he would, he vowed, do anything, even give up the home he loved and take her to Australia.

And when morning came, he was given his first taste of a miracle: his daughter was still alive, ghost pale, sleeping restlessly, but breathing more easily at least.

Now it was up to him to keep her alive.

Hugh didn't want to leave his family home, but if it was the only way to help Adèle, then he'd do whatever was necessary.

Even go to Australia.

He suddenly remembered that his father's cousin had sent his son to Australia. Parker Beaufort was dead now, but Hugh could consult them as to why they'd chosen Australia. Surely they'd know a lot more than he did about the country?

He gazed out of the window at the garden. It was getting a faded autumnal look, after the lushness of summer. Berries already glowed red on the rowan tree, one of his favourites. It looked so beautiful when its foliage was young. There were still flowers here and there, but leaves were starting to fall and collect in sheltered spots.

Anguish speared through him. He'd never expected to move away from Weston Abbas once he'd inherited it. But then, he'd never expected to love his daughter so much, and still didn't understand how Sylvie could have abandoned the child to run away with another man.

He didn't miss his wife, but Adèle longed for a mother, he knew.

That he couldn't provide though. He was never going to marry again.

⋆　⋆　⋆

Maura sagged back in her seat as she stared out of the train window on the last leg of her journey. When they arrived at Enniskillen, she'd have to hire someone to drive her to Shilmara.

Or should she find lodgings for the night?

When she saw Seamus O'Dwyer in his donkey cart, waiting patiently outside the station for a last fare, she decided to go straight to Shilmara. She trusted him.

'Are you looking for work, Seamus?' she called.

He frowned at her as if unable to place her, then his face cleared. 'Is it yourself, Maura Deagan — Phelan, I should say.'

'I go by the name of Deagan again. And yes, it's me. How's Fionulla?'

'She's well and so are the children.'

'How many do you have now?'

'Five living. We lost two.' He crossed himself quickly.

'I'm looking for a ride to Shilmara.'

'Haven't you heard? They've got the typhus there.'

'Yes. The new priest wrote to tell me. I've come to make arrangements for my niece. It seems the rest of my brother Eamon's family have died, his wife *and* the other children.'

He stared at her in shock. 'All of them?'

'All except for my niece Brenna. So . . . can I hire you to take me and my luggage there?'

'As long as you don't want me to go into any of the houses or touch anyone?'

She was surprised at this till he explained that the doctor had spread the word about how the disease was passed on. 'Well, that explains it. We both know my family aren't — weren't the cleanest people in Ireland.' Nor had her husband been, however much she nagged him.

She stood thinking furiously, then said, 'I'd better buy Brenna some new clothes, then.'

'I heard tell Mr Kieran has the survivors in one of his barns, and has cleaned them up. She may be there.'

'He's the one who wrote to me, so I suppose she will be, but I'm still not going empty-handed. We don't need charity. Where can I buy some clothes for her? And I shall have to stay the night, after all. Can you suggest somewhere? And will you drive me to Shilmara in the morning?'

'You always were full of questions. But today I'm full of answers. You can stay with my wife's aunt. She takes in lodgers and she keeps a clean house. She'll know where to buy some clothes, and yes, I'll take you to Shilmara tomorrow morning. Though I'll have to charge you the usual rates. I have a family to feed.'

'I can afford to pay my way, as long as I'm not extravagant.'

'Jump up then and I'll take you to my wife's aunt. It's on my way home, so I won't charge you for that.'

'I insist on paying, Seamus.'

He looked at her, clearly torn both ways.

'You can't afford to be too generous. I'm paying.'

'I'll be thanking you, then.'

*   *   *

In the morning, Maura spent an hour shopping for second-hand clothes, then Seamus arrived to pick her up. As they jogged along, it began to rain and she unbuckled her umbrella from the side of her portmanteau.

'You always did think ahead,' he said with a grin.

'Do you carry nothing to keep yourself dry with?'

He fumbled beneath the driving bench. 'I use a sack for the moment. My cart's hood collapsed a few weeks ago, but I'm getting a better one put on the new cart I've ordered.'

She saw the pride on his face. 'You're doing well if you can buy a new cart.'

'I'm doing all right. I work hard, I don't drink and my Fionulla is a good manager.'

'Vincent was lazy and he drank.'

'You should have taken my brother when he offered.'

'Dan's a full six inches shorter than me. I couldn't.'

'Not six inches. Four maybe. Oh, all right, five.

He's married now anyway. Two children. Tell me about the grand house you work in.'

Seamus was interested in anything and everything. He always had been. So the time passed pleasantly enough.

An hour later they arrived at the big house, which had the same name as the village: Shilmara. 'If Brenna is staying in the barn at the big house, I'd better speak to Mr Kieran first.'

Seamus hesitated as they came to the end of the drive, looking at her questioningly, as if uncertain whether to stop outside the front of the house.

'The back entrance, of course! I'm still a servant.' She knew she was speaking too sharply but was unable to keep her voice calm. She didn't want this burden. Oh, she didn't want it at all!

She glanced towards the small lake to the left of the house, but then they turned to go round the house and she didn't look back at it. The water looked dull and grey today anyway, no glinting ripples. In weather like this, she always felt the water seemed flattened by the rain beating down on it.

There was no lake at Brent Hall, only the nearby moors, rolling in green waves to the horizon. She liked to look out of the attic windows at them, see the shadows of clouds racing across them.

She wished she was back in Lancashire now.

★   ★   ★

36

Hugh waited until Adèle was out of danger before going to see his relatives. They were happy to see him, less happy to talk about their son and he had to drag the information from them. Only by explaining about Adèle did he persuade them to confide in him.

'We don't talk about Parker,' James Beaufort said. 'He . . . made his own bed, was an utter fool with money. It couldn't go on. So we sent him to Australia.'

'Don't I remember that he got married out there?'

'Yes, but she was a nobody. Alice something or other. We don't associate with her now he's gone.'

'She had no children, then?' Silence. He looked at them in surprise. 'Did he have children there?'

'*She* claims her daughter is his. We don't accept that.'

The thought of someone abandoning a child upset Hugh. 'What if she really is his daughter?'

Another silence, then Claudia Beaufort said hesitantly, 'That does worry me, I must admit, Hugh. But how do we find out from this distance?'

'If I go to Australia, I can find the child for you, see if she resembles anyone in our family. After all, the red-gold colour is pretty common in the Beauforts.' He touched his own hair, which was darker than that of most of his relatives, but still on the golden side of brown. 'They were living in Sydney, were they not? Shall I go there? Is it the best place to live?'

'The widow has moved to the Swan River Colony and remarried. She wrote to let us know, asking for money for the child, something she's done several times.'

'It doesn't matter to me where I go as long as the climate is warmer than here. I can just as easily go to the Swan River Colony and look for the child.'

Claudia looked pleadingly at her husband.

James scowled and stared at the floor, drumming his fingers on his chair arm.

Hugh waited. This was obviously a bone of contention between the two of them.

'I suppose you'll never give me any peace if I don't do this, Claudia.'

'Please, James. I can't bear to think of our grandchild in want or being brought up roughly. I weep sometimes to think of it.' She turned to Hugh. 'If she seems to be a Beaufort, perhaps you could arrange for her to be brought back to England? I'd be happy to take her in.'

'What about her mother?'

'Pay her off. I won't have her here. He found her penniless in Singapore. No decent woman would be living in such a place on her own, without husband or family.'

He didn't argue with her that the mother might not want to let the child go. Time enough to worry about that if she did seem like Beaufort's child. 'Very well.' He turned back to James. 'So . . . tell me why you chose to send Parker to Australia? Was it because of the warmer climate?'

'No. It was because it was the furthest away of

38

anywhere in the world. That was the main reason.'

Hugh stared in shock at this blunt response.

'And we paid him to stay there. The money stopped if he came back. They call that being a remittance man. He was still fiddling with his ugly paintings when he was killed. The widow sent one back to us. It's in the attic. I wanted to burn it.'

Hugh hadn't realised how sharp the break had been with Parker. These two had kept their real feelings and reasons quiet, even from their family. Parker had been a fool, and had gone through a small but adequate inheritance in a few short years, but had the poor fellow deserved so distant an exile?

'What did he die of?'

'He was murdered by a deranged neighbour.'

'Good heavens! I'm so sorry.'

'It's a rough life out there. I'd hoped it'd be the making of him, but obviously not.'

Did he and Adèle deserve the same rough life? Hugh wondered. They'd done nothing wrong to merit exile. Hugh sighed. No, he mustn't think like that. There were good reasons for him going to Australia and he could come back if . . . He broke off there. She *would* live. She must.

He'd thought of selling his estate and buying another one in Australia. Now, he was beginning to wonder if he should keep Weston Abbas and rent it out. Yes, that's what he'd do. Maybe one day he'd be able to come back. Maybe.

But he'd take a piano and a guitar with him, because he couldn't live without his music.

Should he try to start some sort of business in Australia? Here, he had his estate to manage, and plenty of musical friends to associate with. But what would he do with himself there? He didn't like to sit idle. He'd already taken a share in various small trading ventures with some like-minded friends. Perhaps he could do some trading on his own behalf out in the colonies. The British Empire was, after all, full of people who needed various basic necessities and a few luxuries too. They might not find everything they needed in the Antipodes.

He'd have to look into it, ask around, learn quickly when he got there. In the meantime, he'd have a lot to do in a short time because they must leave before the winter set in.

Above all, this move was for Adèle. He'd take her nursemaid and perhaps the governess. He must make sure his little girl was well looked after by the two women, in all the ways a man couldn't manage, however much he loved his daughter.

On the way back he made a detour to London, where he purchased a new cottage piano, a beautiful instrument which he fingered lovingly in the shop. He arranged for it to be carefully crated and shipped out on the same vessel he would be sailing on, and would let them know which one it was when everything was settled.

On this visit to London, he didn't go to see his musical friends, wasn't in the mood for playing, couldn't even settle to listening to a concert at the moment, which was unusual for him.

His heart was weary as he took the train

home. Only for his beloved daughter would he even contemplate leaving everything else he loved.

But if she grew better, ah, then it would be worth it. He had to hold on to that hope.

★ ★ ★

When Seamus reined in his horse near the kitchen, Maura closed her umbrella and jumped down from the cart, hurrying across to knock on the door, leaving her umbrella propped against the wall outside.

She asked the woman who opened it if she could see Mr Kieran.

The woman, whom she knew by sight, looked at her warily and kept her distance. 'Have you stopped in the village?'

'No. We've come straight from Enniskillen. Why do you ask?'

'Mr Kieran's orders. We don't want the typhus bringing here. Come in then, Maura Deagan.'

She was taken first to the servants' hall and offered refreshments while Mr Kieran finished talking to his land agent.

'We'll look after Seamus,' Cook told her. 'He can sit in the stables with the men there and we'll send him out refreshments.'

'I can't send him away yet because I'm not sure where I'll be staying tonight.'

'Probably Mr Kieran will find you a bed . . . given the circumstances.'

Maura wasn't hungry, but forced a little food down and drank two cups of tea, trying to be sensible. Sensible! She felt like running away, felt as if some terrible fate was hanging over her head.

When a maid came to summon her, she found Mr Kieran and his wife waiting for her in a small, rather shabby parlour. Even the servants' quarters weren't as shabby as this at Brent Hall.

'Do sit down, Mrs Phelan,' he said.

'I go by the name of Deagan again, if you don't mind, sir. *Miss* Deagan.'

'Miss Deagan, then.' Mr Kieran looked at his wife and she shook her head slightly as if telling him to deal with this.

Why? Maura wondered. She already knew about her niece.

'You'll have got a letter about Brenna being orphaned, I suppose.'

'That's why I came.'

'I'm sorry about your losses.'

'Thank you. The letter was from a Father Hilary, but I've heard you have the orphans here. I've come back to arrange for my niece to be looked after. Then I intend to go back to Brent Hall.' She said that firmly, wanted to make it plain from the start.

'Ah. Well. There's something else happened, and you need to know about that before you come to any decisions.'

She looked from one to the other, alarmed by the sombre tone of his voice.

'The typhus has taken more of your family. Your eldest brother Sean and his wife have also died, leaving his two youngest children orphaned.'

'Dear heaven! What about the rest of his family? My brother Sean had a lot of children, I forget how many. I know my oldest nephew Bram is in Australia — in fact he and I were almost contemporaries — he's only a few years younger than me. But what about the others? There's one in England, isn't there?'

'Two of Sean's sons went to America with their families a while back, so they're safe from the typhus, but we don't know where they are. As to the son who went to England, he didn't let us know where he was. So your young niece and nephew, Noreen and Ryan, are left without family or means of support.'

She stared at them in horror, guessing where this was leading.

They said nothing, but she saw Mrs Julia touch Mr Kieran's arm, as if telling him to keep quiet and let this sink in.

Maura tried to say it calmly. 'I can't take on three children. How would I earn a living for us all? It's just not possible, I'm afraid.'

Relief coursed through her, then guilt followed swiftly at the thought of those two children left orphaned. She startled herself by bursting into tears, she who never allowed herself to weep. But it was all too much. Three children! Three children related to her.

Was she to send Noreen and Ryan into an orphanage? Everything in her cried out against the shame of that. She'd thought to find someone in the village who'd take in Brenna if she sent money regularly, but she couldn't afford to pay for three of them to be looked after.

She managed to stop weeping and blew her nose firmly, muttering, 'Sorry.'

'There is a way for you to manage,' Mr Kieran said quietly.

'I'm not marrying anyone else, whatever they promise.'

'Good heavens, no. We'd not ask you to do that.'

Mrs Julia moved to sit on the small sofa next to Maura, giving her a handkerchief and putting an arm round her shoulders. 'Listen to him.'

Something told Maura she wasn't going to like what she heard. Only she had no choice but to listen to what Mr Kieran was suggesting.

What had they thought up to trap her into taking on the children? Whatever it was, she wasn't going to say yes. She definitely wasn't.

★ ★ ★

In Australia, Bram woke up with a start. He'd been dreaming, a tangle of scenes from Shilmara.

Isabella reached out to take his hand. 'Are you all right? You were tossing and turning, muttering in your sleep.'

'I'm all right now.' He raised her hand to his lips. 'Just a bad dream. No, not bad exactly, but strange. I was back in Shilmara, but though I walked round and round the village, looking for my family, I couldn't find them. My parents' cottage was empty, and so were the others. I felt . . . unhappy.'

'It was just a dream, love.'

'I hope so. Only it felt real.' He shivered. 'In the meantime, Conn will be arriving today. I'll ask him to sell me a piece of land for our house.'

Conn Largan looked happy and rested, in spite of over a day's travel on horseback from his country home. He was a different man these days, now that his name had been cleared and his conviction and transportation overturned. He was even making friends in Perth and Fremantle, coming up from the country three or four times a year to buy or sell horses and meet his own kind.

'I thought you were bringing your wife this time.'

Conn rolled his eyes. 'I can't persuade Maia to come and live part of the year in the town.'

Bram didn't say anything but he guessed his friend's wife was afraid people would despise her because she'd lived with Conn before they were married. He and Isabella had discussed that and were fairly sure that was the reason. But though some snobbish people might shun her, there were plenty of others to make friends with. At least, he'd always found that.

'I wanted to talk to you,' Bram began. 'About some land for a house. I wondered if you'd sell me a corner here?'

Conn looked at him in dismay. 'I don't think there's enough land. I want to build myself a home here. It was one of the reasons I bought this place.'

'Oh. Well, yes. I quite see that. I'll have to look round the nearby streets. I don't want to live too far from the Bazaar. I need to keep an eye on things there.'

'I'll ask around,' Conn said. 'I've a couple of friends in the legal profession now and they often know about houses for sale before anyone else does. In the meantime, perhaps you can find somewhere to rent.' He snapped his fingers. 'What about the house Livia is renting from Dougal?'

'I doubt he'll turn her out.'

'She won't be staying there, surely? A woman on her own. She has to find a way of making a living for herself. We'd expected her to seek a job as a governess.'

'Or she might find another husband,' Isabella said.

'I'm sure we'll find something to rent or even to buy,' Bram said firmly. He didn't want Conn, who had been a good friend to him, feeling guilty about the land.

3

Hugh set about finding a tenant for his Hampshire estate. People wouldn't lease it, however, unless he offered them a five-year lease, and the family he liked best insisted on an option for another five years if he hadn't returned to England by then. And if he was selling it, he had to give them first refusal.

That upset him. It was a long time to give your family home into another's hands. As if he could ever sell Weston Abbas. Though Mr and Mrs Hinton seemed very decent, respectable people and he thought he could trust them to look after his estate and even his beautiful piano. Oh, how he hated to leave that behind!

Actually, in other circumstances he'd probably have liked the family. Now, he bitterly resented their pleasure at the prospect of coming to live at Weston Abbas.

Once that had been settled, it was time to explain to Adèle what was going to happen next. 'Darling, we need to talk.' He looked at the nursemaid. 'You'd better stay and listen as well, Jean.'

He pulled his daughter onto his knee and she nestled against him in the way that always tugged at his heartstrings. 'You know the doctor thinks you'll feel a lot better in a warmer country, and I told you I was making enquiries about going somewhere warmer?'

'Yes.' She cuddled her doll closer to her chest and waited.

'It seems that Australia will be the best place for us to live, so we'll have to start packing our things now and get ready to leave. Mr and Mrs Hinton, who came to visit last week, are going to live here and look after Weston Abbas for us.'

He raised his eyes to look at the maid. 'I'm hoping you'll come with us to Australia and continue to look after Adèle, Jean.'

She stared at him, then at the child, tears filling her eyes. 'I can't do that, Mr Beaufort.'

Adèle cried, 'But you must come, Jeanie!'

'I can't, darling. I was going to tell you, only you've been so busy. I'm getting married.'

'To Tom?'

'Yes, darling. Who else would it be?' Jean turned to Hugh. 'It's Tom Bankson, one of your tenant farmers. We'd thought to wait till next year, but if you're leaving, then I'll marry my Tom straight away.'

'Oh dear! I'll be so sorry to lose you. I wish you well, of course, but we'll miss you greatly. You've been wonderful with Adèle.'

She nodded, her voice thickened with tears. 'I love her, Mr Beaufort. She's like my own.'

'I know.' He looked down at his daughter, who was crying in a quiet, despairing way as Jean pulled her close in a cuddle. It'd be difficult to find someone who cared about the child as this woman had. Jean had raised her from birth.

'We'll find someone else to look after you, darling, someone nice, I promise.'

'It won't be the same.'

'My cousin Carrie might be interested in doing the job,' Jean ventured. 'I'm not certain, because she doesn't know about you going to Australia. But she's good with children and I'd trust her with Adèle.'

'I'd like to meet her, then. If she's a cousin of yours, I'm sure we'll like her.'

Jean hugged the little girl again. 'You've met Carrie, remember? And you liked her.'

'Mmm.' There was silence, then Adèle said, 'Will it really make me better to go to Australia, Daddy?'

'The doctor thinks there's a good chance.'

'You mean, I'll be able to breathe properly there?'

'He thinks so.' Hugh didn't say the doctor hadn't promised anything, except that it was the only chance they had.

'Where is Australia, Daddy? Do we have a map?'

He'd been prepared for that, so took her and Jean down to the library, where he unfolded the modern map of the world he'd bought, as well as pulling out the old globe that had been in his family for decades. The latter didn't show Australia properly, though it showed a rough outline of a piece of land in the right part of the world. He spread out the map and Adèle came to stand beside him, with Jean behind her.

They studied the globe first, then he moved to the map.

Adèle followed his pointing finger with great attention as he showed her how they would travel, and then surprised him by saying, 'I think it'll be exciting to travel round the world, but I don't think my governess will want to come. Miss Fenton doesn't like foreigners.'

'It's mostly British people in Australia.'

'She doesn't like travelling, either. She always complains about it, even when she goes to see her family in Cheltenham.'

'We'll see. I'll speak to her when she comes back from her annual holiday.'

Adèle wrinkled her nose. 'I don't want her to come back.'

'You need a governess, darling.'

'But she's old. She doesn't like playing. When Jean looks after me, we play games. Miss Fenton gives me books or tells me to draw.'

'It's better for you to play quietly.' Miss Fenton took great care of his daughter, or she'd not have stayed with them for the past three years. He'd make it well worth her while to come to Australia for a year or two. 'In the meantime, I think we'd better get Miss Grayling in from the village to make you some more clothes. You've grown taller these past few months.'

She'd grown thinner and frailer too, but he didn't say that. 'Jean, can you see to that for me? Adèle will need at least three dozen of each piece of underwear for the journey, I'm told. Plus plenty of dresses and pinafores. It'll be cold to start off with and then it'll get warmer as we move further south. It'll be very hot sometimes, so she'll need light clothes mainly. It'll be summer when we get to Australia, at the opposite time of year to here.'

'Goodness me, sir. It must be strange to have

Christmas in summer.'

'A lot of things will be strange there, animals and plants too.' He stood up. 'I'd better start clearing out my desk and going through my papers. You can stay with me if you like, Adèle. Jean, could you make a start on clearing out the nursery, please? We've agreed to leave the furniture for the tenants but empty the drawers and cupboards of personal things and store them in the attics.'

When Jean had left, Adèle went across to the big armchair she often sat in when she came to the library. She leaned her head against the chair back, her whole body looking limp and weary. She made no attempt to play with her doll or read a book, just watched him, dozing off after a while.

Hugh prayed they'd be in time to save her, prayed he'd kept a calm smile on his face today, when all he wanted was to rail at fate for making his child so ill . . . and for making him leave his beloved home.

★ ★ ★

In Shilmara, Maura listened to Kieran's explanation about how she could look after her orphaned nieces and nephew.

'I had a letter from your nephew Bram. He's doing really well in Australia and wants me to invite his family to join him there. He'll pay for the fares and whatever they need for the journey, then look after them when they get there.'

'Why did he write to you about that?' Maura

51

asked. 'Why not to his family?'

'He thought his father might throw a letter in the fire, or Father Patrick might forbid anyone to go to Australia.'

'He was probably right. My brother Sean always was pig-headed. He was over twenty years older than me and seemed more like an uncle than a brother. He was a bully.'

A quick glance sideways at Maura showed Kieran that her face had remained expressionless as she said that. She was rather stern-looking, with her dark hair pulled severely back, and she was tall for a woman. Strange, that, when the rest of the Deagans were of small to medium stature.

She'd done well to rise to Assistant House-keeper so quickly. He could imagine her working efficiently in a house like his own, keeping the younger maids in order, making sure things were done properly. She even looked efficient in her plain, dark clothes, the skirts only moderately full. The only trimmings were a small, lace-edged collar in fine white cotton and a couple of strips of braid down the front of her bodice.

He had difficulty imagining her mothering the three orphaned children, certainly not getting herself untidy by playing with them or cuddling them — but then families like theirs didn't display affection as he and Julia did with their children. Poor families were usually too busy trying to earn enough to feed themselves.

'Tell me about the children,' she said.

'Brenna is nine, Noreen six and Ryan twelve.'

She still didn't speak, so Kieran said

encouragingly, 'Your nephew Bram can give you a good life in Australia, you and the children. He's been very successful there as a trader.'

'So he says.'

'So my brother says, too. Conn's his business partner, you know. He owns the land the Bazaar is built on.'

'Well, I have a good life already in England and I don't want it to change.' Her face brightened suddenly. 'But the children could go to live with Bram, couldn't they?'

'How could they travel to the other side of the world on their own?'

'Surely we could find some woman who's making the journey and pay her to look after them?'

'Would you really hand them over to a stranger, Maura? These children have just lost everyone they know.'

'I'm a stranger to them too.'

'But you're family. The blood tie matters a great deal, don't you think?'

She was silent for a long time, staring down at her clasped hands. He exchanged worried glances with his wife, wondering what to say.

Let me, Julia mouthed to him. 'Your niece Brenna is very upset,' she said in that quiet but telling way she had sometimes. 'She wakes in the night sobbing and crying for her next sister Cait, who died in the epidemic. In the daytime she walks round like a lost soul. The woman looking after them tells me she's hardly eating a thing. She's only nine, Maura. A little girl still.'

Kieran saw Maura swallow and blink hard, as

if holding back tears. For the first time he began to hope they would work something out.

'Ryan is twelve and he's angry about what's happened,' Julia went on. 'But I think his anger hides deep grief for the loss of his next brother. Padraig was his closest friend and the two were inseparable. His older brothers all left a while ago, you see, Bram to Australia, the other three going to America and England. Only Bram has kept in touch.'

Julia waited a few moments to let that sink in. 'Ryan quarrels with people, never offers to help and says he'll run away if we try to put him in an orphanage. I'm sure he'll do it, too. He's desperate to stay here because it's all he knows. He's never left the village, never even been into Enniskillen, so doesn't know what a town looks like.'

Kieran remembered something that had been upsetting him, so added his mite to the conversation. 'At twelve, Ryan's old enough to be put to work, but physically he's very underdeveloped. I don't think he's ever eaten well in his whole life. You know what a bad provider your brother Sean was.' He saw Maura nod. 'We can't seem to fill the lad's stomach now, so we're hoping he'll catch up in growth with other lads of his age. But that'll take time.'

'And his little sister Noreen is bewildered by it all,' Julia went on. 'She's only six and she cries for her mammy still. She carries a rag doll everywhere. She doesn't chatter like little girls usually do.'

Julia gave Maura a long, level look. 'I know it's

54

not what you planned for your life, but those children need you desperately. They need to *belong* to someone.'

Maura looked up at last. 'What about me? *I* belong to Brent Hall. It's my home. The staff are like a big family. I feel like weeping at the thought of losing that.' She fiddled with the material of her skirt. 'I lost hope once when they forced me to marry Vincent. Is it fair to ask me to lose it all over again?'

Kieran didn't know what to say to that, except to repeat, 'I'm sorry. I really am. But you're their only close relative left in Ireland. It's your duty.'

'And you won't be losing hope this time, surely?' Julia put in. 'Your nephew Bram will help you make a good life for yourself in Australia and if a life in service is what you want, I gather they're very short of good servants in the colony.'

'I can't . . . think straight.' Maura pressed one hand to her mouth. 'I just can't seem to take it all in. I didn't expect *three* of them to look after. I just . . . don't know what to say. And I won't make a decision without thinking about it. I never rush at things, if I can help it. And I don't let people force me to do things I know are wrong. Not since my marriage.' That dreadful year with Vincent still gave her nightmares.

'You can stay here, meet the children, and take your time to plan what to do,' Julia said. 'We have plenty of spare bedrooms in the house. Take as long as you need.'

Kieran nodded, but he was rather disappointed in Maura's reaction, if truth be told. It wasn't as if they were asking her to marry an unsuitable man again, or live a life of grinding poverty. She'd be well looked after by Bram, and have family and companionship in Australia. Bram might be her nephew, but he was nearly the same age as her and a very personable man. Though of course she hadn't seen him for a long time.

'Come and meet the children now,' Julia said.

Maura stood up, clasping her hands tidily in front of her. If she'd been better dressed, she'd have looked like a lady, Kieran realised suddenly, because she had a natural grace. But those hands bore the signs of years of hard physical work. They were not a lady's hands.

'We'll both go with you,' he said. 'In case Ryan is in one of his angry moods. He'll listen to me sometimes when he won't listen to anyone else.'

Maura's sigh whispered round the room, her shoulders drooped for a moment then she straightened up as if about to face an ordeal.

He pitied her sincerely. Life could be cruel sometimes and didn't always allow you any choice.

But he pitied those three children more. Maura was an adult. How could she even think of shirking her responsibility for them?

★ ★ ★

As they left the house, they saw Father Hilary come out of the barn.

'This is the new priest,' Kieran said. 'Father

56

Patrick died of a seizure.'

'Good riddance to him.'

He looked at her in shock, but Maura didn't apologise. Father Patrick had been one of those who forced her into marriage, shouting and threatening her with eternal damnation, while her father and brothers held her on her knees before him. The old priest had shouted so loudly, been so utterly certain of himself, and her father had beaten her so badly that in the end, she'd given in.

She'd been utterly ignorant in those days, even though, thanks to her mother, she'd managed to attend school often enough to pick up how to read and write, and do simple sums. She wasn't as ignorant now and was working steadily to remedy that.

Today, it felt as if another trap was closing round her, which brought back all her old feelings of helplessness. There didn't seem to be a way of avoiding this one, either.

What if Bram had grown more like her brothers as he grew older? She shuddered at the thought of that. No, surely her nephew would stay as cheerful and kind as he'd always been? Especially if he was doing well for himself.

She stopped walking when the others did, studying the new priest as she was introduced. Father Hilary was young and fresh-faced, but his clothing looked rather unkempt and he'd missed a patch of bristles at the side of his chin when shaving. She liked his face, which was gentle and kindly, for all his youth.

Perhaps this was a man she could talk to?

Perhaps he'd listen to her side of things and offer her some advice. She needed to confide in someone other than Kieran Largan and his wife, because they were thinking mainly of the children.

'Have you found a new housekeeper yet, Father?' Kieran asked.

'Not yet.'

'We'll continue to send you down a meal every evening till you do, also bread and cheese or cold meat for the rest of the day.'

Maura saw a way to gain some thinking time away from the Largans and seized it. 'I could act as housekeeper for a few days, if you like, Father.'

They all turned to stare at her in surprise.

'Are you sure?' Father Hilary asked.

'Why not? I don't like to be idle and I doubt we'll get things sorted out here straight away.'

Mr Kieran frowned. 'What about getting to know the children?'

'I can come up to see them every day, I suppose.'

'Let her do it this way, Kieran,' Mrs Julia said. 'It's been a big shock. She needs time. If that's all right with you, Father?'

'I'd very much welcome your help, Maura. I'm helpless in the house. Why, I haven't even had time to unpack properly. The old housekeeper left as soon as I arrived, you see.'

'Was it still Miss Flynn?'

'Yes. She didn't want to stay with me.' He gave them a guilty smile. 'And I didn't press her to stay, because I didn't take to her at all.'

'Who would? You'll be much more comfortable with someone else,' Mrs Julia said. 'Miss Flynn was as set in her ways as Father Patrick.'

He turned to Maura. 'I'll change my clothes before I come into the house, Miss Deagan, and try not to bring any lice with me. I think you should be safe from the typhus.'

'I keep forgetting about that. There's so much else to think about.'

'We're going to meet the children now, Father,' Kieran said.

'I'll come with you, shall I? Ryan sometimes listens to me.'

The two men exchanged glances and Maura's heart sank. It was beginning to sound as if the boy was difficult.

Kieran turned back to her. 'You can talk to them on your own in this empty cottage whenever you like. I was going to get new tenants in, but then the typhus struck. There is some furniture to sit on, though it'll be chilly without a fire.'

As they waited in the little front room, with its stone-flagged floor and whitewashed walls, Maura decided that Mr Kieran was a better landlord than his father, though he clearly still had a lot to do to bring the estate back in order. Old Mr Largan had not been liked in the district, not even by the gentry.

Mrs Julia didn't seem to expect her to chat while they waited, which was a relief.

The first person to come in was the boy, scowling at someone behind him as if he'd been pushed. Ryan was much smaller than she'd

59

expected, in spite of Mr Kieran's warning. He looked nearer eight than twelve. As he glared at her, she thought he mustn't be sleeping properly. His eyes were sunken and rimmed with dark circles in what looked like an old man's face in a boy's body.

Brenna was next. At least, Maura thought it was Brenna. Fancy not knowing your own niece. Then it hit her once again that the other two were her niece and nephew as well, because they were Bram's little brother and sister. She kept forgetting that, because they were all strangers to her.

Brenna was pale, but her eyes were reddened and swollen with weeping. She was neatly dressed, her hair tied back with a piece of ribbon. Dark hair. Deagan hair. Like Ryan, she was staring at Maura as if they were enemies.

Mr Kieran walked in holding the third child by the hand. Another thin creature. Six years old, but looking more like four. Noreen was sucking her thumb, clutching a rag doll and staring round the bare room as if afraid of what she'd find here.

'Children, this is your Auntie Maura,' Kieran said. 'She's come all the way from England to see you.'

They continued to stare, stiff with hostility, moving to stand closer to one another.

'Aren't you even going to say hello?' he prompted.

The two girls looked at Ryan, as if they'd appointed him leader.

He scowled at his aunt then turned to the

landowner. 'We don't know her. My da always said she ran away because she didn't want to help her family, so why has she come back now?'

That was the last thing Maura had expected to hear from a child. He spoke sharply, using words to hurt.

'She's come because she's the only family you have left now and wants to help you,' Mrs Julia said quietly.

Ryan opened his mouth as if to speak, then saw Mr Kieran look at him warningly, and snapped it shut again. Hunching his shoulders, he thrust his hands deep into his pockets.

Maura made no attempt to touch them. She didn't dare. What if they pushed her away? What would the Largans think of that? 'I'll be staying with Father Hilary for a few days so that we can get to know one another. He needs help till he finds a new housekeeper.'

Brenna looked at the priest accusingly. It was the look of someone who had trusted the man absolutely and been betrayed. 'Is she really staying with you?'

'Yes.'

'Why?'

'To help me in the house, because she's a kind person.'

The scowls deepened. 'Will you still come to see us, Father?'

'Of course I will. And your Auntie Maura will come with me.'

Noreen didn't say anything, just continued to suck her thumb. Mrs Julia held out a hand to her and she went across to huddle against the

61

master's wife, as if desperate for a human touch, as if she'd been cuddled by this kind lady before.

Noreen was so little, her arms and legs like sticks, that Maura felt upset just to see her. She was too little to face the world alone.

'You children look hungry,' Kieran said. 'Why don't you go and get your midday meal now? Your aunt will come to see you again later after she's moved into the presbytery. You can show her the horses, Ryan.'

'She won't want to see them.'

'Yes, I will,' Maura said at once. 'Where I've been living in England, they have a stable full of beautiful horses, but I like the children's pony best. She'll take an apple from your hand without nipping you.'

Ryan stared at her, shrugged his shoulders and left the room. Brenna held out her hand to Noreen and the girls followed him without a word of farewell.

After they'd gone, Maura let out a long sigh. 'Has no one ever fed those children properly?'

'No,' said Mr Kieran. 'Your oldest brother Sean turned into a heavy drinker, and Brenna's father Eamon was following the same path when he died, so there wasn't much left for food.'

'My brothers were like our father, then.' No wonder her brother Eamon's children had had little chance of fighting off the typhus. But it was shocking that out of five children, only Brenna had somehow managed to avoid catching it.

It was at that moment Maura first admitted to herself that she would have to accept responsibility for all the children. But might there be some way of getting them to Australia without tearing her own life apart? She would give up all her precious savings to do it, whether Bram could pay her back or not.

She was unable to banish the memory of those pinched childish faces, with the look of hunger graven deep on them, young as they were. You couldn't have lived in Ireland in the past two or three decades without learning to recognise that look. She'd been hungry quite often herself during her childhood and even during the brief, interminable year of her marriage, so she knew what it felt like.

The words seemed to speak themselves. 'It's not fair, is it, how some people treat their children? And their wives.'

She looked from Mr Kieran and Mrs Julia. 'I'll look after the priest for a day or two. I think best when my hands are busy.'

Desperate to get away now, unable to take in anything else, she turned to him. 'Can we go back to the presbytery now, please, Father Hilary?'

'Yes, of course. I'm grateful for your help. I'll pay you whatever wage is appropriate, of course.'

She inclined her head. She'd need every penny she could get if . . . She shivered, pushing that thought, that decision aside.

'I'll get Cook to send you down some supplies of fresh food,' Mrs Julia said. 'Just ask her if you find anything lacking at the presbytery.'

'I will.'

Maura walked back to the village beside the

priest, grateful when he didn't annoy her with meaningless chatter.

Once they got to his house, he opened the front door for her to go first, then led the way upstairs to the attic. 'This is the housekeeper's room. Come down and make yourself at home in the kitchen when you're ready. They put the food there. I have some left from yesterday, if you're hungry.'

'Thank you.'

'I have to go out now. We can talk tonight, if you wish. Or not, if you don't wish. Just remember that I'm here if you need me.'

She could only nod. When he'd gone, she set her portmanteau on the bed and plumped down beside it, still unable to get the children's faces from her mind — or to forget their hostility towards her.

Would they even want her to look after them, let alone go with them to Australia?

Australia! What in heaven's name was she going to do? How could she bear to give up her hopes and dreams, her secure future?

To go so far away on top of everything else was just too much to ask of anyone. Wasn't it?

★   ★   ★

In Singapore, Dougal McBride studied the ship thoughtfully, then looked at Mr Lee. He liked the Chinese merchant as well as respecting him.

'You say before you want second ship,' Mr Lee repeated. 'I can help you buy this one . . . if you think it good ship . . . if you agree to use it for *my* trade mainly.'

'Hmm. I'll have to think about it.' Now that the opportunity had arrived, Dougal was suddenly afraid of his own ambitions, of trusting his hard-earned capital to another man. It had been such a struggle to buy his first ship.

Mr Lee smiled. 'You have mate. Very clever man, Adam Tregear. Make good captain for new ship.'

Was there anything Mr Lee didn't know? Dougal wondered. 'He's a capable sailor, certainly. But I can't afford a second ship. Not quite yet. And I don't want to borrow money.'

'We buy ship together. Partners. Perhaps Adam like to buy share, too.'

'He won't have the money yet, not for a year or two. He has a share in the *Hannah Grey*, and my brother-in-law wants to buy him out eventually. But Joss can't afford to do that yet.'

'If I buy quarter share in *Hannah Grey* from Adam, then he can take quarter share in new ship. Spreads the risk.'

'You want a fleet of ships?'

'Want a share in many ships. Want to be sure of selling goods where I choose.'

Mr Lee was a cunning devil, Dougal thought admiringly. He was probably much richer than he seemed.

'Take time to arrange all the sales. Can do it, though.'

'It does sound . . . a good idea.'

'Come and look at new ship. You know ships better than me. I know trade better.'

65

And they trusted one another after several years of dealing, which was also very important, Dougal thought.

Mr Lee's godown was very close to the harbour, a very convenient place for a warehouse. They walked to the harbour then stopped next to another schooner. The *Silver Lady* was badly maintained and needed cleaning up.

'The captain hasn't looked after the ship,' Dougal said disapprovingly. 'We'd need to check that she's sound.'

'Have made some check. Seems sound but dirty. You can make better check before we buy.'

'Where is the captain?'

'Dead. Drink too much. Fall and hit his head. Die quickly. Mate bring ship back to port, come see me. Offer me ship.'

'Does he own her?'

'Owns part of it. Captain's wife owns rest. Both want to sell.'

'How much?'

Mr Lee smiled smugly and named a price.

Dougal let out a whistle of surprise. 'If it's that cheap, and if she's sound — and I'd insist on checking everything — then that's a very good price.'

'And Mr Tregear? We make him captain?'

Dougal nodded, noticing the 'we'. He'd already considered this . . . eventually . . . if he found another ship. Adam would make a good captain. More importantly, Dougal would trust the man absolutely. Even if Adam hadn't been married to Bram's sister, Dougal would still trust him. But the Deagans were good people and

Bram was a close friend, so the links were close.

And actually, Dougal trusted Mr Lee as well. He didn't know why. He just did. You could write as many words of an agreement on paper as you wished, but you were still better off trusting those you worked closely with.

'We could think about a partnership,' he said. 'After I've checked the ship thoroughly.'

'Check it today and tomorrow morning. We can talk tomorrow afternoon. We make plans quickly. Don't leave ship sitting idle. Don't give others chance to buy.'

'She'd need a partial refit, probably.'

Mr Lee shrugged. 'I get best prices for that, too, and find best workers.'

⋆ ⋆ ⋆

Dougal hurried back to the ship to explain to his mate what was happening. Adam looked at him in surprise. 'Mr Lee wants to buy into this ship?'

'Yes. As a partner with me and you. I'll pay for half. He'll take over half your share of the *Hannah Grey* and give you a quarter share of this one. So you'll be part owner of two ships.'

There was silence, then slowly Adam smiled and echoed Dougal's words. 'Lee's a cunning old devil. He wants to bind us closely together, give himself trading outlets in Australia managed by people he can trust. People there wouldn't trust a Chinese man, not to deal with directly. They're stupid about that sort of thing. But he can work through us.'

'Yes. I figured that out.'

67

'But we should check out the ship first. Very carefully indeed.'

'Let's make a start, then.'

* * *

The following afternoon, they reached an agreement with Mr Lee, signing the papers the day after that, though only after they'd been translated into English as well as Chinese by people independent of Mr Lee.

He smiled serenely when they insisted on doing that. 'Good idea. I don't want stupid partners.'

Once that was settled, Dougal had another chat with Adam. 'All right. I've got my cargo loaded now, so I can start back to Fremantle at once. Are you comfortable at being left with the refitting of the ship?'

'I have Mr Lee's help.'

'Good. Bring it up to scratch. Make sure every inch of rope is sound, that all the sails and even the spare sails are of good canvas. And then get yourself a cargo similar to mine.'

'I know what's needed. There's just one thing . . . ' He sighed.

Dougal smiled. 'Your wife.'

'Yes. Can you take a letter to Ismay? Tell her I'll be late. Tell her I miss her.'

'I'll tell her you're making the family fortunes.' He clapped Adam on the shoulder. 'She'll be all right. She's with your aunt. Her brother Bram is nearby. And I'll keep an eye on her as well, once I get back.'

'I hate to be away from her for so long.'

'It's what sailors do.'

'But they don't have to like it.'

'Take her with you next time. Run a 'hen frigate' like Joss does.'

'I would, and Ismay would come, too, but there's my aunt. We can't leave poor Harriet on her own and she's a very poor sailor.'

Dougal left Singapore the next morning, feeling good about his purchase. He'd been ready to expand, and Mr Lee had got the schooner at an excellent price. Even his new mate was happy. Pete was a capable fellow, would make a good second in command.

He thought about Mr Lee and smiled. The fellow had surprised everyone in Singapore by starting to build a new house, a very big one. This open display of wealth was something he hadn't done before.

The first Asian had already been appointed to the legislative council there, a man they called Whampoa. Maybe Mr Lee would be the second, if he continued to be so successful.

Dougal was willing to bet that Mr Lee would become one of the richest men in the crown colony of Singapore before he was through.

* * *

That first night, Maura was too tired to do anything but clear up the kitchen and put together a simple meal for herself and Father Hilary from the food sent from the big house.

He insisted they eat together at the kitchen

69

table. 'We'll make things as easy for you as possible.'

After eating neatly and quickly, he looked at her for a moment or two as if wondering whether to speak about her dilemma.

When she said nothing, he excused himself and went into his study as quietly as he did everything else.

She'd expected Father Hilary to try to persuade her to take on the three children and was vaguely disappointed when she didn't have a chance to argue her side of the affair.

She went to bed early. She'd expected to have trouble sleeping in a strange place, but she was so physically exhausted after two days of travelling and making arrangements that she fell asleep almost immediately.

★ ★ ★

In the morning, Father Hilary finished his breakfast then looked at her across the table and asked quietly, 'Do you want to discuss your problem or shall I leave you to think in peace?'

Perversely she said, 'I'd welcome an opportunity to talk about it, if you have time.' Then was angry with herself, but it was too late to take the words back.

'It's a difficult situation for you. I gather you had a hard time in your marriage.'

'Yes, very. I swore I'd never marry again, so I went into service. I've made a good life for myself. I've been happy at Brent Hall.'

'You certainly sound to have done well, rising

to Assistant Housekeeper.'

She allowed herself a quick nod. 'They're good employers.'

Silence fell and when it continued, she looked across at him warily.

He smiled sadly, his head slightly on one side. 'I'm not going to browbeat you, my dear. Only you can reconcile your duty to your family with your own life and conscience. I think you need to get to know those children better before you make any decision.'

'Yes. I suppose so.'

He stood up. 'Perhaps it'd be best if we both thought about it and prayed for guidance today. What do you say? Then we can talk about it again in a day or two. The church is open at any time, if you wish to pray there. It's a peaceful little place. Or you could go for a walk round the grounds at the back of the big house.' He stopped at the door to add, 'But I'd remind you not to get close to people from the village.'

'And yet you visit them.'

'Yes, but I take all the precautions I can. If you'll leave me a bucket of clean water and a towel in the outhouse, I'll change my clothes and have a wash there. I shake my clothes vigorously and examine the seams before I come into the house each night. And of course, lice make you itch, so it's fairly obvious whether you've got them.'

She shuddered. She remembered those days from her girlhood — and from her marriage. It had been such a wonderful thing when she started work as a maid to be able to keep herself clean. The housekeeper had never had to nag her to wash herself properly.

When she looked up, he'd gone.

And oh, the peace and quiet of that house! It was as if the man had scattered peace behind him to comfort her. He was very different from Father Patrick, thank goodness.

★   ★   ★

Two days later Ryan kicked the door of the tack room, then kicked it again because it felt good to vent his anger on it.

'Stop kicking the door, you!' one of the grooms called. 'If you've nothing better to do, come and help me with the hay.'

Ryan scowled and turned to run away but someone grabbed his shoulder and stopped him. He was about to yell at the person when he realised it was Mr Kieran himself.

'Don't you feel you're being unfair — and maybe stupid as well — refusing to help them unless I tell you?' the master said. 'You might actually like working in the stables. Your brother Bram did.'

Ryan shrugged and kicked out at a clump of straw that was just beyond his foot. 'I don't like shovelling dung. It stinks.'

The hand turned him to one side and shook him slightly. 'Well, leave that for now. I want to talk to you, lad.'

At the words, 'I want to talk to you,' Ryan shrank back, one arm up to protect his head, clearly expecting a beating.

72

'I've not done anything wrong,' he said in a whining voice.

'Dear God, can he see nothing but beatings?' Kieran muttered. He began to walk towards the cottage and Ryan had no choice but to go with him, because the master's hand remained tightly clamped to his shoulder.

As he walked into the empty cottage, Ryan looked round for the belt or stick, but saw nothing, so waited for a fist to land somewhere painful.

'Sit down, boy.'

No beating yet, then. He went to the chair furthest away and sat on the edge of it, ready to run if given half a chance.

Mr Kieran spoke loudly and slowly. 'I want to talk to you. *Just talk*. Nothing else.'

Ryan had heard those words before and knew them for a lie.

When the silence continued and he still didn't get thumped, he risked a quick glance. The master had sat down opposite him. Out of reach for the moment. Did he mean what he said, then?

As if he'd read his mind, the master said, 'Talking is all we'll be doing, young Ryan. I don't beat people.'

'What do you want to talk to me about . . . sir?'

'Your future.'

'I'm not going into an orphanage. I'll run away if you put me in one of those places, so I will.'

'Who said anything about orphanages?'

Ryan frowned, trying to work out where else

they could send him.

'Your brother Bram is offering you and Noreen a good life in Australia. It's such a long way away from Ireland, though, it takes more than two months to get there by ship. He writes to me every now and then, you know.'

'He used to write to us. Then he stopped writing. Mammy cried about that.'

'He did write more letters, but we think your father threw them away.'

'Why would Da be doing that?' But Ryan knew really. He just wasn't ready to admit that his oldest brother could be doing the right thing and his father the wrong thing. You weren't supposed to speak ill of the dead.

But the master said it for him. 'Your father probably got rid of the letters because Bram's doing well for himself and your father didn't like his son to do better than him. Bram has a shop in Australia, a big one, and he's making good money, so he can afford to house and feed his brothers and sisters and their families. He wants you to go and live with him. He wrote that without knowing about the typhus. He can give you a much better life.'

Kieran suddenly realised that 'better life' was too vague and he needed to talk in terms Ryan would understand, so added, 'He can give you three good meals a day and extra food at other times if you're still hungry.' Ah, that had caught the lad's attention.

'Is our Bram rich now, then?'

'He's earning good money, so I suppose he's rich by village standards. He's helped your sister

Ismay already, you know. She's living in Australia now, so you'd see her again as well. Bram helped her to go there when she ran away.'

The boy gaped at him. 'She's still alive? Our Ismay? But Da said she died of hunger on the streets of London, and Father Patrick said so too. He said it was the reward of sin.'

The old devil! And he'd called himself a priest. Even to think of him and Sean Deagan telling the children and their mother lies made Kieran angry. Everyone knew how much Bram's mother had grieved for her eldest son and her eldest daughter. 'Ismay definitely didn't die. She went to Australia, to Bram. On a ship. She met a man on the ship and she's married to him now and living just as well as Bram.'

They all lied to you, Ryan thought bitterly. How did you know which one to believe? 'Da said Bram was an eejit and telling lies about Australia.'

'And is my brother Conn an eejit too? Is he telling me lies, do you think? Why should he bother to lie to me about your brother?'

Ryan thought about that, but couldn't work it out, so shrugged.

'Conn is Bram's partner in the shop, and they're both making good money from it every single day. They not only don't go hungry — they're never, ever hungry — they have meat or fish every single day too.'

Ryan knew that was a lie. Even when they ate regularly, poor people like him didn't get much meat. Bram couldn't have changed that much. Or were things really that different in Australia?

He suddenly remembered how his other brothers had said things were different in America, or even in England, and had gone off to make their fortunes. But they'd refused to take Ryan and Padraig with them. They said that Mammy wanted to keep her younger boys at home. They'd quarrelled with Da, big loud arguments, and he'd forbidden them to go. Only they'd gone anyway.

'How do I know who to believe?' he asked, honestly puzzled.

The master's voice softened. 'If I swear on the big Bible in church that I'm telling the truth about Bram and Ismay, will you believe me then?'

'With the priest standing by?'

'Yes.'

Everyone knew you got struck stone dead if you told lies when you placed your hand on the big old Bible in church with a priest watching you. So Ryan had to wonder if the master was telling the truth and Da had been lying. It'd be good if he was.

'We'll do that, then. There's just one problem left after that, Ryan: how to get you and your sister Noreen to Australia. Bram's sent me the money to pay for the passages, so there's no problem about that. But . . . you have to have a grown-up with you on the journey or they won't let you on the ship. So you do need your Auntie Maura to take you there.'

'She doesn't want to go to Australia. She said so. She doesn't want us, either. Nobody wants us now.'

'Bram wants you. And your aunt was shocked because she didn't know your parents had died and had only just found out.'

'And Padraig.'

'Yes, your brother died too. So you see, your Auntie Maura didn't know she'd have three children to look after instead of just Brenna. It'll take a little while for her to get used to that.'

Ryan sighed. He didn't know what the master wanted him to say or do, but if this was true . . . if it was . . . He looked at Mr Kieran and found him smiling, and for some reason that brought tears to his eyes.

'Don't tell me lies,' he begged suddenly, the words bursting out of him. Every grown-up he knew had lied to him, even the old priest.

'I won't lie to you, lad. I promise. No, don't speak. I can tell you don't believe me yet. But we'll go down to the church together, you and I, and I'll swear on the big Bible there, with Father Hilary standing right next to me, that I'll never, ever tell you lies and that all this is true.'

Ryan stared at him and almost believed him there and then. No, let him swear it on the Bible. And it might be better if there were two of them to make sure this was done properly. 'Can Noreen come too?'

'Yes, of course Noreen can come too, and Brenna as well, if you like. Now, let's go and see if Cook has a piece of cake for you. These things are best done on a full stomach.'

Ryan followed the master out, swiping his sleeve quickly across his eyes, so that no one would see any sign of weakness.

If this was all true . . . if it really was . . .

★ ★ ★

Maura, who had been eavesdropping from the back room of the cottage, peeped through into the front room in time to see Ryan wipe his eyes. But he didn't see her as he left. She tiptoed into the front room and stood by the window, watching him walk away next to Mr Kieran, heading for the rear of the big house.

The lad was hunched up, walking a little behind the man.

The man turned a couple of times to look at his young companion, with a compassionate expression.

She hugged her arms round herself, wishing she hadn't heard all that. It had made her want to cry.

It said so much about her poor nephew's life, that conversation did. He'd had a terrible time at home, just as she had.

Those three children were adrift in the world, unless someone reached out to help them.

'Why me?' she whispered. And she too wiped away a tear.

Why not her? She was, after all, their aunt.

★ ★ ★

Ryan waited in the kitchen and found that Mr Kieran had been telling him the truth about the cake, at least. Cook gave him a big piece, all for

78

himself. It was sitting on a white plate with flowers round the edges.

Even though he'd had a good breakfast only three hours ago, his mouth watered at the sight of fruit cake, plump with raisins. He snatched it from the plate and ate it quickly before they could take it away from him.

But though the master and Cook stared at him, they didn't try to stop him eating it.

'Now we'll go down to the church,' the master said once he'd finished the cake. 'Will you go and fetch Brenna and Noreen?'

Ryan ran across to the big barn where all the children were sleeping and eating their meals. He got the other two, then they all followed Mr Kieran into the village. Brenna was holding Noreen's hand but when she got tired and began to cry, the master picked the little girl up and carried her.

He murmured to her as he walked and made her laugh. Ryan marvelled at that. He'd never seen a man play with a little child before, though they said Mr Kieran doted on his own children.

He saw Brenna looking longingly at Noreen and edged closer to her. 'He's kind, isn't he? I didn't know anyone could be kind like that.'

'He's lovely. My da wasn't kind.'

'Mine wasn't, either.'

No one in the village came near them, and Ryan was glad of that, because he didn't want to get the typhus, or even to be dirty again. They'd given him a bath and new clothes when he first went to the big house. Clean, warm water all to himself in a little room off the laundry. He liked being clean, though he hadn't admitted that. It was best to keep important thoughts to yourself or people spoiled them.

The church was dim, with just a few candles twinkling to one side and light shining through the stained glass windows. Lovely colours those windows had.

Ryan half-expected Father Patrick to jump out from behind a pillar and clout him round the ears, even though he knew the old priest was dead.

The new priest came out to see who it was, not shouting but saying hello quietly. The master put Noreen down and explained what they wanted.

'I'll be happy to help you swear a solemn oath,' Father Hilary said.

So perhaps it was going to be true. Perhaps Bram really could help them. Ryan breathed quietly, trying not to upset anyone, trying not to hope for too much as he watched the preparations for the oath.

'Come closer, Ryan lad.'

He moved forward and Brenna came with him.

The master put his hand on the big Bible and swore he was telling the truth about Bram and Ismay and Australia.

Ryan held his breath, but there was no clap of thunder and the master continued to stand there, calm as anything.

'You see,' Mr Kieran said. 'I wasn't telling you lies. Bram really does want you and you'll have a far better life in Australia.'

Ryan looked at the priest, who nodded and smiled. Then he stared round the church, but nothing happened. No clap of thunder. Slowly he nodded acceptance of what the master had said. 'I'll go to Australia, then.'

'So will I,' Brenna said.

Then he saw his aunt walk slowly forward to join them, her face sad. He waited for her to refuse to take them, to spoil their chances. Didn't something always happen to spoil things?

She looked at them, then turned to Mr Kieran and the priest. 'I'd like to swear an oath, too, so that Ryan and Brenna will believe me.'

She put her hand on the Bible and said quietly, 'I swear that I'll take you three children safely to Australia to Bram. I'll look after you on the ship and care for you like a mother, and I won't ever, ever beat you.'

Ryan didn't understand why she was so sad about that. If Bram had a lot of money, it'd be good for her to go there as well. After all, Bram was her nephew too. Family.

He waited a moment or two, just to be sure, but no thunderbolt came to strike her dead, so she must be telling the truth as well.

They were going to Australia.

For the first time he let himself feel excited. He was going to travel on a big ship with his little sister and his cousin Brenna, and their Auntie Maura.

It'd be perfect if only his brother Padraig was still alive and coming with him.

Better not to think of Padraig. Ryan didn't want to cry in front of other people.

'I'll go, then,' he said again.

Ryan stared at his aunt. He supposed he'd have to trust her to take them to this Australia place.

'We'll all go,' Brenna said and smiled at Maura.

Ryan wondered why his aunt got tears in her eyes when Brenna smiled at her.

4

The next morning Maura was summoned to the big house to speak to Mrs Julia. She made sure the kitchen at the presbytery was clean and tidy, set out some food covered in a plate for the father's midday meal, then set off.

She walked slowly through the village and up the drive, feeling as if her whole body was made of lead. Why had she sworn that oath in the church? Given her life and dreams away?

But the thought of her nephew growing up expecting to be beaten, expecting people to lie to him, living without any affection, had been more than she could bear and it still upset her.

Maura's father might not have been a loving man, but her mother had done her best for all her children. It was thanks to her that Maura had learned what it was like to be loved. And her mother had fought for her to get some education, even if that offered at the girls' school in the village wasn't very good. She would always be grateful to her mother for that.

She needed to write to the housekeeper at Brent Hall, explaining the situation, apologising for not giving proper notice and asking if they would send on the rest of her possessions. Why hadn't she written after she left the church yesterday?

She'd sat in the kitchen at the presbytery and

got out the notepaper Father Hilary had said she could use — twice she'd done that now. But she hadn't been able to force herself to dip the pen into the ink bottle, let alone write the words that would end her hopes once and for all.

At the big house, she found Mrs Julia waiting for her in the cosy little sitting room the mistress used in the daytime. 'Come in and sit down, Maura. We need to make plans for your journey. Lots of lists, too.'

Maura took the spindly little chair at the other side of the table from the master's wife, feeling like a prisoner about to be sentenced.

'My husband has been looking into sailing dates, and we think you should take a ship called the SS *Delta* from Southampton.'

'What does SS mean, ma'am, if you don't mind me asking?'

'Steam ship. It's a ship which uses both a steam engine and sails. You travel more quickly on those.'

'Oh. I see. How big would that ship be?' Not that she knew much about ships, but she wasn't going halfway round the world on anything smaller than the ferry to and from Ireland, not for anything.

'I think it's about three hundred foot long.'

Maura tried to imagine that: about a hundred big strides. Longer than the front of Shilmara House, probably, definitely bigger than the ferry. Thank goodness! 'That sounds a decent size of ship.'

'I gather so. Anyway, the SS *Delta* leaves Southampton towards the end of October, so we

84

have only a couple of weeks to get everything sorted out.'

Maura gasped, trying to take in that she'd be leaving Britain for good in two weeks. *Two weeks!*

'Are you all right?'

She took a deep breath and tried to pull herself together. 'Sorry. I didn't mean to be rude. I'm still a bit, um, shocked by it all.'

'Not surprising. You'll have to write to Brent Hall for your things. They can be sent to Southampton to the ship. We'll get you some other clothes and necessities in the meantime, because you'll need extra clothes for the voyage.'

She had a sudden idea. 'Can't I go back to Lancashire and pack my things myself? I'd like to say proper farewells.'

'And leave the children here, wondering if you'll ever come back?'

Maura bowed her head. She was always forgetting the children, thinking only of herself and her own feelings. Father Hilary had talked to her about that last night, gently making her realise she was no longer alone in the world. It was one thing to realise it as a fact, though, quite another to think that way all the time.

'I suppose I can't leave them now. But what if my things don't arrive at the ship on time? They're all I've got in the world.' The last sentence came out sounding pitiful, but she felt so upset she couldn't help it.

'They will, if you write straight away.' She reached out to take Maura's hand. 'You won't be travelling on your own, my dear. My husband

85

and I will be coming with you to Southampton.'

'You will?' She realised how ungrateful that sounded and could have kicked herself for showing her surprise at them being so kind.

'Yes. You've taken on a heavy burden and you're from the village, one of our own. One day, I hope you'll help others in your turn and pay us back that way.'

Maura nodded, the hard lump of fear lodged beneath her ribs easing just a little. Mrs Julia let go of her hand but the warmth of the touch lingered, such a comfort.

'In the meantime we have to get clothes for those children, quite a lot of clothes. They had just about nothing when they came to live in the barn except the dirty rags they were wearing. You and I will take them shopping in Enniskillen and we'll do more shopping for all of you when we get to Southampton.'

'We need to go shopping there as well?' Maura was startled by that.

'Yes. You'll find it useful to buy a ship's kit and perhaps a few books. We can help you with that. We took Ismay to her ship as well, my dear. I know she found it comforting. It's such a big step to take. I do understand that. And we can go and visit my family in England afterwards.' She cocked her head on one side. 'Will our going with you to the ship make you feel easier?'

'Yes.' After a moment she realised how ungrateful she was being and added, 'Thank you.'

'Now. Practicalities. Do you know how to look after children?'

Maura had to admit, 'Not really. It's a long time since I lived at home, and I was the youngest anyway. No one really looked after us either, not in the way you mean by looking after children. Mam did her best, but she wasn't well a lot of the time.'

'Then you must spend some time with our nursemaid and so should the children. Then you can all get to know one another better. At least Ryan now believes he's going, poor lad.'

'He still hardly says a word to me.'

'He doesn't seem to talk to anyone much, even my husband. That boy has been badly hurt by people who should have cared for him. And he's lost his brother and best friend, Padraig. He's still grieving for him. The two of them were inseparable.'

She waited a moment as if expecting Maura to speak, then continued briskly, 'So, if you'll write a letter to your employers, I'll get Kieran to send it off to Brent Hall and they can send your things to Southampton.'

She got out some notepaper, beautiful paper it was too, and set it in front of Maura, who couldn't resist stroking it with one fingertip. Taking the pen her companion was holding out, she dipped it into the ink. Not letting herself think, she wrote a letter of resignation and apology, explaining the circumstances.

Putting the words down on paper made it seem suddenly shockingly real. She'd be sailing from a port town she'd never seen to take children she hardly knew all the way to Australia to her nephew Bram, whom she hadn't seen for ten years.

She read through what she'd written, surprised at how crisp and businesslike it sounded, then suddenly remembered to ask for references in case she wanted to get a new job. Another read through, then she passed the piece of paper to Mrs Julia. 'Would you please check that I've said everything necessary?'

As she stared down at the blotting paper, she heard the page rustle and didn't look up again till the mistress spoke.

'You're very good with words. That's extremely clear.' Mrs Julia suddenly clapped her hands together. 'I know what! I'll give you a notebook and writing materials, then you can keep a diary of your travels.'

'Why a diary?' When had Maura ever had time for such frivolities? She didn't know anyone who kept a diary except rich people.

'For two reasons. One, it helps to pass the time. You'll have two months without occupation, remember. Second, it's such a momentous thing, sailing to Australia. Many people keep diaries as they travel and afterwards they copy them out to send back to their families. I've read two that had been sent to friends of mine in England. One was very moving.' She chuckled suddenly. 'The other was utterly boring, a collection of comments like, *Weather fine. Had salt pork for dinner.* Day after day of that. Was it all the poor fellow noticed, weather and food? He visited some of the most famous port cities in history!'

Maura found herself smiling back, something

88

she'd never expected to do during this interview.

'I'm sure your diary won't be boring, just as I'm sure you'll manage all right on the journey. You're a capable woman and remember, the P&O people are used to passengers who've never travelled on a ship before.'

Mrs Julia was the first person to realise how afraid Maura was of being responsible for three children on such a long journey, where everything around them was strange.

'You'll be travelling steerage, I'm afraid, which is not nearly as comfortable. The richer people have their own cabins.'

Maura looked at her in shock. 'We won't have our own cabin?'

'No. I think, from what I've read, you'll be sleeping in groups and sitting in a day cabin for meals and when the weather's not fine. Ryan will have to travel with the men because he's twelve.'

'You mean the girls and I will have strangers sharing with us?'

'I'm afraid so. I do hope you get congenial people. We'll talk to my husband about the arrangements. I'm sure he knows more than I do.' She clapped her hands together again. 'How stupid I am! Xanthe lives nearby at Ardgullan House. She married Ronan Maguire, you know.'

Maura looked at her in bafflement. What had this to do with her? She knew no one called Xanthe. What sort of name was that, anyway? 'I know of the Maguires,' she admitted.

'You've been away, so you won't know about Ronan inheriting. His wife Xanthe comes from Lancashire originally, but she went to Australia a few years ago and her sister married my brother-in-law, Conn, out there. Xanthe married his friend Ronan Maguire and came back to live in Ireland. They're only just down the road. We'll go and see them before you leave, talk to them about Australia and find out more about what you need to make the journey pleasant.'

'You mean they're the master and mistress of Ardgullan?' She'd never even seen Ardgullan, though it was close enough that she'd heard of it. But she'd moved in the other direction when she married.

'Yes. Ronan and Xanthe are good friends of ours. I can't believe I didn't think of them before. You and I will go tomorrow if it's convenient. I'll send someone across with a message this very day.'

'Thank you. It'll be good to speak to someone who's actually been to Australia and travelled on a big ship,' Maura admitted.

Mrs Julia patted her hand again. 'I'm sure it will. Now, could you make lists of what clothes you'll all need and we'll go through them together this afternoon and again with Xanthe tomorrow. At least two dozen of each item of underwear. No, make that three. While you're drawing up the lists, I'll take your letter of resignation to my husband and get him to send it today. You'll feel more comfortable when you know that's been sorted out. Come back about four o'clock.'

She picked up the envelope and was out of the room with it before Maura had time to blink.

Sitting there on her own, she realised she had

her hand outstretched as if to stop Mrs Julia and get the envelope back. Only it was too late for that, had been too late from the moment she left Brent Hall, though she hadn't known that then.

Fate was determined to send her to Australia and there seemed no way to stop this headlong rush out of the country.

★　★　★

Miss Fenton came back to Weston Abbas after her annual holiday, looking as neat and composed as ever in her grey skirt and jacket over a white blouse, her iron-grey hair in its usual tight bun, from which no stray hair ever seemed to escape.

Hugh met the governess in the hall as her luggage was brought in.

'Welcome back. Could I have a word with you before you unpack, please?'

She looked at him in shock. 'Adèle isn't — '

'In the library, if you don't mind.'

She followed him in, looking anxious.

'Adèle is all right, though no better. I feel I have no choice but to take her to live in a warmer climate, and I've chosen Australia. Indeed, I've already booked our passages on the SS *Delta*.'

'Oh. Then you'll have no more need of my services.'

'On the contrary, I'll have an even greater need of them. Adèle will require a woman to look after her on the voyage so I'm hoping you'll agree to come with us.'

'Go to Australia! I'm afraid I couldn't do that.'

'I'll pay you twenty pounds extra per year if you come to Australia, and should you not like it there, I'll pay your fare back.'

Miss Fenton then proved something he'd long suspected: she was a shrewd bargainer. He already knew that she made the most of her position by getting money or clothes for herself from people chosen to supply Adèle's clothing and other items for the schoolroom.

He didn't like the practice but she was a woman alone in the world and he tried to be sympathetic towards her need to put money aside for her old age, something she mentioned from time to time, so it was clearly on her mind. And after all, the practice of letting shops bribe her to shop there for her employer didn't hurt his daughter.

By the time they'd finished bargaining, they'd agreed that Miss Fenton would come to Australia with them in return for a bonus of fifty pounds after two years, with her return fare to England paid then. She was adamant that she wouldn't stay there any longer.

If anything happened to his daughter en route — did Miss Fenton have to specify that? — the bonus was still to be paid.

When the governess had gone to repack her case and trunk, and sort out other possessions to leave with her family, he scowled at the figures he'd jotted down. He trusted the woman with Adèle. She wasn't loving or fun, but she was extremely careful of the child's health and a good teacher, or he'd not even have considered paying this huge amount of money. Why, you could buy a decent little house for two hundred pounds.

Surely there must be governesses available in Australia for later on? The trouble was, even if he hired a new one here and dispensed with Miss Fenton's services, he wouldn't have time to find out whether the new one was suitable. Then Adèle might suffer. All he could do was pay Miss Fenton her blood money, for his daughter's sake.

That afternoon, he and the governess interviewed Jean's cousin Carrie for the position of nursery maid.

'Has Jean said anything to you about where we're going?'

'No, sir, just that you'll be travelling.'

When he explained what was happening, Carrie squealed loudly in shock.

'Be quiet, girl!' Miss Fenton snapped.

Clapping her hands to her mouth, Carrie stared from one to the other.

'Well?' Hugh asked. 'Might you consider it? It'd mean higher wages and a chance of a new life.'

'I'd have to ask Mam,' she said. 'I can't decide something like that without her say-so. I wouldn't mind doing it, though. And Mam would still have my sisters.'

Carrie's mam was another shrewd bargainer. She not only agreed to Carrie going with them, but negotiated for the first year's wages to be paid to her before her daughter left and for Carrie's next sister to be given the job of under-housemaid, since the staff were being kept on by the tenants.

Miss Fenton looked at him once they were alone. 'As you can see, they aren't a stupid family. That is most important when choosing a nursemaid.'

'I suppose so.'

'Now, we need to make lists of what Adèle and I will need for the journey and for Carrie as well. *She* won't be able to afford enough clothes with her mother taking her money.'

'Right. Carrie as well. I hope you'll see to that for me.'

'Certainly.'

He went to bed, hoping he'd solved his present problems, hoping the journey wouldn't be too taxing for Adèle.

He woke to a decision to buy some more sheet music for his guitar so that he'd have something to keep him occupied on the ship. He couldn't bear to be without music for two whole months. Maybe they'd have a piano on the ship. He'd heard some ships did. Travelling was much more civilised these days, thank goodness.

But it would still take a very long time to get to Australia.

5

Bram turned round to see a young man enter the Bazaar. He didn't look like a customer and Bram had a feeling he'd seen him somewhere before, but couldn't remember where.

The stranger stopped just inside the doorway, completely ignoring the goods displayed on shelves along the walls, or the stall with glass-fronted boxes of lustrous silks, the colours tempting you to look inside. One piece of silk was brought out each day to hang above that area, suspended from two wooden rods.

And unlike most other people, the newcomer didn't even glance at the arrays of household crockery and other items from Singapore which were very popular with local ladies.

When Bram stepped out of the shadows, the stranger's eyes focused on him and he gave a little nod of recognition before walking forward. 'Mr Deagan, isn't it?'

'Yes.'

He offered his hand. 'Charles Perry. I'm a junior partner with Mr Gervase Robinson.'

'The lawyer, yes.' Bram shook hands, then waited to find out what he wanted.

'Mr Conn Largan, who is acquainted with Mr Robinson, told him you were looking for a house or block of land to buy for your family home in Fremantle. Just in case we got any houses to sell for our clients, which sometimes happens.'

95

Bram was only too aware that everyone in the shop was able to hear what they were saying. The wooden floor was beautiful, but it allowed sounds to echo when the shop was empty, as it was now.

His assistant, Freddie, saw him looking across the room and pretended to tidy a shelf which was already perfectly tidy. Mrs Wooston fiddled with her goods. She rented space from him for a stall selling beautiful needlework pieces on behalf of herself and other ladies, some of whom wished to remain anonymous about their need to earn money. She was the only stallholder present at the moment, except for the woman Bram employed to sell good quality second-hand clothing from an area at the rear.

Even the lad who ran errands, kept the floor swept (a never-ending task in this sandy town) and did whatever tasks were needed, stopped to stare till Freddie nudged him. He jerked to attention and carried on dusting the goods and the shelves.

Bram smiled possessively round his little world, proud of it though he tried not to show that too obviously to the world. 'Why don't you come into my office, Mr Perry? We'll be able to talk more privately there.'

He led the way into the small room recently partitioned off from the rest of the large space that formed the Bazaar and offered his visitor a chair. 'Is there a house for sale, then?'

'Yes. Daniel Lawson died two days ago and left the execution of his will in our care.' The young man's face took on a disapproving expression as

96

he added, 'Mr Lawson was an emancipist and his family is still residing in Ireland. They never joined him out here. He asked that we sell the house and send the proceeds to them. It's just about big enough to call a gentleman's residence. Are you interested in looking at it?'

Bram frowned, trying to work out which house the young man was talking about because he didn't have unlimited money to spare for a fancy place. 'Is it the empty house on High Street you're meaning?'

'No. This one is just round the corner from your Bazaar — well, two streets away. It'd be very convenient for you, which Mr Largan stressed was important. But . . . ' He hesitated.

'There is a problem?'

'Yes. Our clerk says the place is in a filthy condition. The neighbour says Mr Lawson grew very strange towards the end. He was convicted for political offences and given a ticket of leave on arrival here. He bought the house, not rented, so must have had some money, but he built the back part on to the building himself, or so the neighbour says. We gather he was hoping his wife and sons would come out to join him here. Sadly, they never did.'

He hesitated, then admitted, 'Mr Lawson was a reasonable carpenter, but not . . . mmm, let us say not a builder, so the part he added will need work doing on it or even perhaps pulling down and rebuilding. Because of that, we're prepared to be very reasonable about the price.'

'I'd have to see it first, and my wife too, of course.'

'Naturally. But we do need to proceed quickly. There is another person interested, you see, a Mr Rory Flynn, but we wanted to give *you* the first chance, because Mr Flynn is not . . . ' Another hesitation, then, 'Not the sort of neighbour the people nearby would want, even if he could afford the house.'

'I know Mr Flynn,' Bram said quietly, not blackening the other man's name because that wasn't his way. But he'd never forgive Rory Flynn for what he'd done to Bram's sister. Never. Flynn must be doing well buying and fattening cows on some land outside the town or he'd not be able to consider buying a house.

It would give Bram some small satisfaction to snap up the house from under the fellow's nose. For all they'd grown up in the same village, they'd never been friends. Nowadays he did no more than offer Flynn a slight nod if they passed in the street because he didn't want to make a spectacle of their differences for the rest of the town to enjoy.

Mr Perry nodded. 'Yes, well, you'll understand how it is, then. It's a quiet street and people want to keep it that way. And since one of the nearby householders is a cousin of Mr Robinson, well, we thought to give *you* first refusal. I'm sure you and your wife would fit in well. There are a few humbler dwellings at one end of the street, but the people in them are all respectable and quiet.'

'It does sound as if the house may be of interest to me.'

'Could you come and see it now, do you

98

think? We really would like to make a quick decision.'

Uppity young devil, Bram thought. He and Mr Robinson probably looked down their noses at Bram as well, for being Irish and not a gentleman, and wouldn't have considered him in connection with the house if Conn hadn't put in a good word for him, and if Isabella hadn't been a lady born and bred. 'Yes, I can come now. We'll take my wife with us, though. Her opinion is the most important of all.'

After all, what did Bram know about large houses or gentlemen's residences, as this young man called them? He'd grown up dirt poor in a two-room house and worked in the stables at Shilmara, never going beyond the kitchen door of the big house.

When he told her the news, Isabella agreed to come. She handed little Arlen over to their young maid and put on her bonnet. She was ready in two minutes, linking her arm in Bram's and walking as briskly as the men, up the gentle slope, past the Bazaar and along the street that ran along the top of their block of land.

As they turned the corner into a second street, Mr Perry led them to a house halfway along it and stopped. 'Here it is.'

Bram stared at it. The place was in great need of attention and wouldn't be called a gentleman's residence in Ireland. But here even the gentry often had to be content with much smaller dwellings. It was a wooden structure with a corrugated tin roof. As with many colonial houses, the planks which formed its walls were unpainted, nailed on to a frame horizontally, overlapping one another to keep the rain out. The wood was silvered by the sun and some of the planks were warped. Yellowing white paint was peeling off the front door and window frames.

'It looks as if it'll fall down at any moment,' he said, not even wanting to go inside.

'I believe the front part of the building is sound though it does need painting.' When Bram said nothing, he added in the tone of a man forced to plead the case against his better instincts, 'I'd also like to point out that it's built on a larger than usual block, with a wide frontage and rear access from a laneway. You'd have room to keep a horse or a small vehicle round the back, should you wish to do so.'

Bram hid another grin at the young man's tone. Hadn't he been a groom for the first fifteen years of his working life? Who knew better than he how to keep a horse? He'd never make some poor animal suffer in a tiny backyard stable, especially in the heat of summer. He realised Mr Perry was speaking again and tried to concentrate.

'I happen to know that the people next door would be willing to sell their house as well, if you're wanting to turn this place into a grander residence. They told our clerk so when he came to check the dwelling.'

Now that made it more interesting, Bram admitted to himself.

'Before we go any further, how much is it?' Isabella asked.

Bram realised he hadn't even thought to ask that. When it came to buying a house, he was amazed he could afford to even think about it so soon after setting up as a trader. His business success was partly thanks to that first trip to Singapore and his ongoing relationship with Mr Lee, his wife's former employer. There was a huge profit on the goods he imported, which were much cheaper to buy in Singapore than if you brought them all the way from Britain.

Buying a house, indeed! What would his mother have said to that? She'd never even had enough to eat properly, thanks to his damned father's drinking.

The sum Mr Perry named had Isabella looking thoughtful, and when she asked about the house next door, a much smaller place with a lower price estimate, she gave no indication of her thoughts.

What a grand woman she is! Bram thought proudly.

When she turned to him, he said at once, 'I think you're the one who should be dealing with this house business, my love. I'm sure you know far better than me what questions to ask.'

Mr Perry looked shocked at that, so Bram added firmly, 'My wife has an excellent business head on her and does all the accounts for the shop. I trust her absolutely when it comes to money.'

The young lawyer stared at her as if she'd suddenly grown two heads.

Isabella squeezed her husband's hand and gave him a quick wink.

'We'll look round it, then,' Bram decided, since Mr Perry was still looking to him for direction in spite of what he'd just said. 'It's in the right part of town, that's for sure, though it does look . . . shabby.'

'Tumbledown,' Isabella added. 'The price may need to be reconsidered if it's as bad inside.'

Mr Perry looked at Bram with ill-concealed indignation, as if he couldn't bring himself to bargain with a woman. 'I'll let you discuss that, my love,' Bram said, winking at her.

Many men couldn't cope with Isabella being involved in the business, or the way she spoke her mind. But having married an intelligent woman, Bram wasn't going to stop her using that intelligence for her family's benefit.

Mr Perry moved forward, then stopped and turned. 'Ah, please be careful of the steps up to the veranda.'

The steps creaked but held his weight, and he was the heaviest of the three of them, so Bram gestured to his wife to follow.

The veranda boards were warped but there was no sign of termites infesting the wood that Bram could see. He'd get someone to crawl underneath the house and check that the wooden stumps it was built on were still free from such pests, who ate the wood till it crumbled. He knew he had to look for that sort of thing, because his friend Mitchell Nash had checked it out when helping renovate the mixture of sheds that now formed the Bazaar.

The front door of the house opened into a long narrow hall that ran all the way through to the back. They called these places breezeways, though on a hot summer day, there was often no breeze at all until the 'Fremantle doctor', an afternoon breeze off the sea, began to bring relief from the heat. The corridor had a nice high ceiling, with an elegant arch part way along separating the front part from the rear.

Isabella wrinkled her nose. 'The place is filthy, smells dreadful, and that's not just from dust or dirt.'

'I hadn't realised quite how dirty it was.' Mr Perry looked round, scowling. 'I should have come here and checked it before fetching you, only Mr Robinson wants the sale made quickly. He's not fond of dealing with emancipists.'

Many people weren't, Bram thought. Though many of the poor sods were only political prisoners and Bram couldn't blame them too much for struggling against the English, who had conquered Ireland centuries before and still didn't want to let go of their prize.

He wished suddenly that Ireland wasn't so far away, that he could go back there for an occasional visit. He missed the greenery sometimes, missed exercising a horse along a leafy lane in the quiet of early morning. He shook his head. None of that, he told himself. You're here and doing well. No one can have everything.

Isabella moved from side to side, checking the rooms and muttering to herself.

The front ones were quite spacious but the furniture in them was pitiful stuff. Bram paced one out: about five yards square. They had fireplaces, full of ash and debris still. The room to the left as they entered seemed to have been used as a bedroom and had grimy, tattered curtains drawn across the window, which presumably looked out on to the veranda at the front. If they bought it, he'd throw out that sagging bed which smelled of stale sweat.

'We need more light in here,' Isabella said. 'I want to check the window frames.'

'I'll see to that.' Mr Perry hurried to draw back the curtains with what was meant to be a flourish, but the whole apparatus fell down on him. The curtain pole hit him hard enough on the head to elicit a yelp and the ragged curtains draped themselves over him as dust rose from them in a cloud.

Bram pulled Isabella back to the doorway, giving her one quick grin, then wiping the amusement from his face as Mr Perry, coughing and spluttering, tore off the shreds of curtain still draping his upper body and hurled them into a corner.

'I must ask you to be very careful and touch nothing,' he said. 'We don't want any injuries. Are you all right?'

'Yes, we are. Thank you. And you?'

The young man brushed vainly at the dust on his clothing and looked round with loathing. 'As I said, the place needs attention, more attention than we'd realised. Shall we continue?'

There were two narrower rooms behind the front ones, looking out on to verandas at each side. All the verandas were quite wide, Bram thought, so they'd keep the hot summer sun off the house walls and windows.

The kitchen ran across the whole of the rear, a huge room with the actual cooking area built on at the right, projecting backwards. That had brick walls, for safety in case of fire. Another door at the left side suggested rooms leading off into a newer part of the building.

Mr Perry had a sour look to him and was occasionally brushing in vain at his clothing. 'I gather there are storerooms too. Do you wish to see them, Mrs Deagan?'

'Yes, of course I do,' Isabella said firmly. 'We need to see everything, even the garden shed, if there is one.'

Bram saw Mr Perry suppress a sigh, so intervened. You got more benefit from keeping people happy than from confronting them. 'You must be a busy man, so why don't you leave us to look round at our leisure?'

He took a deep breath and committed himself further, seeing a good business opportunity to be had. 'I'd be grateful if you'd tell the neighbour we're interested in buying his place before you leave, though. After we've finished looking round here, we'll go next door and look at his place, if that's convenient, then we'll come and see you at your rooms.'

Mr Perry's face brightened. 'That's a very good idea, Mr Deagan. But you will make sure to come and see us this afternoon, will you not?'

'We certainly will.' Armed with facts and figures, and ready to bargain. Bram wouldn't even consider paying full price for this house. But the land, near the centre of town, ah the

105

land was going to be extremely valuable one day, he was sure.

Only when the front door had closed behind the young lawyer, did Isabella give way to laughter.

'A very stiff young fellow, itching to look down his nose at me for being Irish,' Bram said with a chuckle. 'If Conn hadn't spoken up for us, I doubt he'd have let us have first refusal of this place. So, let's have a proper look round now, eh?'

There were cupboards and storerooms at the rear, built on anyhow, with two smaller rooms off the left side of the kitchen beyond them. Two garden sheds, one full of tools and the other containing junk of all sorts, plus a lean-to.

'Was he thinking of setting up as a junk dealer?' Bram wondered.

'Some of it may be useful. You never know. We could offer to clear it ourselves.'

That made him look at her sharply. Had she decided she wanted it already?

When they'd finished, she nodded. 'It has possibilities. What do you think?'

He looked at her with a wry smile. 'You want it, don't you?'

She smiled back. 'Yes, I do. It can be made into a big, beautiful house, and there'll be room for your family to stay with us — and maybe some of them can live next door, if that house is suitable. What do *you* think?'

He stood very still, trying to come to terms with the idea of *owning* this house and land. He didn't own the Bazaar or the land it stood on,

Conn Largan did. If it hadn't been for Conn's money and his trust in his childhood playmate, not to mention Isabella's connections to Lee Kar Ho in Singapore, Bram wouldn't have been able to become a trader or make nearly as much money, let alone buy a house.

Every now and then, he had to pinch himself to make sure he wasn't dreaming all this.

'Bram?' Isabella touched his arm lightly. 'If you don't want it, we can — '

He pulled her close. 'I'm just trying to get used to the idea of owning my own house. Me. Bram Deagan, a groom, who grew up mostly barefoot and went hungry many a time.'

'You've worked hard, but mostly, you've been clever and you have a good eye for an opportunity. Don't you feel this is a good opportunity? If you don't, we'll leave it.'

And his trading instinct kicked in, as it sometimes did. 'Oh, yes, my love. It's an excellent opportunity. If this house was in fine condition, we'd not be able to afford it and they'd not offer it to us. As it is . . . ' He grabbed her by the waist and swung her round, making her cry out in laughing protest. 'As it is, I'll send you home once we've seen the other house, if you don't mind, then I'll go and play the angry husband whose wife insists on buying an unsuitable house, and who for two pennies would tell them to keep their damned house, but might just be persuaded to buy it if the price was lower.'

She threw her head back and laughed. Oh, but he loved the sound of her laughter. 'You're a clever man. If we like the other place, you can be

107

even more outraged at the idea of buying *two* houses.'

As they stood on the front veranda, getting the feel of the street, which was unpaved, its bare sand crunching beneath their feet, a man came towards them from next door.

'Excuse me, but are you the gentleman who wants to buy my house?'

'I may want to buy it, but I haven't seen it yet. My name's Deagan.'

'Yes, my wife said you were Mr and Mrs Deagan.' He bobbed his head vaguely in Isabella's direction. 'She's seen you both at your Bazaar. She likes shopping there. She says to come in and look round when you're ready, because our place is always clean and tidy.'

'How kind of her!' Isabella said. 'Could we come straight away?'

'Of course.'

The house next door was a simple four-bedroomed cottage and was immaculately clean.

'How much do you want for it?' Isabella asked.

It was the woman who replied and the two men exchanged glances then, by unspoken consent, left their wives to barter.

When a price had been agreed, however, it was the men who shook hands on it.

Stupid world where a wife can't buy a house without her husband's permission, Bram thought.

'How soon can you move out?' Isabella asked.

'As soon as you've paid us the money and we

108

can get a passage to Sydney,' the woman said promptly.

'We can pay you as soon as we can get the money from our bank, but I think there will be legal matters to attend to first, contracts of sale and so on. But that said, we'll take it at the price agreed and work as quickly as we can.'

The woman burst into tears of joy and her husband patted her on the shoulder and tried to control his own emotions.

'Our son went to New South Wales, because he said there was no future here. We're desperate to follow him. She's missing her daughter-in-law and the grandchildren. We only stayed behind to sell our house, but people don't want to pay us the full amount in cash and we don't trust them to send payments on to New South Wales once we've left the Swan River Colony.'

'Well, as soon as the lawyers can sort it all out, you can have your money in full,' Bram said. 'All this is, however, on condition we get the other house at a decent price.'

He saw Isabella home, then went off to talk to the lawyers.

When he came out of their rooms, he had trouble restraining himself from laughing and running back to the Bazaar. Thanks to the snobbish Mr Perry being so disgusted with the condition of the place, Bram had bought it at an even lower price than he'd expected.

Oh, what a fine day it was!

When he got to the Bazaar, he saw his wife serving a lady who was selecting a length of silk for a dress.

He waited till the customer had taken her package away, then could hold it in no longer. Grabbing Isabella again, he waltzed her round and round the shop, shouting, 'We got it! We got it!' scattering the laughing customers and staff as he went.

6

The following day, Maura sat in the carriage next to Mrs Julia, looking out of the window, enjoying the scenery. It felt strange to ride along like this. She'd ridden in a carriage before, but not a comfortable vehicle like this one, just an old rattletrap of a thing used for the servants.

However well sprung it was, you still felt the bumps in the road, she thought, and that seemed to fit her life, too. No one was able to avoid the bumps.

They passed through the village of Ardgullan beyond which lay the big house. It stood on a promontory overlooking another of the small lakes that were scattered in between the hills in this area. Mrs Julia said there were dozens of loughs and this wasn't one of the prettiest, but Maura thought the water looked lovely, sparkling in the weak sunlight after a shower, reflecting the lower slopes.

A little further on, she leaned forward to stare out of the window, trying to work out what there was on top of the small hill behind the house.

'Are you looking at the standing stones? They were erected thousands of years ago by primitive men, no one knows why.'

'Just imagine that.' The people might have been primitive by modern standards, but how had they got those huge stones up there? Maura wondered. But she didn't get much more than a glimpse of them, because they reached the entrance to Ardgullan House just then.

The wrought iron gates looked as if they were never closed, because they were pushed right back and grass was growing higher than their bottom edges. The drive itself was clear of weeds, though the gatekeeper's cottage looked to be uninhabited. Irish landowners weren't always rich, she knew.

When they arrived at the house, Mrs Julia told Maura to follow her to the front door, not go round to the servants' entrance.

The door was flung open before they got there and a tall young woman with dark hair came out, beaming at them. She was expecting a child, though she wasn't very far along, and looked to be in blooming health.

This must be Xanthe Maguire, Maura thought. How lovely she looked.

'I'm so glad to see someone on this showery day!' she exclaimed and hugged Mrs Julia.

When she was introduced to Maura, she shook hands, just as if her visitor was a lady, and swept them both into a sitting room which had a cheerful fire burning in the grate, even though it wasn't really cold.

'How is little Andreas?' Mrs Julia asked.

'Lively as ever. He's crawling now, getting into everything he can reach.' She turned to Maura. 'My sisters and I all have Greek names, thanks to my father, so I carried on the tradition with my son. I'll introduce you to him later, if he's awake.'

'I'd love to see him again,' Mrs Julia said. 'But

first, Maura needs to know something about travelling to Australia, as I wrote. She's leaving in a few days.'

'Oh, how I envy you! I do wish it wasn't so far away! Two of my sisters live there and letters take a dreadful long time to go to and fro.'

She sighed and looked sad for a moment, then shook her head as if to banish the mood. 'At least they get there more quickly these days, because they're sent through France to Marseille by train before they're put on a P&O ship. It's amazing that they get there safely, but we've not lost one yet. We number them to be sure.'

She paused for breath, her eyes still twinkling with amusement. 'Am I beating your ears? I do talk a lot, I know. But I see so few people here. Ronan's promised to take me to visit my other sister in England after this child is born. My sister's called Cassandra, another Greek name. I shall hold him to it and we'll talk ourselves hoarse, she and I.'

As the visit continued, Mrs Maguire explained about travelling by ship, pouring out information. She stopped suddenly and said, 'You'll never remember it all. I'll get you some paper and a pencil, and you can take notes.'

Her hostess talked till Maura's head was spinning but she did feel better equipped by having some idea how things were done on board big ships. After a while, Mrs Maguire took her to the kitchen, where she had tea and cakes with the staff, leaving the ladies to chat in peace. She felt more comfortable there.

Now, what she needed most was a bit of peace

113

to think it all through and study the notes she'd taken today, but she doubted she'd get much of that.

As she saw her guests out, Mrs Maguire promised to visit them before Maura and the children left. 'You can ask me about anything else you've thought of then.'

She thrust a parcel wrapped in what looked like an old sheet at Maura. 'I hope you won't be offended but you're tall like me and I know how much you'll need to take with you. These clothes might be useful in a warmer climate. They're of much lighter materials. Not much use for them in rainy old Ireland.' But her fond smile as she said that showed she was happy living here.

No time for false pride, Maura thought. 'I'm grateful, not offended, Mrs Maguire. Thank you very much.'

The information she'd acquired was going to amaze the children as much as the number of clothes they'd need to take, she was sure. She wondered suddenly how good they were at reading, whether they'd been allowed to get much education. If they needed help with reading, she'd teach them on board ship . . . or Mrs Maguire said classes were usually held.

She and Mrs Julia didn't go straight back to Shilmara, but carried on to Enniskillen to visit the shops there. They went to the second-hand one where she'd bought a few clothes for the children when she first arrived. Mrs Julia bought clothes from it regularly to help their poorer tenants.

There wasn't going to be time to make

everything new for Maura and the children, and anyway, you could get some good bargains second-hand if you bought the better stuff. Some of the clothes she was shown were hardly worn. She bought petticoats and chemises for herself, as well as underclothes for the children, who might not be used to wearing them.

They ended up with a huge number of garments and she couldn't have afforded nearly this many if Mr Kieran and his wife weren't paying for the children's clothes.

When they got back to Shilmara, Mrs Julia said, 'Why don't you show the children what we've bought and tell them we've got more things coming? I need to put my feet up for a while.' She added with a smile, 'I'm expecting a child, you see, not for six months yet, but I do get more tired than usual at this stage.'

Heaven help her, Maura walked away feeling deeply envious of that. Two ladies, both blooming and loved. And she was on her own, with only other people's children to look after.

★　★　★

Maura went to find her nieces and nephew. They were listening to a young woman who was reading a story to the group of scrawny children who seemed to be inhabiting the barn now. She waited till it was over, then called her three across.

'Come and see what Mrs Julia and I have bought for you in Enniskillen.' She wasn't quite sure how to speak to them, so settled for treating

115

them as if they were junior housemaids or the boot boy, young but capable of understanding what they had to do.

The three stood there in silence in the cottage, staring at the piles of clothing as she pulled things out of the sacks and laid them on the table in three piles.

'Are they all for us?' Brenna asked in a hushed voice.

'Yes. We'll get them all washed, to make sure they're clean. You'll need more than that, so that your clean clothes will last the whole journey. It takes about two months to get there and we can't wash things on the ship. Mrs Maguire said you have to parcel your clothes up in sets and bring the clean ones up from the trunks in the hold every couple of weeks, leaving the dirty clothes down there.'

They were so quiet she guessed suddenly how they were feeling, as bewildered as she was, so she spoke from the heart. 'I've got a pile of new clothes too. Mrs Julia insisted and Mrs Maguire gave me some of her old things, because she's tall like me. I can't believe it. I never had so many clothes in all my life.'

'But you're rich,' Brenna said sharply. 'Why did she give you clothes?'

'I'm not rich. Whatever gave you that idea?'

'Look at your clothes.'

'They're decent clothes, but they're a working woman's clothes. I have to watch how I spend every penny I earn, believe me. But there's no one to drink away my money like your fathers did, so I can dress decently.' She wondered if

116

she'd gone too far with that, but they just nodded as if they understood that. Well, their fathers had both been drunks. She'd had little time for her brothers because of that.

'Wait till you see the fashionable ladies when we travel to Southampton. They wear crinolines under their skirts to make them stand out. This wide.' She spread out her hands to show them.

'Mrs Julia has crinolines,' Brenna volunteered. 'She wears them sometimes when they're going visiting or to church.'

'They look silly,' Ryan said scornfully, stuffing his hands in his pockets and scowling down at the ground, which seemed to be a habit of his. He hadn't said a word about his own clothes, but he'd looked as astonished as the others.

Maura smiled at Brenna. 'Well, I agree crinolines look silly, but it gives poor seam-stresses plenty of work sewing those huge skirts, so we shouldn't complain about it, should we? Now, can you try each of these pieces of clothing on, please? We'll have to alter some of the clothes to fit you. It's a good thing they let you keep yourselves clean in the barn. We don't want to dirty these.'

'We have to wash every day,' Brenna confided, 'and have a bath on Fridays in the laundry. I like it.'

'You'll have to keep clean on the ship, too. Ryan, you can go into the back room and change into yours there, but I'll need to see each of them so that I can pin them if they need taking in.' And they would for him. She'd bought them too big, because she was sure he'd start growing now that he was eating properly, so she'd try not to cut any material off then they could be let out again.

Still scowling, he did as she asked, but she saw him stroke the jacket that lay on top before he picked the pile up, and guessed he was more pleased about his new clothes than he was letting them see.

Maura used the shiny new pins Mrs Julia had given her to indicate where the clothes needed taking in. The pins had no rust on them so she didn't need to clean them first with the sandpaper.

Once the children had tried everything on, she explained, 'Some of the maids are going to help me alter them, so that they'll fit you properly. I can do alterations, I'm a good needlewoman, but I won't have time to do them all before we leave. We can start teaching you to sew while we work, if you like, Brenna. You're old enough now to mend your own clothes.'

Her niece's face lit up. 'Really? Oh, I'd like that. Shall I help you carry them back to the big house?'

'You can all help me, if you will. I'll carry Noreen's clothes and you two can carry your own. Noreen, you can carry this one.'

The child nodded, taking the little skirt from her. She was nearly as silent as Ryan but she watched everything that went on, wide-eyed at this new way of living, and she responded quickly when asked to do something.

Maura picked up the rest of Noreen's pile. 'We've to take them up to the nursery floor. I

118

don't know where that is, but one of the other servants will show us.'

Ryan followed them in silence. Did the lad never join in conversations? Maura wondered.

The nursery maid came down to the kitchen to show them where to go and the undermaid, who did mending and helped with laundry, joined them in the unused schoolroom. This had been turned over to the task of altering the clothes, since the Largan children weren't yet old enough for proper lessons, and there were several tables to work at.

The two maids looked at Maura for instructions and she suddenly felt like an Assistant Housekeeper again, which made her chest feel tight with sadness for a moment.

'I'll do Ryan's clothes,' she said, 'and you can take one child's pile each. That way, you'll know from one garment to another what's needed. Best leave some room for growth, though. They're eating better now.'

'John from the stables is painting the name DEAGAN on your trunks,' the maid told her. 'Big letters, the master told him, so that there's no mistake whose they are among so many.'

'I'd never have thought of that.'

'Mrs Jamieson said the other maids could come and help for the odd hour,' the other young woman volunteered.

'Then we'll set them to work on the biggest pile left at the time. It'll probably be Ryan's because I still have to look after Father Hilary, who hasn't found a housekeeper yet. He wants to find an older woman, says it looks better for a priest. And he deserves one with a pleasant temper, because he's very easy to look after, doesn't make a mess and always says thank you.' When he said that, it'd made her wonder if he thought her an older woman. A depressing thought.

'My aunt could do that, I reckon,' one of the helpers volunteered. 'Her husband just died and her children are grown up. She's not been a housekeeper before, but she's a good cook and her house is always so clean and tidy you could eat off the floor.'

'I'm sure Mr Kieran would let one of the lads go with a message to her to see Father Hilary about a job. I'm only filling in at the presbytery for a few days. I'd not have volunteered to help him at all if I'd known how much sewing there was to do. It's a pity we don't have one of those new sewing machines. There is one at Brent House, where I work — used to work — but they only use it on straight seams and household linen. Still, it saves a lot of time.'

Maura felt comfortable chatting to the women. She sent the older children back to the barn, where classes were apparently being held, but when she looked, little Noreen was sleeping in a corner, curled up on a rug like a kitten, so she left her there.

By the time she went back to the presbytery to give the priest his evening meal, supplied by the big house still, her fingertips felt rough with the pricks from the needles, but she was happy about progress.

Ryan was outside the back door, kicking a

stone. She wondered if he was waiting to chat to her. She wanted to get to know him better, to take that unhappy look off his face.

'Are you pleased about your clothes?'

He stared at her, then nodded.

'Are you hungry? You need feeding up, my lad. Let's ask Cook for something to put you on till the next meal.'

His face brightened into a smile. 'Thank you, miss.'

'You should call me Auntie Maura.'

'Auntie Maura,' he repeated obediently.

She counted that brief conversation a triumph, especially the fleeting smile he gave her as she passed him a scone Cook had provided.

'I'm always hungry,' he admitted.

'Well, you're a growing boy.'

'Will I? Grow taller, I mean?'

'Don't talk with your mouth full. And yes, of course you will.'

Another lad called to him from near the barn, so he crammed the rest of the scone in his mouth and set off, turning to give her a wave.

One step at a time with him, she told herself.

★ ★ ★

On the day before they were to leave for Southampton, Mrs Julia fell down the stairs after tripping on a frayed piece of carpet.

The household was in uproar as she lay groaning at the bottom, with only Mrs Jamieson and Maura keeping their heads.

'Send for the doctor and the master!' Mrs

121

Jamieson ordered. 'And find two men to carry the mistress.'

'I'll be all right in a few minutes,' Mrs Julia said, but her voice was faint and she looked pale.

Maura beckoned the footman. 'You and I will carry her up to bed now. She'll be better lying down.'

Carefully they took the mistress up to her bedroom, where her maid had rushed ahead to turn back the bedcovers.

As they were laying her on the bed, she grimaced. Maura sent the footman away and sat down beside her, since her maid was young and weeping too much to be of use. She patted Mrs Julia's hand. 'You should lie quietly for a while, ma'am. We've sent for the doctor and the master.'

Before they arrived, Mrs Julia cried out and doubled up in the bed.

Mrs Jamieson, who had joined them, pressed one hand to her bosom. 'What do we do?' she whispered.

'I don't think there's anything we can do but let nature take its course, if she's losing the baby,' Maura whispered back. 'I was there when one of the visitors to Brent Hall lost hers. We'll need towels and water . . . and something to put the mess in.'

By the time the master arrived, Mrs Julia had lost the child, a tiny creature, hardly human in shape as yet. It was Maura who took charge, because Mrs Jamieson's 'Mrs' was purely tradition for a housekeeper and she'd never been married let alone had anything to do with childbirth, as those who'd grown up in big families often had.

Mrs Julia was very brave but afterwards she clutched Maura's hand and wept bitterly. 'I wanted that child, oh, I did.'

'You'll have others, ma'am. This was just an unlucky accident.'

When the master came, they left him with his wife, and showed the doctor up shortly afterwards.

As she went back to the servants' hall, Maura couldn't help wondering what would happen now about her getting to Southampton. It might be selfish, but this couldn't have happened at a worse time for her and the children.

★ ★ ★

Hugh felt like a circus master as he set off for Southampton, accompanied by a governess, nursery maid and, of course, his daughter. His manservant had declined to accompany him to Australia.

Miss Fenton made no attempt to help in any practical way, except for looking after Adèle, who complicated matters by trying to stay with her father rather than her governess. The child seemed to find comfort in clutching his hand, so he let her stay.

He felt utter relief when they got to the hotel in Southampton and managed to book adjoining rooms. If it was such a parade each time they moved on, the journey was going to be very arduous for him, because they all turned to him when they wanted to know something and half the time he had no answer for them. All he knew about travelling to Australia was what he'd read about in books and pamphlets.

Adèle was exhausted and walked slowly into the hotel. He couldn't help glancing enviously at a family with three stout little boys, who were rushing here and there, excited by everything they saw.

What wouldn't he give to have a daughter healthy enough to get into mischief?

When he went to visit Adèle after settling into his own room, she surprised him by beaming at him, seeming to be recovering quickly from the fatigue of the journey.

'The air here tastes salty, Daddy. I like breathing it.'

'You do?'

'Yes. It seems easier to breathe.' She leaned towards him and whispered, 'Miss Fenton says I can't have the window open in case I get a chill, but when she's gone to bed, I'm going to open it again.'

'Just a little bit, then.'

She nodded, eyes dancing.

He had tears in his eyes as he went to his own room.

He'd got his wish. She was planning mischief. Only the most minor of disobediences, but it seemed like a good omen, somehow.

Before he went to bed, he crept into his daughter's room to check that she was all right and found her sleeping peacefully with the window open. Was it his imagination, or was her breath not rasping as much as usual?

He prayed he wasn't mistaken, prayed that the doctor had been right and the sea air and warmer climate would do her good. Just . . . prayed.

Tomorrow they had to see the medical officer, to make sure they weren't bringing contagious diseases on board the ship. Hugh had a small worry about his daughter being refused permission to board. Surely they wouldn't do that? The shipping agent had assured him they wouldn't, but still, the niggling fear remained to disturb his sleep.

★ ★ ★

Maura had planned to go to bed early, but she changed her mind, certain Mr Kieran would want to see her. There could be no question of Mrs Julia travelling anywhere, she knew that, and she doubted he would leave his wife till he was sure she was all right.

Sure enough, at nine o'clock, a maid came to find Maura.

'The master would like to see you, Miss Deagan. He's in the library with Mrs Jamieson. Says you're to knock and go straight in.'

She went at once, worrying what he was going to tell her.

He was looking very serious and so was the housekeeper.

'Do take a seat, Maura.' He waited till she was seated, then said bluntly, 'You must have realised that my wife and I won't be able to travel with you.'

125

'Yes, I had.'

'The thing is, it'd be foolish to wait a month for the next sailing when you're all packed and ready now.'

She knew then that things had got worse for her . . . again.

'Mrs Jamieson and I felt you should go ahead on your own. After all, you're used to taking trains and the ferry, so that part of the journey won't be completely new to you.'

For a moment, she couldn't find the words to answer him.

His voice grew gentler. 'Do you think you can manage?'

No, she didn't. She didn't even want to go, for heaven's sake. But they were both staring at her and somehow she gathered together the shreds of her pride and said, 'I'm sure I can.'

Mrs Jamieson gave one of her rare smiles, nodding approval.

Mr Kieran looked at her with more understanding than the housekeeper. 'I know it's a bit daunting, but you're a very capable woman. Everyone speaks well of you, and we've watched how hard you've worked to get everything ready.'

'Thank you, sir. I always do my best.'

'I can go through what needs to be done when you arrive in Southampton and you can write it all down.'

He pushed a notebook towards her. The house seemed to be full of the things.

'Use this.'

'I have one in my room, if you don't mind me

126

getting it. Then I'll have all the information in one place.'

'Very well. And Maura . . . '

'Yes, sir?'

'I'll give you some extra money so that you're able to take cabs and pay hotel bills.'

She wasn't stupid enough to refuse the money. She knew what a difference that would make with three children, one of them only six, and small for her age. 'Thank you, sir.'

It was well after midnight before she got to bed in the room she'd moved into at the big house when Father Hilary's new housekeeper started. She asked Mrs Jamieson to have her called at five o'clock in the morning.

She lay in bed, her mind buzzing with so many instructions and worries that she was sure she'd never get to sleep.

How on earth would she cope on her own? What if she lost one of the children on the way there? Children wandered off.

What if one of them became ill? Or fell overboard? Or . . .

★ ★ ★

In the morning, Maura woke with a start as someone tapped on her bedroom door. She sat up in bed, thinking it'd be someone there to call her. 'I'm awake.'

To her surprise, Mrs Jamieson entered. 'I thought I'd stay with you till you leave, in case I can do anything to help.'

'That's so very kind of you.'

127

'I can guess what this is costing you and I pray the Lord will reward you for what you're doing. Now . . . come down to my room when you're dressed and we'll have a cup of tea before we get the children ready. The nursery maid has offered to help you with that.'

'People are being very kind.'

'Everyone admires what you're doing, taking on those three youngsters.'

Maura didn't know what to say to that. If they only knew how reluctantly she'd taken on the children, how worried she was that she'd make a mess of looking after them.

Three hours passed in a blur as they got ready, but by eight o'clock, the bags were packed and they went outside. They were to ride to Enniskillen, the nearest town, in the servants' carriage, a huge old vehicle which had room for three trunks and the rest of their luggage. Maura could only pray that her trunk from Brent Hall would be waiting for her in Southampton.

Brenna was jumping about, unable to stand still for excitement. 'I've never ridden in a carriage before.'

Before they could get in, Mr Kieran came running out of the house, looking rumpled with sleep and wearing a dressing gown over his nightshirt. 'I just wanted to wish you well.'

'Thank you. How is Mrs Julia?' Maura asked.

'She had a good night and sends her best wishes.' He turned to Ryan. 'You're the man of the party now and the oldest of the children. Miss Deagan will be depending on you to help her.'

128

Ryan froze, looking surprised, then managed a nod.

That poor boy was constantly being surprised by things that happened in his new life, Maura thought. 'You can get in now, children.'

Mr Kieran shook her hand, closed the carriage door after her and stood waving until they turned out of the drive.

Then the four of them were alone.

'Are you frightened, Auntie Maura?' Brenna asked suddenly. 'You look pale.'

She swallowed hard. Was she showing her fears so clearly? Should she try to pretend? No, they were going to be spending a lot of time together. Better to set an example of being truthful. 'I am nervous, I must admit. We'll be travelling a long way together and I have to look after you.'

'Who looks after you?'

'I don't usually need looking after.'

Brenna wasn't letting go easily. 'What if anything happens to you, though?'

'It won't.' She had a sudden idea and pulled the notebook out of her soft leather handbag, the sort of capacious container for personal possessions which some female servants carried and ladies definitely didn't. 'But if it does, you'd have this to look at. Mrs Maguire told me all sorts of things about travelling, because she's been to Australia and back. I wrote them down, to make sure I don't forget them.'

They stared at the notebook.

'And last night, Mr Largan gave me some more instructions for the journey. They're

129

written in this notebook, too. You can read it, if you want.'

Brenna literally moved backwards, away from the book and Ryan scowled. Only Noreen sat placidly, murmuring to her doll.

'What's the matter?' Maura asked. 'Tell me.'

'I can't read very well,' Ryan said at last. 'Da always said reading and writing don't plant potatoes for your dinner.'

'They can help you get other sorts of jobs that pay for food produced by people like your father, though, and pay well, too. Look at your brother Bram. If he couldn't read and write, he'd not be able to run a shop. But if you want, I'll help you learn to read properly. It's not hard, just takes practice. Then you can check things out in this notebook if you're puzzled.'

Ryan gave her one of his blackest scowls.

'I can read a bit,' Brenna volunteered. 'We learned at school. Only Ma kept me home to help her, so I didn't get very far.'

'We'll have plenty of time on the ship to learn. I'm sure it's what your brother Bram would want you to do, Ryan. After all, you need to be able to read and write if you're to work in his shop.'

'I've never been inside a shop,' Ryan said. 'I wouldn't know what to do.'

'Your brother will no doubt show you. He wanted you to go to him in Australia, so he must have plans for you. It's interesting working in a shop, I'm told.'

'Does Cousin Bram know we're coming?' Brenna asked.

'No, but he'll be happy to see you.'

130

'How do you know that?'

'Because I know Bram.'

'What will I be doing when we get there?' Brenna asked. 'I'm not his sister like Noreen is, so maybe he won't want to help me.'

'I don't know what you'll be doing, but you're my niece so it's up to me to make sure you have some way to earn your bread, and I promise I'll do that. And anyway, Bram wrote that he wanted his family with him in Australia. You're family.'

Noreen didn't talk much, just listened and cuddled the rag doll. Someone had apparently given it to her when she came to the big house. Ryan said it was the first toy she'd ever had and she never went anywhere without it.

The two older children fell silent, staring out of the windows and nudging one another or asking questions because they soon left the village and reached places none of the children had ever seen before.

Noreen whispered to the doll, which was a good sign, Maura thought. The child was starting to speak more, though never loudly.

Maura leaned her head back, feeling exhausted. This was only the start. She had over two months of being responsible for these children. And she had to teach them so much about the world outside Shilmara.

Brenna's question worried her. Who would look after them if Maura fell ill or anything happened to her?

Oh, don't be silly! she told herself. Nothing's going to happen. You're not a sickly person and thirty-five isn't that old.

7

The children were awed by the small railway station at Enniskillen and froze like animals facing a predator when the train arrived. They flinched as it filled the station with noise and clouds of steam, sending out that distinctive sweet-sour smell that only railway steam seemed to have.

Maura tensed as Ryan glanced over his shoulder and hesitated before getting into the carriage. For a moment, she'd thought he might be considering fleeing.

When the train jerked and started to move, all three turned to her, as if for reassurance. Then, when nothing bad happened to them as the train gathered speed, they began to look out of the windows and point things out to one another again.

She'd never heard Ryan say so much.

Even Noreen joined in occasionally now, though she spoke very badly for a child aged six.

'I forgot to tell you: if you want to go to the necessary, you'll have to wait for the train to stop at one of the stations, and go quickly before the train sets off. There is a necessary on the ferry and you can use it any time, but we'll all use it just before we reach England because it'll take time to find our next train.'

It was difficult getting the children on to the

ferry to Liverpool, because they kept stopping to stare at all the new sights on the docks.

Once they were standing on the deck by the rail, Maura said firmly, 'Listen to me. Trains and ships go at a fixed time, so we can't stop and look at things when we're changing from one to the other. They don't wait for anyone. They just . . . set off.'

They frowned at this.

'Not even if they know you're coming?' Ryan asked at last.

'They don't know who is going to get on the train or the ship; they just sell tickets to anyone. This isn't like villages. Nobody knows anyone else.'

They looked round as if checking that.

'And you need to stay close to me, because if you get lost, how will I find you again?'

More silence, then it was Ryan who said, 'Someone will have to hold Noreen's hand all the time, won't they?'

'Yes, please. Can you do that for me?' She waited for his nod and later was relieved to see Ryan holding his little sister's hand tightly as they made their way from the ferry to a train.

Maura heaved a sigh of relief when they sat down in the train. Looking after three ignorant children was exhausting. 'I'm tired. Aren't you? I'll be glad when we get to the hotel in Manchester. We're going to stay the night there, then set off tomorrow morning.'

'What do we do in a hotel?'

She kept assuming they knew what things were like. She'd had to explain so many things to them. But they didn't forget, once told, so she knew they weren't stupid.

Ryan in particular kept asking her the time. None of them could tell the time because they'd not had clocks in their homes, so it was yet another thing she'd have to teach them. She'd better start making a list. When she had a minute to spare . . .

She leaned her head back for a moment and jerked awake as Ryan tugged her arm. 'Is this Manchester?'

She peered out of the window. 'No. But you did right to wake me.' She mustn't let herself doze off again. Oh, but she was tired after only a few hours' sleep.

★ ★ ★

After a rather cursory examination by the medical officer, Hugh took Adèle for a walk round the streets near the hotel, accompanied by Carrie, because Miss Fenton said she needed to rest after the jolting of the train.

'Are we going on board tomorrow?' the child asked.

'Yes. It'll be exciting, won't it?'

'Miss Fenton says it'll be uncomfortable and she was muttering to herself before we went to see the medical officer, saying she felt bilious.'

'Doesn't take much to make her bilious, does it?' Carrie said, then clapped a hand to her mouth and looked at her employer anxiously but with a hint of a smile.

He didn't scold her because she was right: the

governess claimed to be bilious at the slightest thing.

When they got back to the hotel, he took Adèle to eat luncheon in the cafe and sent Carrie off to eat in the staff dining room.

'Shall I go and tell Miss Fenton we're back before I do that?' the young maid asked. 'She might be hungry. I know I am.'

'No. I think we'll let her choose her own time for eating.' He didn't want her sour face across the table from him, was beginning to regret bringing her along, especially now he'd seen how capable Carrie was.

'I think the food's been lovely. It's all been lovely, sir.' Carrie beamed at them and went away.

'I like Carrie,' Adèle said. 'She doesn't fuss and scold like Miss Fenton, and she's always smiling.'

To his delight, his daughter ate well, chatting about all they'd seen on their journey.

However, after the meal, he decided he couldn't neglect Miss Fenton any longer, so took his daughter upstairs with him and tapped on the governess's door.

There was no answer, so he tapped again. 'Are you all right, Miss Fenton?'

A hotel maid came hurrying along the corridor carrying a pile of bed linen.

'You've just missed the lady who had this room, sir.' She pushed the door open. 'I've been sent to change the bed linen in here.'

He followed her in and looked round in shock. No sign of an occupant. 'Do you know where the lady went?'

'No, sir. Just that she had to leave suddenly.'

He walked out to where his daughter was waiting. 'There seems to have been a mix-up. I'll ring for Carrie and you two can wait for me in your room.' When the maid arrived, he explained quickly what had happened and went down to make enquiries.

At the reception desk, the clerk produced a letter. 'The lady was called away suddenly, sir. She left you a note.'

He took it over to a window to read, but he'd already guessed what it was going to say.

Dear Mr Beaufort,

It is with great regret that I must decline to proceed any further on this journey. I am not a good traveller, and even this part of the journey has upset me more than I'd expected. The thought of travelling for weeks on a ship is not to be borne.

I've taken my trunk and other luggage, and shall return to my brother and his wife.

I wish you and Adèle a safe journey.

Eugenia Fenton

He had to read it twice more before he could take it in, then fury filled him. Thank goodness he hadn't paid her the bonus in advance! But he had paid the costs of extra clothing for the voyage.

More important, what was he going to do about Adèle now? Carrie was willing, but young and inexperienced.

He walked slowly back up the broad shallow

136

stairs, pausing for a moment to compose himself before he knocked on his daughter's door.

She and Carrie were staring out of the window, laughing at something. They turned at the sound of the door opening.

'Is Miss Fenton all right?' Adèle asked.

'She's gone back to her family. The travelling upset her.' He looked at Carrie. 'I hope you're going to be all right to travel with us still?'

'Bless you, yes, sir. I'm enjoying myself.'

'You mean, Miss Fenton won't be with us? But who'll do my lessons with me, Daddy?'

'Apart from reading, you can have a holiday from lessons. And Carrie, would you mind sharing Adèle's cabin now Miss Fenton won't be there? It'll be a lot more comfortable than steerage, I promise you.'

She stared at him, eyes narrowed in thought, then surprised him. 'I think Miss Adèle will be a lot happier without that old sourpuss, sir, if you'll pardon the liberty. And I'll take good care of your daughter, don't you worry. I've got younger brothers and sisters and I know how to look after children.'

'Thank you.'

But he was still angry with Miss Fenton. Very.

And angry with himself, too, for being taken in like that. He suspected the woman had never intended to travel to Australia with them, but had seized the opportunity to acquire a whole new wardrobe at his expense.

★   ★   ★

137

As the final train drew near Southampton, Maura sighed in relief, though getting the children on to the ship was an ordeal she now had to face alone. It wouldn't be like taking a ferry, she was sure.

With Mr Kieran by her side, it'd have been easy. People listened to a gentleman and treated him with respect.

Their trunks were loaded on the cab, but their cases had to go inside with them. To her relief the cab driver said he knew a hotel where ordinary people stopped.

'Respectable and clean,' she warned him.

He nodded. 'It is, missus.'

But as the cab turned off the main road, she didn't like the look of the area. And the streets grew rapidly shabbier.

Putting one finger to her lips to warn the children to be quiet, she pulled the string to gain the driver's attention, but he paid no attention to her. Now she was really alarmed. 'Hold tight!' she called to the children and flung the cab door open, slamming it back on its hinges. 'Hoy! We have to go back. I've left a bag at the station.'

He didn't stop but whipped up his horse. For a moment she didn't know what to do, then fortunately she saw a policeman and began to scream for help. He at once blew his whistle and started chasing after the cab, which couldn't get up speed in the narrow streets.

The driver stopped, glaring down at her.

'You all right, miss?' the policeman called, panting as he caught up with them.

'I am now you're here, but this driver wouldn't

138

stop and I don't know where he was taking us. I asked for a respectable hotel.'

He looked up at the cab driver, who said, 'I was taking her to my cousin's boarding house, that's all.'

'I asked for a hotel, not a boarding house! And why didn't you stop when I asked you to?'

'Because we're nearly there.'

The policeman studied the luggage. 'Where are you going, miss?'

'To Australia, on a P&O ship.'

'Travelling steerage, are you?'

'Yes.'

'Why didn't you go to the P&O depot, then? It's where the steerage passengers usually stay as they wait to board. Won't cost you anything, either, as this cab driver no doubt was aware.'

She looked at him in shock. 'I didn't know about it. My employer and his wife were going to see me to the ship, then she became ill and they couldn't come. He told me what to do, but of course he'd only know about the way the gentry travel.'

'No husband to help you? Or are you going out to Australia to join him?'

'I'm the children's aunt. Their parents have died and I'm taking them to their brother in Australia.'

His face softened as he looked at Noreen, leaning against Brenna, almost asleep, but with the rag doll still clutched tightly to her chest. 'She looks about the same age as my youngest. I'll see you to the depot, miss. You'll be all right from there.'

He turned to the driver. 'The depot.'

'Yes, officer.'

When they got to the depot, the policeman saw them and their luggage to the door, decided how much Maura should pay the driver, then said, 'Good luck in your new life, miss.'

'I can't thank you enough for your help.'

'My pleasure as well as my duty.' He turned as the cab horse clopped away. 'I'll remember that one. I think you might have had a lucky escape.'

As the door of the depot closed behind her, Maura closed her eyes for a moment in relief. What if the policeman hadn't been there? She shuddered.

The matron of the depot asked her something, and she turned to give their particulars. These were checked against the passenger list, then they were shown into a big open room with bunk beds, where families stayed. It was clean and Maura immediately felt safe there. She didn't like the idea of sleeping with so many people, but she'd just have to cope with the lack of privacy. It'd be the same on the ship, she supposed. A lot of people crammed into a small space.

By the time she'd got the children to bed, she was so far beyond exhaustion she could have fallen asleep standing up, she was sure.

She woke in the morning because someone was tugging her blanket. 'Noreen wants to go, Auntie Maura.'

She jerked out of sleep and managed to find her coat, which would have to do as a dressing gown. How did mothers manage to keep up with large families? she wondered, as she used the

140

facilities herself. She was finding it difficult with only three children to look after and oh, she felt so guilty for nearly getting them all into trouble yesterday

Back in the big sleeping room, she found Ryan backed up against his bunk with two bigger lads taunting him and shouting 'Dirty Irish'.

She rushed across and yanked them back by the collars. 'Get away from him this minute.' She kept hold of one's collar. 'Where are your parents?'

A man came across the room, looking her up and down insolently. 'What's the matter?'

'He and a friend were bullying my nephew.'

'Ah.' The man cuffed the nearest lad on the ear, making him yowl, then scowled at Maura. 'You should teach him to stand up for himself. You won't always be able to run to his aid. He's a right mammy's boy, isn't he?'

'He's half their size.'

'Then you should feed him better.' He turned and shambled off.

'They tried to bully my son too. You did right sticking up for him. I'm Mrs Baker.'

Maura swung round to find a woman from the next set of bunks smiling at her. 'I'm Miss Deagan. I'm taking my nephew and nieces to Australia to join their brother.' She lowered her voice to add, 'They've just lost their parents.'

'Poor little things.' The other glanced at a clock on the wall. 'You'll have to get them dressed quickly. We have to leave this room soon for our breakfast. We go to the dayroom for that and then stay there all day. They don't let us out

141

of the depot and there's no garden to play in, so the children get very restless. We can't go on board the SS *Delta* till tomorrow, you see.'

With her kind neighbour to guide her, Maura managed to get the children ready and followed the others into the breakfast room.

From then on she didn't have a restful minute till she went to bed, because she was so afraid of the children getting lost or bullied, she felt she had to keep an eye on them all the time.

After a while, they were complaining they were bored.

'So am I,' she said sharply. 'We'll just have to stay bored because we're not allowed out.'

Brenna gave an exaggerated sigh and sat down next to Noreen.

'We have to see the doctor this afternoon,' Mrs Baker told her. 'That'll break the day.'

There was another long queue for that, and the same two lads made a nuisance of themselves till one man with a highly pregnant wife gave them a clip about the ears for bumping into her.

The father then complained about that and the two men fell into an argument till an official separated them and told the father of the naughty boys to keep them in order.

'It was his fault!' He jabbed a finger at the man who'd protested.

The official, a large man, grabbed him by the arm. 'I've got eyes in my head and so have the officers on board ship. If you *don't* keep those two lads in order, they'll be locked below deck all the time.'

The man breathed deeply, looked at the

bystanders, but found no supporters, so stepped back. Next time his sons started wrestling, it was he who slapped them. 'Keep still, you, or I'll take my belt to you.'

That shut them up for a time, at least.

Maura felt as if she'd strayed into a zoo, or maybe she was getting a taste of what hell would be like.

Suddenly she had an idea. Did she dare do it? Why not? She took a deep breath and called out, 'If any of you children would like me to tell you a story, come and sit in a circle round me.'

There was some pushing and a few children held back, but there were about ten sitting waiting, so she concentrated on them and began a story about a naughty elf who played tricks on people.

The children laughed heartily when one little boy got his own back and the elf fell into a pond.

'Tell us another, miss!' one boy called out.

'Yes, tell us another. Please.'

More children came and sat down and to her amazement some of the parents had come to stand behind the circle.

'This is the story of Silly Mary . . . '

She told three stories, then said that was enough for today.

When she turned to collect her three, they were right beside her.

'How do you know the stories?' Ryan asked.

'I made them up.'

'Can you make up others?'

'Yes, of course. But not too many at once. I'll tell you some more another day, if you like.'

He nodded and gave her a quick smile, before putting an arm round his little sister.

She felt so pleased whenever she made him smile. She didn't think he'd ever had much to smile about before.

8

In Fremantle, Dougal McBride was woken from a cosy after-dinner nap in front of his own hearth by someone knocking on his door. After a bare minute's pause, whoever it was began knocking again. He shook his head to clear it, annoyed at being disturbed at this late hour.

In the hall he nearly bumped into his maid. 'I'll get it. I don't like you opening the door at this late hour, Linney.'

When he flung the door open, he found a man and a woman standing there. 'Yes?'

'Captain McBride?'

'Yes.' They were shadowy outlines in the darkness, so he was still on his guard. He hadn't heard Linney close the kitchen door, and knew she was standing there ready to rush to his aid with her rolling pin.

The man was a weedy fellow, with a thin, reedy voice. Dougal could tell at a glance that he posed no threat.

'I'm Mr Malcolm Prescott and this is my wife, Mrs Prescott. We need to see you urgently, to ask if we can hire your schooner.'

'I don't usually hire out my schooner. I make regular trading runs to and from Singapore.'

The woman spoke in a soft, pleading tone. She had a low, musical voice, even now, when she was clearly distressed. 'Please, Captain McBride. Couldn't you even consider it? This is an

145

emergency and we'd pay you well.'

He looked at her. She might have been pretty normally, but tonight she was haggard with exhaustion. Something about her softened his resolve and he stepped back. 'Come in and explain, then, but I'm promising you nothing.'

He led the way into the parlour and gestured to seats. 'Well, what is this emergency?'

'You tell them, Eleanor. I find it too upsetting.' The man covered his eyes with his hand.

'It's Malcolm's brother in England. We had a letter to say Roger was dying of tuberculosis. He begged my husband and me to come back and look after his children, as we'd promised we would if anything happened to him. His wife died two years ago, you see, just after we left for Australia. We'd not have come here if we'd known she was so sick.'

Dougal felt vaguely disappointed that a woman as attractive as her was married to this weakling, a man two or three inches shorter than her, with a silly little wisp of a beard on his chin that made Dougal itch for a pair of scissors to snip it off.

She waited for her husband to speak and when he looked at her expectantly, she sighed and carried on speaking. 'We've come from Melbourne and we need to get to England as quickly as possible. Only we got off the mail ship in Albany to spend a night on shore, because Malcolm had been so dreadfully seasick. And then the ship sailed without us.'

'And people weren't at all sympathetic.'

Mr Prescott had a complaining whine, which

146

grated on Dougal's ears.

'It was my fault,' she said hastily. 'I never thought to ask to be called because I usually wake early, but I was so tired after nursing my husband when he was ill that I overslept.'

'I can't believe no one woke us.' Prescott still had that aggrieved tone. 'But they said they thought we'd left already, because we'd paid in advance for a night's lodging and there was no sound from our room.'

She shot him an irritated glance, as if she was tired of hearing him say this. 'Captain McBride, we've lost nearly all our clothes, everything except what we'd taken off the ship with us for one night, and we've endured several days' jolting in a cart to get to Perth. We're quite desperate to get back to England as soon as possible.'

Dougal couldn't help feeling sorry for her. She was clearly the strong one of the pair. 'You should have waited in Albany for the next mail steamer.'

'We know that now, but we didn't realise how few ships there are sailing from Fremantle. I'm sorry to disturb you at this late hour, but someone told us you're already planning to go to Galle, in Ceylon, and suggested we pay you to take us on there. Do I have that right? Apparently there is considerable traffic to Britain from the Orient by ships going through Galle to Suez?'

Dougal nodded. 'Yes, you'll be able to obtain passage to Suez and the Mediterranean on one ship or another from Galle. The Suez Canal will probably be open too, by the time you get there, if things have gone to schedule. That should speed up your journey.'

'It's such a long voyage, so wearisome,' the man said with a sigh.

She threw an irritated glance at her husband. 'I gather that if we can get to Marseille, it's only five days by train to London.' She looked at Dougal expectantly. 'So could you please take us on from Fremantle to Galle, Captain McBride?'

He was about to say no, because he didn't usually take passengers, especially ones like this fellow, who was sure to be a nuisance and complain about everything. But she looked so distressed he bit back the words. He looked away from her, glanced back, and was tempted by her desperate expression into helping them, for her sake. She was a fine-looking woman and deserved better than this weak fool.

But he wasn't doing it for nothing. He studied her and her husband: well dressed, if somewhat rumpled. 'It'd cost you two hundred guineas.'

She sucked in her breath. 'That seems rather expensive.'

'It seems very reasonable to me,' Dougal retorted, liking the man less and less, and already regretting his offer. 'I'd have to hire a steward.'

Her husband flapped his hand. 'What does the money matter? Once we get to my brother, he'll help us. He'll not leave us without the means to look after his children.'

So they weren't as comfortably circumstanced as they looked, Dougal thought. Well, that was their business. 'Well?' He raised one eyebrow.

'We'll pay what you ask,' she said. 'I gather you sail the day after tomorrow?'

'Yes.'

She looked across at the clock on the mantelpiece. 'It's later than I'd thought. Could you kindly recommend somewhere that will take us in at this late hour?'

Dougal could see the weariness beneath the upright posture and again it was for her sake that he said, 'You can stay here, if you like. My mother used to run the place as a boarding house for gentlefolk, so there's plenty of room. There's only one maid, but she's very obliging.'

She sagged in relief. 'Thank you. We're grateful.'

All her husband did was sigh again.

When Dougal went to ask for Linney's help, she gaped at him in surprise.

'I felt sorry for them,' Dougal explained. 'Well, sorry for her. He's a stupid sort of fellow. Get someone in to help you. Maybe Orla would come?'

Linney smiled. 'You've a kind heart under that gruff manner, Captain McBride.'

'Nonsense. This is purely business. They're paying me good money to take them to Galle.'

She rolled her eyes as if she didn't believe him. 'I'll go and make up the beds.'

A voice came from behind. 'If you only have one maid, I could help to get the rooms ready.'

'Rooms?' He turned round.

Mrs Prescott flushed. 'That's what I was coming to tell you. My husband sleeps so badly, we need separate rooms. If that's all right?'

149

Linney studied her, then nodded, so Dougal knew his maid had also taken to the female visitor.

'Come along then, Mrs Prescott,' Linney said. 'It won't take two of us long to get the rooms ready, then I'll make you a hot drink and let you go to bed.'

'Thank you.' Mrs Prescott turned to Dougal. 'I'm very grateful to you, Captain McBride. I know it's not what you really want to do, but we were desperate.'

'I can probably pick up a cargo for the other leg of the journey.'

When he was on his own, he began thinking. With Adam able to sail to and from Fremantle and Singapore in the second schooner, Dougal wasn't as restricted in where he went. Excitement rose in him. He could go further afield, see what sort of cargoes were available. In fact, now he came to think about it, with two ships to manage, they'd need to find other ways of making a profit.

Fremantle was well situated for trade with places like India, South Africa, Shanghai, and Singapore, and now Suez would surely become more important, with the new canal from the Mediterranean ending there.

He'd leave a message with Ismay for Adam, telling him to return to Singapore as soon as he could find a cargo.

Just this once, for the first time in many years, Dougal was going to do something for himself.

★ ★ ★

The final day started early at the depot in Southampton, as everyone repacked their suitcases, bags and bundles, tidying themselves up ready to go on board ship. Mrs Baker and Brenna held a blanket across a corner so that Maura could wash herself in near privacy and then she held it for them. Others were doing the same, giving their children a quick once-over with a wet flannel.

'But we had a wash all over before we left Shilmara and we wash our hands all the time,' Ryan protested when Maura insisted he wash himself. 'We aren't dirty yet.'

'You'll be having a wash down every single day from now on. Either you get on with it now, or I'll do it for you.'

He scowled at her. 'Da didn't believe in washing a lot. Said it wasn't good for you.'

'Well, he was wrong. People who don't wash smell terrible. You'll see on the ship when you're close to a lot of people. We are going to stay clean.'

They had to walk to the ship from the depot, with some of the men pushing the luggage on handcarts. The trunks had already been taken on board, including Maura's from Brent Hall, which she'd found waiting for her at the depot.

Thank goodness it wasn't raining today, she thought. She felt sad as well as apprehensive when they approached the SS *Delta*, and she wasn't the only one to glance behind her as they lined up on the quay.

As Mrs Julia had said, the ship was about a hundred strides long, which didn't sound huge

151

until you were standing next to her, and had her towering over you. She had a gigantic paddle wheel on each side about halfway along, and two funnels slanting slightly backwards jutted out of the middle part. There was a tall mast for the sails at either end, which would be used for part of the journey, she knew.

When they went on board, the steerage passengers found a man and woman waiting for them at the entrance to the lower decks. The two introduced themselves as the supervisors for the men's and women's quarters.

Mrs Stoddard, the women's supervisor, was tall and thin, clad in dark grey. She was studying the newcomers in just the way the housekeeper at Brent Hall had studied new maids, as if she could see into their very thoughts.

The supervisors led the way below and the passengers followed them down the companionway, which was a cross between a step ladder and a flight of narrow stairs.

The pregnant woman and the older people went down slowly backwards and needed help.

Ryan helped Noreen. It was very touching the way he kept an eye on his little sister.

The supervisors were waiting for them below, checking names on a list and directing the men to one side, the women to the other. Ryan was separated from Maura, as they'd already been told. He would be bunking with the men and boys.

He shot her a terrified glance as he moved away and Maura's heart went out to him. Torn from everything he knew, now he had to make

152

the voyage partly on his own.

Mrs Stoddard directed the women to move along and wait for her in the corridor. When everyone was down, she stood on the bottom step and addressed them. 'I'm in charge of the women's side and if you need anything, you see me, not the ship's officers or crew. That is my cabin.' She pointed.

'What about our husbands?' a younger woman asked. 'When do we see them?'

'The only time you'll be with the men is on deck, and your area for exercise is behind the funnels. First- and second-class passengers have the fore deck. We call stairs companionways, as you've already learned. You'll soon get used to ship terms.'

She began to read names off a list and Maura found that she and the girls would be sharing one of the two cabins allocated to women and female children. It was further divided into two by a wall and open doorway, only it wasn't called a wall here but a bulkhead, it seemed.

The whole area was dimly lit by a couple of portholes. A quick glance round showed Maura that there were nine bunks in the half where she was standing.

'Stay where you are!' the supervisor yelled in a very loud voice as two of the women made a dash to claim the lower bunks. 'Come back!'

They hesitated, then moved slowly back to join the group, scowling.

'*I* will allocate sleeping spaces, and if you want to change later, you will have to find someone to change with, then check with me before doing it.'

Maura was given one lower bunk and the two bunks above it.

'Children usually go on top,' the stewardess told her. 'There's a rail to stop them falling out of bed.'

The bunks were narrow and when Maura bent to feel the nearest mattress, it was very hard. But at least the bedding looked clean.

'These lockers are for your possessions. No leaving things around. Loose items get tossed about in rough weather and can injure folk. I'll give you the keys for the lockers once I've got everyone settled.'

She moved towards the nearer of the two doors. 'The dining room is in the centre, and it's also the day room for when you can't go on deck. The other central cabin is where pregnant women and those with babies sleep. This way.'

They followed her into the day cabin and most peeped into the other one. These two were larger, with skylights in the ceilings. These were still not very brightly lit because it was a dull day.

As if she'd read Maura's mind, the supervisor said, 'There will be oil lamps in here after dark, but no one is to touch them except myself and the leaders of each sleeping cabin.

'Who are the leaders?' someone asked.

'I shall choose people when I get to know you all better.' She began to read out names and hand out keys to the numbered lockers.

As she went to receive hers and the children's, Maura prayed that Ryan would be nowhere near the two bullies. She just . . . prayed. For a safe voyage, for life to be better in Australia, for Bram to be doing as well in his shop as Mr Kieran said he was.

She didn't know what to pray for on her own behalf. Just getting everyone to Australia safely was as far as she could think ahead. She'd have to rely on Bram's guidance for finding another job later. She didn't want to go back to being a mere housemaid, had grown used to organising others and to having some status, but wasn't sure whether there were big houses there.

Of one thing she felt certain, though: unless Bram had changed greatly, he wouldn't let her or the children want. He'd asked Mr Kieran to help his family join him in Australia, so he clearly wanted them and must be able to provide for them. She would take her comfort from that.

Turning her attention to the sleeping cabin, where they'd been sent to unpack their night clothes and put the rest of their things in the lockers, she introduced herself to the women she'd be sharing with, who seemed clean and decent, thank goodness. The two who'd tried to snatch the lower bunks were in the other half of this double cabin.

Mrs Stoddard came back shortly afterwards to show each group how to use the women's necessary, which emptied into the sea. To Maura's relief there was a washroom next to it, but they had to use sea water.

Fresh drinking water would be supplied from a still and would be doled out by the supervisors and cabin leaders.

'What about the men and boys?' someone asked.

'Their quarters are at the other side of the ship, separated from the women's area by the various locked doors you can see. The accommodation can be changed, depending on the numbers of male and female passengers, though there are usually more men. Now . . . food will be brought along to the day room in a few minutes, so hurry up with your unpacking,' Mrs Stoddard said.

When the women went to eat, they found places at tables fixed to the floor, with low wooden frames at each place to keep the plates and utensils from sliding off in rough weather.

Maura whispered to Brenna to save her a seat and waited behind to ask the supervisor, 'How do I check on my nephew? I'm a bit worried about him being bullied by two of the other lads.'

'The boys will be put in the charge of someone suitable. We don't leave lads to make mischief, believe me. You'll be able to see him on deck every day, unless the weather's bad, or at classes.'

'Classes?'

'Those passengers who can usually volunteer to run classes in all sorts of things: reading, of course, and sewing, and whatever else they're good at.'

Maura remembered how children had gathered round her to listen to a story at the depot. 'I could tell the younger children stories, if you like.'

Mrs Stoddard beamed at her. 'That would be very helpful.'

She seemed about to say something else, but

two sailors arrived, carrying huge trays of sandwiches, fruit cake and rather wrinkled apples, and she turned to direct where these should be placed. The sailors brought piles of tin plates to eat from, and enamel beakers.

Maura sat down to eat, nibbling a sandwich, not feeling really hungry because the slight rocking movement of the ship by the quayside and the distinct lack of fresh air below decks was making her feel a little queasy.

She wasn't going to be seasick. She didn't have *time* to be seasick. She was just . . . a little uncomfortable. You had to get used to these conditions, and she would.

Sighing, she looked round. The room wasn't well lit, even with the skylights, and the benches were hard. The other women's voices seemed to echo off the walls, and one kept shouting at her little daughter in a very shrill voice.

Two months in these conditions! Already Maura was dreading it. Then the woman sitting opposite her said something and Maura forced a smile as she answered. If there was one thing she knew about, it was living with other people. You simply had to get on with one another and be as pleasant as you could.

She'd never felt quite so penned in as she did now, though. Or had to contend with so many strangers at once.

She made sure Noreen ate something then put an arm round the little girl's shoulders. When Brenna slipped a hand in hers, she gave it a squeeze and kept hold. They must be feeling far worse than she was.

★ ★ ★

Ryan followed the line of men and boys, feeling nearly sick with fear. How would he manage on his own?

Mr Walker, the supervisor, told the boys travelling without a family member to line up, and to Ryan's relief the two bullies weren't included.

'We're lucky today to have Mr Benford to keep an eye on you boys, and Mr Saville to assist him.'

Ryan could see that Mr Benford was a clergyman, but he wasn't wearing a soutane, just dark clothes and a white collar. Mr Saville had white hair, but though he was older, he had a very upright posture and looked strong. He turned to gesture to Mr Benford to take charge.

The supervisor handed Mr Benford a list and he read out the names, sending the boys to wait in a cabin with Mr Saville. Ryan was one of the last.

Inside the cabin were bunks and they were told which to take, which made it easier. Ryan had been afraid he'd have to fight for bed space, but they each had their own allocated, as well as a locker for their possessions.

Two of the boys smelled bad and Ryan suddenly realised what his aunt had meant. When everyone else was clean, dirty people smelled disgusting. Had he smelled like that all his life? He shuddered.

How different the world was from what he'd expected.

There was plenty of food, and again, everyone

158

behaved in a polite way, no grabbing as it'd been in Ryan's home. Even the two lads who'd tried to bully him were kept in order by some of the younger men.

Maybe being on his own with the men and boys wouldn't be so bad, after all.

He ate several sandwiches, two pieces of cake and an apple. No one stopped him having as much as he wanted.

Some of the other passengers were looking a bit pale and one suddenly rushed out to the necessary. Which made another gulp and follow him.

'They're seasick. Some start before we even leave port. I'll get some buckets,' the supervisor said. 'If you feel sick and there's a queue for the necessary, use a bucket. You, lad. You look nice and rosy still. Come and help me.'

He was pointing to Ryan. 'Not feeling sick, are you?'

'No, sir.'

'Good. You can be Mr Benford's helper and get the buckets for your cabin.'

The supervisor was a bit like Auntie Maura, giving orders and organising people, but in a polite way, not yelling. It must be nice to be in charge of something.

★　★　★

Hugh, Adèle and Carrie left the hotel after a leisurely luncheon to board the ship with the rest of the cabin passengers. He stopped as he got out of the cab to stare at the SS *Delta*, sorry it

159

was a paddle steamer and not a screw-driven vessel. He'd travelled across to visit relatives in France on a paddle steamer and it had bounced about rather a lot.

He'd not attempted to find his wife while he was in France, though he was sure that's where she'd gone. Sylvie had left him because she'd claimed to be desperately homesick for France and her sisters, but she hadn't gone to her family.

They were worried about where she was, but Hugh wasn't. He was quite sure Sylvie was living in luxury with some rich man. She was not the sort of woman to live any other way, had never lifted a finger to do anything but her embroidery while living with him.

She'd not contacted him to ask for a divorce, which had surprised him. Her family might be devout Catholics but she wasn't at all devout. But surely a rich man would have made arrangements for a divorce in England?

Hugh hadn't bothered to seek a divorce, either, because he definitely didn't wish to remarry. Marriage was a tedious business, he'd found. Besides, to obtain a divorce, he'd have had to find Sylvie then prove that she'd committed adultery, or let her prove both adultery and cruelty on his part.

Men often provided such proof to get out of a marriage, but something inside him refused to pretend he'd been unfaithful to her and worse.

He'd written to Sylvie's family to tell them he was taking Adèle to Australia for health reasons, but the letter wouldn't arrive in Abbeville until after the ship had sailed. He didn't want anything upsetting his plans.

The important thing to remember when he felt down-hearted about leaving his beloved home was that he was getting Adèle out of the country before winter really set in. He closed his eyes for a moment and sent up a swift prayer that a warmer climate really would help the poor child.

The cabins were well appointed, though small, and if his felt like a prison cell after his spacious home, Hugh didn't say that to his daughter.

Adèle was fascinated by her cabin, and by the cabin trunk containing her possessions, which opened to show drawers at one side.

Carrie was awed by everything and even seemed thrilled by the narrow but comfortable bed she'd be occupying. 'A bed to myself again? Oh, I do enjoy that, sir.'

'It's very exciting, isn't it, Daddy?'

He smiled down at his child. 'It is, indeed. Um . . . do you need to rest now?'

'No, thank you. I'm not tired and I want to see everything. Will you take me up on deck?'

The steward knocked on the half-open door as she said that. 'Excuse me, sir, but the captain asks that you'll stay below till after we've left Southampton. There is a day cabin where you can sit or I could bring you a cup of tea here, if you prefer it?'

'And could I have something to eat, please?' Adèle asked. 'I'm hungry.'

Hugh looked at her in surprise. She so rarely expressed hunger.

'I'm hungry too, sir,' said Carrie. 'Where do

161

the servants go to eat?'

Hugh explained to the steward about his governess fleeing — there was no other way to describe it — and asked if Carrie could now occupy this cabin with his daughter in Miss Fenton's place. 'And if you could help Carrie settle in, I'd be grateful.' He slipped the man half a guinea and saw a look of satisfaction on his face.

'Happy to help, sir. If it's all right with you, it'll be easier if your maid has a snack here this time. She can't go wandering about the ship.'

So they settled down to wait for the ship to leave port.

He wondered what Miss Fenton had done to entertain his daughter, and couldn't remember her doing anything but read or permit her pupil to draw.

As the time passed and Adèle grew fidgety, he found that Carrie had a store of little games to play and he watched in tolerant amusement as she made Adèle work hard to win a stack of coloured counters.

Maybe it was a good thing Miss Fenton had left them.

But he couldn't feel it was a good thing to be leaving England. It hurt too much.

⋆　⋆　⋆

When the engines started up, the steerage passengers found it very noisy. The whole ship seemed to be vibrating. Maura sniffed and frowned, wondering what the smell was.

Mrs Stoddard was passing at that moment. 'Is

162

something wrong, Miss Deagan?'

'There's an unpleasant smell.'

'Oh, that. You'll soon get used to it. The steerage accommodation is located aft of the paddles and engine rooms, so there's no avoiding it. But it's only the fumes from the coal.' She walked briskly on.

Maura wasn't at all sure about getting used to it. The fumes added to her feeling of nausea. If only she could go up on deck and breathe in some fresh air, she was sure she'd feel better. She turned to check on the children.

Brenna had gone quiet and was looking pale.

'If you feel sick, you must try to reach the necessaries,' she warned.

But though the child did make a sudden run in that direction, there were others before her and she was unable to hold back, but vomited helplessly on the floor.

Mrs Stoddard was dealing with a younger woman who had also made a mess and was in hysterics about being seasick. She looked at Maura pleadingly. 'The cleaning materials are kept in that locker. Would you mind dealing with your niece's mess yourself, Miss Deagan? Only, if we leave it, the smell will make things worse.'

'Yes, of course.' Maura opened the locker door and got out the cleaning materials.

Two other women were trying to push past, both holding their hands to their mouths. There was still a queue at the necessary, so Maura quickly shoved two buckets towards them. 'Use these. You can clean them out in the necessary afterwards.'

She found the mopping equipment and dealt with the mess Brenna had made, and the one the young woman had contributed. This made her feel even more queasy herself, but she couldn't leave Mrs Stoddard to cope on her own.

Maura was determined not to lose control of her own nausea in such a public way. There were a lot of buckets in the cupboard and she could guess why. 'Shall I take some buckets to all the women's cabins, Mrs Stoddard?'

The supervisor, who was helping another sick woman, turned a harassed face towards her. 'That'd be a big help. Thank you so much. It was on my list of things to do. We don't usually have so many being sick early on.'

Organising the buckets and keeping an eye on her nieces helped Maura to ignore her nausea. Luckily, Brenna seemed a lot better once she'd been sick. As for Noreen, she fell asleep in her bunk.

The evening meal was again sandwiches, but quite a few of the women didn't want anything to eat, so Maura used a little of the precious drinking water to dampen the cloths that had covered the trays of sandwiches and wrap up what was left for later.

The supervisor appeared at her elbow as she was doing this. 'You're a godsend, Miss Deagan. Have you had experience of organising people?'

She smiled. 'Oh, yes. I used to be Assistant Housekeeper at Brent Hall, a large country residence.'

'That settles one of my problems then.'

Maura looked at her in puzzlement.

164

'As I said earlier, we usually appoint a woman to take charge of each cabin. I wonder if you would act as leader for your group?'

She hesitated, not at all sure she wanted the responsibility.

'Better you than someone who doesn't have the skill to organise people, Miss Deagan. And it'll give you something to do. Time can hang heavily during a voyage.'

'Oh, very well. I'll try it. As long as it doesn't interfere with looking after the children.'

The supervisor smiled. 'That's a relief. I'll go over your main duties tomorrow morning, after I've found a leader for the other cabin.'

She turned and clapped her hands to get everyone's attention. 'We all go to bed at the same time, ladies, nine o'clock on the dot, so I'd be grateful if you'd bear that in mind. I'll leave a couple of lamps burning low in case you have to go to the necessary during the night.'

Maura put the children to bed at eight o'clock, went to get a final cup of tea in the day room, then took herself off to bed before the rush.

She lay listening to the other women chatting, hating the stuffy air, wondering how she would ever sleep in such conditions.

★　★　★

Hugh and Carrie had agreed that Adèle should go to bed at seven-thirty each night. She was doing better than he'd expected but was looking tired now.

'Do you have anywhere to sit in the evenings, Carrie?'

'The steward showed me the maids' room.' Carrie wriggled uncomfortably. 'But they're all posh maids, sir, and they look down their noses at me.'

'Don't let them stop you using the maids' room. You have a right to some time on your own. And don't let them talk down to you, either. Stand up for yourself.'

She looked at him doubtfully. 'You won't mind if I do that, sir?'

'Not at all. But do it politely, don't shout or show anger.' He grinned. 'It works much better.'

She smiled back, her usual open friendliness with the world back in place. 'I daresay I'll manage to do that. I never did like being bullied, no matter who did it.'

When she'd taken Adèle to bed, Hugh sat chatting to the other passengers, but went to his room at ten o'clock. The cabin might be small, but at least he had his privacy there. He valued that greatly, hadn't even liked sharing a bedroom with Sylvie, to tell the truth.

He got out his guitar and strummed it gently, the melodies that went with the chords playing in his head and relaxing him. He was going to miss playing with other musicians.

As soon as they'd met the salty sea air, Adèle had started to improve, at least, she seemed a lot better to him. That made him feel cautiously optimistic about what he was doing.

He prayed the improvement would continue, that he wasn't fooling himself. Surely he wasn't?

166

9

In Australia, Bram walked round his new house with a carpenter his friend Mitchell Nash had found for him, a ticket of leave man who was having difficulty starting up his own little business because of his background. It was hard to find skilled tradesmen, so Bram was giving this man a chance.

'I hear your timber yard is doing well,' he said to Mitchell.

'Yes. I've found a man to go into the country to scout for timber for me. He's got a good eye for it and knows I won't try to sell rubbish. I've two fellows with bullock carts bringing it to the timber yard.'

'So that you can stay with your son.'

'Yes. I really should find a wife. I miss having a woman around. But there are so few single women here.'

He studied his companion covertly. 'You'll have to ask your family in England to find someone for you.'

Mitchell looked at him, then looked away. 'I've thought of it, I must admit. But what if they sent someone out and I didn't like her?'

'She'd soon find another husband.' Bram waited a minute then changed the subject. 'I think this project is too big for that carpenter. Have you ever thought of setting up as a builder?'

'I have.'

'I think this is too big a job for Horace.'

'He likes to be called Riss.' Mitchell frowned, then shrugged. 'I'll keep an eye on things, if you like. Start small. If your project goes well, I'll maybe take on others.'

Thank goodness! Bram thought. 'Let's go and talk to Riss, then.'

The three men went over the house then stood talking in the kitchen.

'How much do you want to spend on the house, Bram?' Mitchell asked. 'There are ways of doing things more cheaply, though still safely, of course, and ways of making things more beautiful, but that costs more.'

Bram hesitated, torn between economy and beauty, and lost the battle. 'I want it to look as good as you can make it without going silky about spending. I'm not a rich man, but I can afford to do things with a bit of style. I want you to consult my wife as well as me, though. She has an eye for details.'

When Mitchell had left, Riss turned to Bram. 'I want to thank you for giving me this chance, Mr Deagan. You and Mr Nash both. You won't regret it.'

'Would you mind telling me what you were transported for?'

Riss shuffled his feet and it was a few seconds before he replied. 'Greed, sir. I wanted the best for my children. We were doing all right, food on the table, decent clothes, but I got greedy.'

His sigh was almost a groan. 'I started to steal a bit here and there, only I'm a poor thief and I

168

got caught after only a few weeks . . . Now, I don't even know where my children are.'

Bram spoke gently, 'And your wife?'

'She went back to live with her family. She said she hated me for getting into trouble and didn't want anything to do with me again. I didn't need that prison chaplain to tell me to repent after that. I'd lost everything I loved most, and I bitterly regretted what I'd done.'

★   ★   ★

When Bram got home, he found his wife in tears, which was so unusual he rushed across to take her in his arms. 'What is it? What's the matter?'

Then he saw his son behind her, lying on the sofa, instead of toddling round the room or running to meet his father. He rushed across to the poor little lad, who was tossing and turning, wailing fitfully, his face flushed with fever.

Isabella clutched his arm. 'Look how feverish he is, burning up with it. I don't know what to do. Sponging him down doesn't seem to help. I've no experience with sick children.'

Bram forgot the new house completely. He suddenly understood Riss's agony at losing his children. If anything happened to Arlen . . .

From somewhere he found the strength to stay calm. 'Send Sally to fetch her grandma. Mrs Hollins is a wise woman. She's raised several children and grandchildren. If *she* doesn't know what to do, she'll know someone who can help. In the meantime, I'll go and fetch the doctor.'

169

Mrs Hollins arrived first, threw the sheet off little Arlen and asked if any room in the house caught a better breeze.

'Our bedroom. There are windows front and back. If we open them, we get the sea breeze later in the day.'

'Well, the sea breeze is just coming in. It's early today, thank goodness. We'll nurse him up there.'

She took charge of the sickroom in no uncertain manner, hanging a wet sheet near the window and a wet cloth over a chair back near the bed. She directed Sally to make a fan of newspaper and waft it to and fro near the chair to get an even cooler breeze.

Bram brought back the doctor shortly afterwards. With a lurch of his heart, he watched the man shake his head after examining Arlen.

'There's nothing we can do but wait, Mr Deagan. You're doing the right thing trying to keep him cool. I'll leave you some powders, if you can get them down him every four hours they may help. But his own body still has to fight off the fever.' He nodded approval of the wet sheets. 'I've seen that done before. Good idea. And keep sponging him down. Let the moisture dry on his skin, then wet him again.'

When the doctor had left, Bram walked back to the bedroom, putting an arm round Isabella, who was watching Mrs Hollins take her turn at sponging down their son.

The older woman turned to look at them both when she'd finished. 'If we were in England, I'd send for some ice.'

Bram stared at her, then let go of his wife. 'There's a fellow started making ice in Fremantle. I forget his name, but I was talking to him only the other day when I went past his place. I'll see if he's got some.' He rushed out, relieved to have something else to do.

As he hurried through the streets, he tried to remember what the fellow had told him. Someone called Harrison on the other side of Australia had patented an ice-making machine, but the local man was scornful of that, because he felt he could do better. He used ammonia, of all things, to cool the water.

Bram didn't understand how that could work but he knew rich people would pay well for ice in the hottest weather. Only, it was hard starting up and Jim Chilton had come to see Bram at the Bazaar to ask him to finance a bigger manufactory.

Only Bram didn't like to risk his money, didn't really have it to spare, if truth be told.

But if there was ice, and if it helped Arlen, damned if he wouldn't put some money into it.

Ah! There it was. A small place, Chilton's Ice Works. He shoved the door open and pushed past two other customers. 'Can I go first, please? I've a feverish child needs cooling.'

As he paid for the ice, he told Chilton he was still thinking about his business proposition and saw the man's face light up. 'I'll speak to you once my son's better.'

Bram forgot business as he ran back through the streets, carrying a large chunk of the precious ice wrapped in straw inside damp sacking.

Chilton had promised to deliver more ice at nightfall and again in the morning.

Someone called out, but Bram didn't stop. He didn't care what he looked like, or who he missed seeing. It was Arlen he cared about and he had to get back as quickly as possible.

Children were such fragile creatures. Most families lost one or two. What would he do if anything happened to his son?

The mere thought of that made him run even faster.

★　★　★

It was fine, if rather choppy, the first morning of the voyage, so the steerage passengers were allowed up on deck.

Maura's first thought was to find Ryan and make sure he was all right. She told Brenna to keep tight hold of Noreen and searched the crowd of people, glad of her height. To her relief, she saw her nephew almost at once.

Ryan saw her at nearly the same time and gave her a blinding smile, the sort of smile she'd never seen on his face before. Pushing through the crowd, he ran the last few paces towards her and the girls, then hesitated.

She didn't care whether he wanted a public display of affection or not; she simply pulled him into her arms and gave him a big hug. He even hugged her back for a few seconds before pushing away from her and giving his little sister and his cousin an equally awkward hug. It was as if he wasn't used to hugging anyone.

172

'How did you go on?' Maura asked. 'Let's find somewhere to sit down and you can tell me all about it.' She'd been a bit worried about how he'd cope.

They found a raised part of the deck built round one of the skylights and perched on the edge while Ryan explained about the cabin for boys separated from their families, and how he was helping Mr Benford, who was a sort of priest. Brenna told her cousin about being sick.

As words poured out of them, Noreen began to wriggle and look uncomfortable. She kept glancing at her aunt and then at him, as if expecting something bad to happen. In the end, she tugged at her brother's arm and said, 'Shh.'

He patted her hand. 'We can talk here, Noreen.'

Maura was puzzled. 'What do you mean by that? Why wouldn't you be able to talk?'

He shrugged. 'Da used to get angry if we made a noise. He hit Noreen sometimes. Ma was always saying, 'Shh!' to us.'

'Is that why she's so quiet?'

Ryan had a think, then nodded. 'Yes. We were all quiet inside the house, 'specially when Da had been drinking or had one of his headaches. But Noreen hasn't been out and about much, because Mam always kept her at home. She doesn't understand that you can talk as much as you want in other places.'

'Dear heaven, did no one ever love you and play with you?' Her own father hadn't, but her mother had tried to make up for that.

He scuffed the toe of one shoe to and fro on

173

the deck. 'Ismay talked to us and played with us. And I had Padraig. Him and me were special friends . . . only he died. Bram was kind, too, but he was working at the big house so he couldn't be with us much. He brought leftover food home sometimes, though, and gave it to us children secretly, not to Da. After Bram went away, we were hungry a lot.'

'You won't go hungry again if I have anything to do with it.'

He gave her a quick grin. 'I haven't. Not since we went to the big house. And not since we left it, either.'

'They give us a lot of food on the women's side of the ship, more than we can eat.'

'They give us a lot of food on the men's side, too. Some people were sick, but I wasn't.'

'I was sick,' Brenna said. 'But I'm getting better now.' brushed at a speck of black that had landed on her blouse and made a bigger smear, looking at it in consternation. 'I didn't mean to do that, Auntie Maura. Don't get mad at me!'

'I'm not mad.' Maura looked down at her own clothes and saw the odd speck of black here and there. When she looked up, dark smoke was pouring out of both funnels and trailing behind the ship. 'It's the smoke. You're better not brushing the specks. Maybe we can shake them off later. If we can't, they'll look smaller left alone.'

She saw that her niece was still looking doubtful and added, 'How could I be angry when it's not your fault?'

Brenna let out a heartfelt sigh of relief.

174

Mrs Stoddard came up to them just then with a notebook. 'I'm sorting out the classes, Miss Deagan. You said you'd tell stories to the little ones.'

'Yes.' She gave a self-conscious laugh. 'I can tell stories till the cows come home. I used to get into trouble for it with my da, but my mother always liked to hear my tales.'

'Would you mind if we let cabin-class children attend as well? There are a few children among them, and they like stories as much as anyone else.'

'Of course they're welcome.' Maura hesitated. 'I could help with reading classes, too, I mean help someone who was a proper teacher. I'm keen to get my nephew and niece reading better, so they'll be joining those classes. They didn't get much chance of schooling back home.'

'Oh, that's excellent! I wish everyone was as helpful as you.' She walked on to the next group of people.

Ryan scowled at his aunt. 'Do I have to go to reading classes?'

'Not if you want to stay ignorant and make Bram ashamed of you.'

He didn't say a word, but his shoulders drooped. 'I'm stupid at the reading.'

'Why do you say that?'

'Da said I was.'

You shouldn't speak ill of the dead, but she couldn't help it. 'When we were all children, your fathers didn't like anyone else reading because they couldn't do it well themselves. It's not true that you're stupid. You just haven't had

175

a fair chance to learn.'

He shrugged, but there was still anxiety in his eyes.

She didn't say anything more, but she'd make sure he learned to read properly. She didn't intend to waste the time on board ship. She sat quietly for a while, watching Mrs Stoddard carry on through the crowd, asking questions, writing things down. Later, the supervisor went to the front part of the ship, where the cabin passengers were taking the air on a much less crowded deck.

Would the rich people even want to attend classes? Or would they expect to run them all? Maura had known exactly where she stood at Brent Hall, but wasn't at all sure about the rules and expectations in this new situation.

When lists of classes were posted on a notice board in the day room that evening, Maura was as interested as everyone else in what was on offer. She'd only been on the ship just over a day and already she was finding that time dragged. She much preferred to keep busy.

There was a library, too, it seemed, and a class to encourage adults to keep up their reading. She put her name down for that one and to borrow books from the library.

She found out that the books were mostly kept in the cabin passengers' sitting room, except for a few tattered books in the steerage area. Members of the reading class would be allowed to choose from the better books for a short time each morning.

What bliss it would be to have more time to

read. That at least would be one advantage of this voyage.

* * *

To Hugh's delight, Adèle again seemed more lively the following morning. She ate her breakfast without prompting and asked to go and walk round the deck with him.

It was wonderful to get some fresh air, and he enjoyed explaining things to her. Not that he understood everything about ships, by any means, but he was learning fast because some of his fellow passengers had sailed before and were happy to share their knowledge. And the stewards were always helpful if you had a question.

After a while, Adèle got tired of walking about and wanted to play, so he went to sit with some people he'd met at dinner the night before.

He watched an older woman, who must be a crew member, making the rounds of the passengers, asking questions and taking notes, and wondered what she was doing.

When she approached his group, she explained. 'I'm Mrs Stoddard, women's supervisor in the steerage area, and I organise the classes for the whole ship. People are usually very kind about sharing their knowledge and skills, and I wonder if any of you could take a class in something?' There was silence and she said pleadingly, 'It makes the journey so much easier if we have activities. Or concerts. We like to keep people occupied.'

177

Hugh's conscience wouldn't let him keep silent. 'I could organise some singing, if you like. I haven't any music here, but we could work from the words. I have a guitar and I can play the piano by ear.'

The woman beamed at him. 'Oh, that'd be wonderful, sir. We usually manage some sort of concert and people enjoy it. We know it's not professionally done, but people try hard and it makes for enjoyment rehearsing, and then a pleasant evening's entertainment later on.'

'I don't know if we'd find enough singers good enough to perform in a concert,' Hugh said doubtfully. He suppressed a sigh. He'd had experience of amateur choirs before.

'Especially with so few of us.' A man nearby gestured languidly to the group.

'There are the steerage passengers as well, sir, don't forget. The classes are for everyone, and I've seen some excellent singers come out of steerage on other voyages. People do recitations as well.'

The man — what was his name? — gave her a sneering look of disbelief.

'I'd be happy to have anyone in my group who can sing,' Hugh said, remembering that the snobbish fellow was called Grierson.

'Surely not the lower classes!' Grierson insisted. 'I'm certainly not joining any groups with *them* in.' He made a gesture with one hand to squeeze his nostrils, as if he'd smelled something bad.

Mrs Stoddard said nothing, but couldn't completely hide her disapproval as she turned back to Hugh. 'There's a woman who's going to tell stories to the younger children. She did it in the depot and people speak very well of her. Some of the Irish are particularly good storytellers, I find. Perhaps your little daughter would like to attend? Do you like stories, dear?'

Adèle beamed at her. 'I love stories, but I've read all the ones in my books lots of times. Will this lady know some new ones?'

'Indeed she will. She makes them up out of her own head.'

'Can Carrie come with me? She likes stories too!'

'Our maid,' Hugh explained.

'If she'll help out, she'll be very welcome. The storytelling is for younger children and sometimes they need taking to the necessary or helping with something. We might start the stories tomorrow morning, if it's fine.'

After a while, Adèle went back to playing under Carrie's supervision and Hugh managed to move away from Grierson without showing how much he disliked the fellow.

★ ★ ★

The *Bonny Mary* set off from Fremantle only an hour later than Dougal had originally planned, with his new mate's wife Peggy on board as stewardess. He waited until the ship was past Rottnest Island and on her way out into the Indian Ocean, before going across to check on his passengers, who were sitting on deck under an awning rigged up especially for them.

'A fine day for sailing,' he said cheerfully.

Mrs Prescott looked up with a smile. 'Yes, indeed.'

Mr Prescott, sitting with hunched shoulders staring out to sea, muttered something indistinguishable.

His wife looked at him with exasperation before turning back to Dougal and saying quietly, 'You must excuse my husband. He isn't a good sailor and prefers not to chat or talk when sitting on deck.'

Prescott scowled at her. 'You don't need to apologise for me, Eleanor! We've paid our fares and can pass the voyage as suits us best.' He stood up. 'I'll go and lie down in the cabin for a while. I didn't sleep at all well last night.'

The name *Eleanor* suits her, Dougal thought.

She flushed in embarrassment as they watched her husband walk away.

'Don't be upset,' Dougal said. 'It's not your fault if your husband is . . . a trifle grumpy. Some people don't like sea voyages and you'll never change them.'

'No. It's been . . . difficult. By the time we reached Sydney, Malcolm was vowing never to undertake an ocean voyage again. Then we had to go back and that upset him badly.' She looked towards the water and her voice softened. 'But I love it on the water and I think I'm quite a good sailor, so I'll not be much trouble to you.'

'You've met the stewardess?'

'Yes. Peggy was very helpful.'

'Did she mention that you and your husband will be dining in my cabin? I don't have a passenger dining room and it's the only place with a large enough table.' He hesitated, then added, 'There's a space you can use to sit in there too, when you can't go on deck, given that your cabin is so small.'

She didn't say that her cabin was so small it felt like sleeping in a cupboard, or that even so, she preferred it to sharing a bed with Malcolm.

'We didn't have time to make the third cabin ready for passengers before we left — we've been using it to store fragile things. If your husband is incapacitated you may be glad of your own sitting space when the weather is too rough for you to go on deck.'

Her face brightened. 'I'd definitely like that. How soon can I start using it?'

'As soon as Peggy can get it ready.'

Not a loving couple, those two, he thought, as he watched her go. She was only of medium height but she carried herself well and moved gracefully. He went away to give orders. The more he had to deal with Prescott, the sorrier he felt for her. Such a waste her being married to that moaner!

He'd been looking for a wife for a few years now because he wanted children before it was too late, especially a son to follow him to sea. But he'd not met any woman he'd been attracted to and he couldn't marry without some sort of affection, not after seeing the unhappiness in his parents' marriage. How ironic that he found Eleanor Prescott so very attractive!

It was lonely at home without his sister Flora. He hoped her recent marriage to Joss was making her happy, and that they'd been

181

successful in their trading venture between Sydney and Singapore.

He smiled. He'd joked about 'hen frigates' to Adam, but he thought the trading captains like Joss, whose wives travelled with them, as Flora planned to do, were very lucky fellows. They had the best of both worlds.

★ ★ ★

Unfortunately, the following day there were light showers and the sea grew rougher, so the storytelling session couldn't be held on deck. Adèle was disappointed, but Mrs Stoddard, who had come to collect the cabin passengers' children, said there were all sorts of other places they could meet.

'Why not use the dining room?' Hugh asked. 'It seems to be free at this time of day.'

Mrs Stoddard shot a glance sideways at Grierson, who continued to be grumpy about the prospect of the various groups of passenger mingling. 'We'll be all right, sir, though it's kind of you to offer.'

'I think it's foolhardy,' Grierson snapped. 'I don't want our facilities being used by the great unwashed. And if the children bring back fleas, I'll complain to the captain.'

'There's no question of that, sir,' Mrs Stoddard snapped. 'They're a cleanly lot this trip, and if they weren't, I'd deal with it.'

As Grierson always reeked of stale cigar smoke, Hugh felt his protests were unfair. But you couldn't say anything too pointed, because you had to keep the peace when living together in such close quarters.

Out of curiosity, he accompanied Adèle and Carrie to the storytelling, which took place in the smaller of the two day cabins used by the male steerage passengers, who always outnumbered the female passengers.

He was surprised to see that the storyteller was a rather stern-looking woman. He'd noticed her on deck because she stood head and shoulders above most of the other women, and also because she carried herself like a queen.

'Your daughter will be all right with me, sir,' she told him, clearly not wanting him to remain.

'I believe you were asked if my maid could stay and help? She's good with children and can bring Adèle back if she gets tired. My daughter's been ill, you see.'

The woman studied Carrie and seemed to approve of what she saw. 'As long as she'll help with the other little ones as well. I'd welcome that, I must admit.'

'I'll be nearby too,' Mrs Stoddard said. 'We don't usually allow the unmarried women to share an area, unless the weather is inclement. I'll see that your daughter is all right, sir.'

In other words, she was keeping guard over the group and she didn't want him around.

When Adèle joined him later in the day lounge, she skipped across to join him, looking rosy if still very thin.

'How did it go, darling?'

'Lovely, Daddy. Miss Deagan told us a story about a little girl who met a leprechaun. And she

183

had to go hop, hop, hop in a special pattern to get away from him.' She hopped sideways and forwards, then back again, and he had a sudden image of a group of little children hopping round a room. They'd have loved it.

'Damned Irish!' Grierson muttered.

'My mother's Irish,' another passenger said sharply. 'I'll thank you to mind how you speak of them.'

'Oh. Sorry. No offence intended.' But his expression remained sour.

'Daddy, can I draw a picture of the story?'

'Of course you can.'

He went back to the cabin with her to find her crayons and discovered that Carrie was equally excited by the day's tale, since she hadn't had a lot of storytelling in her life.

'Miss Deagan makes it sound so real,' she said. 'I never did hear the likes of it, sir, never. And to think she'd made it all up in her head.'

'I gather the children enjoyed themselves.'

'They loved it, sir. And I didn't have to help, because the children were very well behaved. Miss Deagan only told stories for half an hour, and there were a lot of parts where the children had to repeat things or try out the hopping. She said that even so, half an hour was long enough for little ones.'

'I'm glad you enjoyed it.'

'Oh, I did. I'm looking forward to tomorrow, I can tell you. She's going to do half an hour every morning. She used to be an Assistant House-keeper in a big house in England. Fancy that. And she spoke to me so friendly and kind, and

184

me only a junior maid. As we were tidying the room afterwards, she said she used to tell stories to a neighbour's children when she was a girl and had to look after them. It was the only way of keeping them quiet when it rained.'

Adèle giggled. 'Miss Deagan's not at all like Miss Fenton. She looks a bit fierce, but when she starts telling her stories, her eyes sparkle, and when she gets excited, her hair falls out of its pins. I didn't think she was pretty till then, but she is.'

He was surprised by this comment and decided to study the tall lady more closely. Assistant Housekeeper, eh? He wondered why she was giving that up to go to Australia.

★   ★   ★

In the late afternoon the weather worsened and the *Delta* began to pitch up and down. The passengers were shepherded below deck and 'locked down', as Mrs Stoddard called it.

Maura made sure everyone in her cabin had a bucket to hand. 'And if you miss the bucket, I don't care how ill you are, you'll have to clean it up straight away.'

She could hear that edge to her voice which had always sent junior housemaids scurrying to obey, and it amused her that the other women reacted in a similar manner. But it was so important to keep the cabin clean and as sweet-smelling as possible.

There was a whoosh and water covered the porthole on the outside.

185

One of the women screamed and shouted, 'We're sinking!'

When she fell into hysterics, Maura had no hesitation in slapping her face and telling her to pull herself together. 'Look!' She pointed to the porthole, which was again showing sky. Even as they watched, it was covered in water again, then cleared to show sky.

'It's just the ship dipping in and out of the big waves.'

As the weather worsened, the ship not only bobbed up and down, but began to heave to and fro sideways as well. Maura helped Brenna to be sick in the bucket she'd tied to the bunk leg, and looked at Noreen.

'I don't feel sick,' the child piped.

'If you are, call out to me and we'll make sure you hit the bucket. Sit on Brenna's bunk with her. You'll be closer to it.'

Noreen nodded and clambered down to the middle bunk.

Maura was feeling nauseous as well. The rolling around seemed much worse in the stuffiness of the steerage accommodation. She tried very hard to control her stomach, but after a while gave in to the inevitable and vomited into the bucket.

She lifted her head to see the others staring at her. 'Terrible, isn't it?' she said as lightly as she could manage, wiping her mouth with her handkerchief. 'If someone will keep an eye on my nieces, I'll go and empty our bucket and I can do yours too.'

'I'll keep an eye on them, love,' the woman

next to her said. 'But only if someone will share their bucket with me. Please come back quickly. I'm not feeling so good myself.'

Maura worked quickly and brought back a spare bucket, just to be safe.

When Mrs Stoddard looked in later, even the supervisor was pale. 'This is going to be a bad blow, I'm afraid, ladies. I'm pleased to see you're using the buckets. If you didn't, you'd make it worse for yourselves. Try to drink some water, if you can get to the day room. The bottles are lashed down, and the tin mugs are in the cupboard. Don't leave them lying around once you've had your drink.'

The rough seas seemed to go on and on.

'I wish I'd never come,' one woman moaned.

'We're going to die,' another wailed.

'No, we're not!' Maura shouted. 'Don't you dare say that again!'

Everyone fell silent, staring at her resentfully.

She stared right back. 'It's important to keep up our spirits.'

Mrs Stoddard came back to announce that sandwiches had been brought to the day room, together with tin bottles of tea, which were still quite warm. Several people groaned and only two women said they'd come and get some.

After some thought, Maura roused the girls and took them and the bucket along to the day room. 'You don't have to eat if you don't feel like it, but you should drink something.'

Noreen surprised her by eating a sandwich. Brenna had to be persuaded even to drink. Maura couldn't face any food, but she was thirsty so sipped some lukewarm tea, putting in plenty of sugar.

As they staggered back to the sleeping cabin, Brenna said, 'It felt better in the day room. Couldn't we stay there?'

But Mrs Stoddard overheard and said, 'It'll get worse before it gets better, I'm afraid. I suggest you tie the children into the bunks, Miss Deagan. They'll be safer there.'

So Maura put Noreen, who still hadn't been sick, back into the top bunk and gave Brenna her own bunk at the bottom, since it was nearest to the bucket.

Just as she was thinking it couldn't get any worse, the cabin was lit by a flash of lightning and a moment later, thunder boomed overhead.

One woman was praying loudly, another was moaning and retching.

Maura kept an eye on the children, sparing a thought for Ryan, hoping he wasn't too sick and someone would look after him.

All you could do was wait for the storm to end.

★   ★   ★

As the ship bucked and rolled, Hugh began feeling sick. The steward had left him a bucket, but he was hoping not to have to use it.

He went to check on his daughter, staggering and holding on to the rails on the walls. Now he understood why they were there. He found that Carrie had already been sick and was looking white and limp. 'How are you feeling, Adèle?'

188

'I don't feel sick, Daddy, but I don't want anything to eat and I don't like it when the ship jumps about.'

'I think you'd both better come into my cabin and we'll all look after one another. Carrie, don't forget your bucket.'

'I'd rather stay here, sir. But I'd be grateful if you could look after Miss Adèle. I'm sorry to — ' She leaned over the bucket again.

'Will you be all right on your own?'

'I'd rather be on my own. I'm sorry to let you down.'

'You're not letting anyone down. Who can help getting sick?'

He left her to her miseries and took his daughter into his own cabin.

But the storm got worse, and in the end, the rolling around got the better of his stomach and he had to use the damned bucket.

He lifted his head to see Adèle sitting upright, hands clasped around her knees.

'Are you all right, darling? You're not feeling sick at all?'

'Not really. I just want to sit here quietly. I don't want to do anything.'

The steward appeared some time later, taking the soiled bucket and leaving a clean one. 'I should try to drink a bit, sir, and get the little girl to do so too. Just sips of water or cold sweet tea, which I'll be bringing round in a few minutes. It'll have to be in tin bottles, I'm afraid. Daren't risk glass in weather like this.'

'Have you any idea how long the storm will last?'

'It's set in, sir. Listen to that thunder. Be bad all night, I should think, perhaps longer. You never know in the Bay.'

Hugh understood now why some people chose to take the train to Marseille to avoid the Bay of Biscay, and wished he'd done the same. He'd thought it'd be easier not having to change trains and hotels, but he'd been wrong. It'd have been worth any extra trouble to avoid this.

Groaning, he bent his head over the bucket again.

10

Bram and Isabella spent two days watching over Arlen, sharing the duties, day and night. At first they were terrified of losing their son, then started to feel hopeful as the fever abated and the little boy began to recover.

'There. Didn't I tell you the ice would do it?' Mrs Hollins said with satisfaction.

'If you ever find another child who needs ice and whose family can't afford it, come to me,' Bram told her. He couldn't bear to think of anyone losing a child for lack of a shilling or two.

Once he was assured that Arlen was better, Bram went back to Chilton and offered to consider some financial investment in the expansion of the ice works.

Chilton stared at him in delight then shook hands vigorously, before blowing his nose hard. 'I know if you are involved, things will go well for me, Mr Deagan.'

'I'm not promising anything till I know more about it. And I haven't got unlimited money.'

So Chilton took Bram through to the back, insisting on giving him a tour of the works and a full explanation of what new equipment was needed. The technicalities didn't mean much to Bram, and he'd not like to work in a place that smelled of ammonia.

He was glad to leave the small, damp ice works and sat down with Chilton to work out an approximate figure for what it'd cost to expand the place. It wasn't as much as Bram had feared, because Chilton would be building the apparatus himself. It wasn't something you could buy ready made. But it was still more than he'd wanted to lay out at the moment.

'Could we not take smaller steps?' he asked when Chilton ran out of facts and figures.

'False economy, Mr Deagan. We'd have to spend twice as much to gain a bigger output if we do it that way.'

'Well, I can't give you that much.' The other man's face fell so dramatically, he sought for a compromise. 'How about I ask my friend Conn Largan if he'll take a share, too?'

'Please do.'

'And of course, we'll have to talk to a lawyer. I'm doing nothing without a signed agreement. In the meantime, I want to see all your figures for selling ice. Get your account books up to date and send them to me at the Bazaar.'

Chilton looked at him in dismay. 'I'm not . . . good at accounts. It's all a bit messy. In fact . . . well, to tell you the truth, it's mostly in my head.'

'Then send me what you have. And write down what's in your head, if you can. I need to see something.'

★　★　★

After he left the ice works, Bram walked along to the new house. It still looked dilapidated from the outside, but from inside came the sounds of hammering.

192

When he went to see how it was going, he found utter chaos, with walls stripped and beams propping up rafters. He followed the sounds of whistling to discover Riss, covered in sawdust and working with a lad. Bram was pleased to see that the ex-convict knew how to work hard without being supervised.

'Just calling in to see how you're going,' he called.

Riss turned his head, spitting some nails out of his mouth into his hand before he could speak. 'Good morning, Mr Deagan. We're putting the frame of the house to rights before we go any further. Get on with your work, lad.'

He went to join Bram, easing his back a little. 'I've been wondering if you'd like me to put in some attics for your servants while we're at it. There's plenty of space under such a high, sloping roof. I'm surprised they didn't do that before.'

'Will it be safe to put rooms up there? Will the structure be strong enough?'

'It will by the time I've finished.'

'And will it cost a great deal more?'

'I don't think so. I've been doing some calculations, which Mr Nash told me to do. It's a question of whether he can get us some good long timbers that'll bear extra weight here and there. I'll go and call on him later today, if you want the attics.'

Bram swallowed hard. Things were galloping ahead so fast, he felt as if his head was spinning. 'Have you ever done such a big job before, Riss?'

'Not on my own, no. But I've worked on them and Mr Nash knows what needs doing.' He studied what he'd done, his hands moulding the air, as if he was handling pieces of timber. 'I know wood, sir, know what it can do. My father was a carpenter before me. If he hadn't died, I'd not have been tempted and I'd still be working in the family business.'

'Go ahead and order the timber, then,' Bram said. 'But keep it simple and make sure Mr Nash approves of every stage.'

'Oh, he does already, sir. He was going to talk to you about it, only you came round here first, so I thought I'd mention it.'

So Bram went to call on Mitchell, who confirmed what Riss had said.

⋆ ⋆ ⋆

When he got home, Bram went to tell Isabella. After all, she kept the accounts and was his partner in every way. Had he gone too far without consulting her? Bazaar, ice works, big new house. He'd gone barefoot as a child and now he was a man of property, a trader respected in the town and an investor in other men's businesses. Was he taking too many risks?

She was sitting drinking a cup of tea, while Arlen slept on the sofa nearby. She looked tired, her skirt crumpled, but her smile was back.

He gave her a kiss first, because he could never resist touching her, then sat down, holding her hand in his as he explained what he'd agreed to.

She listened carefully, then got out the account books and went over them with him. 'We can afford it, but only just. Don't take on

194

anything else for a while, not a single thing. Even this will leave us without as much in reserve as I'd like.'

He nodded. 'I'm sorry. I didn't plan to invest in the ice works. It was just . . . the ice saved Arlen and I wanted to have ice for other children in need.'

'You've a soft heart, Bram Deagan.' She gave him one of her glorious, loving smiles. 'And don't ever change.'

★   ★   ★

In the middle of the night, Maura woke up with a start as a loud bang reverberated through the tossing ship. At first she thought an engine had exploded, but the engines kept running, and there was another bang, then another.

Everyone else had woken up as well and the timid woman nearby started wailing.

The dim light from the corridor brightened and Mrs Stoddard poked her head in, clutching the door frame to keep herself and her lantern steady. 'In case you're worried about the noise, it's just the paddle wheels. In stormy weather, they sometimes take turns to come out of the water and when they hit it again, that causes the bang. It's quite normal.'

It might be normal, Maura thought grimly, but how could you sleep with such loud noises? The ever-present engine was bad enough down here.

To her surprise, however, she did manage to doze a bit.

The weather was no better in the morning. Maura took the girls to breakfast and though they didn't want their toast buttering, they ate it slathered with jam and seemed to relish it.

She tried a piece herself and found the sweetness comforting. There were only a few other people trying to eat breakfast.

Mrs Stoddard came hurrying in just as they were finishing. 'Oh, dear,' she said cheerfully. 'Everyone does seem to be laid low. I was hoping someone would be able to help one of the gentlemen. Both he and his nursemaid are very ill, and little Adèle, who's eight, has no one to look after her. She comes to your storytelling, Miss Deagan, a slender child with red-gold hair. She's like Noreen here, not ill at all. I think you two girls are the best sailors of us all.'

Noreen smiled proudly.

'You could bring the little girl here,' Brenna suggested before Maura could stop her. 'She could play with us. I'm feeling better now I've eaten something.'

Mrs Stoddard shot a glance at Maura. 'How are you feeling, Miss Deagan?'

'Somewhat better. Look, if it helps, bring the child here. I'll keep an eye on her.'

'Thank you so much. They're a sickly lot in the cabins this trip. None of the ladies is in a fit state to take on extra responsibility, and of course we can't give a little girl to a man to look after.'

'How will you get her here? Surely you can't bring her along the deck?'

'No, of course not. There's a way through the

196

crew's quarters if we unlock the connecting door.'

She brought Adèle back with her shortly afterwards. The child looked quite unaffected by the rough weather and even laughed as she was tossed from side to side and had to grab hold of the rails on the walls.

Strange, thought Maura, how the frailest are sometimes the strongest. Adèle and Noreen were the two she'd have thought least likely to weather these stormy seas without problems.

To keep them occupied, Maura told the children stories, her three and any who weren't too sick to join them.

At other times, Adèle shared her crayons and Mrs Stoddard provided some more paper for Brenna and Noreen's use. The supervisor seemed to be doing a heroic job of looking after the other sick passengers, with a couple of women's help.

'We'll be out of the Bay soon and into the Mediterranean, then things will calm down,' she said cheerfully, when she came to check on Adèle later.

★ ★ ★

After two days, the storm began to abate. Mrs Stoddard had relieved Maura's worries about Ryan by telling her he was helping Mr Benford look after the others and had settled down well in the boys' cabin. But Maura would still be glad to see him again and make sure he was all right.

She kept Adèle with them, sending messages

of reassurance to her father, who was apparently still not well. The child was sleeping in the bottom bunk with Noreen, leaving Brenna to climb to the top.

'Can Brenna and Noreen come and play with me when I go back to my own cabin?' Adèle asked. 'I'm sure Daddy and Carrie won't mind.'

'If your father says it's all right, I'm sure they'd love to.' Maura didn't think he would approve. She had years of experience in a 'them' and 'us' way of life. It was mainly children who crossed the boundaries, but not for long. Those looking after them soon pulled them back into line.

She couldn't imagine Mr Beaufort being any different from other people of his class, though Adèle seemed to think him perfect in every way. The child had only once spoken of her mother, to say casually, 'She left us when I was little. I don't remember her at all.'

How could you ever leave your child? Maura wondered.

Soon, Mrs Stoddard's prediction was proved true. They sailed into the Mediterranean, heading for Gibraltar and almost immediately, the winds abated, the rough seas calmed and the sun began to shine.

However, they'd fallen behind their normal schedule because of the severity of the storm, and it seemed that this would not do with a P&O vessel.

'The captain isn't pleased about not being on time,' Mrs Stoddard confided in Maura. 'But sometimes the weather prevents you from doing

198

what you want. 'Man proposes, God disposes.' '

'I don't suppose it'll make much difference in the long run.'

The supervisor shook her head. 'You never can tell. And don't mention it to the other passengers, but we're picking up some bigwigs from the company at Marseille. He'll want everything perfect by the time they come on board, if I know our captain. I gather they're going to the opening of the Suez Canal.'

★ ★ ★

Mr Prescott continued to spend most of his time in his cabin as the *Bonny Mary* sailed towards Galle. He took most of his meals there as well, though they were snacks rather than meals as far as the stewardess was concerned. Peggy grumbled that it was no pleasure taking good food to him to be wasted.

Even when Prescott went on deck, he hardly bothered to say a word to anyone, his wife included, and never stayed there for longer than an hour.

Mrs Prescott, on the other hand, spent as much time as she could on deck, welcoming any opportunity to chat to Dougal, his officers or the stewardess. She also borrowed books from him, confessing she loved to read.

'She's a nice lady, that one is,' was Peggy's summing up. 'Never causes any trouble, if she can help it. I feel sorry for her, married to that scraggy old fool, I do indeed.'

Dougal didn't reprimand her. It'd have done

no good anyway. Peggy had a heart of gold, but she would speak her piece, even to Queen Victoria, he was sure, if she ever met Her Majesty.

The weather was kind to them, with only a couple of days of rougher seas. Inevitably, Dougal found himself lingering after the evening meal to chat to his guest. Apart from his sister, he'd never found a woman as easy to talk to as Eleanor, who was interested in anything and everything, pelting him with questions about the ship and how things worked. He'd not expected her to understand his explanations, but she did and remembered what he'd told her, too.

'I hope you'll be in time to see your brother-in-law again,' he said one evening. 'You've still a long way to travel.'

'I hope so too. I'm fond of Roger and was sad to hear he was so ill.' She sighed. 'He and Malcolm have always been delicate, though. As a result, their mother spoiled them. Roger's wife was good for him and he grew more cheerful, but she was killed in a train accident, poor Mary. I wish I had her skill and could help Malcolm to develop a more cheerful attitude to life.'

She flushed. 'I shouldn't have said that. It sounds so disloyal.'

'I think you're amazingly loyal . . . given the circumstances.' He dared to add, 'Some people seem to enjoy playing the invalid.'

'Yes. If only I could find out whether Malcolm's woes are imaginary or real. Some doctors say one thing, some another.'

'It must be hard for you.'

'What choice do I have?' she asked bitterly. 'I married him for better or for worse. I had no money of my own, so it was a relief to feel secure. I have no close family left at all now.'

'I'm sorry.'

She looked down for a moment then raised her eyes to meet his and smiled ruefully. 'I feel as if I can say anything to you and not shock you.'

'I hope so. I wish — ' He broke off, not wanting to drive her away.

'What do you wish?'

'That we'd met before you were married.'

She swallowed hard.

'I can't help how I feel, but please believe that I'll never knowingly upset you.'

She stared at him and whispered, 'I wish so, too.' Then she vanished into her cabin for an hour.

He wondered if she'd join him for dinner the next night, but she came to table as usual. She didn't say a word about what he'd confessed and of course he didn't mention her last comment, either. She was a lady worthy of respect.

But he'd meant every word. He wished this voyage would last for ever, that he could at least go on enjoying her company, but a fresh breeze on a following sea was powering the *Bonny Mary* towards Galle in near record time.

Perhaps he could take them on to Suez. He could explore the possibilities there for trade while he was at it.

He knew he was only making excuses. But he knew he'd go on to Suez if at all possible.

Some of the first-class passengers got off the SS *Delta* at Gibraltar to enjoy a few hours on shore, but the steerage passengers weren't given the choice. They had to stay on board, and could only gaze enviously at the first foreign country most of them had ever come so close to.

Mrs Stoddard said Gibraltar wasn't a foreign country because it belonged to Great Britain, but it looked foreign to them, very different from an English port.

Maura spent as much time as she could on deck, but the supervisor kept an eye on them, insisting they mustn't get burned by the sun.

The ladies sitting on the foredeck had awnings and parasols to protect their complexions, lucky things. Maura watched them enviously. Travelling in style must be wonderful. In the meantime, the children had been out in the sun long enough, so she insisted on them going below, even Ryan.

'Do you want to look like a boiled lobster?' she asked when they protested.

'What's a boiled lobster?' he asked at once.

'It's a sea creature and when they boil it to eat, it turns bright red. As you're doing now. Away with you and practise your reading, Ryan Deagan.'

Fortunately, the various classes offered to passengers kept people out of the sun for part of the time. Her storytelling had resumed and she'd joined the reading class, who were taking it in turns to read aloud and discuss *Our Mutual*

Friend. Maura had read other tales by Mr Dickens and was enjoying this one, but she was also reading extra books on her own. She'd never had such a feast of reading.

Mr Beaufort came with his maid to collect his daughter from Maura's story class and asked to speak to her. She let the other children leave and turned to find herself alone with him. The maid must have taken Adèle away.

'I wanted to thank you properly for looking after Adèle, Miss Deagan, and to give you this.' He held out a book.

'There's no need to give me anything. I was glad to do it.'

'It's only a book.'

Only a book! Each one she managed to buy was a treasure to her. She looked at its title. 'Oh, it's *Sonnets from the Portuguese.* I've seen this book at Brent Hall and I love Elizabeth Barrett Browning's poems. I shall enjoy having my own copy.'

'I'm glad. Adèle enjoyed her stay with you very much. She's had rather a lonely childhood, because she's always been rather sickly. I wondered if you'd permit Noreen and Brenna to come and play with her?'

'Would that be allowed — or even wise?'

He smiled as if he perfectly understood what she was hinting at. 'I think it'd be good for Adèle and I'm sure your two nieces would enjoy playing with her toys, which is more important to me than society's rules. You could come with them the first time or two, just to satisfy yourself that Carrie can handle the three of them.'

203

'Well. All right, then. Thank you.' Why not? Anything to pass the time on this long journey. And it'd be good for Noreen and Brenna to play with a child from a different background, she was sure. They'd had such limited lives until now.

He turned, then swung back. 'Adèle says you've been singing to them and she thinks you have a nice voice.'

'I'm nothing special. Children are easily satisfied.'

He was thoughtful. 'Not Adèle. She's very musical. Why don't you try out for the choir? We're putting on a concert before we get to Alexandria, you know.'

'Sing in public!'

'Only with a group. It's a very pleasant way of passing the time.'

'I have the children to care for.'

'Carrie can do that while you practise.'

Maura hesitated and gave in to temptation. She loved music of any sort.

'Well, all right. We servants used to have sing-songs sometimes at Brent Hall. I always enjoyed it.'

'I knew it when I heard you speak!'

'Knew what?'

'That you'd have a good singing voice. Your speaking voice is beautifully modulated.'

★　★　★

The first time she went to the singing group, leaving the children with Carrie and Adèle, even

Ryan, Maura felt guilty. She was embarrassed when she had to sing alone for Mr Beaufort to assess her voice, but soon settled into the group, beginning to enjoy herself hugely.

Mr Beaufort had chosen a selection of simple songs, not hard to learn: cheerful old songs like, 'Now is the Month of Maying', sentimental songs like 'The Last Rose of Summer', poignant songs like 'Home Sweet Home', which brought tears to quite a few people's eyes, given that most of them were leaving their home for ever.

Two people also came forward to volunteer to recite poems. Maura listened to them, as she had listened surreptitiously with other servants at Brent Hall when the family and its friends were entertaining one another.

One of the poems was a miserable tale of a child's death, and she'd as soon not listen to that after losing so many family members. But the other poem spoke to her heart: 'A Psalm of Life' it was called, by an American gentleman called Longfellow. She decided to find a book of his poetry, if she could, and learn this one by heart. She knew the third verse already:

> Not enjoyment, and not sorrow,
> Is our destined end or way;
> But to act, that each tomorrow,
> Find us farther than today.

She loved the idea of that.

★ ★ ★

After a couple of days of rehearsing, Mr Beaufort asked Maura if she'd sing a duet with him.

She gazed at him in shock. 'Me? I couldn't!'

'Why not? I think your voice and mine would go well together. A baritone and alto can sound very sweet if the timbre is right, and I think it is with us.'

'Sing with you?' She was sounding like the village idiot. 'I couldn't, Mr Beaufort. Not in front of all those people.'

'Let's just try it quietly and see how it sounds. Could you wait behind when the others have left?'

She made up her mind to slip out, which would surely tell him she couldn't face doing it, but something made her stay, because it was cowardly to run away. Mr Beaufort had a lovely voice and surely he'd know if she was good enough, wouldn't want to make a fool of himself.

Anyway, it wouldn't hurt to try, now would it? Why was she being so timid?

He sat down at the piano when the two of them were alone together. 'I was thinking of 'Beautiful Dreamer'. Do you know it?'

'Yes. My employers at Brent Hall were very fond of music, so we heard all the latest songs, some of them all the way from America.' She smiled reminiscently. 'And we didn't scruple to eavesdrop more than they realised. I love music.'

'I could tell you did.' His voice was soft, his smile warm and approving. 'Let's sing it in unison first.' He gave her a note and then started off. She sang softly, afraid of making a mistake.

But it was a song she loved and soon she forgot her nerves, joining in wholeheartedly.

When they'd finished, he was silent for so long, she looked at him anxiously. Had she been fooling herself about how good they sounded?

'I don't think I've ever sung with anyone whose voice goes so well with mine.'

She let out her breath in a great whoosh of relief and he gave her a sympathetic smile.

'This duet is going to be a pleasure, Miss Deagan. No, a great pleasure.' He sat thinking for a moment, then, 'Could you do the harmonies, do you think? My voice is a bit stronger so I think it would be better for carrying the melody.'

'If you teach them to me.'

And she was lost, knew she'd stepped out of her place in the world, was risking making a fool of herself if her nerves got the better of her. But it was such a joy to sing with him that for once she ignored common sense.

There was some grumbling among the other passengers that she was 'putting herself forward', but she ignored that too.

She didn't ignore a request to lead an occasional sing-song with the other women in steerage, though, and began to teach a few simple songs to the children.

How strange! She'd expected this voyage to be sheer tedium and instead, it was proving to be one of the most enjoyable times of her life. She'd never had so much leisure to do what she wanted.

Her nieces and nephew weren't nearly as

much trouble as she'd expected, because Ryan and the other boys away from their families were being supervised by a kindly old gentleman. It was as if they'd all acquired a grandfather.

Now that the storms had abated, most people were enjoying life on board ship, joining in the classes, or the games organised officially and unofficially for children. And Ryan, at least, seemed to be growing visibly. Good food and fresh air. You couldn't beat it for young bodies.

Little Adèle needed more of that sort of thing as well, Maura was sure. Being rich wasn't enough to guarantee health and happiness. She's seen that at Brent Hall, with its many visitors.

She wondered sometimes what she'd need to make her truly happy once she got to Australia? She didn't know, couldn't seem to think beyond the moment. Her world had been turned upside down, so she'd have to take one step at a time and hope she found a new path that suited her.

Maybe Bram would help her to care for the children? Was he earning enough for that? She couldn't imagine her nephew a rich man. But if he could send for his family from Ireland, he must be comfortable, at least.

Oh, what did she know about anything? She began to hum a new tune Mr Beaufort had taught her. One of several.

It was enough for now to relax and enjoy herself, as she'd never done in her whole life before.

11

Thanks to the storm, the *Delta* was over a day late arriving in Marseille. There was a big fuss on board to get the ship immaculate before she docked — well, as immaculate as possible. The storm had damaged the rigging and one of the sails, which would cause further delays for repairs before they could continue their journey.

The captain went about looking tight-lipped, snapping out orders. Mrs Stoddard whispered to Maura that no P&O captain liked to be late with the mails, even when it was unavoidable.

Maura stood on deck with the children beside her. They watched signal flags being raised and lowered on the ship to communicate with the port authorities, then they turned their attention to the city itself.

'Isn't it pretty?' she said. 'Look at the way the houses cling to the side of the hill.'

'White houses with red roofs,' Ryan said. 'They're not like the houses in Shilmara, are they? And a lot of houses we saw from the train in England had grey roofs.'

Brenna pointed. 'Look how big that church on top of the hill is. But the square tower doesn't look finished.'

A man's voice said, 'I stood on that hill, years ago, before they finished the new church. It's called Notre Dame de la Garde. They're going to put a huge statue of the Madonna and Child on top of it, but the statue has to be hollow and made of copper, because of the weight, so it's taking time to get it right.'

Maura swung round to see Mr Beaufort standing beside them, holding Adèle's hand. The child let go and went to stand next to Brenna, smiling shyly at the older girl.

'She really enjoys being with your children,' he said in a low voice. 'Do you mind if we chat for a while so that they can be together? I've asked the head steward and he suggests we stand at the rear of the foredeck. The other cabin passengers don't seem to frequent that area, so we shouldn't be interrupted, though as we're taking other people on board here, that may change once we set sail again.'

'Oh. Well. If you're sure.' But Maura could see some of the other steerage passengers staring at her jealously as she and the children went forward with him. Some of the cabin passengers stared too. Well, let them stare. At least she'd be out of the way of those dratted smuts here.

And would enjoy some interesting conversation. She and Mr Beaufort were never short of things to talk about, if it was only their mutual pleasure in seeing the children so happy.

The young ones moved a short distance away to stand by the rail, commenting to each other on the busy port and the other ships. Ryan was holding one of Noreen's hands. It was touching how careful he always was with his little sister. Adèle and Brenna put their heads together and started giggling. Maura couldn't help smiling at that.

'I remain deeply in your debt for looking after Adèle,' he said suddenly. 'And it's good to see her with other children.'

'She looks better altogether. Perhaps the fresh sea air really does help. I find it invigorating.' She hesitated, then asked, 'What exactly has been wrong with her? She looks reasonably well and happy now, just a little delicate.'

'Weak chest, the doctor said. She wheezed a lot and had to fight for breath sometimes. She had pneumonia during each of the past two winters. Weston Abbas was a cold house, with stone floors on the ground floor. I feared for her life last time and the doctor believed another winter might kill her. He was right that she needed to get away. It was so strange . . . the minute we reached sea air, she started to get better, stopped wheezing as much. Now she's hardly wheezing at all.'

'Then you must find somewhere by the sea to live once you arrive in Australia.' Maura saw a sadness come into his expression. 'Is that going to cause problems?'

'I'm free to live where I want, and can afford to do so. But if Adèle does well in Australia, it'll mean never going back to Weston Abbas. The house and estate have been my family's home for several generations, and I love it.'

'That's a difficult choice for you to make.'

'Not difficult in one sense, because I'd do anything for Adèle, but the thought of losing the family home does hurt, I must admit.' His eyes lingered on his daughter, who was laughing at something Ryan had said, and who was now

211

holding Noreen's other hand as the little girl jigged up and down.

The ship came to rest by the dock and they watched the frenetic activity as the sailors tied up. Almost immediately, three men came into view, striding towards the ship, formally dressed. They were followed by porters wheeling their luggage.

'What are they here for?' Maura wondered aloud as some smartly dressed members of the crew ran to line the gangway and the captain went to wait at the top.

'I'm not sure. They look full of their own importance to me, as if they know they're superior to most other people.'

'They do, don't they? A lot of the gentry have that air. You aren't at all like that.' She clapped one hand to her mouth, but couldn't keep back a smile. 'Sorry. I shouldn't have said that.'

'You don't have to watch what you say when you're with me. I don't think I'm snobbish, perhaps because of my love of music. What people are like, what they can do, matters far more to me than whether their parents are rich or not. You find beautiful voices or great musical skills in people of all classes, and it used to annoy my wife that I invited 'unsuitable' people to our house to make music.'

Maura opened her mouth to ask where his wife was now, but shut it again. It wasn't her business.

'Sylvie went back to live with her family in France when Adèle was less than two,' he said abruptly, staring at the docks rather than meeting her eyes.

'She must be unhappy at you taking Adèle to Australia. It's so far away.'

'She's been gone five years and during that time has made no attempt whatsoever to see our daughter, who doesn't remember her at all. I doubt Sylvie will be in the least concerned about where Adèle goes. She believes in leaving children to the care of nursemaids and governesses. It was another bone of contention between us that I spent so much time with Adèle, 'spoiling her'.'

'Children need love.'

He nodded. 'I did write to let Sylvie know where we were going, but I didn't post the letter till we were about to leave. I didn't want to risk her causing trouble.'

Maura heard the grim note in his voice. 'If I had a daughter, I'd not leave her for others to bring up, not for anything. But I'd only been married a year when my husband died.'

He looked at her in surprise. 'You've been married?'

'Yes. We didn't have any children, though, and I was glad of that.'

'You disliked him that much?'

'Yes.' She refused to pretend that she'd cared about Vincent, because he certainly hadn't cared about her.

'Then why did you marry him in the first place?'

'My family wanted it, especially my father, who made his point very forcefully. And the

213

village priest went on and on about it being my duty. In the end I gave in, not just because of what they said, but because there was no one else offering to marry a maypole of a woman like me and I did want children. But the marriage was worse than I'd expected, like living with a lump of wood, for all he talked to me.'

Oh, the lonely hours she'd spent during that interminable year, dreading those evenings — fortunately not many — when he would grab her and relieve himself, without caring whether he gave her pleasure too, or even whether he hurt her. And she'd been angry at having to manage on only part of his wages while he drank the rest. She'd gone hungry more than once.

'After Vincent was killed in an accident, I left Ireland before my family could find me another husband. That might have been cowardly, but it led to a happy life in service.'

'You don't contradict people when they call you Miss Deagan.'

'I went back to my maiden name, didn't want any reminders of *him*.'

'And now you've had to leave your position in service.'

She couldn't hold back a sigh of regret. 'Yes. Family duty again, but this time I undertook the care of the children willingly — well, I did once I'd got used to the idea. I couldn't let them be put into orphanages, now could I? None of them had had easy lives.'

'You've a kind heart. It shows in how you deal with your nieces and nephew, and the other children, too. You're an absolute marvel with the

214

storytelling. It's a real gift you have.'

She could feel herself blushing.

'Ah, there you are, Mr Beaufort,' a voice said sharply behind them. 'We wondered where you'd got to.'

'I'm spending some time with my daughter and her friends, as you can see, Mrs Halligan.'

A woman dressed far too finely for travelling on a ship stopped a short distance from the group, staring disapprovingly at Maura and the children. 'Are you rehearsing your duet?'

As if she needed to ask that when they'd not been singing, Maura thought. But it was clear her presence here was annoying the woman. She shouldn't have moved out of her proper place on the ship. Never mind that no one else had been sitting here or that Mr Beaufort had invited her.

'We'd better go now, Mr Beaufort,' she said. 'Thank you for letting the children play with your daughter.'

'Thank you again for helping me with Adèle, Miss Deagan.'

His face had gone instantly expressionless, Maura thought as she walked away. She was getting to know his moods, had seen the change before and watched him completely lose the charm and warmth that were so obvious when he talked to his daughter. Or her, she realised suddenly.

She wondered why he disliked this woman so much.

Well, Maura didn't like her either, especially the way Mrs Halligan stared down her nose at the group of small children — as if they smelled bad, which they didn't.

Even Ryan was managing to keep himself clean nowadays. He was a quick learner, that lad, just like his brother Bram.

She realised in that moment that she wouldn't change her new life now, not if it meant losing her nieces and nephew. She might have been reluctant to take charge of them at first, but she'd grown to love them all, and felt they cared about her, too.

★   ★   ★

As the three children walked away with their aunt, Adèle went to take her father's hand and whisper, 'I wanted to go on playing with them.'

Mrs Halligan clicked her tongue in exasperation as if this remark annoyed her. 'I wonder if I might have a private word with you, Mr Beaufort.' She looked meaningfully at his daughter.

'Why don't you go and find Carrie, darling? Get her to play some of those new card games with you.'

'I suppose.'

When Adèle was out of hearing, he turned to Mrs Halligan. 'How may I help you?' He could guess what she wanted to say, though, and to hell with her.

'I felt I must drop a word of warning in your ear.'

'Did you? I wonder why.' He didn't attempt to hide his annoyance. She'd been attaching herself to him whenever she could, trying to match make for her lump of a daughter. Well, even if he was free, he'd not look twice at the girl, who was not only much younger than him, but must be the dullest female he'd ever met, with a harsh voice that grated on his ears. He could never live with such a voice. And who'd marry a woman with a mother like that?

Mrs Halligan lowered her voice. 'It doesn't look good, you know, Mr Beaufort?'

'I beg your pardon?'

'It doesn't look good you spending so much time with *that woman*.'

'*That woman?* Whoever can you mean?'

'You know very well who I mean. That Miss Deagan, putting herself forward, trying to push her way into our circles. She's a steerage passenger and she should stay with her own class.'

'I wasn't aware that Miss Deagan had been pushing herself anywhere. Indeed, I had trouble persuading her to join me in a duet for the concert.'

She tittered. 'Persuade! She was only pretending. Women of her class shouldn't be involved in a ship's concert anyway. What do they know about music? They should just be grateful to be allowed to attend it.'

'Miss Deagan has a truly beautiful voice. Class doesn't come into it where music is concerned, only talent. Moreover, not only did she help with my daughter when I was incapacitated, but Adèle is enjoying playing with Miss Deagan's nieces, who are well-behaved children.'

'And who knows what they bring with them from steerage.'

217

He looked at her in genuine puzzlement this time. 'What do you mean?'

'Dirty people breed lice, if I must put it plainly.'

He took a deep breath to calm himself before speaking. 'Ah. I see. You think all people from the lower classes are dirty. You're completely wrong about that. Now, please excuse me, but I must go and write my diary.' He wasn't writing a diary, but it made as good an excuse as any to get away from her or other boring people, so he kept up the pretence.

He'd learned not to say he was going to play his guitar, because he'd found out the hard way that they insisted he bring it to the day cabin and entertain them. Only they didn't really listen, and tried to talk to him while he was playing. He simply couldn't talk and play at the same time.

Anyway, he was only a competent guitar player, doing it for his own pleasure not to entertain others. He'd bought a guitar and learned to play it while travelling in Spain as a young man. He'd had a wonderfully free year wandering round the safer parts of Europe, till he met Sylvie on the way back and fell in love with her beauty. *Don't judge a book by its cover.*

Sometimes Adèle came into his cabin to listen and sing softly to his accompaniment. He enjoyed that, was delighted that she shared his love of music. At such times he sent Carrie off to chat to the other young female servants she'd made friends with, because she couldn't keep quiet for long.

His anger at the gratuitous insults to Maura

gradually subsided. It'd only make matters worse for her if he argued with Mrs Halligan. But even in the peace of his cabin, he was unable to settle to music or reading, unable to do anything but pace to and fro. If you could call three steps each way pacing.

He missed having a piano even more than he'd expected. He was looking forward to unpacking the cottage piano he'd brought, which was sitting in its wooden crate in the hold. So near and yet so far. He'd learned how to tune pianos himself when he was younger, because there were no good piano tuners in Upper Weston. And he doubted there would be many in Australia, either. He had a good ear, if he said so himself.

He hoped the new piano hadn't been damaged by the ship rolling about in the storm.

He sighed. He'd been enjoying his conversation when that Halligan woman interrupted. He really liked Maura, whatever her so-called social class, and always felt happy and relaxed in her company. And he enjoyed her voice, too. It was so beautiful, she could have sung professionally — except that women from small Irish villages didn't get much chance to do that, and anyway, she didn't have the flamboyant personality she'd need to succeed as a singer.

Oh, he was fooling himself if he tried to pretend he was just interested in Maura's voice. It was the woman herself who interested him. Highly intelligent, so loving with the children. He was beginning to care about her, something he hadn't thought possible after his experiences with his wife.

Perhaps getting out of the comfortable rut of his home was making him view the world differently. When he was younger, he'd travelled and benefitted from it. But he'd never expected travel to lead him to another woman.

Should he stay away from Maura from now on?

Could he do that?

No. And why should he? She was so very special.

For the first time ever, he wished he had sought a divorce from Sylvie. For the first time, he regretted the shackles still locking him into a marriage he could never, ever go back to.

How quickly he had grown to care about Maura! That surprised him. Meeting her had made him realise that he'd been lonely for long enough. He was a man with all a man's needs.

Did she care about him? He thought so.

Only what could he do about their relationship while he was trapped on a ship on the way to Australia? Nothing, that's what. He couldn't court her in such a public setting.

But perhaps one day . . . ? Oh, he was being a fool.

⋆ ⋆ ⋆

Maura continued to stare out at the city from the steerage deck, jostled by her fellow passengers, their noisy chattering and the yells of a group of older lads beating at her ears.

The day seemed to have lost its colour. The way that woman on the foredeck had looked at her . . . as if she was dirt. It had upset her. There was no denying that.

She should have known better than to go openly on to the cabin passengers' deck, though, even when invited. She should also beware of getting too friendly with a wealthy man like Mr Beaufort, even though their friendship was quite innocent, because it would still cause talk and could lead nowhere.

The trouble was, he was the most congenial person she'd met on the ship . . . had ever met, in fact.

She felt as if she could talk to him about anything. She'd not told anyone at Brent Hall how unhappy her marriage had been. Vincent had seen her only as his servant . . . no, his *slave*. It wasn't too strong a word.

That's what had decided her after he died. If she was going to be a servant, she intended to get paid for it.

But she'd told Hugh Beaufort about it.

She'd better be more careful what she did on the ship in future, though. She didn't want people to gossip about her. Gossip had a way of spreading, and she couldn't risk that because she'd need to find employment in Australia once she'd delivered the children to Bram.

She'd better not spend any more time than she had to with Hugh from now on. She would still have to rehearse the duet and the concert songs with him, but apart from that, she'd keep her distance.

She sighed at that decision.

Only, how could she stop the children from

playing with one another? Adèle seemed to be the only little girl of that age among the first- and second-class passengers, and she and Brenna got on as well as any two sisters.

* * *

Once the *Delta* was under way again, after being delayed another day by the need for repairs, final rehearsals started in earnest for the concert. Mrs Stoddard was right, Maura thought ruefully. Everyone was thankful for the time this took. People needed something to occupy them on a long voyage and rehearsing was a very pleasant way of passing the time.

The concert was to take place on the foredeck on the evening of the third day out from Marseille. They'd been told the journey to Alexandria would take five days in all, so this would fit in nicely.

Of course, the other passengers must have heard all the music being rehearsed over and over again, but they didn't complain. Indeed, from what she'd overheard, they were very much looking forward to an evening's entertainment.

Hugh was tireless, rehearsing individual performers in the mornings and the whole choir in the afternoons. He also listened to the people who were doing recitations, able to make suggestions that improved their performance. He was very good at bringing out the best in people, correcting them without upsetting them.

He still found time to rehearse the duet with Maura twice a day, but she made sure to have

222

the children nearby at those times. Their duet was going so well, she wondered if it was necessary to rehearse at all, but he insisted, and added another song, in case an encore was needed. She had no trouble remembering the words and harmonies to the new one, and once they started singing together, she lost herself in the music . . . singing with all her heart . . . enjoying it. As he clearly did.

'I didn't know you had a beautiful voice, Auntie Maura,' Ryan said thoughtfully one day. 'No one ever told me that.'

'No one cared about singing in our family. They were too busy trying to put food on the table.'

'And the women were always having babies.'

She looked at him in shock. It was such a strange remark coming from a lad of twelve.

'Mam had a lot of babies, didn't she? She was always looking after one, or feeling tired because she was going to have another one.' He shrugged. 'She never said anything, but I couldn't help noticing when she got fatter with Noreen.'

'She did have a rather large family.'

'I heard some of the men in the next cabin talking last night. They were saying you don't need to have so many children if you're careful. Is that true, Auntie Maura?'

She hesitated. A priest would tell her it was a sin to prevent children being made, and indeed, most men didn't have the willpower to do it, but she too had heard of ways. You overheard a lot in a forward-thinking household like Brent Hall.

223

'Don't you know?' he pressed.

'Yes. But it's not something people usually talk about, unless they're married. Still . . . you're growing up and you'll be a man one day, so perhaps it'll help you and your wife both.'

She thought she heard someone nearby, so she moved a little apart from the crowd before explaining what she knew, speaking in a low voice and blushing as she told him. She knew people would be horrified at her speaking about such things, especially to a lad, but Ryan had grown up surrounded by farms and animals, so he already knew what was needed to create babies.

Maura had sometimes had to speak about delicate matters to the junior maids who had not grown up on farms, or stand by while her mistress did, so perhaps she was more hardened than other women. When she'd finished, she waited to see how he took it.

'I'll remember that when I grow up. *If* I ever get married, which I'm not sure I will.' Ryan walked away, hands thrust into his pockets, head slightly on one side as if still considering the information.

Once again, he reminded her so much of Bram, who had also been hungry for knowledge and not afraid to ask. And now that he was eating well, Ryan also had that same cheerful, friendly air as his brother.

Seeing the three children flower and grow rosy-cheeked was a reward in itself. She might not be able to have children of her own now, but she could mother these three, couldn't she?

How her ambitions had changed!

224

* ★ *

On the afternoon of the concert, Maura began to feel nervous. Who was she to be performing in front of people who considered themselves her betters? Why, they'd probably heard great singers in London, been to the opera or to concerts played by whole orchestras. They'd probably laugh at her untrained voice.

She stood on deck by the rail, watching a group of children play a clapping, singing game, her stomach churning. When she caught herself wringing her hands, she stopped at once, but she still felt tense and yes, afraid.

Someone came to stand beside her. Hugh. She tried to speak and failed.

'Nervous?'

She nodded.

'Don't be. You have a beautiful voice.'

'I wish I hadn't agreed to do this. I've never wanted to put myself forward, whatever Mrs Halligan says.'

'Ignore her. She's a fool. And it's only a ship's concert. You'll probably never see most of the people again.' His eyes crinkled at the corners and he leaned closer to whisper, 'If anyone upsets you, just imagine them sitting in a bathtub *without any clothes on.*'

She gasped in shock, then her sense of the ridiculous betrayed her into a smile. 'And that'll stop me feeling nervous, will it?'

'It's already done so, to judge by your lovely smile. I'd better not stay to chat, for your sake. The Halligan witch is watching us.'

Lovely smile, Maura thought. What a nice compliment.

He nodded and walked away, pausing to speak to one of the women who was to recite a poem, then to a man singing a solo piece, finally chatting to Ryan and Noreen, making them laugh.

Making sure she wasn't singled out. Clever of him. Yet he'd taken the time to calm her nerves. Bathtub, indeed!

The three gentlemen who'd joined the ship in Marseille, whom the steerage passengers had dubbed 'the bigwigs', came to sit in the front row at the concert. They were surrounded by those cabin passengers not performing, who included Mrs Halligan and her tone-deaf daughter.

The steerage passengers either found somewhere to perch or stood around the edges of the space. Children from the first- and second-class cabins were brought to sit at the feet of the bigwigs. Other children had to manage as best they could.

The choir filed into the open space and stood waiting, arranged in two rows. Maura was relieved that her height put her in the back row.

Hugh walked forward to stand in front of them, and the lady who was providing the accompaniments on the rather battered cottage piano brought out from the first-class passengers' day cabin for the occasion, took her place to polite applause.

Maura felt butterflies multiplying in her stomach, but once the choir began their first song, her fear left her. It was just singing, after all. She'd sung in front of the other people in the servants' hall many a time. This wasn't that much different.

When it came time for the duet, she walked forward to take her place beside Hugh, her breath catching as Mrs Halligan scowled at her and muttered something to the lady next to her.

Maura summoned up an image of the scrawny old woman sitting naked in a bathtub and was nearly betrayed into laughing.

Then the opening chords sounded and she took a deep breath, readying herself, determined not to let Hugh down.

As the two of them began to sing, there was complete silence from the audience. Their voices echoed out, seeming to rise to the stars sparkling in the sky above them and fill the world with music.

The applause was so enthusiastic, Hugh whispered, 'We'll do the encore now. Told you so.'

She'd not thought it possible that they'd be asked to do an encore. Letting him take her hand, she sang with all her heart and soul. Just this one night of pleasure at his side. She'd have it to think about always, a wonderful memory.

When the song ended, she inclined her head in response to the applause, then went back to join the choir.

Afterwards the bigwigs came to congratulate the whole concert party.

'Were you on the stage before, my dear?' one gentleman asked Maura.

'No, sir. I was an Assistant Housekeeper. I'd

not like to go on the stage. I sing for the pleasure of it.'

'Well, you certainly gave me a great deal of pleasure tonight. You have a beautiful voice.'

As the crowd dispersed, she thanked Ryan for looking after the girls, saw them to bed and turned towards her own bunk, wanting to lie quietly and mull over the evening. But her cabin mates insisted on chatting about the concert, wanting her to sing to them again. She refused, laughing and insisting they'd get into trouble for waking up the other passengers.

In the end, the only way she could shut them up was to say, 'We'll all have a sing-song tomorrow night, if you like. It's good for children to sing.'

As she got into her bunk, Brenna whispered, 'It was lovely, Auntie Maura, just lovely.'

Maura bent to kiss the child and Brenna's arms came round her neck in a big hug.

That was worth a dozen concerts.

★ ★ ★

In the morning, everyone was told to assemble on the foredeck after breakfast for an announcement by the captain. Since Marseille, there was nearly a full complement of passengers, so there would be about a hundred and seventy people there, Mrs Stoddard had said. This gathering was so unusual, there was much discussion over breakfast as to what it could be about.

When they were all assembled, the captain cleared his throat, glanced at the bigwigs, who were standing to one side, and began to speak.

'I think you must all have heard about the Suez Canal, which has just been completed so that ships can sail from the Mediterranean into the Red Sea and thence into the Indian Ocean, thus shortening the journey to the East. Of course, no one is sure whether the canal will silt up again or how safe it will be, so it's a rather risky venture at this time, while our company's usual way of getting passengers to Suez, taking them overland from the Mediterranean by train from Alexandria to Suez, is tried and tested, but still . . . '

Some people nodded, others near Maura looked as if they didn't know what he was talking about. She'd no doubt some of the women in her cabin would ask her what it all meant later, so she listened intently.

'The canal is due to open very shortly and these important gentlemen,' he gestured to the bigwigs, 'have come on board especially to attend the opening. Sadly, our ship was delayed because of the storm and then the repairs, so we no longer have enough time left to set passengers ashore at Alexandria before attending the opening, which is to take place over two hundred miles away at Port Said, where the canal begins. Consequently, it has been decided that the *Delta* will proceed straight to Port Said and join the flotilla of ships. They'll be the first ones to pass through the canal. The *Delta* will stay with them at least for the first part of the journey, before returning to Port Said and from there to Alexandria.'

He paused to allow a buzz of comments to subside. 'We regret any inconvenience to our passengers, but this will only delay you by a few days and you will have the satisfaction of being present at a momentous occasion, something to tell your grandchildren about one day.'

He waited to let a buzz of comments subside. 'Unfortunately, you'll miss the planned ship connection at Suez, but the company will pay for your accommodation in one of our own hotels there until you can get on the next ship, so you won't be out of pocket.'

Maura frowned, not sure how she felt about this. On the one hand, she and the children would be present at a momentous event; on the other, the journey would be extended by several days, perhaps more. She looked across at Hugh and saw him smiling and nodding, seeming happy about this.

He glanced round at the people nearby, as if wondering whether other cabin passengers might protest. But no one did and there were only a few mutters of annoyance.

The steerage passengers were dismissed and Maura caught Hugh's eyes on her, but she immediately looked away. Safer to do that. But she'd have liked to talk to him about it, see what more he knew about this canal. He'd already spoken about it enthusiastically, but the captain had sounded dubious about the use of a canal, which had surprised her. Who was right?

When they got back to their own area of the deck, some of the women from the cabin crowded round Maura to ask what it all meant, and she explained it carefully, well, as much as she understood herself.

'So we're going to be late arriving,' one woman grumbled. 'That's not fair. They should have set us down somewhere first.'

'The captain said there was no time,' another woman said. 'And anyway, when do they ever bother about people like us? At least they're paying for the extra stay. I hope the food's good in this hotel of theirs.'

Maura repeated what Hugh had said about the P&O company being rather short-sighted about the canal. 'I was told — '

'By Mr Beaufort,' someone called and people laughed, not unkindly.

She could feel herself flushing. 'They say it'll never take over from their system of a railway and their own hotels, with food supplied from their own nearby farms. And certainly, they look after us very well, don't you think?'

If you can't say something pleasant, say nothing, the housekeeper at Brent Hall always used to tell the younger maids if they got upset with one another. It was a good rule for life.

'Well, it'll give us something else to talk about,' one woman said.

They needed that, Maura thought. So did she. Now that the concert was over, things felt rather flat. But she couldn't get excited about going to see a canal.

She'd already seen plenty of them in England and didn't find them particularly exciting. Though of course this one would have to be far

231

bigger if it was to accommodate ocean-going ships.

Oh, well. Since there was no choice about what was happening, she'd just make the best of it.

* * *

Prescott grudgingly agreed to pay Captain McBride extra to be taken right to Suez.

It was Eleanor's glowing smile that made it all worthwhile to Dougal. And her company in the evenings. She was so easy to be with, so pleasant-tempered.

He felt sad as the second part of the voyage approached its end. He needed to make a quick turnaround if he was to avoid unfavourable winds and weather in the Bay of Bengal on the way back to Galle. At least the monsoon season was over now. He'd never risk going near the Bay from May to August, because it was so shallow it could be treacherous in storms.

Once Eleanor had left the ship, he'd check whether he could pick up a cargo to make his detour more worthwhile. He had a long list of trade goods he carried regularly from Singapore for Bram so had a fair idea of what would sell best. He hoped Bram would forgive him for the delay.

But he'd miss Eleanor's company greatly once she left the ship. He could hardly bear the thought.

Oh, he was a fool to care about a married woman, who was nothing if not proper. And yet,

232

he knew there was an answering warmth in her eyes sometimes, knew instinctively that she could have cared for him too, if circumstances were different.

Her husband continued to play the invalid and she stayed with him when he wished her to. If Prescott wished to be alone, she entertained herself by reading or painting in water colours, skilled paintings that showed glimpses of the everyday life of the crew on the *Bonny Mary*.

Prescott seemed to spend more time alone than with her, and what he did with himself, Dougal couldn't think. The fellow didn't ask to borrow books, his fingers weren't ink-stained. Did he just lie there all the time?

In the evenings, Dougal and Eleanor either dined alone, or finished their meal together after Malcolm had joined them for the first course. He always excused himself after that on the grounds of tiredness, not even seeming to notice that he was leaving his wife alone with another man.

He was skeletally thin and pale now, seeming to be losing weight visibly. Was that because he avoided the sun, because he ate so poorly or because he was ill? He ascribed his poor health to the sea, saying he'd be well again once he was back on dry land.

Eleanor carefully avoided discussing her husband's health, or anything else personal, and Dougal could only respect her wishes.

But she didn't follow her husband's example and retire to her cabin straight after the meal. She enjoyed chatting to Dougal and they were never short of something to talk about.

That worried him. How was he ever to find a wife if he let himself care for a married woman like this . . . if he compared other women he knew to her and found them lacking?

And yet, how could he not care for a woman like her? She wasn't perfect, she'd laugh at the very idea of that. But she was *right*. She was just right for him, somehow.

He wished he'd never agreed to take them to Suez.

No, he didn't. He had at least had these weeks with her, the best weeks of his life.

12

There was great excitement among the passengers and crew as the *Delta* drew closer to Port Said, which was seen first as a darker patch on the horizon.

Even the bigwigs came on deck and of course, everyone else spent as much time there as they could, the steerage passengers taking turns by the short stretch of rail they were allowed. The coastline grew clearer on the horizon, but it seemed to be happening very slowly.

The engines had been running all the time for the past few hours, even though there was a brisk wind and the ship was fairly racing through the clear blue water.

The noise of the engines was wearing Maura down. It was so close to the steerage area, you couldn't get away from it and there was also an unpleasant smell from the engine fumes. Was it sulphur she could detect? Whatever it was, it made her feel slightly nauseous. She spent every minute she could on the deck, but the engines seemed to throb through her very bones.

They reached Port Said later in the day on the 16th November. The *Delta* had to slow down as she moved into the port area, because there were so many ships anchored just a short distance away from the docks. They were flying a variety of flags, both national and the message flags, but today the crew were too busy to explain what the

235

latter meant to the passengers.

Ships' horns began to blast as the *Delta* passed some of the smaller ships, and each time she blew her horn in response.

'It's called Passing Honours,' one of the crew called. 'Blowing horns like that.'

'Where are we going, do you think?' Maura winced as yet another horn blasted its noisy message. Noreen and Brenna covered their ears with their hands.

Ryan didn't seem as upset by the noise as the girls. Since the crew had threatened that any lad getting in their way would be instantly sent below, he stayed near his aunt, for once, and other lads had also joined their families.

No one wanted to miss a single thing. They were all waiting, though they weren't quite sure what they were waiting for, exactly. How did you open a canal? What happened? Why were so many ships there?

Small boats were moving from ship to ship and people were yelling at one another across the water. It was a wonder none of the small boats collided.

The *Delta* slowed right down, almost drifting along now, so there was time to take a good look at the other ships.

The three bigwigs must have gone up on the bridge with the captain, Maura thought, because they weren't on the foredeck that she could see. Darkness was fast approaching as the ship came to a halt.

'I've counted nearly a hundred ships,' Ryan announced.

Maura didn't bother to contradict him. He was making such progress with arithmetic and reading. Besides, it was difficult to tell exactly how many vessels there were. Even the adults were disagreeing with one another about the total number.

Now, smaller boats began pulling towards the shore from the various ships, carrying people wearing what looked to Maura like evening dress. Was there going to be a party somewhere? Probably. Grand folk loved their parties.

No one was worrying about getting the children to bed, even though the light was very poor now.

When Hugh joined Maura by the rail, she was torn between being happy to see him and feeling worried that his singling her out might give rise to more talk.

'I doubt anyone will notice me if I stay in the shadows,' he said quietly, guessing what was making her look worried. 'I thought you'd like to know there's a grand banquet taking place on shore for the dignitaries and our bigwigs are furious that we've arrived too late for them to be invited to attend.'

'They don't seem happy about anything, judging from their scowls.'

'Well, their company's profits are threatened by this canal and from what they've said, they sound as if they're hoping it'll fail. Apparently there was a panic earlier today when the engineers found a rocky ledge in the canal itself that would have holed a ship. The bigwigs were gleeful about that. I'm surprised the canal builders could have missed something of that size, but I suppose it's inevitable with such a huge project.'

Other steerage passengers had gathered round them to listen to Hugh. So much for no one noticing he was here, Maura thought. But still, it was interesting to hear what was going on.

'How did you find out about the ledge?'

'The captain asked me to translate what a French officer in a small boat was telling him, since the man's English was very poor. The Empress of France herself is attending the banquet, apparently, and will lead the flotilla through the canal tomorrow in a ship called *L'Aigle*, which means the *Eagle*.'

He smiled and moved along a few steps to signal that he had finished talking to the group, but beckoned to Maura. When they were away from the others, he pulled a wry face at her. 'One thing about having a French wife who refused to speak English unless she had guests was that my command of the French language improved by leaps and bounds.'

Imagine being able to speak other languages, she thought enviously. Didn't he see how different he was from her? Why did he insist on seeking her out?

She couldn't tell him to leave her alone, not when so many people were within hearing, but she would have to find an opportunity to insist, for her reputation's sake.

Just then a ship's officer came up to them, looking annoyed. 'Miss Deagan, the captain would like a word with you immediately.'

'With me?'

'Yes. I'm afraid there's been a complaint about your behaviour.'

Hugh stepped forward. 'Who from?'

'I'm not at liberty to say, sir.' He turned back to Maura. 'If you could hurry, miss. The captain's a busy man.'

She couldn't help throwing a startled glance at Hugh, but turned to follow the officer, sure it was a misunderstanding.

Hugh fell in beside her.

'The captain wishes to see her on her own, sir,' the officer said pointedly.

'I'll wait for her outside his cabin, then.'

The officer hesitated. 'I shouldn't do that, sir. It'd only make matters worse, given the nature of the complaint.'

'I don't understand and she's going nowhere until I do.'

'Look, let me get her to the captain. I'll explain it to you afterwards. Believe me, it'll be much better for her if you stay out of it.'

Hugh could see he'd get no further information and stopped at some distance from the captain's cabin, but in a place where he could see Maura come out.

Mrs Stoddard, who had been waiting outside, followed her and the officer inside, then the door closed.

★　★　★

'Stand there,' the supervisor whispered, pointing.

Maura stopped in front of the captain's desk.

239

He looked up, clearly angry. 'I can't afford to waste much time on this. A complaint has been made against you by a cabin passenger, so I'm confining you below till we arrive back at Alexandria.'

She had trouble speaking for a moment, then shook off Mrs Stoddard's hand as the supervisor tried to tug her away. 'A complaint about what? I'm not aware that I've done anything wrong.'

He glanced at his pocket watch then said in an irritated tone, 'The complaint is that you've been talking lewdly to the children on board and that you've been pursuing one of the male cabin-class passengers, who is too embarrassed to complain himself.'

'I deny all of this absolutely.'

'Are you suggesting the passenger was lying?'

'I most certainly am.'

'I'm afraid I'll have to take a lady's word against yours.'

Fury swelled up inside her, but he gestured again, and Mrs Stoddard and the officer pulled her outside.

'You'll have to do as he says. A captain's word is law,' the officer whispered.

'But I haven't done anything wrong! It's only one person's word against mine and whoever it is, she's lying.' She could guess who it was, though.

'She's a lady,' Mrs Stoddard said. 'And I heard she was related to one of the bigwigs. You'd stand no chance against her.'

'It's only for a few days, then you'll be leaving the ship,' the officer said soothingly.

* * *

'Ah, Mr Beaufort. Do come and join us for refreshments,' a voice cooed beside him and he turned to see Mrs Halligan standing there. If she hadn't thrown a triumphant glance towards the captain's cabin, he'd never have suspected her, but when she did that, he suddenly guessed who had been complaining about Maura.

'What the hell have you done?' he demanded.

She froze, then shrugged. 'I've done what's right, Mr Beaufort, and so would you if you hadn't been besotted with *that woman*. Let me tell you that decent people object to the filth she discusses openly, and if *you* can't see that she's pursuing you, I can.'

Hugh glared at her. 'She is not pursuing me. It's you who won't leave me alone. Well, *do not — speak to me — ever again*, madam. And leave Miss Deagan alone.'

'I shall tell everyone what *that woman* is like.'

He turned away without a word.

'Do you hear me? I won't share a ship with a woman of loose morals.'

He turned back to say loudly and clearly, 'Miss Deagan's morals are impeccable. What's more *she* doesn't tell lies, as you clearly do.'

She let out a shriek of anger and stormed away.

Hugh went back to staring at the door of the captain's cabin. He didn't dare push inside, because that would be disrespectful, but he intended to find out what had happened from Maura as soon as she came out.

While he was waiting, someone hailed him from a nearby ship and he turned to see one of the officers grinning across the stretch of water at him.

'*Que fais-tu là, mon vieux?*' the man yelled, his voice carrying clearly across the water.

'*Gérard!*' He was amazed to see his old friend. Keeping an eye on the captain's cabin door, he explained quickly that he was on his way to Australia. Then he heard the captain's door opening and called out that he had urgent business to attend to and would try to speak to Gérard later.

Maura came out of the captain's cabin, accompanied by the supervisor and an officer. She looked angry and was arguing with them in a low voice.

When Hugh stepped forward, the stewardess held up her hand to keep him back.

'Captain's orders, sir. Miss Deagan is not to speak to anyone except steerage passengers and crew from now on.'

Maura ignored this. 'They say I've been talking lewdly and pestering you.'

'*What?* I'll see the captain about that, then, right away.'

He turned but the officer stepped in front of him. 'Won't change a thing, sir, except to cause more trouble — and for her, not you.'

'The captain's made his mind up already,' Maura called back as the supervisor continued to pull her along. 'But it's all lies.'

She shook off the woman's hand and, head held proudly high, followed her down the companionway.

242

Hugh turned to the officer. 'Unless you want me to push into the captain's cabin this minute, kindly explain what's going on.'

When this had been done, Hugh went to his cabin to try to work out what to do. Seeing Maura being so unfairly treated made him realise how very much he cared for her. He wanted to rush to her rescue.

But a captain had complete power on his ship.

And Hugh hadn't spoken of his feelings, had no right to consider Maura his until he knew she returned them.

★ ★ ★

Bram walked round the smaller of the two houses he'd bought. There hadn't been much work needed here and he was wondering whether to move in himself while he waited for the renovations to be completed on the larger dwelling. Only that would mean moving twice, which would be troublesome.

Riss was proving a steady worker and as far as Bram could tell, was doing a good job, with the help of his lad.

As he went into the bigger of the two houses, Bram still found it hard to believe that he owned it and would be living here soon.

There were footsteps behind him and he turned to see Mitchell Nash coming down the hall towards him. He waited till they were closer to ask quietly, 'How are things going?'

'Riss is doing an excellent job,' Mitchell replied. 'He has a good eye for spaces, but

243

sometimes needs guidance. I'm going to offer him a permanent job with me and then I hope to build houses for people.'

'How long is the work on this house going to take, do you think?'

'I can't say exactly. But once the structure is sound, things will move more quickly. No use rushing this part of the job. We want it done right.'

'I'm wondering whether to move into the other house.'

'Ah. I was going to ask you if you'd be renting it out. I need somewhere to live temporarily, because the cottage at the timber yard is far too small to hire a live-in housekeeper. People talk if you don't have servants' quarters.' He scowled briefly at the memories that brought back. 'Then I'm going to extend my own home and move it to the side of my timber yard, where there is some spare land.' He smiled. 'One thing about wooden houses. You can move them or add to them quite easily.'

Bram made a quick decision without even asking Isabella, sure she'd approve. 'I'd be happy to rent the smaller house to you.' And even happier to have some extra money coming in. The ice works was costing more to extend than had originally been estimated, and Bram was beginning to wonder if it'd ever make money for him, if Chilton knew what he was doing.

He was starting to lie awake at night, worrying, and he knew that Isabella was worried about their financial situation, too. Not that the Bazaar wasn't doing well. It was.

But he had taken on too much. The ice works on top of the house, and not just one house, but two.

★ ★ ★

Hugh stood up and moved to another seat when Mrs Halligan came to sit beside him for the evening meal. People fell silent at that obvious insult and her cheeks burned red against her sallow skin. Her daughter sat with bowed head, not eating much and not speaking throughout the meal.

When he'd eaten as much as he could force down, Hugh went to check on Adèle then went to stand on deck alone.

Somewhere in the distance were lights and sounds of revelry.

Somewhere closer to hand, a small boat was being rowed gently along. When it came closer, he saw that Gérard was sitting in it, with a sailor rowing steadily.

'Ahoy the ship!' his friend called softly. 'Permission to come aboard?'

Hugh leaned over the rail before the sailor on watch could say anything. 'I'd rather come and visit you.' He turned to the sailor. 'Would that be all right?'

'We're not going anywhere tonight, sir. Do you need any help getting down?'

'No, I'll be fine.' Hugh had always loved climbing and made nothing of descending the big rope nets on the side of the ship.

'Something wrong?' Gérard asked.

He nodded. 'Can we go somewhere private?'

'I know a little bar on the docks. Not a fancy place, but we could have a drink or two there.'

Hugh nodded, feeling comfortable in his old friend's presence. They'd seen a lot of one another a few years ago, when Hugh was courting Sylvie. Indeed, Gérard had expressed doubts about the proposed marriage, though he'd never explained why.

When they were settled with tiny cups of strong coffee, the Frenchman said, 'You might as well tell me what's wrong, *mon vieux*.'

So Hugh explained because he trusted Gérard completely.

'You should have divorced Sylvie, you know.'

'I thought I'd never want to marry again and anyway, I didn't know where she was. Even if I had known, I was damned if I'd pretend I'd been unfaithful *and* cruel or some other form of ill-treatment in order to give *her* a divorce.'

Gérard nodded. 'Especially when it's she who has been unfaithful with her cousin Jacques.'

'*What?*'

'You didn't know?'

'I knew there must be some man, but not who he was.'

The Frenchman sighed, shrugging his shoulders expressively as only the French could. 'She's loved him since she was a girl but they couldn't afford to marry, so she married you. He went off to make his fortune and he did. Her family refuse to talk about it, but he was the one she ran off with.'

'If I can prove that, I'll definitely divorce her.'

246

'*If* you can prove it. You're on your way to Australia and can do nothing now. In the meantime, what are you going to do about this lady you have started to love?'

'What can I do? If that Halligan woman really is related to one of the bigwigs, the captain won't risk upsetting him. At least we'll be getting off the ship in Suez.'

'What if they send a message to the next ship warning them about her? What if the Halligan woman is on her and refuses to continue if your lady is allowed on board? Spiteful people will go to great lengths to hurt others if they feel slighted. I'd guess your new lady — *comment s'appelle-t-elle?* — is in for a long and uncomfortable voyage.'

'*Elle s'appelle Maura.*'

Hugh thought this through, then thumped his fist on the table. 'Damnation! What am I to do?'

'You could try to find another ship at Suez to take you all on to Galle.'

'Would that be possible?'

'Very possible these days. The place is getting busier all the time.' He traced a line in the moisture on the table, then snapped his finger. '*Tiens!* If you're desperate now, you could always transfer to our ship. One group of passengers didn't turn up and since the captain owns a share in the ship, he's always eager to make more money. It's only for a night or so, after all. We could take you to Suez from here. It's only a short journey. I've heard that your ship is returning to Port Said, of all the stupid things.'

'Thank you for the offer, but we have passage

247

booked in the P&O system, so we will have to put up with delays. And surely it won't be necessary to change ships? Not even that woman would go to such lengths to hurt my Maura.'

Gérard shrugged. 'Who knows? Always better to have an emergency plan.'

Hugh changed the subject. He didn't believe there would be any need for such extremes. He'd speak to the captain about it all, explain why Mrs Halligan was lying.

★   ★   ★

The following day most of the passengers were up early, well before their usual time, to go on deck. They were there even before word was sent that the *Delta* was to join the first flotilla ever to go through the canal.

Hugh looked in vain for Maura, hoping the captain had changed his mind. When he saw the women's supervisor he made his way across to her to ask about Maura.

Mrs Stoddard looked at him warily. 'I can't take a message to her. It's more than my job's worth.'

'How is she?'

'Upset.'

'She's done nothing wrong, I'm sure of it.'

The supervisor hesitated, then said even more quietly, 'I agree with you. But I still can't go against the captain's orders.'

'Could you take her a verbal message?'

She shook her head, as if refusing, but said, 'Mmm.'

He hoped he'd understood her properly. 'Tell her I'll find a way to get her released.'

Mrs Stoddard gave him a sharp look. 'I doubt you can do that, sir. When someone has connections to the management of the P&O line, their wishes get priority with every captain.'

'But this is all so unjust.'

She shrugged and moved on.

Later he tried to speak to the ship's officer again, but was told the same thing.

'The captain's word is law on a ship, sir.'

Hugh walked away to stand by the rail till he'd got control of his anger.

Gérard waved at him from the next ship and Hugh waved back. He studied the French ship. Much smaller than the *Delta*. Would it be possible to move from one ship to the next in the middle of a journey? What about the luggage? How would they get that across? And his piano. He'd have to leave it behind and trust it'd be delivered safely to Australia.

He feared it might become necessary to change ships if this went on, bizarre as that idea had seemed last night. He couldn't leave Maura incarcerated like that. She didn't deserve it. She'd helped him with Adèle and he'd have felt duty-bound to help her in return even if he hadn't cared for her.

Now . . . he wanted to help Maura. In every way possible. If he were free, he'd do a lot more than that to help her.

If he were free. He sighed.

★ ★ ★

Maura sat on her bunk and willed herself not to weep. She hadn't said anything to the girls the night before but now she had to explain why she couldn't go on deck. She told them briefly what she'd been accused of and said bluntly that she hadn't done it.

Is suddenly occurred to her that the 'lewd' talk must refer to the conversation she'd had with Ryan about limiting the size of families. Well, it had been a private conversation and if that old hag had been eavesdropping, she should mind her own business.

'You'd never do anything wrong,' Brenna said at once.

'I try not to.'

'That lady is telling lies, then.'

'I'm afraid so. But she has important friends, so she's getting her own way.'

'That's not fair.'

'No, Brenna. Not at all fair.' She tried to think what to do. 'Look, will you go up on deck and tell Ryan what's happened? Tell him not to make a fuss. We'll not be on this ship much longer, anyway, just a week or so.'

'Does that mean we have to stay down here in this smelly old cabin for a whole week?'

She shrugged. 'I do. You don't.'

'But it's so hot down here.'

'Sometimes you can't help what happens to you. Sometimes you just have to put up with it. But you and Noreen can go up on deck if you promise me to be careful and keep hold of her hand all the time.'

'We're not going on deck if you can't.'

'We're staying with you,' Noreen said, for once not waiting for Brenna to speak.

Maura was touched that quiet little Noreen would say this. She was sure the girls would change their minds about staying down as it got hotter, so she didn't argue. 'Go and tell Ryan for me, will you, Brenna love?'

The older girl followed the others up to the deck and Noreen snuggled down next to her aunt.

'It's nice and quiet down here now the engine's stopped. I don't like noisy places.'

'No. Neither do I.'

Maura had held her head high last night, refusing to act as if she had done something to be ashamed of. But she couldn't help feeling very upset. She might have wept now if it wasn't for the children.

*   ★   ★

Hugh saw Brenna come up on deck and began to make his way towards her. But the officer blocked his path.

'Please don't go aft, sir.'

As Hugh stood there, he saw Brenna staring towards them — no, she was looking past them.

'What's that child doing?' the officer asked as Brenna suddenly set off running, pushing past people in a way she'd never done before, her face set and determined.

Hugh thought for a minute she was coming towards him, but she veered to one side and stopped in front of Mrs Halligan.

251

'Why are you telling lies about my aunt?' the girl yelled in a piercing voice. 'It's wrong to tell lies. She's not done anything bad.'

Hugh and the officer exchanged horrified glances and set off towards them, but by now, everyone nearby had swung round to gape at the indignant child.

Mrs Halligan's face had turned a bright red and she was making gobbling noises as if she didn't know what to say.

'I'm going to tell the captain about your lies,' Brenna went on. 'My aunt is a lovely woman. She's looking after us now our parents are dead. You're wicked, you are, missus, wicked.'

Hugh reached Brenna and put his arm round her.

She swung round indignantly, then saw who it was and sobbed loudly. 'Tell her to stop lying about my aunt, Mr Beaufort. Tell her.'

There was no doubting that the child was telling the truth. It rang in every word she spoke. And guilt showed in the older woman's face as she turned away.

People were murmuring to one another, but none of the other ladies went to Mrs Halligan's side. Indeed, they were all drawing back from her and her daughter. She'd tried to spread her poisonous remarks about Maura last night and Hugh had wanted to give her a dressing down. But a gentleman didn't do that to a lady in public.

He watched in grim satisfaction as people continued to move right away, turning their backs on Mrs Halligan. He remembered

252

suddenly how kind Maura had been to the others involved in the concert. She'd helped out when she could, encouraging those who were nervous, not putting on airs because she was performing the duet.

'The biter bit,' he murmured.

But that didn't help Maura because the Halligan witch still had connections and the captain wouldn't cross her and risk upsetting his superiors or the major shareholders.

Ryan had now joined his cousin and Brenna was whispering to him. He looked shocked and asked a couple of questions, then he too stared across at the old lady standing there so stiffly.

'God hears every lie you tell,' he yelled across the deck. 'Leave my aunt alone.'

This time the officer didn't stop Hugh from accompanying the two children to the steerage deck.

'Shh, now. Come back to the other deck,' he said softly to them both. 'No, Ryan. It won't do any good shouting. Trust me, it'll make things worse for your aunt.'

'What's going on?' someone from steerage asked him before he could get the children away. 'Why is that nice Miss Deagan shut up below?'

A cabin passenger joined in. 'I didn't believe what Mrs Halligan was saying about her last night, just couldn't believe it.'

'It's a . . . misunderstanding,' Hugh said, afraid of making matters worse.

'It's that old lady telling lies about my aunt!' Brenna said fiercely.

'Can't you tell the captain he's wrong, Mr

253

Beaufort?' one woman who'd been in the concert party asked.

'You can't tell captains what to do on their own ships. If I could do anything, I would have done it already, I promise you.'

'Well, it's pretty poor, that's what it is. A damned shame,' a cabin passenger said.

'It's not right.'

Other voices joined in till there was quite a hubbub and for once both steerage and cabin passengers were united.

Hugh and Ryan guided Brenna back to sit on the edge of one of the hatches. They both had their arms round her and she was still sobbing.

Mrs Stoddard came to join them. 'I'll see to her now, sir. She'll be better below with her aunt for the time being.'

'I want to go and see my aunt,' Ryan said.

'Yes, how is Miss Deagan going to see her nephew?' Hugh asked. 'She'll be worried about him.'

Mrs Stoddard sighed. 'I'll let him come to visit her later. Leave that to me and the male supervisor.'

'Is that all you can do?'

She glanced round quickly. 'I can take that verbal message. Though I'll deny doing it if anyone asks me.'

'Tell her I'll work something out, that I won't let her be kept there.'

She looked sceptical, hesitated, then whispered, 'As long as she's on this ship, he'll keep her there, now that he's given the order.'

'Then I'll have to get her off the ship, won't I?'

254

He could see that now. How lucky that he'd met Gérard!

He went to find Carrie and Adèle, explaining the misunderstanding and telling Carrie to pack their things in case he found another ship for them to travel on.

She looked at him wide-eyed. 'Does that mean we'll have to climb down the side of the ship like you did last night?'

'It might. It's not difficult and the sailors will help you and Adèle.'

She grinned. 'Bless you, sir, I'm better at climbing trees than any of my brothers. I'd enjoy climbing down. And I'll tell Adèle how to do it, as well.'

His daughter nodded.

'You're a good lass, Carrie. Do what you can without showing exactly what we're planning, then stay close to Adèle.'

But how was he to manage it?

★　★　★

All the passengers stayed on deck as the procession of ships formed.

'They're calling it the Voyage of the Monarchs,' the man next to Hugh said. 'The Empress of France is there with Monsieur Lesseps, who was in charge of building the canal, plus Prince Henry of the Netherlands, and someone said the Emperor of Austria is here too.'

'It's certainly an amazing sight.' Upset as he was, Hugh couldn't help watching as the first ship in the flotilla entered the canal, moving slowly past the big stone obelisks at the entrance. Since it was a French project, *L'Aigle* was leading them, with the Empress Eugénie on board. Other vessels fell in behind them one by one, at carefully spaced intervals.

There were more like forty ships than the hundred Ryan had claimed to have counted the night before, but that made for an impressive convoy. Apparently another convoy was setting off from the southern end of the canal, to meet in the middle.

Smaller ships moved alongside the larger steam vessels, but were soon left behind. Here and there groups of spectators in flowing Arab robes waved from the sandy sides of the canal.

The first stop would be at Lake Timsah, where a banquet was to be held for a thousand guests under the desert stars, with fireworks and an equestrian fantasia to entertain them, whatever the latter might mean.

Only Hugh wouldn't be there, even as a spectator. It would be the best opportunity he'd get to speak to Maura, something he was determined to do.

Everyone on the ship was taking a great deal of interest in even the smallest scrap of information.

He fanned himself. It was so hot. And Maura was penned up in the stifling cabins below, which didn't even have portholes that opened, she said. Hugh couldn't concentrate on the festivities, and he made very sure he kept his distance from Mrs Halligan and her red-eyed daughter.

Mid-afternoon he saw Mrs Stoddard come and speak to the officer who seemed to be dealing with Maura's affair.

Hugh moved so that he could eavesdrop.

'I think Miss Deagan's suffering badly from the heat, sir. It's like an oven down there. And so are the two little girls. Could you please ask the captain if they can come up for some fresh air? The smallest child is so little . . . we wouldn't want a death on the ship, would we? You know how quickly a child can fade.'

The officer hesitated, then said, 'Get the doctor to see her and recommend that, then I'll speak to the captain.'

Mrs Stoddard hurried off and shortly afterwards, the doctor followed her below decks, looking irritated at having to miss part of the grand arrival at Lake Timsah.

Hugh watched as thousands of spectators cheered the flotilla, and French warships fired several salvos.

'This is only the beginning of the celebrations,' a man near him said. 'Amazing, isn't it?'

'Yes. A momentous occasion.' But Hugh kept turning round to see whether the doctor had come back up on deck.

13

Maura felt increasingly faint in the heat below decks and was feeling so unwell that when Mrs Stoddard came to check on her, she found it hard to answer her questions coherently.

The two little girls had stayed by her side and refused point-blank to go up on deck without her, which was very touching. But it meant they too were suffering.

She looked at the supervisor. 'Please could you take Noreen and Brenna out into the fresh air for a while. They're so hot and uncomfortable down here.'

'I'm not going without my auntie,' Brenna said.

Noreen just lay limply against her, eyes closed.

The voice seemed to come from a great distance. 'How are you feeling, Miss Deagan?'

'Not . . . well. So . . . hot.'

Mrs Stoddard went away and returned with the ship's doctor.

He came up to Maura and felt her pulse, laying one hand on her forehead. 'Ridiculous!' he snorted. 'It's appallingly hot down here. I'll have a word with the captain myself. This is no time to incarcerate people for supposed crimes. And why are the children here?'

'They won't leave her.'

'Does he want a death on his hands?'

Maura roused herself to make the protest

she'd been repeating every time anyone came near her. 'I've done nothing wrong, doctor. I don't understand why Mrs Halligan made those accusations.'

He snorted again. 'Because Beaufort was ignoring her daughter and talking to you. Everyone in first class knows that. You have a beautiful voice, my dear. Bound to make people jealous. I've seen for myself how Beaufort loves music. He's very talented.'

'I wish I hadn't . . . joined the choir.' Maura wiped the sweat away from her face.

'We'll get you out of here, at least.' He went away and she let her aching head fall back on the pillow.

Mrs Stoddard lingered to shake her gently. 'You need to drink more water and make sure the children do as well. Sip it, don't gulp. It doesn't taste pleasant when it's lukewarm, but I've seen people fall seriously ill for lack of drinking enough in hot climates. Yes, I'm coming, doctor.' She bustled off again.

Maura dragged herself into the dining area and gradually forced down a glass of water from the supply there, making sure the girls drank a whole glass each as well.

When footsteps sounded on the companion-way some time later, she didn't even look up until Mrs Stoddard said, 'The captain says you can come up on deck, but you're not to speak to anyone, and if you'll take my advice, you won't even look in Mr Beaufort's direction. I'm sure you and the children will feel better in the fresh air.'

She could only nod and follow her. She tried to carry Noreen up the companionway, but couldn't summon up the strength even for that.

Clicking her tongue in annoyance, Mrs Stoddard took the child from her. 'Get up those stairs. I'll bring her.'

★ ★ ★

Hugh had been watching the rear deck carefully. It wasn't long before the doctor and Mrs Stoddard came up talking earnestly. She waited near the companionway as he went off to see the captain.

Hugh ignored the celebrations and cheering crowds. He saw the doctor come back a few minutes later, so moved close enough to hear what he was saying to the supervisor.

'The captain says she can come up on deck, for the children's sake, but she's not to go near the foredeck or to speak to anyone at all.'

Mrs Stoddard looked surprised. 'Can't she even speak to the children?'

'I didn't like to ask the captain to interpret that, in case he changed his mind. I'm sure she can speak to the three children who are with her, though. Now, if there's nothing else that's urgent, I'd like to watch this momentous event. These accusations against Miss Deagan are a lot of fuss about nothing, if you want my opinion.'

Her voice was toneless as she replied, 'Yes, sir.' The doctor might say it was all nonsense, but he was doing nothing to challenge the captain. No one was except that nice Mr Beaufort. It made her feel angry.

Hugh continued to watch as Maura was brought up. She looked dreadfully pale and her hair was plastered to her head by sweat. The supervisor was carrying Noreen, and Maura was walking slowly, as if it was an effort to move. Brenna trailed behind her, drooping visibly.

Someone stopped beside him, one of the men he'd chatted to occasionally. 'Your songbird doesn't look at all well today, Beaufort.'

'No. She's suffering because of that harridan's lies.'

'Are they lies?'

'Oh, yes. All of them.'

'My wife said the same thing. Seems a bit unfair to punish the poor woman because you won't flirt with the Halligan girl. Better watch out. Mrs Halligan will be accusing *you* of something next.'

There was a pause while they both studied Maura, who was talking quietly to the children. She leaned closer to wipe the sweat gently off Noreen's face, smiling tenderly.

'The wife said to tell you to get that poor woman away from the ship, if you possibly can. Hattie knows something about the old woman, because the Halligans come from near her family home. She refuses to tell me what she knows, just muttered something about spite and said to pass a warning on to you.'

'Thank her for me.' It only confirmed that he'd made the right decision.

261

Hugh kept willing Maura to look his way, but she was avoiding looking in his direction. She still seemed exhausted and was so pale it worried him. What if they sent her below again and kept her there? She might become ill . . . die, even.

And what if that old witch tried to stir up more trouble? She'd certainly looked angry this morning.

No, he couldn't allow this to go on. Maura was too important to him now. She hadn't tried to attract his attention, or anyone else's. It was enough that she was . . . Maura. Brisk and upright, hiding her tender heart from the world, but revealing it occasionally in her dealings with children.

Hugh saw that his companion was waiting for a reply. 'I intend to do exactly what your wife has advised. Thank her for confirming that I've made the right decision.'

'If I can help in any way, you only have to ask.' He grinned. 'I doubt the captain will dare take it out on the cousin of an earl, so I'm safe enough.'

Hugh had never bothered about connections and influence, despised all that social jostling. He just wanted to enjoy his life, his family, his music. Was that such a bad thing to wish for?

And a new ambition had been growing on him: to have more children and lead a happy family life with a real wife, not someone as vain and selfish as Sylvie. A life filled with music and simple family pleasures.

There was another thing he needed to do before he could achieve that: write to his lawyer in England from Suez and ask him to set things in motion for a divorce from Sylvie, no matter what it cost.

He should have done it years ago, instead of standing on his foolish pride.

* * *

As soon as Maura was settled on deck, Ryan came over to join her, frowning.

'You don't look at all well, Auntie.'

'It was too hot below deck. I'll be better now I'm up here.'

'It's hot up here too.' He glanced round and leaned closer, whispering, 'I've got a message for you. Mr Beaufort is trying to find another ship for us all to change to. If you agree, he said you should pack your things and be ready to move at a moment's notice.'

She gaped at him. 'Did *he* tell you that?'

'No. Carrie did. I'm to give her your answer. But not straight away, in case anyone's watching us.' He grinned, obviously enjoying the plotting.

'How can Mr Beaufort find another ship?'

Ryan shrugged. 'I don't know. But perhaps it's one of those.' He gestured to the line of ships making their way slowly and majestically along the canal in front of and behind the *Delta*. For a few moments they all stared at them.

Maura's voice was wistful. 'It's a magnificent sight, isn't it? I wish there weren't all this bother to spoil it for us.'

'Well, we can still see them, can't we? And I don't want to stay on this ship, if they treat you

263

like this.' He scowled in the direction of the bridge.

She still felt too muzzy-headed to think clearly, but oh, she'd love to get off this ship too. 'Tell Mr Beaufort I'll do whatever he thinks best. Tell him . . . I trust him absolutely.'

Ryan beamed at her, turned to walk away, then swung back to give her a quick hug, before running off to play with the other lads.

She didn't watch him, just sat in the shade and tried to pull herself together. The girls sat with her.

'Why don't you go and play for a while?'

They shook their heads. 'We're staying with you,' Brenna said. 'They might try to hurt you, and if they do, I'll kick and bite them.'

'Oh, darling, you mustn't say that.'

But Brenna's lips were pressed together in a straight, determined line. And her expression said she'd take on the world if necessary.

Maura was so touched by this she spoke from the heart. 'Thank you for caring about me. I love you both very much and I won't let anyone hurt you without a fight, either.'

She reached out her hand to clasp Brenna's and they smiled at one another, then Noreen wriggled between them and took their hands as well.

★   ★   ★

In the evening, when the celebratory banquet was under way, and the sky was lit by fireworks and flares, Hugh summoned one of the little

264

boats that seemed to have appeared out of nowhere to take people not attending the ceremonies for rides on the water.

'I'm going across to see my friend on the *Vitesse*,' he said to the sailor on duty.

'Right, Mr Beaufort. Duly noted. There's a few people gone for a ride round.' The sailor wrote his name in a notebook.

Hugh climbed down and pointed to the ship he wanted, giving the man rowing it a coin when they arrived. 'Wait for me here.' He pointed to himself and the ship, then pantomimed climbing back down again, before holding out another coin.

After gaining permission to go on board, Hugh climbed up then looked back to check that the boatman had understood and was still waiting.

'*Encore de problèmes?*' Gérard asked as they stood side by side on the deck, leaning on the rail.

'Yes. I've come about your offer. Were you serious about us taking passage on this ship from here to Suez? And if so, how much will that cost?'

'I didn't think you'd take me up on it, but yes, I was serious. You'd be a bit crowded, though. We're not as big as the *Delta*.'

'That doesn't matter for such a short time.'

'We'd better talk to the captain about it, then. He likes to do the bargaining.'

After a lively discussion, during which Hugh specified exactly how many people would be joining the ship, the captain stuck out his hand

and they shook on the bargain.

Hugh accepted a glass of wine, talking about the practicalities of the changeover the following evening, then was rowed back to the *Delta*.

The die was cast. From now on, he would be totally responsible for Maura, Carrie and four children.

Actually, he rather liked the idea of that. He'd never seen himself as a *pater familias* before, but he was thoroughly enjoying having a group of people who belonged to him, so to speak, or he had been enjoying their company until this incident. The Irish children were delightful and Maura had become . . . very special.

Adèle too was much happier having other children to play with and she continued in better health, putting on weight noticeably. He was even daring to hope that this trip to a warmer climate would do the trick permanently.

★   ★   ★

When he got back to the *Delta*, Hugh found the decks still well populated, in spite of the late hour. He sought out the officer he'd dealt with before, who was sitting down, looking half-asleep. No one wanted to go to their cabins in this sweltering heat.

When he explained what he'd arranged, the man whistled softly. 'The captain won't like that. It'll look bad for him.'

'I don't care. We're not prisoners here. We're customers and are free to do what we wish. Dissatisfied customers, moreover, who've been unfairly treated. I shall write to the company to complain afterwards.'

'I wish you luck.' The officer bit his lip, then added, 'I'd better warn you. The old lady has asked to see the captain again. She was very agitated tonight. The steward thinks it's because no one would sit next to her at the evening meal.'

'Serves her right.' Hugh frowned. 'I wonder what she wants to see him about now? She surely can't blame anything else on Miss Deagan.'

The man shrugged, hiding a yawn behind his hand.

'When would be the best time to speak to the captain?'

'Not tonight. He's gone off to the feast. After we're under way to the Bitter Lakes might be best. He'll have less to do then. I'd let madam speak to him first, then go in straight afterwards, in case you have to deny anything.'

'Thanks for your advice. I'd better get some sleep, then.'

As he walked back Hugh couldn't help glancing across at where Maura had been sitting but she was no longer there. Nor could he see Ryan on deck. It was a little cooler now. People were seeking their beds. He'd better seek his. Tomorrow would be a busy day.

* * *

Maura slept badly. She didn't feel at all well, and it might be cooler now, but it still wasn't cool enough to suit her. At least the engines weren't

267

running tonight, so it was quiet.

Above her, the two girls were sleeping peacefully in their bunks. She'd got up twice to check them.

From across the cabin came that faint whiffling sound from one of the other passengers, a sound everyone had got used to because it happened every night, except when the storm drowned out all other noise.

If only her head didn't ache. She went to get another drink of water, and dampened a handkerchief to put on her forehead. It was eerie in the day cabin with no one there and only the dim light from one lamp.

Could Hugh Beaufort really get them off this ship? That would mean she owed him money. Or Bram would owe him.

It couldn't be helped. Things couldn't go on like this. The girls had looked so drained of energy today after staying with her in the stifling heat below decks that she'd felt very worried about them.

Back in her narrow bunk, she tossed and turned, dozing fitfully.

Would the night never end?

★ ★ ★

Hugh waited impatiently for breakfast to finish, then went across to the part of the deck nearest the captain's cabin to wait.

They had left Lake Timsah now and were moving slowly down the canal under steam power. Once again, the flotilla was a magnificent sight and he wished the day hadn't been marred by this spitefulness.

Mrs Halligan sailed past him, nose in the air, and was shown straight into the captain's cabin.

He walked slowly back to the part of the deck near the funnel, just to have a quick look at the rear deck. Maura was sitting in the shade. She looked even more exhausted today, as if she'd slept badly.

A group of children had gathered round her and she was telling them a story. They were quiet and well-behaved, clearly enjoying the tale.

No one was rushing round in this heat. Some of the parents were watching, smiling in approval, and quite a few had drawn closer, to listen surreptitiously.

The door of the captain's cabin opened and a junior officer came out, looking embarrassed. He walked along the deck to where Maura was sitting and bent his head to speak to her.

She gaped at him in shock, then stood up and addressed the nearby people. 'I don't know why, but I've been told to stop telling stories to the children.'

Hugh wanted to rush forward and give her his support, but held back. He intended to do nothing the captain could complain about. Anyway, he didn't have to, because others were taking up the cause.

There was a roar of disapproval and some of the men moved to surround Maura and the children, jostling the young officer out of the way.

'Who's picking on our children?'

'Get away from here and let the children enjoy themselves.'

The officer looked distressed. 'Sir, it's captain's orders.'

'It's that old hag's doing!' someone yelled loudly. 'She's telling lies about Miss Deagan again.'

A senior officer moved forward, beckoning to two sailors and they pushed through the crowd.

'I'm afraid the captain's word is law, so please take your children away from this woman or I'll have to send her below again.'

Maura sat down again, head bent. She flicked away a tear with one finger, then pulled out a handkerchief.

'Let's go and ask the captain why he's picking on our children!' a man yelled.

There was a roar of agreement and a large group turned to make their way towards the foredeck, looking angry.

The officer hurried to catch up to them. Hugh smiled as he heard the man begging them to go back to their own area and let him tell the captain.

'We'll tell him ourselves, thank you very much.'

'Miss Deagan has paid her fare like anyone else. Why is she being treated like a criminal?'

Hugh stepped back and watched in amusement as they banged on the captain's door. The officers were trying to push past them, but the men held them back and a group of women from steerage had come to join them now as well.

When the cabin door opened, it was the

270

captain himself. He looked amazed to see the large group of angry people.

One of them turned round and raised his hands. 'Shush now. Let me speak to the captain.' There was instant silence as he turned back.

'Whatever's the matter?' the captain asked.

'Why have you stopped Miss Deagan telling stories to our children? She's done nothing wrong, and it's keeping them quiet and well-behaved.'

Hugh saw the captain's mouth open and shut, as he sought for words. *Get out of that, if you can!* he thought, with savage satisfaction. There were too many men involved to put them in the lock-up and if they were shut up below decks there would be more people falling sick.

There was no sign of Mrs Halligan, but she must still be inside the cabin.

'There have been complaints about Miss Deagan's behaviour,' the captain said. 'And I — '

'What's she supposed to have done? Us and our wives have been living cheek by jowl with her, and we'd have seen it if she'd done anything wrong.'

'Bring out the old lady. Let *her* tell us what's wrong?'

'Yes, bring her out! She's making it all up.'

The captain prudently shut his cabin door behind him. 'I — um, didn't realise Miss Deagan was telling stories to the children. I was told she was making trouble.'

Another roar of anger greeted that.

'She'd be more likely to stop trouble than start it, that one,' the spokesman said.

'And we're not letting you lock her below decks again, either, not in this heat,' a woman called. 'She near died of it yesterday, yes, and the little lass too. Are you trying to *murder* them?'

The captain beckoned to his first officer, saying something in a low voice.

The officer shrugged as he answered. If his expression was anything to judge by, he too thought it an injustice.

As the captain wiped his brow, a shrill voice called from inside the cabin. 'She's related to two members of the board,' he said, forgetting to speak quietly.

'She's related to the devil himself,' replied the first mate.

People began talking angrily to one another, shouting at the captain and officer.

Hugh moved through the crowd and to his relief, when they saw who he was, they let him pass. 'I think I can help you with this, Captain. I've been waiting to see you.'

'Oh?'

Hugh glanced towards the crowd. 'In private, if you please.'

'I'll talk to you in your cabin. Mrs Halligan had better stay in mine.' He wiped his brow again and someone called out.

'It *is* hot, isn't it? Going to make them Deagan kids ill, are you, while you stay up here in the fresh air?'

'Certainly not. I hadn't realised.' The captain flung up his arms in a gesture of helpless acceptance. 'Let the woman continue the storytelling. But I don't want her getting into conversation with anyone, not till I've investigated this more thoroughly.'

There was more growling and muttering.

Hugh turned to the ringleader and said quietly, 'It might be wise to go back to the rear deck now. Leave me to see if I can help. I'm on Miss Deagan's side, I promise you.'

'We're not letting them torment her any more.'

'No. I'm not, either. You have my word on that.'

The man turned away.

A voice called out loudly, 'Bloody old hag.'

There was a general laugh and they went back to cluster round Maura, who was sitting clutching her handkerchief, looking upset.

'Do you want to finish the story now, miss?' one asked gently. 'The captain says you can.'

She looked as if she was about to say no, then one child called out, 'Ooh, yes. I want to find out if the princess escapes.'

Maura nodded. 'Give me a minute or two, then I'll start again.'

'I don't like that captain, Da,' one child said.

'It's not polite for children to pass remarks on grown-ups.'

'Well, I don't,' the child muttered.

$$\star \quad \star \quad \star$$

Hugh went to his cabin, expecting to be kept waiting for a while. However, the captain joined him a few minutes later.

'I'm sorry about all this, Beaufort.'

273

'So am I. You're persecuting an innocent woman.'

'It's a case of damned if I do, damned if I don't. Mind if I sit down?'

He subsided on to a chair, fanning himself with a paper. 'That Halligan woman is out for blood, I'm afraid. She's now refusing to travel any further with a 'lewd and immoral woman on board' — her words not mine. She wants me to toss Miss Deagan *and* the children off the ship.'

'She's mad.'

'I'm beginning to think so, and I'd never put people off the ship, but I am caught in a cleft stick.' There was a knock on the door. 'I hope you don't mind, but I asked my steward to bring us some cognac.'

'If there was ever a day for having an early drink, this is one,' Hugh agreed. 'Did you find out why she's calling Miss Deagan lewd?'

'Sounds to me as if Miss Deagan was giving her nephew a lesson in the facts of life, instructing him in how to limit his family.' The captain gave a wry smile. 'She was doing it in private, from what the old woman said, so *she* could only have heard it by eavesdropping on them.'

'I don't consider that lewd, but sensible. Having huge families keeps people in poverty. They can't feed and clothe them properly.'

'I agree.' He took a slow sip of cognac, rolling it round his mouth. 'You — er — said you might be able to offer a solution?'

'I think I can get Miss Deagan and the

274

children off the ship without putting them at risk. I've booked places for us all on *Vitesse*, which is going right through to Suez, unlike the *Delta*.'

'That'll leave the matter unresolved.'

'If we're no longer on the ship, why is there a need to resolve it?'

'She'll insist.'

'Well, that's up to you. I'll do my part. You insist on letting the matter drop.'

As the captain still hesitated, Hugh added, 'I have to say that we're leaving anyway, unless you intend to lock us all up in our cabins. I'm not having Maura persecuted or made ill.'

The captain gave him a suspicious look. 'Got an interest there, have you? That won't look good.'

Oh hell, Hugh thought, if I don't watch out here, I'll make matters worse.

★ ★ ★

Maura took a few moments to calm herself, helped by Mrs Stoddard, who brought her a glass of water, a gesture of unspoken support, accompanied by a quick half-smile.

She thought she'd have difficulty going on with the storytelling, but with the group of little children looking up at her expectantly, she soon slipped back into the tale.

When she'd finished, they clamoured for more. 'Another time, my dears. I'm feeling a bit tired today.'

To her relief, the parents intervened, coming

to collect them. One or two told her what a shame it was, and how badly they thought she was being treated.

She moved her seat into a patch of deeper shade, thankful for the canvas awnings the sailors had erected above them. 'We should watch the procession of ships now,' she told Brenna. 'This is an important occasion.'

'They're just a lot of old ships. I'm tired of being on one. I wish Australia wasn't so far away.'

'I do too, love. But watch the procession of ships anyway. One day people will talk about the opening of the Suez Canal and you'll be proud to say you were there.'

They sat quietly. Maura kept waiting for someone else to come and harangue her or send her below again, but no one did. When refreshments were brought out for the passengers, two women brought some across for her and the girls.

'*You* may not be supposed to speak to us, but they're not stopping *me* speaking to you, or to anyone else I want,' one of them said. 'That old woman wants locking up. She's mad as a hatter. Thinks she's Queen Victoria, we reckon. Only she isn't.'

'We're British, we are,' the other added. 'Land of the free, we come from, and we're not putting up with bullying from anyone.'

Maura smiled, but didn't say anything. She wasn't risking being sent below again for speaking to them.

The woman patted her arm. 'We're keeping an

eye on things. Nearly all of us are on your side. Don't you worry. We won't let them hurt you and those little bairns.'

Her words left a warm feeling in Maura's heart. First Hugh, then her fellow passengers. She was a lucky woman to have fallen among such lovely people. Lucky to have the children, too.

Would Hugh really manage to get them off the ship? She did hope so. The *Delta* was turning around — not even stopping in Suez — so if they stayed on board, they'd be stuck with the ghastly Mrs Halligan and probably imprisoned for yet another day's travel back to Port Said. And even then, they'd have to catch a train across the isthmus with her. All this to take them back to where they already were!

No, if Maura could avoid continuing her journey with that woman, she would do so. And hope they could find another ship to take them to Australia from Suez! But what about their trunks, which were in the hold? What about the cost of it all?

The sun continued to beat down, and although she was sitting in the shade, she still felt so uncomfortable and hot, she didn't know what to do with herself.

She hadn't recovered from being kept below, which was strange because she was usually so healthy. She just had to give herself time. Take things easy.

But she kept finding herself doing what she'd promised herself not to — looking towards the foredeck, waiting for Hugh to appear.

And that made her angry with herself for caring about someone so far out of her reach.

* * *

Hugh took a deep breath, looked the captain in the eyes and said, 'I've definitely got an interest in Miss Deagan. In fact, we are engaged to be married.'

The captain looked startled. '*Engaged?* But she's — '

'A woman I admire greatly.' He leaned forward to emphasise his point. 'And believe me, Captain, I'll take it very much amiss if you or anyone else blacken her name. Mrs Halligan was lying.'

'Whether she was or not, you'll not stop her. I've never seen such hatred.'

'I won't be here to stop her, but I hope you will try. I shall certainly be contacting your company later and asking for a refund of my fare. It won't look good if you continue to countenance such unreasonable behaviour. It's driving us off the ship already. What if Mrs Halligan turns her spite on others? What if that gets known about? The company won't want to lose more custom.'

The captain said nothing, but his lips tightened into a narrow, bloodless line.

'It would improve matters if you could help us transfer to the *Vitesse*. I should be much obliged for your help there and would mention it when I write to the company. We have trunks in the hold which we'll want to take with us. The piano will

278

have to continue on its way to Australia with you, but I'm sure you'll make sure it gets safely to its destination.'

'Very well. If you give me the details. I'll send people to find your trunks.'

'And I'll need to speak to Miss Deagan. I had to send her a message via the children. Who knows how they twisted it? She must be dreadfully worried about the lies being told about her.'

'I'll send word to the *Vitesse* after we anchor tonight.'

'Captain Pierremont is expecting us. And about my meeting with Miss Deagan . . . ?'

'It had better take place in my cabin with the door open. I shall be on the bridge.'

'What about Mrs Halligan?'

'I shall have a word with her. If you don't object, I'll let her think I've arranged for you to leave the ship in answer to her complaint.'

Hugh immediately promised himself to spread the word among the other passengers that the old lady's spite had driven them off the *Delta*. He had no intention of giving her the opportunity to further blacken their names.

But what would Maura say when she found out about his deception? Would she agree to pretend they were engaged? After all, *she* knew he was still married.

Perhaps they might one day make the engagement more than a pretence? Would she be willing to wait until he had won his freedom? Would she consider linking her life to his?

A man could dream.

14

When the flotilla arrived at Bitter Lakes later that day, the royal guests were rowed to and fro in the dark to visit one another. The lanterns on their small boats sent trails of light flickering across the calm water.

It seemed very quiet here after the huge celebrations at Lake Timsah, and people who'd been expecting another spectacle grumbled.

'Pity we're not going on to Suez tomorrow,' the first mate told a group from steerage. 'They're planning to put on a big show there.'

So, for lack of anything else, the passengers on the *Delta* turned their attention to what was happening on their own ship, watching with interest as sailors puffed up from the hold, bringing trunks and piling them on the deck.

Hugh and Carrie watched them even more carefully, counting the pieces until all except the piano had been brought up.

Maura and the children came up from steerage to check their luggage, but they had only four battered trunks, so that was soon sorted out.

'We'll take you across to the other ship first thing in the morning, Miss Deagan,' the officer in charge of the transfer said. 'Much safer for both you and your luggage to do it by daylight. I should try to get a good night's sleep now, if I were you.'

Hugh came across to join them. 'Miss Deagan, may I have a word with you in private?'

'The captain says — ' the officer began.

'The captain says I can speak to Miss Deagan, but it's too hot in his cabin.' Hugh spoke with cheerful confidence. 'We'll only be over there by the rail. Maura, Carrie will keep an eye on the children.' He held out his arm.

She took it and they moved to one side.

'Are you feeling all right about this move to another ship? You know you can trust me absolutely to look after you all.' He watched her smile, her teeth showing white in the dim light from a nearby oil lamp. Such a lovely smile she had, not lightly given but worth waiting for.

'I'll be glad to leave this ship, and of course I trust you, Mr Beaufort.'

'Hugh.'

She looked at him, then said, 'Hugh, then.'

'We'll go to Suez in the *Vitesse*, then stay in a hotel till we see our way clear. Other passengers are apparently joining the *Vitesse* in Suez, so we have to find another ship to travel on, *not*, I hope, a P&O vessel.' Even in the light of the deck lamps, he could see her flush and her voice sounded strained.

'I'll have to rely on you to pay for things, I'm afraid, Mr — um, Hugh. But if you keep careful note of how much you spend, I'm sure my nephew Bram will pay you back once we arrive in Fremantle.'

'I shan't need paying back. It's partly because of me that you're in this pickle. I wonder . . . could we send the piano, via P&O cargo, to

281

your nephew's? Would he look after it for us?'

'I'm sure he would if you label it carefully and I send a letter with it.'

'I'll do that.' He hesitated, then leaned closer to speak in a very low voice, knowing how sounds carried on the water. 'There's something you need to know. The captain was very suspicious about why I was helping you. I had to say . . . that we were engaged to be married.'

'*What*? But — '

'Shh.'

' — you're married already. Why did you say that?'

'If I hadn't given a good reason for helping you, I doubt he'd have allowed us to leave the ship at all.'

'Oh.'

'But I also . . . wish it were true.'

She looked at him in shock.

'I mean that.'

'But you're a gentleman and I'm only a maid.'

'You're not *only* anything, Maura. And just so that we set matters straight, I intend to seek a divorce from my wife as soon as I can.'

'The priest would say you'd still be married, even if you got one,' she said with a sigh.

'What would you say?'

'I'd say . . . you weren't married any longer if you had a divorce. I've been unhappily married and I know what it's like. I think divorce can be a good thing. Why should people be tied together for life in a union that brings only misery?'

'I agree.'

'Isn't it expensive getting a divorce, though?

Are you rich enough?'

'Things changed in 1857 when they passed a new law. They set up a special new court and allowed ordinary people to get divorces through it, without needing an act of parliament. Though it's still harder for women to get a divorce than for men.'

'Isn't everything harder for women?' she murmured with a sigh.

'I've written a letter to my lawyer in England, asking him to set matters in train for obtaining a divorce. I'll post it in Suez.' He clasped her hands and kept tight hold when she tried to pull away, not caring that the officer was still watching them. 'Am I wrong in thinking you have feelings for me?'

She raised her eyes, meeting his very directly. 'No. You're not wrong. But I've never expected anything to come of it.' But if it did . . . ah, if it did, she'd be the happiest woman on earth.

'I never thought I'd want to marry again. Sylvie was . . . not easy. Very temperamental. But now that I've met you, I've changed my mind. You will marry me, won't you?'

She suddenly gave him a luminous smile and gave in to temptation. 'Yes, Hugh. If you manage to free yourself, I'd love to marry you.'

'I want to kiss you, but I daren't give that old harridan anything else to complain about.'

They stood clasping hands, smiling foolishly at one another. After a while, she pulled away. This time he let her go.

'I'd better get the children to bed, though I doubt they'll get much sleeping done.'

'Adèle was bouncing on her bed while we were packing her things and Carrie was nearly as excited. That maid is a real treasure. Adèle has hardly stopped talking about changing ships all day. I never thought to see her so energetic and *normal*. The voyage is doing her so much good.'

'She's a dear child, a pleasure to be with. My three are very fond of her.'

'Good. That'll make things easier after we're married.' He escorted Maura to the hatch that led down to the steerage quarters. The children were waiting for her there.

As he turned to go back to his cabin, he couldn't stop smiling. Then he remembered Carrie and went to knock on the door of the cabin she shared with his daughter. 'I'm just checking that you're all right. Are all your things ready for the morning?'

'Yes, sir. Don't forget your guitar tomorrow. I do like to hear you play it.'

'They'll wake us very early.'

'I'm still awake, Daddy. I can't get to sleep.'

He made a growling noise like a bear and said 'Go to sleep, little girl!' in a deep voice. It was a game they had played since she was tiny.

He heard her chuckle and smiled.

Once back in his own cabin, he undressed and went to bed, but he doubted he'd get much sleep. He kept smiling, because Maura hadn't pretended about her feelings. She loved him and had been quite open about it. You couldn't mistake the look in her eyes, the tone of voice, the happiness in her smile. Such a difference from — He cut off that thought. He must forget

Sylvie now. He was going to marry Maura, whatever it took, however long they had to wait. That was all that mattered.

For the first time, he felt completely happy to have come on this long, wearisome journey. Everything was turning out for the best, the very best.

★ ★ ★

On the final evening of the voyage to Suez, Prescott ate even more lightly than usual.

'I shall be glad to get on dry land again,' he said with a sigh. 'Please excuse me, Captain McBride.'

Dougal saw him to the door, closed it behind him and came back to join Eleanor at the table.

'I apologise for my husband. I did remind him to thank you for your care of us on this voyage.'

Dougal shrugged. 'He's not been much trouble. I've hardly seen anything of him.'

'He's always like this on the ocean. He doesn't enjoy sailing, so sleeps away most of the voyage.'

'And yet, you enjoy it.'

She lifted her head. 'Yes. I love being on the water. He and I are . . . very different.'

He dared to ask, 'Are you happy with him?'

She gave a tiny shake of the head and began to fiddle with her dessert spoon.

'You must realise how attracted I am to you, Eleanor.'

She went very still, then gave him one long, anguished look before bowing her head again. 'I would never break my marriage vows, Dougal.'

'No. I realise that. But I want to say one thing, and to assure you that I mean it with all my heart.'

'Please don't!'

'It's not what you think. It's just . . . Eleanor, if you are ever free, or even just in need of a friend, it will always be my privilege to help you.'

'I'm not likely to be free. Malcolm seems ill now, but he'll recover after a few days on land. He always does.'

'Nonetheless, I've written it all down.' Dougal pulled a paper out of his pocket and put it on the table in front of her. 'This tells you how to find me, or to find good friends who live nearby in Fremantle if I'm away on a voyage. It also tells you how to access funds in England. I'll send enough money there to pay your fare, if you need it.'

She looked at him in shock. 'Why would you think that? Malcolm's brother has enough to look after me for the rest of my life.'

'I don't know why I think it, I just do. The money will be there, in the care of Adam's old lawyer, who has moved from Liverpool to London. I meant what I said. If you're ever in need, come to me. Or if you're free.'

She tried to speak lightly. 'Oh, you'll no doubt get married in a year or two and have a family of your own. You should definitely do that, Dougal. Don't waste your life waiting for the impossible.'

His voice became suddenly harsh. 'You're the only woman I've ever wanted to marry in my whole life, so it's not likely now that I'll meet anyone else. My sister will be the one to give the

286

family heirs with her new husband. She seems very happy with Joss, thank heaven. Her husband captains another ship. She doesn't stay at home, but goes to sea with him, as a few captains' wives do.'

'How lucky she is.' Eleanor closed her eyes for a moment, then opened them. As she stared at him, all the longing showed in her face. 'I wish things were different.'

'May I ask for one kiss to seal our bargain, and to remember you by?' he asked. 'Just . . . one kiss.'

She nodded.

He walked slowly round the table and drew her to her feet. Oh, the softness of her, the beauty of her skin, the glory of her dark hair! Slowly, giving her time to draw away, he pulled her closer, holding her against him, breathing in the light perfume she always wore. It was a while before he bent his head and kissed her, and in those wonderful minutes of closeness she didn't attempt to move away but nestled close to him as if born to fit into his arms.

As his lips met hers, she put her arms round him and returned the kiss with passion and yet tenderness too.

'Eleanor — '

She pulled out of his arms with an inarticulate cry, snatched the piece of paper from the table and rushed out of the cabin on to the shadowed darkness of the deck.

He stood and watched her, but didn't follow.

She stayed by the rail for some time, then heaved a great sigh, followed by another. He could see how her body moved, though not hear the sighs.

After that, she walked quietly along to her cabin, not looking in his direction.

He thought he saw a tear glistening on her cheek. His own eyes were full. Life could be so cruel — show you happiness, then snatch it away.

In the morning, Eleanor was as composed as ever.

She stopped to hold out her hand to him at the foot of the gangway. 'Thank you for an excellent voyage, Captain McBride. You've taken good care of us.'

'Remember,' was all he allowed himself to say.

She gave a quick little nod.

'Eleanor, do hurry up. It's dreadfully hot in this sun,' Prescott called in his whining, spoiled child's voice. He hadn't bothered to say thank you to Dougal, only nodded goodbye.

'Coming.' She walked across to take her husband's arm and didn't look back.

Dougal stood there watching till they were out of sight. They were following the guide he had found for them and he knew they'd get to a hotel safely. He hoped they would find a quick passage to England and that Malcolm's brother wouldn't have died in the meantime.

He also hoped she'd find some measure of happiness.

He realised they'd been out of sight a while ago, and he was watching nothing but a blur of busy people.

Going back on to the ship, he did something

very unusual for him: he poured himself a stiff shot of brandy and downed it in one.

It seemed necessary to mark the occasion. After all, it might be the last time he ever saw her. Probably would be.

No! Something deep inside him clung to the hope that he would see her again. Surely fate couldn't have brought them together for no reason?

★ ★ ★

Maura and the children were woken at half past five in the morning, when it was still dark. For once, the two girls came wide awake immediately. They wanted to fling on their clothes, but Maura made them have a good wash in the day room, which was empty at that hour. She'd made Ryan promise to do the same.

Mrs Stoddard joined them. 'They've got tea and some food waiting for you up on deck. It'll be easier if you eat with Mr Beaufort and his party.'

Maura didn't feel like eating, but the children did justice to new bread hot from the oven, with strawberry conserve and butter, plus glasses of fresh milk from one of the poor milking cows kept penned up on board the ship.

There was a sort of greyish light by this time, so faint that the sailors moving about on deck looked unreal. She smiled shyly at Hugh, then watched the men getting the trunks down to the first of three boats that were to transfer the passengers to the *Vitesse*.

There was no sign of the captain, only a tired officer yawning as he supervised the men. He counted the trunks and bags, ticking them off on a list.

Footsteps sounded behind them and Maura swung round to find a few of her defenders from steerage standing hesitantly nearby.

'We've come to say goodbye,' the fellow who had acted as spokesman announced. 'And to wish you well.'

'The children are going to miss your stories,' another man told her.

A woman came across to give Maura a quick peck on the cheek. 'My Lettie hasn't stopped talking about that princess in your story, says she's going to learn to read so that she can find more stories.'

'I'm sure she'll do well.'

The woman nodded, then turned to the group of four children. 'You look after your auntie.'

'*She* is supposed to look after us,' Brenna pointed out.

'Well, you can all look after each other, can't you.'

'She isn't *my* aunt,' Adèle said. 'But I wish she was. She looks after me sometimes as well.'

'Not yet she isn't,' the woman muttered under her breath, winking at Maura.

She could feel herself blushing and didn't dare glance in Hugh's direction.

And then it was time for them to clamber down into the last boat.

As she stepped off the ship into it, the rocking movement made Maura's head spin. For a moment she thought she was going to fall, then a sailor grabbed her arm.

'Careful how you go, miss. Come and sit over here. There you are.'

The children had no such difficulties, clambering aboard and sitting perched on the wooden plank seats like a row of little birds. Hugh sat silently beside her.

She didn't look back, didn't want to, was still angry at how badly she'd been treated. And anyway, the sun was rising now, gilding the masts and even the sooty funnels, making the group of ships look quite splendid. She wanted to look round, take it all in, remember it.

It seemed to promise so much, that clear pale sun lifting slowly above the horizon.

* * *

Sailors were ready to help them board the *Vitesse*, sailors who spoke French not English.

Maura had to turn to Hugh for help in understanding what they wanted.

This time there was no gangway let down. They had to climb up big rope nets slung over the side of this smaller ship, and her heart was in her mouth the whole time, not only for herself, because she definitely didn't like heights, but for the children, in case they fell.

'They'll be fine,' Hugh said quietly. 'Look, they're climbing up like little monkeys, not waiting for us older folk. And Carrie's the same.'

A few seconds later Maura heard Brenna's distinctive gurgle of laughter from the deck. 'I

291

wish I was as nimble as them.' Even if she had been, her long skirt and petticoats hampered her, and she was so nervous her knees felt stiff. Thank goodness it wasn't windy, because she hadn't thought to tie a scarf round her skirt at the knees.

'I'll stay beside you, my love. It's not far.'

She was glad of his presence, shuddering with relief when she got on board the ship through a sort of gate in the rail.

The luggage was still being winched on board, and she couldn't help worrying they'd let it fall into the water, and then how would she manage?

'Maura, this is Captain Villiers. And this is my friend Gérard Colbert.'

She shook their hands and waited for Hugh to tell her what to do next.

The captain stayed only briefly, leaving them to Mr Colbert's care.

'I'll show you the cabins.' He spoke English, to Maura's relief, though with a marked French accent.

She looked over her shoulder. 'Children, we're going to see our cabins now. Stay close behind.'

There were only two cabins.

'I was not sure 'ow you would wish to sleep,' Mr Colbert said with a wicked little smile.

Maura flushed, guessing what he meant. 'I'll sleep with the children, of course.'

'We can sling hammocks for them. It's only for one night, after all.'

Behind her, they jumped up and down with pleasure at that thought.

Maura studied first one cabin, then the other.

There wasn't nearly enough room for themselves and their luggage, so the trunks had been left outside, lashed to stanchions.

'I think Ryan, Adèle and I should take the smaller cabin,' Hugh said after a moment's thought. He grinned at the lad. 'Don't worry. They can sling a hammock for you.'

Ryan beamed at him.

'Do you mind sharing with Carrie and your nieces, Maura?'

'No, of course not.'

'I want to go with the girls,' Adèle protested.

'We can fit three hammocks in here . . . if the little girl doesn't mind a hammock,' Mr Colbert said. 'And if you two ladies don't mind sharing the bed.'

Maura eyed the narrow bed, hoping her dismay hadn't shown.

'We can sleep top to tail, miss. It's only for one night,' Carrie said cheerfully. 'I'm not a kicker.'

'Yes, of course.'

'I'll show you the amenities,' Mr Colbert said. 'When you've sorted yourselves out, please come to the dining cabin and 'ave something to eat.'

'We've already eaten breakfast,' Maura said.

'Aw, that was hours ago. I'm hungry again.' Ryan looked at her pleadingly.

'He has a good appetite,' she said apologetically.

'Growing boys do. After you've eaten, you can watch the procession set off. Miss Deagan, you'll be welcome on the foredeck with Hugh. I'm sure your maid will be happy to keep an eye on the children.'

'*I* always keep an eye on my sister,' Ryan said at once. 'Noreen's only little and I don't want her falling overboard.'

'You're a good, kind brother, then,' Gérard told him, winning a smile. '*Un bon frère*. We'll teach you some French words, *hein?*'

Ryan nodded, repeating '*un bon frère*' and letting Monsieur Colbert correct his pronunciation.

'Isn't it exciting?' Adèle was jigging up and down. 'I want to learn some more French words, too, please. I've forgotten most of the ones *Maman* taught me when I was little.'

'Never mind that now,' her father said. 'While you're watching the procession, you're to stay close to Carrie and Brenna.'

But then he saw that she was already holding Brenna's hand, which brought a lump to his throat.

★ ★ ★

After their late breakfast, they went out to join the other passengers, who were promenading round the deck. Not nearly as many as on the *Delta*.

Most stopped to introduce themselves. Hugh translated what they said to Maura and she tried to memorise a few words. *Bonjour* meant Good day, it seemed. That was easy. And *Merci beaucoup* meant thank you very much, but the R was pronounced differently, at the back of the tongue.

'They're not standing on their dignity as much

294

as the passengers on the *Delta*,' she confided to Hugh.

'They're a smaller group. If they quarrel with one another, they'll have no one to talk to.'

Even with the flotilla to watch, and conversations with one or two of the ladies who could manage a few words of English, the day seemed to pass slowly. The weather was just as hot as the day before, which made her feel tired out.

'Does it never rain here?' Maura fanned herself with a piece of folded paper.

'It doesn't look as if it does. You seem uncomfortable.'

'I'm still not myself. I confess I don't cope well with such heat.'

Hugh's expression darkened. 'That Halligan woman has a lot to answer for. You were all right till they shut you up below decks.'

'Forget her. I'll be all right once we get to sea again and feel a cooler breeze on my face. The ships are travelling so much more slowly along the canal.'

In the afternoon, the officers came round to tell everyone they were nearly there. The leading ship raised some extra colourful flags and all the other ships followed suit as they rounded the last bend in the canal.

Cannon began to fire, which made people jump in shock, even though they'd seen the sailors making preparations, then cheer loudly.

From the shore and from other ships came the sounds of bands playing cheerfully, if not always accurately.

Hugh winced as they passed one or two of

them, looking so pained, Maura laughed at him.

'It's like street bands. You have to accept the joyfulness of the sound and forget the discords and wrong notes. The players are doing their best.'

Once they'd dropped anchor, the officers hurried round asking the passengers to gather as the captain wished to speak to them. He made a short speech in French, which Hugh translated for Maura, about how this canal was due to French engineering brilliance, and they should be very proud of their nation's engineers.

'The Suez Canal is now open,' he said in conclusion. 'And you were here for the occasion.'

The 19th of November, 1869. I shall indeed always remember this day, Maura thought. Who'd have thought I'd witness such an event. She turned as Hugh spoke to her.

'I've been asking Gérard's advice and I'm sorry to tell you the best hotels in Suez are run by the P&O. I don't really wish to deal with that company again. Fortunately, the *Delta* turned back towards Port Said, so we won't see anyone we know from the ship here.'

'Thank goodness.'

'I'll get you and the children settled in and the luggage offloaded, then I'll see if I can book passage on another ship.'

'The sooner we leave Suez, the better.' Maura was still worried about her reputation being tarnished.

She didn't intend to tell people they were engaged, because it wouldn't be right with Hugh still married to someone else. Later, she would need to look for a job, or perhaps she might work for Bram until Hugh was free.

But oh, she'd miss Hugh. And she couldn't help wishing their engagement could quickly lead to a marriage.

It might do one day. If she was very lucky. Mightn't it?

A man like Hugh would be worth waiting for.

15

Dougal hadn't realised his arrival in Suez would coincide with the actual day of the opening of the canal. No one in the town seemed even remotely interested in doing business, only in celebrating.

Since he'd been here before, he was able to avoid passing the hotel he'd recommended to Eleanor and her husband. He'd said his goodbyes. Why rub salt in the wound?

As he strolled round the town, his spirits felt heavy with loss. He knew his crew would probably have guessed what was wrong with him, but they'd not comment, he was sure. Most of them had been with him for a while and were very loyal, as he hoped he was to them.

If Adam had still been his mate, he could have talked to him.

But his new mate Pete, although a good man and an experienced sailor, was not a close friend as Adam had quickly become.

Dougal went to watch the arrival of the ships, and even in his present sad mood, couldn't help admiring the magnificence of the flotilla and joining in the excited calls as it came slowly into sight, one ship following another.

Flags fluttered in the breeze, both on land and on the ships, cannon roared a series of salutes. But Dougal was not so lost in the spectacle that he didn't notice when a lad tried to pick his pocket. He caught the young fellow's arm just as the would-be thief was discovering the short silver chain that clipped the wallet to his victim's belt.

Terror showed on the young face and the lad cringed back, his free arm flung up to protect his head from possible blows.

'Anyone speak English?' Dougal shouted, keeping hold of the struggling lad.

'Can I help you, sir?' A man who looked like a clerk stepped forward. He was dark-skinned but spoke perfect English.

'Yes, please. I've just caught this lad picking my pocket. Could you please ask him where his family lives?'

'I doubt he has one, sir.'

'Ask him anyway.'

The man did so.

The lad cringed back if anyone so much as looked at him and it took him a few moments before he could be brought to answer the question.

He couldn't be more than twelve, Dougal decided, as a tear tracked down the dirt in the youngster's face.

The man turned back to him. 'The boy has no one left now. All have died. Shall I call for the watch to take him away, sir?'

Poor little devil! thought Dougal. That makes two of us in distress today. 'No, ask him if he wants a job on my ship. I'm looking for a cabin boy. But tell him, and say it very strongly, that if he ever steals anything again, I'll throw him overboard myself.'

There was a quick exchange of conversation and both the man and the lad looked at Dougal in such a suspicious way that he suddenly guessed what they were thinking.

'Tell him also that I love women, not little boys or men. He has nothing like that to fear from me or any of my crew. This is just a day when I feel I must do a good deed.'

The man nodded and spoke again.

The lad's expression lightened a little and he studied the captain again.

'So, does he want the job?'

The man translated and the lad nodded, kneeling to clutch Dougal's jacket and pour out words.

'He says he will work hard for you all the days of his life.'

'Ask him his name.'

'Ahmed.'

Dougal let go of the boy's arm. 'Tell him to follow me.' That would ensure Ahmed was a willing worker, because it'd be easy enough for him to run away now.

As he walked back towards the *Bonny Mary*, Dougal glanced behind occasionally, pleased to see that the lad was still following.

At the foot of the gangway, he stopped and gestured to the ship and then to himself. 'This is my ship.'

The lad hesitated, then muttered what was obviously a prayer and followed him up the gangway.

He handed the boy over to Peggy. 'This is our new cabin boy. Ahmed. He's lost all his family and was begging on the streets, so treat him kindly and teach him English.'

'He doesn't look very strong.'

'I doubt he's been eating well.'

'I'll see to him, sir, then pass him to my husband. Let's hope he's a hard worker.'

Dougal went to his cabin and stayed on the ship that evening, leaving the noise and merrymaking to those on the shore who had lighter hearts than his. He checked a couple of times that Ahmed had been fed well and wasn't being teased too much by the crew.

'He's a quick learner, I'll give him that,' the mate said. 'Not like you to pick 'em up off the streets, though, Captain.'

'I must have been in a generous mood. And we've been wanting a cabin boy for a while.'

'Well, Lascars usually make good sailors. I've sailed with a few in my time. I couldn't do what they do, leave home and family to wander round the world.'

'Lascar isn't really the name for where they come from. They're from a lot of different countries in the east.'

'Lascar will do for me — and for our new cabin boy.'

★ ★ ★

The following morning, Hugh set off after breakfast to try to find a ship sailing to Australia, or at least to Galle, in Ceylon.

To his dismay, there were no places on steamships going in that direction, and wouldn't be for a week or two. The ships in the harbour had all converged on Suez from the east, it seemed, wanting to be among the first to pass through the canal and try it out. The ones that had come through the canal from Europe to Suez were chock full of passengers who'd wanted to participate in the event.

'What am I to do?' he asked the shipping agent. 'My family and I need to get to the Swan River Colony.'

A man who was waiting to speak to the agent looked at him very searchingly, then moved forward. 'I'm a ship's captain and I can give you passage to Western Australia. Fremantle is my home port, actually. But I don't have a steamship, just a schooner, so it'll take longer.'

Hugh stuck out his hand and introduced himself. 'I'd be interested, but I'd like to see the ship first, of course.'

'Naturally. Just let me discuss possible cargoes, then I'll be with you.'

After a brief and clearly unsatisfactory conversation with the agent, Captain McBride turned round and led the way out of the office. 'Looks as if I'm going to have to buy my own cargo. There are no other loads needing shipping unless I wait a week or two. I brought some passengers here so want to make the return journey as profitable as possible.'

'When will you be sailing?'

'As soon as I can acquire and load a cargo. A couple of days at most. Look, how about I take you to see the ship and the cabins now, then if you're interested, we can discuss details.'

302

'I don't wish to travel steerage.'

Captain McBride chuckled. 'There are three cabins and that's all. One's large, one's small and the other is tiny. The *Bonny Mary* is a cargo ship mainly. How many are there in your party? If there are too many, we might not have enough room for you.'

Hugh explained.

'We can fit everyone in if you and the boy can share a cabin. The girls can take the biggest cabin with the maid, and your fiancée can take the smallest cabin. We used to have only two cabins, but we made space for another because it's sometimes profitable to take people to places where the big ships don't go.'

The two men walked along to the harbour and boarded the ship, which was a clean, tidy vessel, Hugh noted. It looked particularly well maintained and the crew didn't have sulky faces.

The cabins were small, except for the largest, which the girls would have to share with Carrie. He knew Maura well enough to be sure she wouldn't stand on her dignity about occupying the tiny cabin.

'How long will it take to get to Fremantle, Captain?'

He shrugged. 'About six weeks, given favourable weather.'

Hugh sighed. 'It takes such a long time to get from England to Australia. I feel as if we've been travelling for ever.' Then he remembered Adèle and how much good the sea air had done her. Perhaps an extended sea voyage would be just the thing. That thought cheered him instantly.

'May I bring the rest of them to see the ship? My — um, fiancée, is the aunt of three of the children. We met on board the ship coming from England.'

'If you've found a woman to love, count yourself fortunate.'

The captain sounded bitter, as if he hadn't been lucky in love. Hugh waited a moment or two before forcing himself to smile and say, 'I do count myself lucky, believe me.'

'Why didn't you stay with your previous ship?'

'It was going back to Port Said because the bigwigs had to return to Europe. The rest of the passengers were to be left at Alexandria to come to Suez by the overland route. The P&O people seem to think the Suez Canal won't last and will silt up or something.'

'I very much doubt that. I've heard the French have made a good job of building it.'

'The flotilla went through without any problems. It was quite a sight.'

He explained about Adèle. 'She's been near to death with pneumonia twice now in England's cold and damp climate, and the doctor thought a sea voyage was her last chance.'

'I'm glad to hear it's doing her good.'

'Yes. It makes everything worthwhile. So . . . when should we come on board? Or will we be in the way if we come now?'

'You can come on board as soon as you like. In fact, I wonder if your Miss Deagan would have time to help me to choose some trade goods that might appeal to women?'

Hugh had a sudden idea. 'I'd not mind buying

a few goods myself, if there's some way to sell them in Fremantle.'

'You're a trader?'

'Only a dabbler, but I've had some success. I have independent means, though I'm not rich. But it's always good to make more money and I find the exercise of choosing and selling goods very interesting.'

Dougal frowned. 'You say your fiancée is called Deagan. Would she be related to Bram Deagan, by any chance?'

'Yes. He's her nephew, though there are only a couple of years between them. I'm not sure whether he knows they're all coming. I gather a letter has probably been sent to him by someone called Largan, the local landowner in Ireland.'

'Conn Largan's brother. Yes. Actually, Bram's a good friend of mine and he often speaks of bringing his family to Australia, so I know he'll be delighted to see them all.'

'You think so, Captain?'

'I'm sure of it.'

'I'm delighted to hear that. Small world, isn't it?'

'Sometimes it seems very large.'

The captain was silent for a moment, the sad expression back on his face, then continued, 'Bram owns a very successful bazaar and can either sell the goods for you on commission, or hire a stall to you. Very enterprising fellow, our Bram.' Captain McBride stuck out his hand. 'So it's a bargain?'

'It is.'

Hugh hoped his intense relief hadn't shown in his face.

★ ★ ★

The hotel was quiet and inside the room, the children were sitting sulking. They'd been scolded (with excruciating politeness) by the manager for making too much noise in the guests' sitting room, so Maura had brought them up to the bedroom.

She went to stare out of the window. Like them, she was dying to go out and explore the town. But Hugh had made a point of asking her to stay in the hotel and keep the children with her till he could escort them for a walk.

He hadn't taken account of four lively children being penned up in a hot building for several hours. She'd told them several stories. Carrie had played games with them and was now cuddling Noreen, who was sleepy because of the heat.

Brenna and Ryan suddenly began to quarrel, shoving one another, which upset Adèle, who wasn't used to how quickly a quarrel could pass.

'It doesn't matter who got up first this morning, Brenna,' Maura said wearily. 'And stop kicking the chair leg, Ryan.'

He looked down as if surprised at what his foot was doing. 'Couldn't I just go out to the front of the hotel and wait there?'

'No. Mr Beaufort wants us to stay inside.' Anyway, she was sure Ryan would wander off without meaning to.

She tried to tell herself it was good that they'd recovered from their underfed lives and were bursting with energy. And it was. But still, their bickering was making her head ache. Even Adèle, usually very biddable, was complaining about being bored.

Just as Maura was getting to screaming point, there was a knock on the door. Ryan flew to answer it, bumping into Brenna. They pulled one another away, arguing about who should open it.

Carrie rolled her eyes at Maura and slipped past them. 'Mr Beaufort. Oh, we're so glad to see you, sir. The children are a-twitching to do something.'

He gave the four of them one severe look and they fell silent.

Why couldn't she do that? Maura wondered.

'If you are going to be troublesome, I've a good mind not to take you to see our new ship.'

Adèle ran across the room to take his hand. 'Have you found one for us already, Daddy?'

Ryan followed her, his face eager. 'What's it like, Mr Beaufort?'

'Auntie Maura, did you hear that? We're going to see our new ship?' Noreen said.

They'd been happy to get off the *Vitesse*, she thought; now they were happy to be going to another ship. So was she. This hotel was so stuffy. She realised Hugh had come to stand beside her. 'Sorry. Did you say something? My thoughts were miles away.'

'Have they been driving you mad?'

She saw apprehension on four faces but couldn't tell a complete lie, not to Hugh.

'They've been . . . rather fidgety. Tell us about the ship.'

After he'd finished explaining, she smiled. 'It's good to hear he knows Bram.'

By now, the children's tempers had improved and they all got ready to go out, helping one another now instead of bickering.

'Am I to stay here?' Carrie whispered to Maura.

'Certainly not. You'll be travelling on the ship too. Besides, we need as many eyes as possible to make sure these four don't get into trouble.'

Ryan turned to her and grinned, looking so like his brother Bram when he was little that she was startled for a minute or two.

They set off for the ship, the children surprised to be told it had no engine. Maura was delighted about that, even if it was going to take longer to get anywhere. She'd had more than enough of thumping noises and bad smells from burning coal.

She found herself walking next to Hugh, while the others stayed in a group that formed and reformed as they followed behind them with Carrie. Always, though, Ryan kept hold of Noreen's hand, and Adèle of Brenna's.

Maura liked Captain McBride on sight. He had such a solid, dependable face. And not only was the ship trim and neat, but she was delighted at the thought of having a cabin all to herself, however tiny it might be.

After a quick tour of the passenger facilities, the captain entertained them to tea and cakes in a shady corner of the deck, then asked her if she'd be prepared to give him advice about buying trade items which would appeal to women.

'I don't mind trying, but what if I'm wrong?'

He laughed. 'It's all guesswork, though there are some things which always sell well. For the ladies, it's beautiful materials, silks, taffeta and muslins especially. Your nephew's wife Isabella specialises in silks, so you wouldn't want to buy those, but you couldn't go wrong if you chose a selection of light cotton fabrics. Do you know what's fashionable at the moment in England? Ladies in Australia love to keep up with the fashions.'

'Well, as it happens, I do, because I was Assistant Housekeeper in a large country mansion, and we had a lot of company. Very fashionable people, some of them.'

'There you are, then. But we'll have to buy things quickly. How about we leave these rascals here in the charge of young Carrie, with my stewardess Peggy to help her, and make a start on buying goods today?'

She stared at him in surprise, glancing quickly sideways to see if Hugh minded.

'We'll all three go out shopping, and I'll buy a few trade goods too,' he suggested.

She went back to join the men and they set off into the town, along narrow streets where camels walked by carrying loads. People were wearing clothes very different from anything she was used to. Some of the men had baggy trousers, some were wearing what looked like nightshirts that reached their ankles. There weren't many women to be seen, but the locals must be used to

European women because they didn't seem to find her presence or clothing strange. Or perhaps they were being polite and not staring.

By the time the three of them got back to the ship, she was exhausted. She could normally walk for miles, but she'd lost the habit of walking briskly while she was on the *Delta*.

'I'll have your cabins ready for you tomorrow,' Dougal said. 'Just come any time that's convenient.'

The children had gathered round them, trying to tell them what they'd been doing. The crew seemed to have been giving them a lot of attention.

'We'd better start back to the hotel now,' Hugh said.

Ryan left Noreen with Carrie and came to walk beside him and Maura. 'What did you buy for trading today, please? I'd like to learn about it, if you don't mind, because that's what my big brother Bram does.'

'All sorts of things, materials for ladies, some light wraps and shawls, crockery, glasses, a few rugs. I can't believe how much the captain bought. What did you do?'

'Brenna and I had a look round the ship with Pete. He's the mate and he's got a brother my age. He showed us how to tie knots. Noreen and Adèle talked to the man who mends the sails. He showed them his sewing needles, great big ones they were. Adèle likes sewing, especially embroidery, but Miss Fenton forgot to pack extra embroidery materials and Adèle's used everything up. She says she'll teach Noreen to embroider when we get to Australia.'

Hugh made a mental note to find some embroidery silks and needles for the girls before they set sail. Perhaps Maura would know what was needed. 'So you enjoyed yourselves, eh?'

'Yes. I like to learn new things.' Ryan beamed at them both.

Hugh clapped him on the shoulder. 'Good for you, lad.'

★ ★ ★

They set sail from Suez two days later, making for Galle on the island of Ceylon, which would take between two and three weeks, depending on the winds. Captain McBride gathered them together and pointed it out on a map, promising to show them how far they'd come each day.

'I never saw a map till we were leaving Ireland,' Ryan commented, running a finger round the shape of Australia. 'Just a dirty old globe in the village school and the teacher didn't tell us much about other countries, just which were in the British Empire.'

'And now we're travelling across a map.' Brenna corrected herself as her cousin opened his mouth. 'I didn't mean we were *on* the map, silly, you know I didn't.'

Their words showed Maura yet again how limited their lives had been. She found a seat in the shade and settled down beside Hugh with a book borrowed from the captain. 'It's lovely to know this ship will be taking us all the way to Fremantle.'

311

'With one stop in Galle. The captain says it's a pretty little town and we can pick up some more trade goods there.'

She smiled, feeling lazy and relaxed. 'As long as the children don't fall overboard.'

'I think the crew will keep an eye on them. They seem to have taken a fancy to them. We'll have them all turned into sailors by the time we get back.'

But she couldn't settle down to reading. Her thoughts kept going back to the children. They needed more schooling. At the very least they must be able to read fluently, know their tables and be able to handle simple arithmetic.

They might not like that, but she'd get Hugh on her side and start giving them lessons during this voyage. Ryan hung on his every word, so if Hugh said schooling was important, then the boy would try much harder, she was sure.

He talked a lot about his brother, whom he remembered clearly, even after a few years apart. She thought a lot about Bram, too. And trusted him. That was a good thing, because her whole future depended on what he wanted to do about her and the children.

She did hope he hadn't changed, grown mercenary, as some men did when they became successful. No, not Bram.

★　★　★

On a hot summer's day in November, Bram paced to and fro in the Bazaar. He was getting a bit short of goods, if truth be told. Dougal had

312

undertaken an extra trip to Suez, and although Adam was due back in the new schooner, he was late, should have been here before now. There was cargo for Singapore waiting for him here for the next trip.

Of course, the sea was always chancy. You couldn't rely on it for time or for safety. Bram prayed Adam would be all right on several counts. More important than the trade goods was the fact that if anything happened to her husband, his sister Ismay would be heartbroken. He hadn't realised till Ismay married a sailor how much their families worried about them while they were away.

Less important was the money the trade brought, but it was still needed, because it was the lifeblood of their business. Thank goodness the ships and their cargoes were insured.

Isabella came to link her arm in his. 'Stop worrying.'

He turned to her. 'I can't help it. We don't know what's going on out there.' He gestured in the direction of the ocean. 'And we need to be selling far more than we are in the Bazaar.'

'We're doing all right.'

'Are we? You keep the accounts. Are we really doing all right?'

'Yes, we are. It's only . . . ' She looked at him, seeming to be choosing her words with great care. 'I don't think we should spend a lot of money on furniture for the new house. In fact, I think we should move in with what we've got and buy more only if needed. And we should let the Hollinses move into our cottage here and pay us rent, or Sim could continue to act as night watchman in return for the cottage.'

'So you are a bit concerned about money.'

'Well . . . I do like to have something saved for a rainy day. It won't hurt to be careful, just until we get past these recent expenses.'

So he said it for her. 'And until the ice works is functioning properly. Chilton is still having trouble with the new machinery.'

'I'm not sure he knows how to build it, not really.'

Bram sighed. 'No. I'm beginning to wonder about that. Maybe I shouldn't have bought into the business. I was so relieved at Arlen recovering that I didn't want any other child to go without if they needed ice to help reduce a fever.'

She squeezed his arm in an unspoken gesture of comfort. 'It'll all work out, even if it's taking more time than we expected. People *do* need ice during the hot summers and Mr Chilton still sells all he can make with his old equipment.'

Bram nodded, then changed the subject back to their other problem. 'It's not easy in Australia, getting stock to sell, I mean. Especially here in the west. We're so far from everywhere else in the world.'

'It's a problem for those producing goods, too: wheat, wool, sandalwood. There aren't enough people to buy them here. Dougal never quite knows what he'll be taking as a cargo, whether it'll be several smaller loads from different people, or whether the whole *Bonny Mary* will be hired by one of the big Fremantle merchants.'

'He's done well, though. Not many ships go to Singapore from here and he has good contacts there with your Mr Lee. You know, they say three good trading voyages will pay for a ship. So he's more than paid for the *Bonny Mary*. And now that he has two ships, it won't be long before he's earning nearly double.'

She looked at him suspiciously. 'We're not buying a ship, Bram.'

He grinned, pushing his worries aside. 'A man can dream, can't he?' he said provocatively.

'I'll lock you in a cupboard if you try to buy even part of a ship. I mean it.'

'As long as you'll come and sit in the cupboard with me.'

They paused at the rear of the shop, not talking, both looking down the interior of the Bazaar, which was a rambling, odd-shaped building made from several old sheds. One day he'd refurbish it, or build a fine new bazaar, or even one of the newfangled department stores he'd read about, where they had nearly everything under one roof. Imagine that. A fine stone building, with different sections for different goods.

That was a much better dream than a ship, to his mind. Ships were too risky and what did he know about them, except that travelling on them made him sick?

He wasn't doing badly, though his ideas always raced ahead of his purse. There were people here in the Bazaar all the time, buying and selling, money coming into his hands. But it was going out rather quickly, too, at the moment.

315

It was the fault of that house. He should have rented somewhere, waited to buy a house of his own. Most people rented, after all, even those comfortably off.

Isabella squeezed his arm to get his attention. 'Let's go and sort through the second-hand furniture in the lean-to. We're going to need a proper dining table and chairs, and a couple more beds in the new house. Didn't you say someone sold you a whole houseful of stuff yesterday?'

'They did. I bought it as a job lot without going through it in detail, I got it so cheaply, I couldn't lose. I'd meant to start going through it yesterday, but I got distracted.'

'Well, let's look through it now together.'

Still arm in arm, they went outside to the lean-to and only then did they move apart.

'Look! They didn't even empty the drawers,' she said in astonishment.

'Once their parents had died, the sons wanted to clear the house and get rid of every single thing, so they crammed them in. They're moving to Sydney or they'd not have taken our low offer.'

'There are too many people moving to the east from the Swan River Colony. Why can't they stay here? We need more people in this colony, not fewer.'

He patted her hand. 'They'll come here gradually.'

'And if they don't? What will we do for customers?'

'We'll manage with the people we have here already.'

'I suppose so.'

He stepped back. 'Look how we had to pile things up to fit them in. It was starting to get dark when the last load came in. I'm not a big man, so I'm going to need help to get things down.'

She wrinkled her nose in disgust. 'They smell a bit. We'll need to spread them about to air them, maybe out in the sunshine.

'We'll use some ourselves, then we'll put the rest of the decent things up for sale in the second-hand section.'

She reached up as if to pull something down.

He grabbed her by the waist and tugged her back. 'I'm not having you lifting stuff.'

She looked at him. 'You've guessed, haven't you?'

'Of course I've guessed. Do you think I can't count? You're having another child. I'm sorry about that. I tried so hard not to get you pregnant again. It's the curse of the Deagans to get children so easily.'

'I'll be fine.'

'You'll be thirty-three by the time you have this baby, and you had a hard time of it with Arlen.'

She shrugged. 'Too late to worry about that now. I want a daughter this time. I hope you've given me one.'

He smiled at that. 'I don't mind which it is. I'll love it anyway. It'll be due in what? Another seven months? At least we'll be in the new house then and we'll get another full-time maid as well as Sally.'

'We're not going to extra expense. I can manage with Sally.'

'We are definitely getting more help if you're expecting a child.' He pulled her towards him, clasping both her hands between his. 'I love you too much to see you worn down with child-bearing, like my mother.'

She smiled and cuddled up to him for a moment, even though people could see them from the street.

He sighed. 'I'm going to ask advice about how to be even more careful in future. I don't want to stop loving you but I do want to keep you safe. Maybe Mr Lee knows some way of preventing children.'

She gave him one of her serene smiles and his heart melted. Ah, but she was beautiful, with her red hair and her bright eyes. He must look after her.

But how could you help making love to your wife? It was one of the things that brought you closest together.

16

When they were three days away from Galle, a storm blew up, and Dougal could see that it was going to be a bad one. He ordered most of the sails to be taken in and made sure everything was lashed down. He warned his passengers to stay in their cabins, sparing an extra stern look for Ryan.

'If you don't stay down here, if I see so much as the tip of your nose on deck, I'll *lock* you in. The sea can be cruel and this is no time to disobey orders.'

The boy nodded, but he had an air of only accepting this because it made sense.

Dougal turned to Hugh. 'Is it all right if I put Ahmed in with you folk? His English is improving all the time, but I don't want him loose on the ship in a storm, unable to understand instructions.'

'It's going to be a bad one, then, this storm?'

'Very bad.'

'You're sure there's nothing I can do to help?'

'Keep your party in the cabins, Beaufort. Keep the children within sight at all times. Don't expect to be waited on, even if you have to go hungry. Don't even go to the head, after one final visit. We'll put buckets with lids in your cabin to use instead. They'll be lashed in place.'

Maura, who had been listening from inside the cabin, slipped out to stand behind Hugh, feeling

319

worried about their safety. What if she had saved the children and brought them here to die?

As if he'd understood how she felt, the captain turned to her. 'My *Bonny Mary* is a good ship, Miss Deagan, well found. Trust in her. I might add that storms always seem worse to people who aren't sailors. The main thing is not to panic and to leave dealing with the ship to those whose trade it is.'

She nodded and as Dougal hurried away, linked her arm in Hugh's for a moment. 'I hope the children will be all right.'

'Adèle coped well when we met rough weather in the Bay of Biscay, didn't she? It's I who don't cope well with storms,' he added ruefully.

'Then we'll have to look after you. In the meantime I think we should all stay together in the biggest cabin. I'm not letting those children out of my sight.'

Ahmed came to join them. His English was still strongly accented, but was improving all the time. 'Captain say I stay with you, pliz.'

'Yes. Come inside the cabin.'

When the children pulled him into their game, Ahmed seemed at first baffled, and kept looking at Hugh, as if to check that it was all right to play. Gradually, he forgot to worry and got lost in a game of dominoes, which didn't need words once the others had demonstrated how to play it.

Without the deck space, they couldn't play whip and top, or push the little horse and cart about. It belonged to Adèle, as did most of the toys, but she shared them generously and they featured in everyone's make-believe games, even

320

Ryan condescending to play sometimes.

When Adèle got out her doll and began to change its clothes, Ahmed first looked shocked, then began to sneak a few peeps. He was startled when Ryan began to discuss which clothes the doll should wear. He looked from the doll to the other children, open-mouthed.

When Adèle pulled out a boy doll to be 'daddy' in her game and undressed it too, he watched again.

'I don't think he knew what ladies wore under their clothes,' Maura said quietly to Hugh with a smile. 'Or European gentlemen, either.'

'In his religion, I think boys and girls are segregated from an early age.'

'I'd like to see anyone keep Ryan away from his little sister for long now he's off that P&O ship. I don't know whether he loves Noreen more or she loves him.'

'They're very close. That happens sometimes when there's little love from the parents. I never saw my wife kissing or cuddling Adèle. The nursemaid brought her in to be viewed once a day.'

'I couldn't keep my distance. I've grown to love these children so much,' she said softly.

The movement of the ship grew more violent and after a while, Hugh stopped trying to hold a conversation.

When Maura looked at him surreptitiously, she was surprised at how pale he'd become. 'Why don't you go and lie down in your own cabin?' She saw Ryan swing round. That boy had very sharp hearing.

321

'Are you feeling sick, Mr Beaufort?'

'Unfortunately, yes. I'm not a good sailor in rough weather. If you don't mind, Maura, I will go and lie down.'

She looked round the cabin after he'd gone and repeated what had been said earlier. 'If anyone wants to be sick, please try to reach the bucket. Go and stand next to it if you feel even a little bit sick.'

Ahmed looked at her in puzzlement, this clearly beyond his understanding.

Ryan lifted the lid off one of the buckets and pantomimed being sick into it.

Ahmed nodded understanding. 'I no get sick. Good sailor, me.'

'I was sick in the last storm,' Ryan admitted. 'But after I'd emptied my stomach, I got used to the ship moving about. I think this time it's going to be worse, though.'

'I'm feeling a bit sick myself,' Carrie said suddenly. 'Very sick.' She looked at the buckets and hesitated. 'Shouldn't I go out to the head?'

'Certainly not,' Maura said firmly. 'It's dangerous out there. We've been told to stay here.'

The door opened and the stewardess slipped into the cabin. Peggy's hair was windblown, ends escaping from the scarf she'd tied round it, and her clothes were damp. She shut the door on the noise of the wind and leaned against it, letting her breath out in a sound of relief. 'Everyone all right here?'

'Mr Beaufort was feeling bad,' Brenna told her. 'He's gone to lie down. And Carrie isn't

322

feeling very well, either.'

Peggy studied the rest of them. 'You look a bit pale, too, Miss Deagan.'

'In the Bay of Biscay I felt nauseous, but it wasn't too bad. And anyway, someone has to look after the children.'

'I'm the oldest. I can look after the others,' Ryan said at once.

'You can certainly help me,' Maura said tactfully. It touched her how he was sometimes a child, sometimes trying to be an adult.

'Why don't we send Carrie to lie down on your bed, Miss Deagan?' Peggy suggested. 'I've put a bucket in there as well. You and the children will have more chance of staying well if people aren't vomiting right next to you. I'll try to bring you some food and fresh water later.'

As she opened the door and the wind howled into the cabin, the ship gave an extra big lurch downwards. Carrie gulped and clapped one hand to her mouth, leaving at a run. They heard the door of Maura's tiny cabin next door bang open, then Peggy closed their door again from outside.

The children looked at Maura expectantly, as if assessing her condition.

'I'm not going to be sick,' she said firmly. 'What game do you want to play now?'

'I don't want to play anything,' Adèle said. 'I just want to lie down, and not in a hammock, please. Look at the way they're swinging about. I'd fall out.'

'We'll put your bedding on the floor, then.'

None of the girls wanted to play, so Maura

323

found a book and insisted Ryan read to her. It was an effort to listen patiently to his stumbling words, because while she didn't feel badly seasick, there was no denying the tossing around made her feel uncomfortable.

He grew quieter and after a while, used the bucket, then came back saying firmly, 'I feel better now. I'll help you with the girls.'

She couldn't resist hugging him.

★   ★   ★

The buffeting continued to get worse. It seemed as if the ship had no sooner tossed in one direction, than she heaved in another, jerking them every which way. Though the girls weren't actually sick, they were all very quiet. Finally the two older girls huddled down in the corner with Ryan, who seemed much better now. Ahmed curled up on another blanket and went to sleep.

Maura lay on the bed, cuddling the sleeping Noreen, envying the cabin boy's tranquil slumber.

After a while, she tried to slip out of bed without waking Noreen, but the little girl cried and clutched hold of her.

'I'm frightened, Auntie Maura.'

She looked across at Ryan. 'Can I trust you to go directly next door and nowhere else?'

'To check on Mr Beaufort?'

'Yes. And then on Carrie. We can't leave her on her own.'

'Why don't we ask Ahmed to stay with Mr Beaufort?' Ryan suggested.

'Good idea.' She tried to explain to Ahmed what they wanted, but only succeeded in confusing him.

'I'll do it when we're next door,' Ryan said. 'If I can point, maybe he'll understand better.'

But Ahmed refused point-blank to leave the cabin.

'Captain say stay. Captain say stay,' he kept repeating.

Ryan rolled his eyes. 'I'll go and see if Mr Beaufort or Carrie need help.'

'But nowhere else.'

He shuddered. 'Nowhere else. I don't know how they stand it up on deck in a storm.' He hesitated. 'Are we . . . in danger?'

'I suppose so. But Captain McBride said to trust in the ship.'

He came back a few minutes later, grinning. 'Mr Beaufort says he prefers to be sick in private. And Carrie's fast asleep. She's been sick in the bucket, though.'

'Then all we can do is wait.'

The daylight gradually faded.

Peggy turned up with a large enamel container of water, bread and a jar of jam. 'Can't make you a drink of tea, I'm afraid,' she said cheerfully.

'How are things going?' Ryan asked. 'Is the ship . . . all right?'

'She's a good ship.'

Even as she spoke, they were thrown about like skittles and there was a thumping sound above them on the deck.

'Stay here!' she yelled and ran out, fighting to close the door.

The girls and Ahmed jerked awake.

'What's happening, Auntie Maura?' Brenna asked.

'I don't know. Whatever it is, we need to keep out of their way. They'll fetch us . . . if they need us to do something.'

They waited and this time fear waited with them. Maura could feel it like a dark presence in the cabin. She didn't speak, but she couldn't help thinking that ships were lost in storms at sea.

The minutes continued to tick away slowly. She tried counting the seconds but couldn't seem to concentrate.

'I can hear shouting,' Ryan said. 'At least, I think I can.'

The ship was bucking and lurching, her movement somehow different from before.

'We should pray,' Maura said. 'That's what we should do: pray to be safe.'

They all bowed their heads and she said the Lord's Prayer slowly and clearly.

'What if the ship sinks?' Brenna asked.

'We won't think about that. She's a good ship. The captain says to trust in her, so we'll do that.'

She noticed that Brenna and Adèle had their arms round one another. She hadn't seen Ryan sit down on the bed with her, but there he was, holding Noreen, who was sitting between them.

They were such good children. She prayed they'd have a chance to live happy and useful lives.

It seemed a long time before Peggy came back. Every face turned towards her apprehensively as she entered the cabin, but they waited for her to speak.

'We've lost the top part of a mast. They had to go aloft and cut it away. And one of the sails came adrift, so they had to lash that down. It's a wonder they managed to keep themselves from falling about up there, but they did.'

Maura nodded. 'It's good that the men are safe.'

'Captain McBride says to tell you the storm's abating and we'll be all right, even with the damage.'

'It doesn't feel as if it's abating,' Brenna muttered.

'If *he* thinks it's turned, that's what's happening,' Peggy said firmly. 'He's got a good sense of the weather, our captain has. Now, I'll leave you to eat.'

None of them looked as if they liked the idea, so she added, 'And if you don't want to eat, you *must* drink something. At least a cupful of water each, in mouthfuls, not all at once.'

'Could you look in on Mr Beaufort and Carrie, please?' Maura asked.

Peggy poked her head back round the door a few minutes later. 'I made sure Mr Beaufort knows it's important to keep sipping water. As for your maid, she's still sleeping.'

When she'd gone, Brenna looked at Maura. 'Well! How can anyone sleep with the ship heaving to and fro?'

Adèle giggled. 'Carrie is a very good sleeper. If I want her in the night, I have to shake her to wake her up.'

'I envy her,' Maura said. 'I doubt we'll get any sleep at all.'

'It doesn't matter, does it?' Ryan said. 'We're going to be all right. That's what matters.'

★ ★ ★

Morning came with seas still rough, but it was clear the worst of the storm was past. Dougal surveyed the damage to his ship and let his hand linger on the rail in a caress that contained a promise: he'd make the *Bonny Mary* good again.

He turned as Pete came up to him. 'We survived.'

'She's a good ship, with a good captain. We're lucky no one went overboard, though. I was feared for the men.'

'Me too. What about Ahmed?'

Pete grinned. 'My Peggy says he slept soundly through most of it.'

'We'll make a sailor of him yet.'

'We could do with his help in the galley now.'

'Ask your wife to fetch him, then. She can check on our passengers at the same time.'

Ahmed appeared briefly, gaping at the damage on deck, then was sent to help out in the galley.

Peggy came to report to the captain. 'Mr Beaufort was the worst, sir. The maid vomited then went off to sleep. Miss Deagan looks very tired. I don't think she got much sleep for worrying about the children.'

'Are the youngsters all right?'

'Ryan was sick once, then he was fine.' Her smile broadened. 'I could tell he was miffed about that, because his cousin Brenna wasn't sick at all. The two youngest girls slept most of the time.'

'I'll go and speak to them later to tell them what's happening. In the meantime, if you can find something warm for them, even if it's just a pot of tea, I think they'd appreciate it.'

She nodded and bustled off.

'She's a good worker, your wife, Pete. Do you think she'd like to travel with us permanently and help with the cooking? We seem to be getting passengers fairly regularly these days.'

Pete beamed at his captain. 'I know she'd jump at the chance. She gets lonely left at home on her own, since we've never been blessed with children.'

* * *

Dougal went to see the passengers in the afternoon, by which time the sea was merely choppy. He was glad to see that Mr Beaufort had joined the others again, but the poor fellow still looked wan.

'Well, as you've no doubt heard, we suffered some damage. Not too bad, considering, but we'll have to get some repairs done in Galle before going on to Perth. That'll delay us for a few days, I'm afraid. It's a pleasant little town, though, so I don't think you'll be too bored while you're waiting. You may even be able to arrange a visit to a tea plantation inland.'

He waited a moment or two, then said, 'And if you want some fresh air, you're welcome to come on deck again, but don't go near the rails.'

When the children had been sent to bed, not without protests, Hugh followed Maura out to get some fresh air. He was feeling hollow and weak still.

'Thank you, Maura.'

She looked at him in surprise. 'What for?'

'Once again, you looked after the children when I couldn't. I don't think I'm cut out to be a sailor.'

'I'm not fond of stormy weather myself.' She sighed. 'I must admit, I'll be glad to get this journey over and done with. Captain McBride says it'll be another two to three weeks from Galle to the Swan River Colony.'

'Perhaps we should have waited for a P&O ship. That'd have been faster.'

'I didn't want to find myself in the same sort of steerage quarters. It was horribly noisy because of being so close to the engine, and stuffy as well as smelly. I hope I never have to travel back to Britain. I don't think I could face it.'

He was silent. He still hoped to see his home again one day. 'I didn't get a letter off to my lawyer in England before we left Suez. We were so busy and . . . well, I wasn't sure what to say, or whether he's the sort of fellow to handle a divorce. I think I should find a competent lawyer in the colony and get him to arrange matters for me. Unfortunately, that'll take time. Will you wait for me?'

She smiled. 'I've not exactly got suitors queuing at my door, and anyway . . . I seem to have grown fond of a certain tall, musical fellow.'

He took hold of her hand. 'I'm glad.'

'I don't want to tell my family we're engaged, though. Not with you still married.'

'I suppose not,' he agreed reluctantly. Because if it was up to him he'd like to tell the world.

★ ★ ★

Two days after the storm, the passengers stood at the ship's rail, bathed in sunshine now, looking across a stretch of pale turquoise sea towards the island of Ceylon. There was a range of hills along the interior with one standing out.

'It's called Adam's Peak,' the captain told them. 'There's a lighthouse to guide people in, but you can't see that yet, so we use that mountain as our first landmark.'

They spent most of the day on deck. The ship was sailing more slowly than usual, due to reduced sail.

When they arrived, they were able to anchor in the port itself, because there was deep water close to the shore. Stone ramparts framed the harbour.

'You'll be able to stroll along the ramparts and into the town, or watch other ships in the harbour,' the captain had said earlier.

'It looks a beautiful place.' Maura fanned herself. 'But it's very hot and humid, isn't it?'

Peggy saw how hot she was getting and came up. 'Could I have a word with you and Carrie, please?'

When they were in the cabin, she said bluntly,

'You'd be better reducing the number of clothes and undergarments you wear — if you want to stay comfortable, that is. I always do in the tropics. One petticoat is enough, and a light cotton skirt and bodice. If you haven't anything, it's very cheap to buy something and have it made up. They produce beautiful fabrics here.'

'I have some lighter clothes that one of the neighbouring ladies gave me before I left Ireland. They're lovely. I shall be very happy to wear them. Luckily she had dark hair too and the colours suit me.'

'I think Adèle should wear less too,' Carrie said. 'I'll see to that. Your two don't have a lot of petticoats and such, do they, Miss Deagan?'

'No. They had almost nothing till we got them ready for this voyage, as you may have guessed from what they say.'

'Can't help noticing, miss. They're a clever bunch, pick things up quickly, don't they?'

They didn't leave the ship to go into the town that evening, but the following morning saw the passengers all eager to go off and explore.

There were other ships in the harbour, including a P&O steamship which was travelling on towards the East.

'They come here to coal,' Hugh said. 'Dirty stuff, but steamships certainly cut down the time it takes to go round the world.'

'I can't believe I'm here,' Maura said. 'I never even expected to leave England.'

A little later, she murmured, almost to herself, 'I wonder what Bram will say when we arrive.'

She was still worrying about that.

17

The following day was just as fine and sunny, and even though it was a steamy sort of heat, Hugh enjoyed strolling round the town and ramparts with his little brood. The children were full of questions and exclamations about the strange new things they kept seeing. Maura was more restrained but she too was enjoying herself, he could tell.

They met several people from the P&O ship they'd seen in the harbour, so stopped to exchange greetings out of courtesy. But as they got further along the ramparts, they met fewer people.

The last man they met stopped only for a moment, explaining that it was nearly time for the midday meal on board the ship. 'I never trust foreign food, so I'm not risking the local dishes.'

'I rather fancy trying new sorts of food,' Hugh said once they were away from the man.

'And Captain McBride said he loved the spicy eastern dishes.' Maura smiled. 'I've never tried them, but I'd love to, and I'm quite sure Ryan would try anything.'

'That lad can certainly eat.'

'He's grown visibly on this journey. Well, they all have, but him most.'

Brenna came up to ask her aunt to settle an argument between her and Ryan just then. Smiling at the girl's passionate defence of her own opinions, Hugh fell a little behind the others. He loved the harbour scene spread out below them. It made him wish he had some artistic talent and could sketch it.

He wasn't looking where he was going and when a couple turned a corner, they had to stop to avoid bumping into him.

'Sorry, I — ' He stared at the woman in shock. His wife! Sylvie was the last person he'd have expected to see here, the very last.

She was equally dumbfounded, clutching her companion's arm and cringing away from Hugh.

A quick glance showed that Maura and the children were strolling on, thank goodness. Hugh stood stock still, not knowing what to say. *What the hell was Sylvie doing here?* And she wasn't on her own, judging by the way she was clinging to the man beside her. He must be the one she'd run away to.

He heard her whisper, '*Mon dieu! C'est Hugh Beaufort.*'

The man gaped first at her, then at him.

Hugh tried to remember the fellow's surname. Durand! Yes, that was it. Jacques Durand.

'Do not hurt her!' Durand said in heavily accented English, pushing in front of Sylvie as if to protect her.

'I have no intention of touching her. But I do want to know what she's doing here. Sylvie? *Que fais-tu ici?*'

She didn't answer, still clinging to Durand, looking so pale Hugh feared she was going to faint.

Another glance ahead showed him that Maura

and the children were waiting for him at the corner. 'I must tell my companions to go on without me. Do not attempt to run away.'

'I 'ave no intention of running away.' Durand struck a heroic pose.

With Sylvie clinging to his arm, the pair of them looked like some stupid sentimental painting, Hugh thought in irritation.

Trying to keep calm, he ran up to the others. 'Something's happened. I can't explain it now, Maura. Could you go on without me, please? I'll meet you back at the ship and explain then.'

To his relief, she only shot a quick glance at the two people waiting for him, then nodded and started walking again.

He hurried back to where Sylvie and Durand were still clutching one another. He'd found early on in his marriage that his wife wasn't quick-witted, to put it mildly. Could she do nothing but stand there like an idiot struck by lightning?

Once again, Durand positioned himself between her and Hugh.

'For heaven's sake, why do you think I'm going to hurt her?'

The man switched to French. 'You 'ave beaten her in the past. But you shall not do it again.'

'What? I've never laid a finger on her. She's lying if she's told you that.' He saw her blush.

Durand also looked at her face, frowning a little. 'Whether you 'ave or not, she is afraid of you, and I will not 'ave you bullying her.'

Bullying, indeed! Hugh didn't waste time arguing about that. He wished he hadn't seen them, but now that he had, this needed sorting out.

Sylvie began to sob delicately into her lace handkerchief. He'd bet her eyes were not in the slightest bit moist. She could put on a show like this at the drop of a hat.

He didn't even try to contain his impatience, but looked round. 'We need to talk. Is there somewhere we can go to be private?'

'Don't let him near me, Jacques!' she whispered.

Durand put his arm round her. '*Chérie*, we have to talk to him. We must decide what to do. It cannot now be avoided.'

'He will want me to go back to him.'

'No, I won't. I have no desire whatsoever to live with you again!' Hugh snapped. 'In fact, after today, I hope I never see you again as long as I live.'

She stopped pretending to sob and glared at him.

'There is a stone bench on the ramparts where we can sit. *Calme-toi, chérie.*' With soft, coaxing words, Durand persuaded Sylvie to walk back to it and installed her at one end, sitting guard between her and her husband.

Hugh scowled equally at them both. Two fools, well matched. Since they didn't speak, he did. 'As I said before, I presume you've run away together.'

Durand gave a very French shrug. 'As you say. I 'ave money now, so we can live comfortably. Not in France, of course. We make a *scandale* there. We had intended to make a home for

336

ourselves *en Australie*, thinking no one would follow us to such a distant place. How did you find us?'

'I didn't find you. This meeting has happened by the merest chance. Adèle has been ill, near death's door. The doctors thought a warmer climate was her only hope, so we set sail for Australia.'

He waited for Sylvie to ask for more details, but she didn't bother. Durand seemed to be waiting for her to speak, too. When she didn't, he gave her a nudge.

'*La pauvre!*' Sylvie managed at last, fluttering the handkerchief to her eyes again. 'But she is your concern now, Hugh. I shall stay with my Jacques.'

'Stay with him. I don't care. As soon as we reach Australia, I shall sue for divorce. If you tell me where you're going, I'll make sure they send the necessary papers to you there and you'll be free. This time, I'm willing to pretend to be at fault to speed things up.'

She looked at him in horror, then turned to Jacques. 'Stop him!'

'Will you please stop talking so foolishly? Once we're divorced, you can spend your whole life with him.'

Sylvie looked at Jacques, biting her lip. When he gave her a questioning look, she shook her head.

'Don't let him goad you, *chérie*. We can . . . work something out.' Jacques looked at Hugh as if something had struck him. 'Who was that woman you went to speak to? Are *you* living

337

with someone else now?'

'Of course not. She's a fellow passenger, that's all.'

Jacques smirked. 'The way you looked at one another, she's a bit more than that. Is she a widow? She had several children.'

'She's their aunt. Their parents died.'

Sylvie's eyes narrowed. 'You wish to marry her. Me, I can tell such things. That's why you're seeking a divorce now.'

Jacques leaned his head against the stone wall, staring thoughtfully into space. 'It seems to me the best thing you can do from now on is pretend that Sylvie has died and not waste your time on a divorce. Why not just marry your lady?'

'Because I'm not free. It'd be a lie. I could be put in prison for bigamy.'

'Who is to know that in a far country, unless you tell them?'

Hugh stared at them in shock. He'd always known that Sylvie's only morals were to do what suited her best. But he wasn't like that, and couldn't do such a thing to Maura.

Only, if he didn't pretend to marry her, he might lose her, and he couldn't bear the thought of that.

'Our ship leaves tonight,' Jacques said. 'And when we get to the next port, we'll go somewhere else and change our names. We shall not now go to Australia, definitely not. So . . . you need never see or think about us again after today.'

Sylvie nodded and a message seemed to pass between the two of them.

Jacques hesitated, frowning in thought. 'However, you will be better with some sort of document to prove things are as you say. I could, if you like, supply you with a signed declaration that I know for certain your wife has died. I can get the captain to witness it.'

Sylvie clapped her hands. 'So clever, my Jacques. But Hugh won't do it. He's too much of a coward.'

Jacques studied Hugh. 'I think you will do it, n'est-ce pas?'

'No, I don't think so.'

'You will change your mind when you think about it. But you have only this afternoon before we leave, so you must act quickly. Come to the ship this afternoon if you wish me to give you this document.'

Hugh was very tempted.

Jacques turned to Sylvie. 'Come, my darling. Let us return now. You will need to lie down to recover from this terrible shock.'

Hugh didn't try to stop them or to call goodbye. They didn't even turn their heads, but began to whisper to one another.

As he watched them walk away, his emotions were in turmoil. It would be so easy to do as Durand had said. Only it'd be living a lie.

But how would anyone find out, unless he told them? He was quite sure Sylvie wouldn't tell anyone — she'd probably forget she wasn't properly married to Jacques, knowing her.

He began to walk back towards the ship. One thing he'd decided already. He wasn't going to try to stop Sylvie leaving. He'd told the truth when he said he didn't want her back, not just for his own sake, but for Adèle's. Sylvie had been as bad a mother as a wife.

Only . . . once Sylvie and Durand had gone, there would be no way of finding her again. A sworn statement that she had died might be useful.

What the hell was he to do? He couldn't ask Maura to commit bigamy. Could he get a divorce now?

Arguments for and against were going round and round in his mind, but one thing seemed obvious. Whether he used it or not, he should get that statement from Durand . . . just in case.

He'd go to their ship and ask Jacques to sign a document to the effect that Sylvie Beaufort was dead.

To all intents and purposes, she was. Or would be once her ship set sail.

When he thought of Maura's quiet integrity and loving nature, he had to wonder what he'd ever seen in Sylvie.

Or she in him. That had soon puzzled him, still did. If it had been money, he probably had as much as Durand, yet she'd run away to him.

He'd never understood Sylvie.

* * *

Bram whistled cheerfully as he left the Bazaar and went to find Isabella. She was sitting on the sofa, bouncing little Arlen on her knee, playing a game that made the child roar with laughter as she said, 'Boo!' If only you could take a

340

photograph of such a moment, instead of having to sit still for a minute, so that the photograph came out with you looking wooden, or with young children looking blurred because they'd moved.

He'd heard that they had new ways of taking 'instant' photographs, but he didn't think there was anyone in the Swan River Colony with that sort of equipment. If someone came here, they could make money from it. No, he mustn't even think like that. He could afford no more business ventures.

When he saw his father, Arlen wriggled down and ran to be picked up. 'Go for a walk, Daddy. Go for a walk.'

'He's a clever one, isn't he? Listen to how well he's speaking, and him only twenty months old.'

'That's because Sally and I talk to him, and when we don't, Louisa does.'

'Where is she?'

'Where do you think?' She winked at him and jerked her head towards the sofa. Louisa loved to hide behind it and bob out to surprise people.

'I wonder where Louisa is?' he said loudly.

A stifled giggle came from behind the sofa.

'There she is!' Arlen shouted and ran to find his second cousin.

They rolled on the floor, laughing together.

Isabella looked at him, head on one side. 'It's not like you to leave the Bazaar at this time of day.'

'I got word the house is so near to being finished that they want us to check everything. Mitchell is very efficient, isn't he? Can you leave

341

these two little demons with Sally and come with me now to check the house?'

'Yes.' She stood up at once.

'You're eager to move in, aren't you?'

'Very eager. We're far too crowded here.'

'I shall miss being right next to the Bazaar.'

'You'll only be a couple of streets away, for goodness' sake.'

'Not close enough to nip down for a cuddle and cup of tea. I shall miss that.'

She wondered if that might be a good thing for the business. Dear Bram always had time for a chat, no matter who with, giving courteous attention to anyone, no matter how lowly.

It was one of his strengths — and perhaps one of his weaknesses, too.

★　★　★

The door of the house stood open. From inside came a mixture of smells: newly sawn wood, paint, boiling varnish.

They stood still for a moment on the doorstep, then with a laugh, he swept her off her feet. 'You're supposed to carry your wife over the threshold, are you not?' He staggered inside with her, letting her down gently in the hall.

'That's for newly-weds, silly.' Flushing at the sight of Mitchell standing smiling at their antics from the top of the stairs, she straightened her skirts.

'I still feel the marvel of being married to you,' Bram whispered. 'And I always will.' Then he looked up. 'Good morning, old fellow. Are you

342

ready to show us round?'

'As if you haven't been coming here several times a week.' Mitchell ran lightly down to join them. 'Shall we start with the downstairs?'

Bram fell silent as they walked through the spacious rooms, swept clean of shavings now, the floors gleaming with varnish.

Upstairs he shook his head, muttering, 'To think of all these bedrooms just for one family.' Then they went up to the attics, which hadn't been there before the renovations.

'I think Sally should still sleep with the children,' Isabella worried. 'She might not hear them from the attic.'

'Whatever you say, my love.'

'Is it all to your liking?' Mitchell asked.

'Very much to our liking,' Isabella replied, seeing that Bram was still overwhelmed and understanding why. 'Riss has done a wonderful job with the woodwork. But I'm glad *you* were there to manage things.'

'I've discovered that I like building, seeing things come together, having the necessary equipment and supplies ready for each stage. I'd thought to continue to earn my living as a timber merchant here in Australia, but I think now I'm going to set up as a builder too.'

'Well, if anyone can supply the wood, it's you, and a good quality of wood too.'

'And some to spare,' Mitchell said with a smile. 'Did I tell you Adam's found a market for good quality pieces of jarrah in Singapore. It's a very hard wood, but it's beautiful, such a rich deep colour when polished. Mr Lee wants

343

regular supplies of it.'

'You'll have to take on more employees,' Bram said idly.

'I will be doing.' He smiled. 'Some say the Swan River Colony isn't a place to get rich in. Well, let them move to Sydney and Melbourne. You and I are doing just fine here.'

'Are you hankering to be rich, then?'

'Not rich so much as comfortable. Too much money brings its own problems, I think. I've seen it before. Men who made a fortune then had to spend all their time caring for their money and worrying about it. I care about my son most of all.' He sighed. 'Though I'd love to have other children before it's too late.'

'I agree with you,' Bram cast a loving look sideways at his wife. 'Family come first. And though I used to think I'd like to be rich, what is that? The money Isabella and I are making now from the Bazaar and trading with Mr Lee in Singapore would have seemed like unbelievable riches to me when I was a young fellow working in the stables.'

'Well, I'd like to make more money.' Isabella looked challengingly at the men. 'I know women are supposed only to care for their homes and children, but I enjoy working in the Bazaar and I like handling the money, too. I've got an idea for selling clothes that are mostly finished. I can get them done cheaply in Singapore. For mourning especially, they'd be very popular. But I'll need somewhere else to sell them. There isn't space in the Bazaar and it's not . . . elegant enough.'

Bram rolled his eyes and took her arm again.

344

'What will you think of next, woman?'

'You're a fine one to talk.' She didn't move on with him, because she was still thinking aloud. 'I think living with the Lees in Singapore taught me a lot. Xiu Mei managed the silk shop and she wrote to tell me she's going to open a bigger place once they've moved into the new house. She's very ambitious and her brother will support her in that venture. With her help, I can make my idea work. I trust her like a sister.'

'I'll support you in anything you want to do, my darling,' Bram said at once. 'You're too intelligent to spend your days in housework. But you must let me hire you a housekeeper.'

As she smiled at him she saw Mitchell looking at them enviously. Poor man. He was left to bring up his son on his own. If she could, Isabella would find him a wife. It was such a pity their friend Livia and he weren't attracted to one another, but they weren't and you couldn't make someone like a person in that way.

⋆ ⋆ ⋆

Hugh found Maura and the children on the docks near the ship, buying food from a hawker, with the help of Captain McBride.

'Is it safe to eat this?' he asked involuntarily.

The captain smiled. 'I've bought from this hawker before when we've come to Galle, and the food has always been good. Try it. But eat it while it's hot.' He accepted a package wrapped in a big leaf, nodded and made his way back to the ship.

The children were each holding a rolled leaf of food, so Hugh bought one for himself as well. The four youngsters were jumping up and down in excitement at the prospect of eating something exotic as they led the way back to the ship.

'Hurry up, Auntie Maura!'

'Hurry up, Daddy!'

Hugh took a cautious bite. Mmm. The captain was right. The spicy rice and vegetable mixture was very good. The children thought it hilarious that it was meant to be eaten with the fingers, as the vendor had shown them.

Hugh ate his quickly, keeping an eye on Maura. As soon as she had finished and pushed away her leaf with some rice still on it, he said, 'I wonder if I can have a word? Something's cropped up.'

'Can I finish your rice, Auntie Maura?' Ryan asked.

'Of course. Share it with the others if they want some.' She looked at Hugh, waiting for him to speak.

'In private.' He led the way to the rear of the deck.

When it came to speaking, to saying that he'd just met his wife, he couldn't get the words out to tell Maura, just couldn't.

'Is something wrong?'

'I . . . maybe. Look, I know I promised to take you all out again this afternoon, but I have to see the man I met during our walk. He's someone I know from France and . . . um, he may have some information about my wife. I couldn't

346

speak to him openly then, but I've arranged to go and see him before his ship leaves.'

'Then you must do so. Is it bad news, do you think?'

So Hugh had to tell a direct lie, which he hated doing. 'He wouldn't say in front of his wife, so I'm not sure.'

'We'll be all right. We'll probably go into town again. I promise we won't go far, but I want to tire those children out.'

'Thank you.'

'For what?'

'For being so understanding. Not prying.'

'I trust you, Hugh. You must do as you see best.'

Her trusting smile made him feel even worse. He didn't deserve her trust, didn't deserve her love, even.

You couldn't ask a woman like her to commit bigamy and risk going to jail.

* * *

He stopped at the foot of the gangway, staring up at the P&O vessel, which wasn't as new as the *Delta*, but looked well cared for.

A sailor stopped him at the top of the gangway. 'May I help you, sir?'

'I've come to see Monsieur Durand. He's expecting me.'

'I'll send someone to fetch him, sir. If you'd like to take a seat?' He indicated a bench nearby, waiting till Hugh had sat down before beckoning a cabin boy over.

347

It seemed a long time before Jacques came in sight.

They went to stand in a corner where they'd have some privacy. Jacques was looking amused, damn him.

'How can I help you, Beaufort?' He spoke French and Hugh followed suit.

'You know very well why I've come.'

'You wish me to provide proof of your wife's death.'

'You can hardly provide proof.'

'No. But I can give you a sworn statement, which people will take as proof.'

'I think it'd be better if Sylvie also signed it, using her new name.'

There was silence, then. 'I'll have to persuade her. First I'll let them know we wish to see the captain, for him to witness our document.' He stood up and left, stopping next to the sailor on duty to say, 'I need to fetch my wife, so my friend will be waiting for me.'

Hugh sat there for what seemed a very long time. Glances at his pocket watch showed that fifteen minutes had passed, then twenty, then thirty.

Durand was doing this on purpose. And Hugh had no choice but to wait on the fellow's pleasure.

Thirty-five minutes had passed when Durand reappeared, with a drooping Sylvie on his arm. She completely avoided Hugh's eyes, dabbing away with another of those flimsy lace handkerchiefs.

'My wife is upset, since she knew your wife

well,' Durand said loudly.

'I'm . . . sorry to hear that.' Hugh waited. He would not beg.

'I have arranged for us to see the captain. In the meantime, this is the paper I drew up after we left you earlier.'

'You were so sure I'd come?'

'*Mais oui*. It is the only practical thing to do.' He turned to Sylvie. 'Please sit down, my love, while Beaufort reads the deposition.'

Hugh scanned the paper. 'It's in French. It needs to be in English as well.'

Durand produced another paper. 'This I am not so sure of. I know the legal terms necessary in French but not in English.'

Hugh ran his eyes over it. 'It's clear enough. We don't need legal terms. You're prepared to sign this, Sylvie?'

She scowled at him. 'Jacques has assured me that it is needed, for the child's sake, so I shall do it. I would not do it for you. After this, I hope never to see you again as long as I live.'

The virulence in her voice surprised Hugh. Had he been so bad a husband? He didn't think so.

Durand offered her his arm. '*Eh bien*. Let us go to see the captain. Try to look sad, Beaufort, or he will think you heartless.'

Hugh didn't think he could manage that. He didn't feel at all sad, just angry.

The captain listened to their explanation, offered Hugh his commiserations, and witnessed the signatures on the pieces of paper. He behaved with great gallantry towards Sylvie, who was clearly a favourite with him.

When they left his cabin, she walked away without another word, handkerchief pressed to her eyes.

Durand escorted his visitor to the gangway. 'I should also tell you that if you do try to gain a divorce, we faked Sylvie's death before we left, so they'll tell you there's no need.'

His smirk as he said this made Hugh, normally a peaceable man, want to punch him good and hard.

'We did it rather cleverly. Lost at sea. No body to worry about.'

Hugh managed to scrape out a couple of words. 'I see.'

'We shall not now go to Australia, so don't try to find us.'

'I won't.' Hugh had had enough. He turned without a word of farewell and strode down to the quay. He felt sick at what he'd done, but the only other choice would have been to claim Sylvie as his wife.

If he was lucky, he would never see the pair of them again. Which suited him just fine.

He still didn't know whether he would use the statements, whether he *could* lie to Maura.

But what else could he do but provide for all eventualities?

Only . . . there seemed nothing he could do to get out of his marriage legally now. Nothing at all. He was trapped.

18

The *Bonny Mary* left Galle on what would be, the passengers hoped, the last leg of their journey. Though there were regular tropical downpours in the afternoons, they enjoyed mainly favourable winds and encountered no more storms, just a couple of brisk, windy days that had Hugh sitting quietly and eating very little.

'What will happen once we get to Australia?' Ryan asked one day, after his reading lesson with his aunt had ended.

'You'll probably go and live with Bram.' She'd said this several times, but Ryan still seemed to need reassuring.

'And he doesn't hit people?'

'No, never. He's a lovely fellow.' How sad that a child didn't know his own brother well enough to worry so much about being beaten.

'And there will be enough to eat at his house?'

'Oh, yes. Plenty.'

Ryan began scraping his shoe toe about on the deck as if he was drawing a pattern. 'I'd rather stay with you. You never say what *you* will do when we get there. Won't you want us any more?'

'Of course I will. It's just — I know Bram will want you too. After all he's your and Noreen's brother. I don't know whether I'll be able to keep you because I may not have enough money.

351

I'll have to find a job, you see, and they don't pay women as much as they pay men, so it'll be . . . difficult.'

She had no one to talk to about it, but she found it hard to believe that Hugh's fondness for her would last once they were back in a situation where there were the usual divisions between upper and lower classes. How could it? He was a gentleman. She was from Irish peasant stock.

'But if you did have enough money, then you'd want us to live with you?'

Ryan wasn't looking at her, but Maura noticed that Brenna was listening carefully to this conversation as well. 'I'd love to have you, all of you, to be a family together. You know that.'

'Adèle too?'

'Well, she has her father. It's not quite the same for her.'

'But she's like another cousin now. She and Brenna are best friends and they help me look after Noreen, so we *fit* together.'

'You'll still be able to see Adèle sometimes, I'm sure.'

'I'm going to ask Mr Beaufort to live near us, then. He's rich so he can choose where he lives. I'm going to be rich when I grow up. Like Bram. Like Mr Beaufort. I'll work hard and get rich.'

'Then you'd better put a lot of effort into your arithmetic or you'll not be able to count all your money.'

Ryan gave her one of his fleeting smiles, knowing this was a joke, because once she'd shown him the rules of arithmetic, he had proved really good at dealing with figures. He went across the deck to sit with the three girls, who were chattering to one another, as usual.

Hugh came to sit beside her. 'I couldn't help overhearing what Ryan said just now. Adèle keeps saying the same thing: she wants to live with them. I'd be happy to have them all, more than happy, and I hope — somehow — we can arrange that, you and I.'

But he didn't sound confident. There! she thought. She'd guessed something would prevent him from marrying her, even if that was still his wish while they were together on the ship.

She studied him surreptitiously. Something had happened in Galle, and though he said he'd received news of his wife, he hadn't gone into details, and he'd not talked about a future with Maura since then. She often caught him staring into space, looking worried.

He hadn't played his guitar half as much as he usually did, either. Only when the children pleaded for a singsong did he take it out and lose himself in the music for a while. But the worried frown soon came back once he stopped playing.

This leg of the journey would take just over two weeks if the weather stayed good and the winds favourable, Captain McBride said. She was determined to find out what Hugh's problem was before the journey ended. Well, she had to know what was going on before she asked Bram to help her make a new life.

Who were those French people he'd met in Galle? What could they have told him to make him so distant?

Had the news about Hugh's wife meant he

had to take Adèle's mother back? Was that it?

Maura sighed. Perhaps he was now trying to work out how to tell her? It seemed a possibility, no, a probability. It was so hard for people to break up a marriage, except through death.

Two weeks after they left Galle, with Fremantle only about three days away, according to the captain, she decided that today she would insist Hugh talk about what was wrong. She had to know where she stood.

She waited till evening, then once she'd persuaded the children to go to bed and had left Carrie keeping an eye on them, she went to find Hugh.

He was sitting chatting to the captain and both men stood up politely as she came up on deck again.

'Don't tell me they're asleep already?' Hugh teased.

'Not quite, but Carrie's with them and they soon will be, I'm sure. I, um, wonder if I could have a private word, Hugh?'

The captain moved away. 'I'll leave you in peace then. Do sit down, Miss Deagan. Take my place. This is a nice spot for a cosy chat.'

When he'd gone, Maura tried to think how to start.

Hugh spoke first, his voice harsher than usual. 'It's time we had a talk, I know that.'

'Yes, it is. Something's worrying you. If you've changed your mind about me, you have only to say. I won't make a nuisance of myself.'

'I'd never change my mind, my dear one.'

He reached out and took her hand and she

turned hers to clasp his properly. Oh, she loved holding his hand. It was so warm and strong. 'Tell me what's wrong, then, Hugh.'

He let go of her hand and stared down at the deck. The silence went on for so long she didn't know whether to say something or not. Then suddenly he began to speak in a low voice.

'In Galle . . . those people I met — ' He broke off and suddenly buried his head in his hands, his voice muffled. 'Maura, that woman was my wife.'

It was her turn to be lost for words. She tried to remember the woman. Short and pretty in a doll-like way. Only, she'd been clinging to the man she was with. 'Your wife? But she was with another man, surely?'

'Yes. She's always loved that fellow — Jacques Durand, he's called, though he goes under another name now. He's some sort of cousin to her, and it caused a scandal in the family. I didn't know about him when we married, but I soon found out.'

'She left you for him?' Maura couldn't understand that. The other man was quite short, with a weak chin and receding hair of a faded brown, while Hugh was tall and . . . a proper man, somehow.

'She wrote that she was leaving me because she hated being married to me. She'd refused to share my bed after Adèle was born, and wasn't at all interested in looking after our child. I didn't go after her, assumed her family would look after her. They were comfortably off. She used to get letters from France regularly. I thought they were

355

from her family. Perhaps they were from him.'

'But if she loved him, why did she marry you in the first place?'

'I suppose her parents forced her to. He had no money then; I did.'

Maura knew what that was like to be forced, oh, she did! 'So she and this Durand are living in sin?'

'Yes. And I don't care about that, not one bit, but I do care about . . . I'm afraid it gets worse.' He sighed and took her hand again, raising it to his lips for a kiss.

'They were going to Australia to live as far away as possible from me — ironic, isn't it? But Durand said they'd be going somewhere else now and would change their names. He swore he'd make certain I never found them again.'

'Oh.'

'He suggested I pretend to marry you. They're now claiming to be husband and wife.'

She drew back. 'I couldn't do that.'

'No. And I wouldn't ask you. You deserve better.'

'You deserve better, too, than a wife like that.' She had to ask it. 'I thought you were going to get a divorce? Surely she's given you ample grounds for that now.'

'The problem is, they've faked her death. If I try to get a divorce, I'll be told I'm a widower and don't need one. In fact — ' His voice broke.

'Tell me everything,' she insisted gently. 'I'd rather know the truth.'

'You'll hate me.'

'I could never do that, Hugh.'

'They both signed a declaration, with the captain as witness. It said they knew for a fact that Sylvie Beaufort was dead, drowned at sea. And I . . . let them do it and give me the document. I must have been mad. I thought I might use it to marry you once we get to Australia. Only I can't lie to you, even if the truth keeps us apart.'

She wished he had lied without telling her. Now that she knew, it'd be a mortal sin for her to marry him, knowing she was committing bigamy, as well as a crime. But still, she couldn't help wishing he'd done it.

'Do you hate me, Maura?'

'No, of course not. I love you, Hugh.'

'And I love you, too. So much, so very much.' Another silence, then, 'As a result, we're trapped in a situation of their making. I shall be known as a widower, only I won't be able to marry you.'

She stood up, unable to keep her distress hidden any longer. 'I have to be alone. I need to take it all in.'

'Yes, of course.' He stood up, looking at her, all his feelings showing in his face. 'Take in this as well, when you do your thinking. I love you deeply, Maura, and I always will. That will never change.'

A sob escaped her and she was half blinded by tears as she hurried down to her cabin. It was so tiny, it was more like a cupboard, but oh, she was relieved to have it, to be alone tonight.

She let the tears flow, muffling her sobs in her pillow and weeping for a long time.

She'd lost him. She'd thought she could

manage without Hugh if he changed his mind, but now she knew she couldn't. She'd feel like only half a person and the mere thought of spending the rest of her life without him broke her heart.

The tears stopped eventually, but it felt as if anguish was running through her veins instead of blood. She crossed her arms over her chest, as if to give herself comfort. But she wanted him to be the one holding her. There was no comfort in a spinster embracing herself.

After a while she tried to be practical, think of the future. What was she to do with her life now? She hadn't realised till tonight how used she'd grown to his company, to turning to him with a question, or to share amusement at what the children said or did. All the small things that made up a life together.

Like singing with him. The music added another layer of joy to their relationship. Or it had done.

She hadn't understood before just how much you could love someone.

With another sob, she remembered a poem she'd read in the book of poetry he'd given her. It was a sonnet and so beautiful, she'd learned it by heart, sad that the woman who'd written it was dead. Elizabeth Barrett Browning had had a difficult life too, had had to fight to be with the man she loved.

Maura murmured the first line, 'How do I love thee? Let me count the ways' but it was the later lines that seemed to echo her own feelings most:

> *I love thee with the breath,*
> *Smiles, tears, of all my life! — and if God*
> *choose,*
> *I shall but love thee better after death.*

She'd met it before, in a book at Brent Hall, and had thought the words truly beautiful, but exaggerated to make the poetry more telling, showing an idealised love. Now she knew there was nothing idealised about it. This was the outpouring of genuine love by a woman who truly loved her husband.

And it was exactly how Maura felt about Hugh.

★   ★   ★

During the next two days, Hugh watched Maura carefully, but didn't know how to approach her or talk to her privately, because she seemed to be keeping her distance from him.

What else was there to say, anyway? He couldn't change the circumstances. He couldn't ask her to help him commit bigamy.

Perhaps he should have gone ahead and married her.

Her eyes were reddened and slightly swollen. She'd obviously been weeping, not just once, but both nights.

He wished men could weep as freely as women did. He'd never felt closer to it in his whole life, but his pain was more like a heavy stone in his chest, hurting . . . hurting so much.

And yet, somehow he managed to speak to the

children and if they noticed anything different about his mood, they didn't comment. He even played his guitar for them. But he didn't find his usual comfort in the music.

He chatted to the captain and ship's crew, though what he'd said was a mystery to him afterwards.

When he spoke to Maura, their conversation sounded stilted and wrong. They were mouthing meaningless phrases, as if they were strangers, as if they weren't hurt to the core by what life and a heartless woman had done to them.

And yet, if he hadn't married Sylvie, he wouldn't have Adèle. He loved his daughter very much, and the one bright spot in his life at the moment was how well she was looking.

'We'll be arriving in Fremantle tomorrow,' the captain told them on the third evening. 'We'll anchor at the New Jetty, as long as the weather is calm. It was only completed last year, and about time too. It'll make it so much easier to unload the cargo, as well as the passengers.'

They woke next day to see Rottnest Island sitting on a calm sea, with just a low swell painting the occasional white crest on the waves close to it.

A pilot came out to guide them in, to make sure the ship reached the jetty safely, though Captain McBride said he could have done it perfectly well himself, since this was his home port.

The children were fascinated by all the activity on board and by the signal flags the ship was now flying, but most of all they were excited by the thought that they'd nearly reached journey's end. They pointed things out to one another as the town of Fremantle became clearer.

All Maura could think of was that soon she'd be separated from Hugh.

★　★　★

As the ship moved towards the port, all four children managed to corner Hugh. They stood in a circle round him, looking solemn.

'We need to talk to you, Daddy,' Adèle said. 'We've chosen Ryan to say it because he's best with words.'

Hugh watched her turn to smile at the boy standing next to her, a boy who had grown a couple of inches on the journey and who now held himself with confidence.

'Mr Beaufort, we four have decided we don't want to be separated. Auntie Maura says it's for you to decide what happens to Adèle, because you're her father, but we want you to know that we like being together.'

'They feel like part of me,' Adèle said simply. 'You know I've always wanted brothers and sisters.'

Brenna looked towards her cousin and when Ryan didn't speak, she said, 'We wondered if you'd consider marrying Auntie Maura. Then it'd be all right and we could all stay together. No one would be lonely. She's been crying at night, you know.'

'We think it's because she might lose us,' Ryan said. 'And you don't have to worry. We wouldn't mind at all if you had more children with her, which is what happens when people marry, I know. You would have enough money to make sure they didn't go hungry.'

They waited, expectant as a row of fledglings sitting on a fence waiting to be fed.

When he didn't speak, Adèle asked anxiously, 'You're not angry at us for asking you, are you, Daddy? I still love you very much.'

'No, I'm not at all angry. I'm glad you like being together, and whatever happens, I'll make sure you continue to see one another. I can't promise more than that because even when you're grown up, you can't always do what you want.'

'That's because of my mother, isn't it?' she said with a sigh. 'Because she ran away. I thought you could get a divorce when you didn't want to be married any more, then you could marry someone else.'

He was startled. 'How did you know about that?'

'I heard Miss Fenton talking about it one day to the housekeeper, saying you should do that and find another wife, a proper lady, not a foreign one.'

'Father Patrick said people who get divorced roast in hell,' Ryan said. 'A friend of Mr Kieran's got divorced and when he came to visit, the priest went up to the big house and shouted at him. He said the master shouldn't invite godless, sinful heathens into a Christian village. Mr Kieran was very angry.'

'Oh dear.' Brenna looked disappointed. 'Does

362

that mean you couldn't marry Auntie Maura, even if you wanted to? We never thought of that. It just seemed right, somehow, because you smile a lot when you're together.'

'I think that's enough for now.' Maura came out from where she'd been listening to them, so touched by their innocent concern, she'd hardly been able to breathe. 'We'll have to leave Mr Beaufort to plan his own life.'

Hugh looked at her sadly, then turned to the children. 'I promise you that whatever happens, I'll make sure Adèle and I are living close enough for you children to see one another. More than that I can't promise.'

The children went to sit together and whisper about it.

He looked at Maura. 'How much did you hear of what they said?'

'Most of it.'

'I wish Sylvie really were dead!' he exclaimed.

'Don't wish ill on someone.'

'I can't help it. She's ruined my life in all ways but one.'

She could guess what he meant. 'Adèle.'

'Yes. My daughter. It doesn't even feel as if Sylvie is Adèle's mother.'

'Your wife has ruined my life, too. And the children's. She's done a lot of harm, hasn't she?'

Maura couldn't bear to talk about it any more, so moved away, joining the children to make sure they stayed out of the sailors' way as they got the ship ready to dock. And to make sure Hugh didn't catch her on her own again.

Why did life have to be so cruel?

Once the ship had docked, Dougal beckoned to one of the lads loitering on the quay hoping for an odd job or two. He handed over two letters, one with a big X on the back in case the lad couldn't read. This one was to be taken to Mr Bram Deagan at the Bazaar, and taken first of all. The other was to be taken to his own house to ask Linney to make things ready for himself and his two guests: Mr Beaufort and his little daughter Adèle.

Then he turned back to his passengers. 'I should think Bram will come here to fetch you himself, Miss Deagan, once he receives the letter.'

'I'm looking forward to seeing him again. He was always my favourite relative.' She looked sideways at the children and smiled. 'Until I met you three.'

'It's kind of you to invite me and Adèle to stay with you, Captain McBride,' Hugh said.

'I'll enjoy the company. Besides, I have plenty of room, and my maid Linney is used to visitors. My sister used to run a guest house when I was first making my way with my own ship. Now Flora is married, but I still have Linney, who is very capable.'

Half an hour later, as the children were walking up and down the quay, laughing at the way the ground felt to be moving beneath their feet, a man came into view. A small man, dark haired, running flat out.

He stopped dead at the sight of the little group

364

and brushed away a tear before starting to walk briskly forward, his face so filled with love, it was radiant.

Maura called to the children to wait together and moved towards him. She had to speak to him before he met them, make sure he was willing to look after them.

'You've come,' he said, holding out his arms and hugging her close, though she was taller than him. 'Oh Maura, you've come to Australia and brought some of the family! It's been my dream to have them here. It made me so happy when I got your letter from Suez. It arrived before you did with the piano. Fancy you travelling with Dougal!'

She hugged him back, tears of relief in her eyes at the undoubted welcome, the sheer joy on his face.

He stepped back a little and grinned. 'Or should I call you Auntie Maura and treat you with more respect?'

'Don't you dare! You'd make me feel old.' She hugged him again for the sheer pleasure of seeing him.

'You speak with an English accent now, Maura Deagan.'

'It was better to speak like that when I was in service in England.'

His eyes went beyond her to the group of children. They were staring at him with unabashed curiosity, with Carrie standing behind them, watchful as ever. 'Whose exactly are the children, Maura? You didn't give details in your letter.'

365

'I wrote it in such a hurry, I can't even remember what I said.'

'The lad's Ryan, isn't he? But I don't recognise the girls at all. There were so many children in our family.'

She took a deep breath, had been dreading telling him what had happened. 'These three are the only ones left out of our family in Ireland.' She saw the smile fade and a horrified expression replace it.

'They're *all* dead?' His voice was barely above a whisper.

'No, no. Not all of them, though several of them are, including your mother and father. I'm sorry to be the one to tell you that.'

'Don't be. I lost any feeling for them after the way they treated my sister Ismay. Anyway, I had a letter from Kieran Largan telling me that they were dead. If my relatives are not all dead, where are the others?'

'One brother has gone to live in England. Two have gone to America and taken their families with them. That probably saved their lives. There was an outbreak of typhus in the village, you see, a bad one. Mr Kieran has done a lot to clean things up, but he can't afford to replace all the cottages, and some people just won't keep themselves clean.'

She gestured towards the children, smiling again. 'As you guessed, the lad is your youngest brother Ryan and the smaller girl is your sister Noreen.'

'What about Padraig?'

'He's dead, I'm afraid.'

366

'I've not seen Noreen since she was very small. I'd never have recognised her. Ryan looks a fine young fellow now, doesn't he?'

'He is, and so like you.'

'Is he now?' He smiled at that. 'And the other girl?'

'She's your cousin Brenna — my niece. She's Eamon's only surviving child.'

Bram looked at her in shock. '*Only* surviving child? But he had several. What happened to them?'

'A couple died earlier, and then the typhus took the rest. I'll tell you all the details later, when we're alone. The children have mostly recovered from their grief now, and I don't want to upset them again by talking of the sad details in front of them.'

He nodded. 'Yes, we'll do that. I'll need to know. You'll all come to live with my wife and me, of course.'

'Will that not be too many? The children will need supporting, but I can look for work and pay my own way.'

'You'll not need to do that, Maura. I'm bringing in more than enough to feed us all, and I have a house big enough to lodge us all in comfort, as well.' He smiled. 'Though we'll have to buy some more beds because we've only just moved into the house from a small cottage so it's not all furnished yet.'

She closed her eyes in relief.

'Were you worried I wouldn't want you?' he asked softly.

'It's a lot to ask, taking in four of us, but Mr

367

Kieran seemed to think you'd want us.'

'He was right. Now, introduce me to the children. They're looking anxious. We'll discuss the details later.' He set one hand on her shoulder and kissed her cheek. 'You are so very welcome, my dear aunt, and I thank you for bringing my brother and sister and Brenna to me.'

As he turned towards the children, he slowed to ask, 'Who's the fourth child, the one holding the man's hand? Is he her father?'

'That's Adèle Beaufort. And yes, Hugh's her father. They've come out here for her health. She's grown very close to the other children during the journey.'

'Beaufort?'

'Yes. I believe a second cousin or some such relative came out to Australia with his wife, and then he died. Hugh has agreed to search for the man's widow. She's been claiming to have borne him a child, and the family aren't sure whether to believe her or not.'

Bram sucked in his breath. 'Well, I can tell them that she did bear her husband a child, in wedlock, and both child and mother were in great distress for a while because his family wouldn't help them. I'm the one rearing the little girl now, and I'm not likely to give Louisa back to people who care so little for her that they've waited all this time to find out if she exists or needs help.'

There was a new authority to Bram, Maura thought. He spoke like a man used to dealing with the world and doing it to his own benefit, too. It already felt as if he'd taken a load off her shoulders. She'd worried about how to look after the children if he didn't want them. Now, her main concern would be to stay with them. She'd grown to love them so.

She beckoned to the three Deagans. 'Come and meet Bram and stop looking so worried.'

'I'm really happy to see you,' Bram said.

She introduced them one by one, taking care to say something positive about each child. 'I told you how much you resembled your brother, Ryan, did I not? And Bram, your brother is a fine young fellow, who has cared for your youngest sister devotedly.'

Ryan nodded to his brother, looking surprised to see a hand held out towards him. He shook it gravely but kept one hand on his little sister's shoulder the whole time. 'I'm happy to meet you again, Bram, but we all want to stay with Auntie Maura, if you don't mind.'

Before Maura could intervene after this tactless response, Bram smiled. 'And why should you be separated? I've a house big enough for us all.'

'We'll work to pay for ourselves, so that there's enough food.'

From the expression on Bram's face, he knew exactly why Ryan had said that, Maura thought.

His voice grew gentler. 'I've enough money to buy food, don't worry, lad. But I'd appreciate some help in the shop from time to time. It's never too soon to learn about business. I'm hoping, though, that you'll go to school and learn as much as you can there. In these modern times it doesn't pay to be ignorant.'

Maura could have hugged Bram for saying this and unconsciously echoing what she'd been telling Ryan. She gave him a nod and smile to show her approval and he winked at her, before bending to speak to Noreen.

'And what about you, little sister? Will you come and live with me?'

'And Auntie Maura too?'

'Yes, and your aunt. And I've a wife at home, so you'll have a grown-up sister-in-law Isabella as well and my baby son is your nephew. You're an aunt now.'

She looked at him in surprise, then chuckled at the thought of that.

Brenna stepped forward, head up, looking him straight in the eye. 'I'm Brenna, and I'm your cousin, not your sister. And *I* want to stay with Auntie Maura too. We all do. This is our friend Adèle, and we want to be with her as well.'

Maura gestured to the other two. 'Let me introduce you to Hugh Beaufort and his daughter. Hugh was very helpful when there was trouble on the P&O ship. He found us all passage on the *Bonny Mary*. I don't know what I'd have done without him. I'll tell you about that later.'

Hugh had been waiting patiently, holding his daughter's hand while Adèle watched the other children wistfully. Now he moved forward with her to shake Bram's hand.

The two men took their time about this, giving each other assessing looks as men often do. Maura watched with some amusement. She was still hurt and upset about Hugh and his wife, but she felt better for being with her nephew. At least Bram really seemed to want them.

'Do you have somewhere to stay, Mr Beaufort?' Bram asked. 'If not, I can maybe help.'

Ah, he is such a kind man, she thought. That hadn't changed at all. Bram had always been kind to anyone and everyone.

'Captain McBride has offered us accommodation,' Hugh said. 'But I hope we can call on you and of course, the children will want to see one another often. They've grown very close during the voyage.'

'That's good. You need all the friends you can get in this world.'

'Adèle is more like a cousin,' Brenna said. 'We wanted Mr Beaufort to marry Auntie Maura so that we could all live together, but he has a wife already, only she doesn't live with him.'

'Brenna, be quiet!' Maura said hastily. 'We don't talk about things like that.'

The girl looked puzzled but said no more.

Bram looked at Hugh and then Maura, but thank goodness he didn't comment. Maura could feel herself flushing and hoped he hadn't noticed it.

'Right then,' he said briskly. 'It's only a short walk to our new house. Dougal knows where it is, so he'll tell you how to find us, Mr Beaufort.'

Bram waved to his friend, who had been watching the meeting from the ship, then turned back to Hugh. 'I gather you wish to meet my ward, Louisa Beaufort. You must come and take tea with us tomorrow afternoon. But I'll warn you now — we regard Louisa as our child and we're not sending her to the other end of the world to people she doesn't know.'

'I'd not ask it of you. But they do wish to know whether they have a grandchild by their son. And if she's all right.'

Bram took a step backwards. 'Well, my wife is waiting eagerly to meet my family, so we'll say goodbye for the time being.'

Maura saw Adèle's face crumple and couldn't resist bending down to give her another hug. 'We'll see you tomorrow, darling.'

But Adèle continued to sob and Maura had to leave her with Hugh.

Sure, she felt like sobbing herself as she whispered a goodbye to him, hearing her Irish accent come back, as it did sometimes under stress.

The look he gave her was so full of love, she had to swallow hard and pretend to blow her nose before she could turn and follow Bram, who was now holding Noreen's other hand.

'It's not far,' he said gently. 'We'll look after you all. And you will see them again. Fremantle isn't a large town, only about three thousand people live here.'

But she knew it wouldn't be the same. Never the same again.

19

Bram offered Maura his arm. Though he was a couple of inches shorter than she was, she felt him to be a tower of strength. And his smile — ah, that hadn't changed at all. He had the warmest smile in the world.

'The children seem to be very good friends,' he said, after they'd walked along a couple of streets.

'Yes, very. I've grown to love Adèle, as well.'

'And you seem rather fond of her father?'

She forgot to watch where she was going and stumbled. 'How on earth did you know that?'

'The way you looked at him. And he looks at you the same way.'

She tried to change the subject. 'Goodness, it's warm today.'

'It's summer. Don't change the subject. What about Mr Beaufort?'

'I . . . can't talk about it. It's not possible between us. He has a wife, even though she left him. He might be able to get a divorce, though.'

Frowning, he patted her hand as it lay on his arm. 'Then I won't press you. But if you ever need to talk, or ask advice, I'll be happy to help you in any way I can. Just one thing: don't let his station in life stop you, or even that he has to get divorced. Seize love while you can. Look at me. I married a lady born and bred, and we're extremely happy together.'

Maura nodded, unable to talk for the lump of emotion that came into her throat at the mere thought that she'd lost Hugh completely now.

She didn't notice much of what they were passing, so was surprised when Bram stopped.

'Here we are, then, Maura.'

The house had a raw, new look to it, though the wood in one part was silvered with age. It was big, far bigger than she'd expected. 'That's a fine house, Bram.'

'Yes. We've not got the inside furnished properly yet, though, so it's not the welcome I'd like to offer you.'

He turned to the children, waiting patiently behind them. 'My Arlen's not two yet but he's a fine little fellow.'

They smiled politely.

'And then there's our Louisa, who is related to Mr Beaufort and Adèle. She's nearly five now.'

The front door opened and his face lit up as a woman came out. 'Isabella, come and meet our family.'

The way he spoke his wife's name was a caress, Maura thought. And no wonder. Isabella was beautiful, with lovely dark red hair. But it was the warm smile she gave Bram before turning to her guests that told Maura she loved her husband just as much as he loved her.

Had she looked at Hugh like that? Maura wondered. Did you give away your feelings so easily?

Isabella made a beckoning gesture. 'Come in, do, and welcome! We'll introduce ourselves properly inside, where it's cooler. We have to

374

keep the doors and windows closed here during the day to keep the heat out.'

Maura and the children followed her, and it was indeed cooler inside, thank goodness.

'This is a fine, big house. Is it really yours, Bram?' Ryan's voice echoed in the hall and stairwell, which were uncarpeted.

His brother looked round his home, smiling. 'It is, yes. And what a lucky thing I bought it just in time for your arrival.'

The children clustered together to one side, waiting, staring from one person to another.

'What a mix-up our family is!' Bram turned to his wife and introduced each person in turn, explaining how they were all related.

'What do we call you, please, ma'am?' Ryan asked her.

'Well, I'm your sister-in-law since I'm married to Bram, so how about using my name, Isabella?'

'But you're not Brenna's sister. What does *she* call you?'

'The same. We don't stand on ceremony in Australia and it'd seem strange for one of you to call me by a different name. Now, are you hungry, or do you want to come and choose your rooms first?'

Maura waited in resignation for Ryan to ask for food, but Brenna got in first.

'I'd like to see the house, please, Isabella. I've never even been inside such a big place before, except for the kitchen at Shilmara. Are we really going to live here?'

'I hope so.' Isabella gave them another of her glorious smiles. 'I'm so glad you came. Bram's

375

been longing for his family to join us here. How about Sally and I get some food ready while Bram shows you round? I think Arlen's still asleep.' She put a hand on Louisa's shoulder. 'Will you help me to set the table, darling?'

The child nodded, seeming shy, so Maura didn't try to talk to her. Let her get used to them all first.

As they were shown round, she could hear the pride in Bram's voice, but there was something else as well. Was it anxiety? Why would that be? Her immediate thought was to wonder if he'd over-extended himself and they were the final straw that broke the camel's back? His money was recently earned, after all, and this was a big house, which had been completely transformed, according to what he'd told them. That must have cost a lot.

She didn't ask him about that, of course she didn't.

When they got to the spare bedrooms, there was nothing but bare boards, with no furniture at all.

He sighed at the empty rooms. 'I'm sorry it's such a poor welcome. I'll get some mattresses in before night and we'll find you some bedsteads to put them on soon, if you don't mind sleeping on the floor for a day or two.'

He hesitated, looking round. 'I'm wondering if you'd rather be up in the attics. They're proper bedrooms, mind, except they have dormer windows, but it'll mean you're all sleeping next to one another.'

'That sounds like an excellent idea.' Maura

followed him up another flight of stairs. 'I love the smell of newly sawn wood up here.'

'So do I,' Bram confessed. 'The whole house smells clean and fresh now. Here you are.'

'We'll be more than comfortable here,' Maura said. 'Thank you, Bram.'

'We used to sleep on strawbags in the roof space when we lived at home,' Ryan said. 'They didn't smell nice after the first few weeks. This smells lovely.'

'I remember those. Scratchy, they were, as well as lumpy. I won't be asking you to do that here. You'll be getting proper mattresses and bedding. Oh, excuse me!'

There was a knock on the front door and he went bounding down the stairs to answer it.

When she looked out of the window, Maura saw a couple of lads with pushcarts full of their luggage.

Bram brought them inside and showed them where to take each trunk and bag. Then he went outside with them, talking vigorously, to much nodding, dismissing them with an easy word and a coin slipped into their hands.

'So,' he said when he rejoined the group. 'They'll go and fetch us some mattresses. My name's good enough to get them here today, if there are any to be had.' He frowned. 'Maybe we should put you downstairs after all. It sounds bad to be housing your relatives in the attics.'

'Bram, we'll be fine up here,' Maura said, and the children nodded. Who wouldn't be fine with a decent-sized room and a window that looked out onto the street? But with the way sounds echoed through rooms with bare boards, she mustn't allow herself to weep at night or the children might hear her.

Anyway, she was done with weeping now. Had to get on with her life without Hugh.

'Are you all right, Maura?'

She came out of her reverie to find Bram looking at her in concern. 'What? Oh, yes. Just thinking.'

He patted her shoulder gently, as if he could guess she was thinking about something that made her feel unhappy. 'Let's go down and have something to eat and drink.'

Ryan beamed at his big brother. 'Yes, let's. I get very hungry. Auntie Maura says I have hollow legs.'

'So did I at your age. You'll be growing fast.'

Maura lingered for a moment in her bedroom as the others clattered down the wooden stairs. The room could be made pretty. But she'd rather sleep in a tiny cabin on a ship and spend her days at least with the man she loved — even if they couldn't have their nights together.

Oh, she was being silly again. What choice did she have?

What choice did Hugh have, either?

She walked slowly down the stairs, looking forward to getting to know her niece-in-law, Isabella, who seemed a friendly woman, as you'd expect from anyone Bram married. And Isabella seemed only a couple of years younger than herself.

She went to bed early, claiming tiredness, but in reality, she just wanted to be alone.

As she lay there, she wished again that Hugh had pretended to be a widower and had simply gone ahead and married her, legally or not. It surprised her how much she wished it.

*　　*　　*

Adèle held her father's hand tightly all the way to Captain McBride's house. When she was shown a small bedroom to herself, her lips quivered at the thought of being on her own again.

Carrie noticed, however.

'Do you want me to sleep with you?' she whispered.

Adèle nodded.

'Sir, I think Miss Adèle will be happier with company at night,' Carrie said.

'Yes, of course. Do what you think best. There are two beds in here, anyway, so it's no trouble to our host.'

The beds were comfortable and there was a pleasant sitting room. Carrie suggested Adèle eat in the kitchen with her and Linney, because the child was already dropping with weariness.

Hugh was grateful for some time to himself before Captain McBride joined him for the evening meal.

But though he felt as exhausted as his daughter, Hugh had trouble getting to sleep, then woke a couple of times during the night. Each time he wondered where he was, then remembered with a sigh of regret.

It felt wrong to be away from Maura. Wrong to

be away from the other children, too. He missed Ryan's sharp comments, Brenna's impulsive remarks and Noreen's shyly whispered confidences.

Damn Sylvie. She'd taken all hope of happiness away from him.

⋆   ⋆   ⋆

In the morning, Maura got up early. She listened but there were no sounds coming from the children's rooms.

There was a bowl and jug of cold water in her bedroom, not a matching set and standing on the floor. She didn't go in search of hot water, because it was quite warm enough, even at this early hour, to wash in cold. It still seemed strange to have summer at this time of year.

When she went down, she followed the sound of voices to the rear of the house.

'I'm making a list of what we need,' Isabella was saying. 'We don't want them to be uncomfortable, but we must manage as cheaply as we can, just till we recover from the cost of this house . . . and that investment.'

Maura stopped in the hall, then turned and tiptoed back up the stairs. Her guess was right, then. They'd arrived at a time when Bram was short of spare money.

Turning, she walked down the last few stairs again, humming to make her presence felt.

In the kitchen she found Bram and Isabella sharing a pot of tea.

He smiled and gestured towards it. 'Would

you like a cup to start the day, Maura?'

'I'd love one.'

Isabella studied her shrewdly. 'You look as if you slept badly. Were you not comfortable?'

'The mattress was fine. It was just me. You know how it is in a strange place. And it seemed strange not to have the sounds of the ship and water.'

'How are the children?'

'Still asleep. I peeped into their rooms. I think most children can sleep anywhere.'

She waited till she had a cup of tea before her and had taken a sip. 'Mmm. That's good.' Then she said firmly, 'Look, I don't want to be a nuisance or an expense to you, so I intend to find work. If you'll let me live here, I can pay my way.'

Bram looked at her, frowning, then said, 'Ah! You overheard us talking just now, didn't you?'

She nodded, surprised at how quickly he'd realised what she was doing. 'I didn't mean to eavesdrop. Sorry.'

'It's only a temporary thing, being short of money,' he said. 'Give me a few weeks and things will be just fine again, especially if Dougal has some goods for me in his cargo. So you've no need to go looking for work.'

'I've every need. I'm not used to sitting around like a lady. Um, ought we to go somewhere else to speak about this? Won't your servants be up soon? You don't want them hearing about your . . . difficulties.'

'Servants!' Bram's laugh wasn't one of amusement. 'That's another point of issue

381

between Isabella and myself. We're expecting another child and she's trying to work all the hours God sends, in the shop and then in the house, too. Our only live-in servant is Sally, though we have a scrubbing woman three times a week.'

Maura stared at him in delight. 'Then that's it. Let me take charge of the house, Bram. You won't need to pay me any wages. I was an Assistant Housekeeper, and there isn't a job in a house that I don't understand. Nor am I afraid to get my hands dirty.'

He looked at her indignantly. 'I'm not bringing my family here to scrub my floors.'

'Better I scrub your floors than I scrub them for a stranger. Besides, you said you already had a scrubbing woman.'

'And we send our clothes out to a washerwoman, so she won't have that to do,' Isabella said thoughtfully. 'I think it's a good idea, and I thank you for suggesting it, Maura.'

'There you are,' Maura said. 'We women have settled it.'

Bram was still shaking his head.

'Please let me do it. I'll go mad if I have nothing to occupy myself with. And the children can help me till we find them a school. They know nothing about how to run a proper house. You know what the living conditions were for our families, Bram. I want to teach them so much about how to live decently.'

'I do remember what it was like, yes. Dirt floors and hens wandering in and out. No underclothes and not even spare clothes to wash,

382

thanks to my father's drinking. Oh, I know all right. But still . . . '

Maura put her cup down. 'If you don't let me help out, I'll find a job elsewhere.'

'So thank her and accept.' Isabella took her husband's hand and gave it a little squeeze. 'You can't do everything for everybody, Bram. People like to help themselves.'

'Oh, very well! As for the children, well, let's give them a few weeks to settle in before we find them a school. Things are very different here. I remember how strange it all seemed when I first came here. Conn Largan was wonderful to me and so was Ronan Maguire.'

'What made you decide to become a shopkeeper, Bram?'

'Talking to other passengers on the ship. I'd never met people like them before. And talking to Conn and Ronan man to man, instead of like a servant who wasn't allowed to speak his thoughts and ask questions. But it was Conn who gave me my start. He lives in the country but he bought some land in Fremantle and invested in my dreams, trusting me to make money for him . . . which I have. I'll tell you the whole tale another time.'

'We can let Ryan help out in the Bazaar sometimes,' Isabella suggested. 'He'll learn a lot. We both enjoy working there.'

'If he does that, Brenna will want to help, too. She's determined to do everything he does.'

'And why not? She can help me with the silks, if she's interested. We bring them in from Singapore. We import a lot of goods from there.

We're traders as well as shopkeepers.'

'And Isabella does the accounts for me,' Bram added. 'She's better at figures than I am, though I'm not too bad.'

'But he's much better at selling to people. They enjoy him serving them. He has a knack for finding them something they'll love. That brings them back time after time, which is important.'

Maura was fascinated by it all. 'Oh! I just remembered . . . Hugh bought some trading goods to sell here. Perhaps you can help him dispose of them?'

'I can if he'll wait for payment,' Bram sighed. 'Ready cash isn't easy to come by here in the Swan River Colony. They do a lot of the selling on credit. Some of the bigger merchants in Fremantle take wool from the pastoralists and give credit against that. I don't. I've no means of dealing with wool, and I can't compete with merchants who're loaded with money and connections overseas. I'm just a little fish in their pond.'

'Don't let him belittle himself,' Isabella said. 'He's more than a little fish.'

Bram grinned. 'Medium fish, then.' His smile faded. 'It's just, there have been a lot of expenses lately. This house for one. And I bought into an ice works, only it's not profitable yet and it's cost me more than I expected.'

'An ice works?' Maura gaped at him.

Isabella pushed the teapot across the table. 'We'll tell you all the details later. Bram's always seeing opportunities. Forget all that and have

384

another cup to celebrate your new job, Maura. You can be my housekeeper. You can definitely be in charge of food. I won't miss worrying about that. I buy my bread from the baker's, but perhaps you'll know how many loaves to order from now on. I gather Ryan is a hearty eater.'

'The children all are.'

'Making up for lost time,' Bram said sadly. 'If only I could have brought the others out here before the typhus took them.'

Isabella rolled her eyes. 'He wants to help everyone in the world, this man does.'

'He was always kind, even as a boy.' Maura heard the sound of voices upstairs and stood up. 'Excuse me. I'll just go and check on the children.'

She went up to the attics to find the three of them scrambling to get dressed. 'Stop that at once! Things haven't changed since the ship. You need to have a proper wash before you come down. I'll not be feeding you till you're clean.'

When she went back into the kitchen, Bram was smiling.

'You're a born mother, Maura.'

But that upset her, because she'd never be a mother now. She took a gulp of tea and pretended to choke. She didn't think she'd fooled them, but they said nothing, thank goodness.

★   ★   ★

Hugh came awake to find Adèle standing at the foot of his bed. He fumbled for his pocket watch,

385

which he always set on the bedside table at night. 'Six o'clock. Go back to bed.'

'I can't. I've no one to talk to. Carrie won't be awake for ages.' Adèle came to perch on the edge of the bed near him.

He took her hand. 'We spoke about that last night. You'll still see the others sometimes. Why, we've been invited round to tea at Mr Deagan's house this very afternoon.'

'That's a long time to wait. Me and Brenna usually lie and talk in the morning.' Tears began to fall. 'I want to be back with them.'

'Oh, darling.' He pulled her into the bed with him. 'Lie and chat to me instead.'

'I love you, Daddy, but it isn't the same. Why can't you marry Auntie Maura and let us all live together?'

'It's complicated.'

'You always say that.'

'Because it's true. There are things you won't understand till you grow up yourself, things between men and women.'

'I think you love her.'

'I do.'

'Well, then — '

'That's the last word I'm going to say about it. It's private, darling. Between me and Maura.'

She pulled away and rolled out of bed, yelling, 'You don't *want* to make things right!' as she ran out of his bedroom.

She was wrong. He wanted nothing more.

★ ★ ★

After breakfast, Bram insisted on taking them to see his Bazaar before they did anything else.

'But the house — ' Maura began.

'The house can wait. We have some second-hand goods in the store. We take them on consignment usually, no sale, no payment to the owner. But we also have a few pieces we've bought outright. You could look through them and see if any are suitable for your rooms.'

'And then you won't get the money for selling them.'

'A few shillings won't make that much difference, Maura darlin'.'

'Every penny counts when you're short. I learned that the hard way when I was married.'

'Vincent Phelan was a stupid brute and they shouldn't have forced you to marry him.'

'It was a long time ago. After he died, and I went to England I got a job at Brent Hall. They treated their staff well and I was happy to stay on there. I was Assistant Housekeeper when I left, very grand I was, with my own bedroom and eating at the top table in the servants' hall.'

'You always were a clever woman.'

★ ★ ★

The two older children were dying to get out and explore. But Noreen decided she wanted to stay with Louisa, who was another quiet child. The two had quickly made friends.

It relieved Maura's worries about Noreen being so quiet to see the two little girls whispering to one another as they played with their dolls.

When they got to the foot of the slope on which the Bazaar stood, the three newcomers stopped dead.

'Bram, it's huge!'

'It is, isn't it?' He beamed at his big sign saying *Deagan's Bazaar*. 'It used to be a series of sheds, but we put them together and smartened them up. Now you'd never know they used to be sheds.'

'Don't touch anything!' she warned the children before they went inside.

'We know that.'

'We're not babies, you know.'

Bram led them through, showing them the various sorts of goods he brought in from Singapore. He introduced them to a couple of people who rented space in the Bazaar to sell their own things. At the back was the second-hand goods section, with another door leading to the outside from it.

That area too was bigger than Maura had expected.

'It's good quality stuff,' she said after wandering round. 'No rubbish here.'

'There are other shops that sell cheap stuff. We find there's a market for quality second-hand pieces of furniture, or curtains and rugs. Things come and go. So do people. A lot leave the colony for Sydney or Melbourne. We never know what will be offered to us next. Anyway, have a look round. You all need furniture for your bedrooms, so take anything that catches your fancy. Oh, and there are some books there too. You always did like reading.'

388

'Are you sure?'

He gave her a sudden hug. 'Of course I'm sure. And if you don't choose enough to furnish your rooms properly, I'll bring more home myself.' He pulled out his silver pocket watch. 'Isabella will be along to join us once the morning sickness has passed.'

Maura kept the children with her as she examined the goods. Ryan was interested in everything about the store, Brenna less so, but they made her proud of how well-behaved they were, not making a nuisance of themselves in any way.

She found a couple of bed frames, rather dusty, but when she wet one fingertip and rubbed it across the wood, she could see that they'd polish up nicely. There were several chests of drawers, so she chose one for each of them. They'd be able to put their washing bowls and jugs on the top. No need for separate wash stands.

'There are some nice rugs,' Brenna said wistfully.

Maura looked over her shoulder to make sure her nephew wasn't near. 'We don't want to be making too much expense for Bram. If he hasn't got these to sell to other people, he's losing money because of us.'

'Oh. I didn't think of that.'

Isabella came into the shop half an hour later. She was clearly feeling better now because she'd regained the colour in her cheeks. She showed Maura some of her silks. Ryan wasn't interested but Brenna stood beside them, looking in wonderment at the beautiful, glowing colours.

Isabella had put on white cotton gloves to handle them. 'Please don't touch them without gloves, Brenna. We don't want threads pulling or the fabric marking. These are quite expensive silks. One day, I'm going to have my own silk shop in Fremantle.'

'Where do you get them from?' Brenna asked.

'My friend Xiu Mei sends the dress lengths to me from Singapore. She has such an eye for beautiful materials.' Isabella explained how she'd lived with the Chinese family for two years there after her mother died, till she'd met and married Bram. 'Sometimes we eat food Chinese style. It's delicious.'

Afterwards, Maura and the children walked home, leaving Bram and his wife to go about their business.

But when the goods she'd chosen were delivered to the house later that day, she found they included rugs and curtains, as well as four chairs, one for each bedroom. They weren't a matching set but they were well made, the type of chairs usually reserved for the gentry.

How kind that was! She vowed that she'd work her fingers to the bone, if necessary. Bram and Isabella weren't going to regret taking her in.

★ ★ ★

Isabella came home from the Bazaar in time to help entertain Hugh and Adèle to tea, by which time Maura had made a difference to the kitchen, enlisting Sally and the children's help in

390

her first efforts to teach them how to run a decent home.

Bram joined them just before their guests were due to arrive. 'I thought I'd steal an hour to be with you all. It's a quiet day.'

When Adèle entered the house with her father, the four children rushed to greet one another, Noreen dragging Louisa with her to join the group. Maura was touched by their reunion and was so glad to see Adèle, she found tears welling in her eyes. She was already missing her as well as Hugh.

She glanced across at him and tried to smile, but failed. She tried to think of something casual to say, but failed to find even one word.

He was looking sad. 'I'm happy to see you safe with your family, Maura.'

'I'm . . . glad to be here.'

Their conversation was jerky and trite, but underneath it, she seemed to feel the questions they couldn't ask publicly.

How are you managing?

Not well. And you?

Missing you dreadfully.

She wanted to weep for the waste of their love, the waste of their lives.

'Have you found a house for yourself yet?' Bram asked Hugh.

'It's a bit early, but Linney thinks she knows of one we can rent for a year while the family goes to England, by which time we should have more idea of what we want to do. So I told her to go ahead and arrange it, if she could. We're going to see it tomorrow morning.'

'Maura says you've brought some trade goods,' Bram said. 'I'd be happy to talk to you about them later.'

But Hugh was looking across the room like a man who'd seen a ghost. 'That's Louisa, isn't it?'

Isabella spoke quietly. 'Yes. She's rather shy with strangers, though it's lovely to see her making friends with Noreen. She saw some dreadful things, including her father being stabbed to death in front of her, and though she doesn't understand it fully — at least, I think she doesn't — she still gets nightmares about it and wakes sobbing and screaming.'

The two youngest girls were playing on a rug on the floor, while Brenna and Adèle sat nearby, laughing, their eyes lit up and their hands gesticulating. Ryan was standing next to them, joining in but keeping an eye on Noreen.

Hugh was already certain Louisa was Parker Beaufort's daughter, because you couldn't mistake the Beaufort hair. Rippling waves of a red-gold colour, the same as his and his daughter's. She had a look of the family, too, and was tall for her age, another Beaufort trait. No, he didn't have any doubts about who'd fathered her.

'She resembles my Adèle,' he said to his hostess.

Isabella nodded. 'I noticed that. Was Parker a close relative of yours?'

'No, not close. Some sort of second cousin, I think.'

'I hope you're not going to try to take Louisa away from us. We feel she's our daughter now.'

'Is her mother dead, then?'

'No.' Isabella moved away from the children and he followed her.

She began fiddling with some crockery on the side table, speaking in a much lower voice now. 'My cousin Alice is . . . a weak-willed woman. She has to have a man to live with and her new husband isn't interested in Louisa, only in Alice bearing him children, sons preferably. He pays us a yearly sum for her keep and we put it in a savings bank for when Louisa is grown up, so that she'll have a little money behind her, at least.'

'I'm not here to take her away from you, though if she had nowhere to go, I'd have stepped in. I've only been asked to report on whether she's Parker's daughter or not. I'll write to my family at once and tell them she is, no doubt about it, but that you love her dearly. They can decide whether to get in contact with you or not. I'm hoping they'll at least send her a small inheritance — he was their son, after all — which will give you something else to save for her future.'

Isabella let out her breath in a whoosh of relief.

'She's lucky to have found you.'

'We're lucky to have her. She's a clever little thing, for all she's so quiet.'

'I'd like to tell her we're related, if you don't mind, then see her regularly so that she and Adèle get to know one another. It's always good to have family.'

'Her mother is my only remaining close family,

but we're not close these days.' Isabella sighed, then shook her head as if to banish sadness. 'It's a good thing Bram has so many relatives, even if they are scattered round the world.'

'He loves people, doesn't he?'

'Yes. Do you think you'll be staying in the colony?'

'Probably. Adèle's health is so much better near the sea that I can't take her back to England, though I'll miss my home.'

'Well, you'll no doubt make new friends and come to consider the Swan River Colony your home as the years pass. I have done, already. No doubt you'll be keeping in contact with Maura and the children, so your daughter will grow up knowing Louisa.'

'Yes. Of course.'

He'd agonised over whether to stay away from Maura or not, even wondered if he should move to one of the other colonies. But he couldn't separate the children now. They'd been so ecstatic to see one another today — and that after only one day apart.

Adèle had been sulky over breakfast, because he wouldn't agree to bring her here again in the morning.

What were he and Maura going to do about the situation? Would they get used to it?

Would she marry someone else? He couldn't bear the thought of that.

He didn't think he'd ever get used to living a separate life from the woman he loved so dearly. She felt like half of him, somehow. He wasn't complete without her.

20

The following day Maura started assessing the house and working out what was needed to keep it running smoothly and efficiently. A lavish amount of money wasn't necessary. There had been a lot of waste at Brent Hall, to 'keep up standards'. She could manage very economically, she was sure.

She'd already found that Isabella stayed home until her morning sickness had passed, then went to the Bazaar to sell her beautiful silks. So she was able to talk to her nephew's wife about what was important to them about their home and what wasn't.

Maura had liked the cheerful young maid on sight and Sally did a huge amount of housework, as well as looking after Louisa and the son and heir. But there would be far more work now.

Arlen was a proper Deagan, she thought, pausing to give the little boy a cuddle. He had the dark hair and birdlike alertness that characterised his father and his young Uncle Ryan.

She was amused by the way Ryan enjoyed being an uncle, mentioning it as often as he could.

'Come to your uncle, Arlen.'

'Let your uncle fix that, Arlen.'

The scrubbing woman, Joan, was older than Maura, at least she looked older, and had a careworn air, as if life had treated her harshly. She came three days a week and they always provided her with a midday meal.

'I don't think she gets much to eat at home,' Isabella confided. 'Her husband's a brute and her sons are bigger than her now.'

With extra people in the house, they would need Joan's services more often, Maura decided.

Isabella frowned when asked if this was possible, then sighed and said yes, of course they'd need extra help.

Were they so short of money, then, that a few shillings mattered? Maura wondered.

When offered regular work six days a week, Joan beamed at them both. 'That'll save me looking for other jobs, Miss Deagan. And the meal I get here is a godsend. It's the only time I get to eat in peace, with my lot at home.'

Maura spoke to the children that evening as they were getting ready for bed. 'You'll have to help keep your own rooms clean — yes, even you, Ryan — because we don't want to cost Bram more money than we have to.'

Of course Ryan frowned and protested. 'But he's rich.'

'He's not rich, just comfortably off, but it's still not right to expect other people to pay for looking after you, even if they are relatives. So you'll all be learning to keep yourselves and your rooms clean.'

Ryan's scowl grew darker. 'That's girls' work. Da said a man shouldn't have to lift a finger in the house, and he never did.'

'It isn't girls' work in any house I'm living in,

thank you very much. Just think about this: your mother might have been in better health if she'd had more help, poor woman. She might even have survived the typhus.'

There was silence for a few moments, then, 'It's still girls' work.'

'Isabella goes to work in the Bazaar. Is that men's work? Should she stay home and mop floors instead?'

Ryan opened his mouth, looked at her expression and shut it again.

*   *   *

Over breakfast Adèle asked, 'What time are we going to see the children today, Daddy?'

Hugh put his fork down. 'We aren't going to see them today, darling. We're going to look at the house I told you about, to see if we'd like to live there for a year or so.'

'Why just for a year? We're not going back to England after that, are we?' She looked at him in dismay. 'Please don't make me go back. I can't breathe properly sometimes there and I get frightened.'

'I know, and I won't take you back. But the people who own the house are going to visit their family in England and would like to find someone to look after it while they're away. If we live there, we can look round for a place of our own and make sure we get somewhere that truly suits us.'

'Couldn't we just stay here? Carrie and I like Linney.'

'No, we can't. This is Captain McBride's house and we're only visitors here. We need a place of our own. Besides, we can't leave the piano in its packing case at Bram's. The wood needs to breathe and be cared for, and the piano needs to be tuned and played if it's to keep its tone. I'd like to teach you to play it, too.'

'Yes. It'd be nice to play tunes. But not just scales and exercises like Miss Fenton used to make me do.' She changed her tone of voice, pleading now. 'I still need to see Brenna every day, Daddy. We're best friends.'

'I'm sorry, darling. I'm afraid you won't be able to see her that often.'

Adèle surprised him by bursting into tears and slamming her glass down so hard that milk splashed out of it all over the table. When he scolded her, she ran out of the room, sobbing.

He was glad Dougal had eaten breakfast earlier and gone out to the ship. He'd have hated to spoil his kind host's meal with a scene like this one. He pushed the rest of his food away, sighing.

* * *

When it was time to go and see the house, he went to find Adèle, who was sitting with Carrie in the bedroom, kicking her heels against the chair legs.

'Time to go out now.' He tried to sound cheerful, but it was hard with his daughter still scowling at him.

'I don't want to see your horrid old house. I want to see my friends.'

398

Carrie gave her a little shake. 'What did I tell you, Miss Adèle?'

'I don't care.'

Hugh turned to the nursemaid. 'I hope you'll come with us too, Carrie. I'll need your opinion about the house as well.'

'I'm happy to come, sir. Leave me to get Miss Adèle ready.'

His daughter was scowling impartially at them both. He couldn't think how to bring her round. 'I'll wait for you in the hall.'

They came down to join him seven minutes later, but he noticed that Carrie had a firm hold of Adèle's arm. The child was still scowling and sulking as they walked across town.

The Martins' house was adequate, smaller than Hugh was used to, not nearly as big as Dougal's home. But it seemed clean and well furnished.

'Do you have any maids who'd like to work for us?' Hugh asked Mrs Martin.

'Well, there is Pippie. We're used to her now, and she's a hard worker, but . . . ' She leaned forward to whisper, 'She doesn't know her place and will say anything to anyone.'

'It'd make things easier if she continued to work here, don't you think?'

'Well, yes.' She leaned forward again. 'Her name's Philippa, but she won't answer to anything but Pippie.'

The maid appeared in the doorway, had obviously been eavesdropping. 'If I'm staying on, I'll need to show Carrie where she's to sleep. I'm not sharing a bedroom with anyone.'

'Why don't you show her round now?' Hugh asked. 'I'm sure Adèle will wait for you both in the kitchen.'

The two maids went off with the little girl trailing behind them and Hugh turned to Mrs Martin. 'My daughter's missing her playmates from the ship. I'm sorry she's so sulky.'

'It's a big change for her, coming to Australia,' she said comfortably.

'And you won't mind my bringing my piano here?'

'Bless you, no. We aren't musical, so we haven't got one, but you can move things round and fit it in where you like.'

They discussed the changeover date and how much rent he should pay them. Mrs Martin shared information with a casual openness he hadn't often found in England. He liked that.

By the time everything was settled, the two maids had returned.

Carrie looked round the room. 'Isn't Miss Adèle with you, sir?'

'I thought she was with you. I haven't seen her since you left us.'

'Oh dear! She isn't in the kitchen, either.'

'Perhaps she's out on the back veranda,' Mrs Martin suggested. 'It's cooler there.'

'I'll go and look,' Pippie said.

'I'll come too.' Hugh followed her out. But there was no sign of Adèle on the veranda or anywhere near the kitchen.

'I'll check the inside of the house,' Mrs Martin said. 'She's probably hiding, having a bit of fun, as children do.'

'I don't think so, ma'am. She was in such a bad mood today. I'll go and look round again.' Carrie hurried out to the back garden with Pippie close behind her.

Adèle wasn't anywhere in the house or garden.

'This isn't like her.' Hugh was beginning to feel worried.

'You don't suppose . . . ' Carrie stopped and looked at him.

'I don't suppose what?'

'That she's gone to find the other children.'

'On her own?'

'She was very upset, sir. She thinks of them as brother and sisters, not just friends. And I think they feel the same way about her. Even Ryan does, for all he pretends to be scornful of girls and more grown up than the others.'

Hugh turned to their hostess. 'I'll have to go and look for her. If she comes back here, can you please keep her and send a message to Captain McBride's house?'

'Of course I will.'

'Carrie, would you go and wait there, in case she turns up?'

'I'd rather go out and look for her, sir.'

'Someone needs to be there, just in case. Linney was going out shopping this morning, I heard her say so. Anyway, you don't know your way round the town.'

'Very well, sir. And won't I give Adèle what for once we find her! She's never been this naughty before.'

Hugh set off with Pippie to show him the way to Mr Deagan's house. She seemed to know where everyone lived. They walked slowly, stopping to stare down each side street. He kept scanning the street ahead and sometimes turned to stare behind him, desperate to catch sight of his daughter.

But there was no sign of her.

★ ★ ★

Adèle knew it was wrong to go out on her own. But she didn't want to sit in a kitchen and wait for people when she could be with her friends. She wasn't going to let them be separated. This would show her father she meant what she said.

She knew which direction the Deagans' house was, because she'd recognised a street they passed as they walked to the Martins. That was the way they'd taken yesterday, she was sure.

She hurried back the way they'd come, eager to see her friends again.

But though the street looked similar at first, it led her to some smaller houses in an area that didn't smell very nice.

She stopped, disappointed, but there was nothing to do except turn and go back the way she'd come. She soon realised she'd taken another wrong turn and stopped again. How was she to find the Deagans' house?

Near to tears, she stopped walking to seek a passerby's help.

'Excuse me, ma'am, but could you please tell me the way to the Deagans' house? It's near the High Street.' The woman looked at her for so long, she began to feel uneasy.

'Are you lost, dear?'

'Yes. We've only just arrived from England.'

'And you're staying with the Deagans?'

'Yes. They're relatives of mine.' It didn't feel like a lie, not really.

'Well, I'm happy to set you on your way, but we'll just have to stop at my house first to get my shopping bag. This way.'

Adèle followed her, feeling relieved.

They turned into a little side alley, so narrow a cart couldn't have gone down it.

'I live at the back here, all on my own.' The woman opened a door. 'Sorry about the mess. I haven't been well. Do come in.'

'I can wait outside.'

'No, come in.' She took hold of the girl's arm and dragged her inside.

Feeling suddenly afraid, Adèle began to struggle and cry out, but the woman was stronger than she was. However hard she fought she couldn't stop her from tying her arms to a chair and stuffing a dirty handkerchief in her mouth to stop her calling out for help.

Feeling terrified and short of breath, Adèle waited, sure something dreadful was going to happen to her.

★ ★ ★

By the time he and Pippie arrived at Bram's house, Hugh was feeling so anxious he hammered on the door, hoping desperately that his daughter would be there.

It was Maura who opened it.

403

'Is Adèle here?'

'No. We've not seen her today.'

'She's run away.'

'Oh, no. Come in.'

He looked up and down the street, then did as she asked. 'This is Pippie, Mrs Martin's maid. She's helping me search for Adèle.'

Ryan peered out of the kitchen door, with the others standing behind him. 'Isn't Adèle with you, sir?'

When Hugh explained again, they all looked at him in dismay.

'She'll have got lost,' Maura said in a calm voice. 'It's easy to do that in a strange town.'

'The trouble is, I don't know the town well enough to search for her.'

'I think we should send a message to Bram.'

'I remember the way to the Bazaar,' Ryan said at once. 'I can take Mr Beaufort there to see Bram.'

'Are you certain you know how to get there?'

'Yes. It's only two streets away.'

'I'll take a walk round the town centre,' Pippie said. 'I'll spread the word in all the shops that we have a little girl lost.'

'Can you wait here, in case she turns up?' Hugh asked Maura.

'Yes, I can — ' she began but he'd already set off, striding along the street beside Ryan, both of them looking round as they walked.

She had a bad feeling about this. Adèle was normally very biddable, but the bond between the children had grown very strong.

'I don't want Adèle to be lost,' Brenna said, tears in her eyes.

'They'll soon find her.' Maura gave the child a hug and tried to keep her occupied as they waited.

She kept looking at the clock, but each time only a few minutes had passed. Time seemed to pass very slowly.

Surely Adèle would be all right? Children were lost and found again all the time.

★ ★ ★

Hugh and Ryan got to the Bazaar without seeing a sign of the little girl.

Bram and Isabella were upset to hear that Adèle was missing and he said at once that he'd come out and help search for her.

'I can manage here,' Isabella said at once. 'I'm sure you'll find her soon.'

They spent the next hour combing the town centre, returning to the shop and Bram's house to check Adèle hadn't been found.

But there was no sign of the little girl anywhere.

They widened their search, going further afield, asking everyone they met if they'd seen a little girl with red-gold hair wearing a blue dress. But no one had.

At one stage they met Pippie, standing with her hands on her hips, staring round. As they approached her, she said, 'I've left word in all the shops. They'll ask all their customers. Someone is bound to have seen her. Are you coming back to the Martins' house, sir?'

'No. I'll go back to Captain McBride's house,

where we're staying, just to check that she's not returned.'

'I'll come with you.'

But there was still no sign of Adèle and by now Hugh was feeling frantic with anxiety.

'We'll try my house next,' Bram said, once they had searched everywhere he could think of. 'She's more likely to have gone there to find the other children.'

Maura opened the door to them before they had time to knock. 'You've not found her?'

'No. We've left word everywhere that a little girl is missing, but no one seems to have even seen her.'

'Oh, Hugh.' He was in such anguish that without thinking what it looked like, she put her arms round him. 'We'll find her. Somehow we will find her.'

He held her close for a moment or two, resting his head against her dark, soft hair. 'I pray you're right.'

When she pulled away, they found themselves alone in the hall. They could hear Bram speaking to Carrie and the children in the kitchen.

'Bram can tell how we feel about one another,' she said with a wry smile.

'I can't pretend I don't care for you.'

'No. I can't, either. Once we've found her, we'll have to talk about ourselves.' She bit back more words. This wasn't the time to tell him what she'd been thinking, not with that poor child missing.

Adèle wouldn't be missing if their group had stayed together, Maura was sure of that. But they'd have been able to do that only if she and Hugh could marry.

All the children were unhappy about their separation.

But not as unhappy as she was about losing Hugh.

21

Rory Flynn was doing very nicely in Australia, he thought, as he loaded some food into his little cart. He wasn't doing as nicely as that damned Bram Deagan, but better than he'd ever have expected to back in Ireland. He had a way with cows that few could match, could bring them into plumper, better health.

He'd rented a small piece of land south of Fremantle, one with a good well and plenty of shade. He now had a couple of cows of his own in milk and was fattening others for the farmers who'd raised them. Most of the so-called gentlemen farmers didn't know nearly as much as he did about looking after animals, and they didn't have very skilled men working for them.

He and Bram had grown up in the same village, but mostly they avoided one another, nodding briefly as they passed in the street. They noticed one another. Oh yes, they did.

Rory should have been the one to marry Bram's sister Ismay and that still made him feel angry. She'd been promised to him by her father. Ever since he was a lad, he'd wanted her. Only she'd fled to join her brother in Australia and Bram had helped her marry a damned Englishman instead.

The trouble was, no other woman had ever tempted Rory. Well, not to marriage, anyway. Only now he was needing a wife, needing one badly to look after him and his house. But how did you find one in a land where there were ten men to every woman?

He might have to write back to his cousins in Shilmara asking them to send him out a wife. Wouldn't he look a fool then, and him telling them all — when he left to follow Ismay Deagan to Australia — that he'd find her and put things right between them.

He heard about the missing child when he took the day's milk to the two shops he supplied. 'Whose child is she?' He was touched by the thought of a little girl lost and crying for her mammy. He'd lost a little sister once to illness. Mary had been such a pretty child.

'I'm not sure,' the shopkeeper told him. 'Some say she's a Deagan.' He grinned. 'And I thought how glad you'd be that he'd got something to upset him.'

Rory had a think about that, then shook his head. 'No. I'd like to hear of Deagan in trouble, sure enough, but not about a child getting lost. Any child. I've got no quarrel with a child, even if she is from that damned family.'

He got himself something to eat then went for his usual glass of beer afterwards. They were talking about the missing child in the boozer as well.

'It can't be Deagan's daughter because he hasn't got one,' he said, as they seemed to know more about it all.

'No, not his,' an old fellow told him. 'It's the daughter of a new arrival, who's a friend of the family. Tall, lanky fellow with yellow hair. Only eight, she is.'

Rory was about to finish his drink and leave when he saw the woman standing near the door, studying the drinkers. He knew her. Madge. Used to run a brothel, but it'd been closed down by Deagan's brother-in-law. Ismay's husband Adam had inherited it and been too moral to profit from that trade. Nev, Madge's protector, had tried to kill Bram and been put in prison. Looked like Madge had fallen on hard times since then.

When she saw Rory, her face brightened and she came across to him.

He felt sorry for the poor old bitch, so he bought her a glass of gin.

She gulped a mouthful down and sighed in pleasure. 'Thanks. I needed that.'

Which only made him glad he'd stopped drinking heavily. Look where it could lead you. She looked worse every time he saw her. *He* wasn't going to fall into the booze trap. If Bram Deagan could make a pile of money, then so could he.

When she'd finished the gin, she eyed him sideways. 'You don't like the Deagans, do you, Rory?'

'I do not.'

'Maybe you'd like to upset them and make some easy money at the same time?'

'I might. Depends what'd need doing.'

She glanced over her shoulder. 'Not in here. Come outside and I'll tell you about it.'

★ ★ ★

Hugh couldn't settle to anything. He kept walking to the front door to stare up and down the street, then walking back to the kitchen, shaking his head in response to Maura's unspoken question.

He'd brought his daughter to Australia to save her life and he blamed himself most bitterly for letting Adèle out of his sight so soon after their arrival, before she knew her way round Fremantle. She wasn't used to towns, having grown up in a village. Just thinking of the trouble she might be in made his blood run cold.

'I think I'll go and walk round the streets again,' he said. 'At least I'm now very familiar with the centre of town and I can't see why she'd go further out.'

Maura stood up. 'I'll come with you. Two pairs of eyes are better than one.'

Bram also stood up. 'I'll search a little further out of town. But first I'll go and tell Dougal and my sister Ismay. They can keep their eyes open for her, as well.'

'I wish I could help, sir,' Sally said. 'It's so dreadful to be able to do nothing.' Her eyes went to Arlen and Louisa, sitting on either side of Noreen, who was pretending to read them a story, but making it up as she went along. Brenna was sitting by the window on her own. She'd been crying.

'You're needed here to look after the other children.'

Outside, Bram said, 'I'll go this way, to the east. Once you've done another check of the town centre, go in a southerly direction if you

411

want to search further out. We don't want to both go over the same ground.' He strode off down the street.

Hugh offered Maura his arm and she took it immediately, hugging it closely to her in a gesture of comfort. They were together again, he thought, worrying and working together as if they were already married. He shouldn't be thinking of that, should be concentrating on his daughter, but it felt so comforting to have Maura's arm in his.

'Adèle will turn up, I'm sure she will,' she said. 'She must have got lost and walked further than she realised.'

A dreadful thought struck him. 'Perhaps she went down to the harbour and fell into the water?'

'Someone would have seen her. Bram will have told Dougal now and he'll keep an eye on the harbour. It's not very big, after all.'

They walked for a while, not quickly because they wanted to check every garden and alley they passed. But still, there was no sign of Adèle.

When they reached a church, she said quietly, 'It wouldn't hurt to pop inside and say a quick prayer.'

★ ★ ★

Rory went outside the boozer with Madge. 'What did you want to tell me?'

'I might know where that little girl is. The thing is, I'd want to be paid to tell her family.'

He stared at her in shock, then disgust filled

412

him. She'd got the child. He knew it as surely as he knew his own name.

He was no saint and never wanted to be either, but he drew the line at ill-treating a child to get back at a grown-up. By hell he did!

Madge stepped back. 'Don't you look at me like that. If you're too fussy to help me, I'll find someone else.'

As she tried to walk away, he managed a soft laugh and pulled her back. 'I was just surprised, that's all.'

She looked at him suspiciously, then tossed her lank hair back, the sort of gesture that looked right on a pretty young woman but not on a scrawny, raddled older one, whose unwashed body made his nose wrinkle in disgust.

'You'll need to do this carefully, Madge, or they'll put you in prison.'

She nodded. 'I know. I need a letter writ, then they won't see who's got her. I'm not good with the writing, though, and I want it writ proper.'

Rory was better educated than he used to be, thanks to lessons on the ship coming out. And he'd kept improving his reading with the newspaper. 'I write a fair hand.'

'We need some paper and ink. We'll have to buy some.'

Again he pulled her back. 'Hold on a minute. First you need to prove to me that you've got the child. And then we need to make an agreement. Half and half would be fair.'

She screeched loudly. 'That's not right. I found her and I thought of this, so I should get most.'

'You don't get anything if I don't help you, and I won't do that till I've seen the child. She might be dead, for all I know. I'm not getting involved in murder, not for you or anyone.'

'She ain't dead.'

'Prove it.'

He bought her a bottle of gin to put her in a good mood and walked with her to the squalid room she lived in, wrinkling his nose at the filth and stink of the alley.

Inside the room, a little girl was tied to a chair, her face white and tear-stained. She seemed to be struggling for breath, poor thing. He pulled the rag out of her mouth, whispering, 'I'll get you away from her.'

He turned back to Madge, who was pouring gin into a dirty cup. 'I'll just untie her and let her move about a bit.'

She slammed the bottle and cup down and rushed across the room. 'Don't you loose her. I'm not havin' her run away.'

'You've tied her up too tight. There's no need for that.'

Madge went back to take a big gulp of gin. 'We have to keep her safe till we get the money.'

He tried to undo the knots but they were far too tight. Annoyed, he took out his pocket knife and slashed the rags tying the child to the chair.

Madge shrieked and tried to stop him, flailing around like a madwoman, but missing him most of the time.

'Get behind me,' he said to the child. 'She's out of her mind with the booze. We'll move slowly towards the door and then we'll take you back to your family.' And wouldn't he rub Bram's nose in it? You and your fancy friends can't even look after a child, he'd say.

He opened the door, smiling. 'Come on.'

She rushed to cling to his hand.

That reminded him of his little sister again.

★ ★ ★

Bram walked round the streets on the eastern side of town, feeling dreadful about little Adèle. He'd racked his brains and couldn't think where to look next.

Surely no one had taken her out of town? Why would they?

He detoured into a slum area, disgusted by the filth and smells, but determined to look everywhere. The town council ought to do something about this area, though, they really ought.

Though he looked everywhere he could think of, he found no sign of the child. And though he kept asking everyone he met if they'd seen her, no one had.

Dear God, what must Hugh be feeling?

He turned a corner and saw Rory Flynn disappearing down an alley with a woman Bram knew by sight. On the streets, she was, and selling her body to those who couldn't afford a younger woman. She looked ill and worn. He'd seen her drunk more often than sober.

He paused at the end of the alley, wondering what Rory was doing there. Suddenly, he heard a screeching and yelling from the back of the building. He hesitated. Not his business if that fellow ill-treated women.

A door banged open and Rory stumbled out of it with a little girl behind him. He was trying to fend off the woman, who was howling and hitting out at him.

The child had red-gold hair. It was Adèle!

Bram started down the alley and as he got to the end, Rory saw him and thrust the child into his arms. 'Get her away while I deal with this stupid bitch!' He grabbed the woman who was now trying to claw his face and threw her back into the room, yelling, 'Don't you ever touch a child again.'

Bram gaped at him, but before there could be any explanations, he had to calm the little girl, who was sobbing uncontrollably against him. He fumbled for his handkerchief, but Adèle was clinging so tightly to him, he couldn't get it out.

'Here.' Rory took out a handkerchief, clean but crumpled, and thrust it into Adèle's hand.

'Let's sit down for a minute,' Bram said. 'Shh now. Shh, Adèle. You're all right.'

They both perched on a nearby wall as he rocked and soothed the child.

'What happened, darling?' Bram asked her, still a bit suspicious of Rory's involvement.

'A horrible woman. She took me home. Tied me up.' More sobs, then, 'I couldn't breathe properly. This kind man came and untied me.'

Kind man! Rory. As kind as a mad bull, that one.

Rory looked at Bram. 'I'd never hurt a child.'

Bram suddenly stuck out his hand. 'Then I thank you.'

Rory looked at the hand, shrugged and shook it.

Bram turned back to the little girl. 'Are you all right to go home now, Adèle? I can't carry you that far, you're too big for me, but — '

'I'll carry her. She's only a little 'un.' Rory held out his arms and she went to him gladly.

The world was turning upside down on him, Bram thought. His greatest enemy had turned into a hero.

For the second time, dammit. Rory had saved them from an attack at Ismay and Adam's wedding celebration. He'd been as surprised to be a hero then as Bram had to see him do the right thing.

* * *

Even before they got to Bram's house, there was a yell and Hugh came pounding along the street towards them, with Maura running behind him.

'Daddy!' yelled Adèle.

Hugh took her from Rory, smothering her face with kisses. 'Are you all right? No one's hurt you? Where have you *been?*'

'Let's go into the house before we explain.' Bram turned to Rory, who was looking as if he didn't know whether to stay or go. 'You'll come with us and tell your tale over a cup of tea?'

'I will. Afterwards, we need to do something about that Madge. She's lost her wits with the booze. We don't want her kidnapping other children.'

Bram turned to Maura. 'Are you all right?'

417

'I am.' She looked at Hugh who was murmuring to his daughter.

She listened to the explanations, then studied Adèle. The child was filthy. 'I think before we do much more, we'd better give her a bath. She might have picked up lice or something in that place.'

'We'll bath her in the washhouse at the back,' Sally said. 'The water's still warm from this morning.'

'Can you children go and play in the garden?' Maura asked. 'I think the men need to talk.'

Ryan looked mutinous, but she gave him one of her stern looks.

Maura relented. 'You can take Adèle up to your bedroom and talk once she's had her bath.' She followed Sally into the washhouse.

'I'll make us all a cup of tea,' Bram said.

Rory was still looking as if he didn't know whether to stay or not.

'You're included in that, Rory.' Bram grimaced. 'Damned if I expected to be grateful to you *again*.'

'Damned if I expected to be helping you again. But I won't say no to a cup of tea.'

When Rory had drunk the tea and eaten a huge slice of cake, he took his leave.

'Not a friend of yours?' Hugh asked.

'Definitely not. But this is the second time he's stepped in to help the family, so you have to give the devil his due. He saved your daughter today.'

From the washhouse came the sound of a child laughing and Hugh found tears welling in his eyes.

'Here.' Bram thrust a pot towel at him and went to look out of the window till his companion had calmed down.

After her bath, Adèle kissed her father then went upstairs with the other children.

'I ought to take her home,' Hugh said.

'Let her play for a while,' Bram said. 'It'll make everything feel normal again.'

When Ryan came down to say Adèle had fallen asleep in Brenna's bed, Bram said at once. 'Then you must both stay here tonight, Beaufort.'

As he hesitated, Maura added, 'I think Bram's right: what that child needs is time with other children — some normal, happy time.'

'I'll go back and fetch some clothes for us both, then. A sofa or anywhere will do for me, Deagan.'

'How about a mattress on the floor in one of the spare bedrooms?'

'Luxury.'

As he stood up, Maura followed suit. 'I'll walk back with you, Hugh. We need to talk.'

Behind her, Bram sighed sentimentally at the loving look Hugh gave her.

22

Again, Hugh offered her his arm, but this time Maura shook her head. 'Let's walk briskly and wait till we get back to your house to talk.'

'Very well.'

They walked across town in silence, striding out, stopping a couple of times to answer queries about the little girl from complete strangers they must have spoken to during their search.

Just before they got to Captain McBride's house, she reached out to Hugh. 'Can we go somewhere private? I don't want to be interrupted.'

'There's a small room with a very poor piano in it. I'll ask Dougal if we can use that to be private.'

When they were settled, he leaned back and studied her face. 'What do you want to talk about?'

'Us.'

'Why prolong the pain? There is no 'us', can't be.'

'I thought that at first, but now I don't agree.'

'I won't ruin your life by making you my mistress.'

'If it's the only way to be together, I'll do that willingly. Before we go any further, do you love me, Hugh?'

'Of course I do. You know that.'

'And do you truly wish to marry me?'

'I can't think of anything I'd like better.'

She gathered her courage together and said baldly, 'Then we should get married.'

He stiffened. 'It'd be bigamy.'

'No one need know that but us.'

'Maura, no! I think more of you than that.'

'Do you? Or are you worried about being caught out and sent to prison?'

He shook his head slowly. 'I'm not worried about me; it's you I'm concerned about.'

'Then think about it logically.' She moved to sit next to him on the sofa and took his hand. His fingers twisted to clasp hers tightly, and oh, it felt so right. That gave her the strength to continue. She raised his hand to her lips. 'Sylvie has provided proof to her family that she's dead. As far as people here are concerned, a couple you met in Galle, whom you knew slightly, told you that your wife was dead. They provided you with a witnessed declaration of that, which you believed, since they swore on the captain's Bible that it was true.'

'But you and I know differently.'

'Who's to tell anyone that?'

He spoke slowly, still sounding doubtful. 'I doubt I'd be able to find Sylvie and Jacques again, even if I wanted to. They'll do their best to stay hidden.'

'If you have no way of proving she's still alive, neither will anyone else. Even her family believes her dead.'

'But *we* still know she's alive.'

'We can ignore it. Hugh, it would be stupid to blight our whole lives because of Sylvie. You

421

can't divorce her because people think she's dead, so this is the only way we can be together.'

He sighed. 'You shouldn't tempt me.'

'I've not finished. This isn't just for us. I've always believed you shouldn't tell lies and that's what I've tried to show the children, but in this instance, there's far more at stake than just our happiness. There are the children to think of as well. Their happiness is so important. Adèle ran away today rather than be separated from the others. She was rescued, but it might have turned out badly.'

He shuddered.

Maura gave him a brief smile. 'Or do you not want to be father to four children?'

'I'd love to be their father. You know I would.'

'I've lain awake and prayed for guidance, and I can't feel it'd be morally wrong for us to marry, given the circumstances. Four children would also benefit.'

He was staring at her with a strange intensity, so she played her final card. 'I've experienced one unhappy marriage. I could never make another match like that. I didn't even realise it was possible to love someone as much as I love you, Hugh. So if you won't marry me, you'll be condemning me to a life of spinsterhood, helping out with Bram's children, on the fringes of a real family life.' She felt a sudden surge of emotion. 'Hugh, I don't want that. I want to have you *and* the children. I want a normal family life. Children of my own.'

'Oh, my darling!' He pulled her into his arms

and cuddled her very close. 'My very precious darling.'

For a while they stood pressed against one another. Then he held her at arm's length and gazed into her eyes. 'Are you sure?'

'I'm very sure.'

His kiss was so tender, so loving she began to weep.

'What is it?'

'I'm so very happy.'

His smile was radiant. 'Strange way to show it.'

She reached out to brush away a tear from his cheek. 'You're showing it the same way. I'm not . . . pushing you too hard to do this?'

'No, my darling. You're giving me the greatest gift a woman could. Yourself. Let us decide now and for all time that we shall consider ourselves truly married, whatever the law says.'

It was only when the mantelpiece clock chimed that Maura realised they'd been sitting there for over an hour.

She pulled him to his feet. 'Then let's get the clothes you need for tonight and go and tell the children. We'll wake them up, if necessary.' She kissed his cheek. 'Don't worry, for I shan't. We'll be happy together.'

'You deserve better.'

★ ★ ★

As they went out into the hall, Dougal came out of the sitting room. 'Oh, there you are. I forgot to tell you earlier. I picked up my mail today and

423

there's a letter for you, Hugh, care of me in Fremantle — amazing that it got to me. You have to give the P&O one thing: they are very efficient at getting the mail through.'

He held the letter out, then pulled out his pocket watch. 'Please excuse me. I have to meet someone.'

Hugh started to put the letter in his pocket, then stared at the envelope. 'This handwriting . . . It looks French.'

'Open it, then.'

He tore it open, letting the pieces of envelope fall to the floor. The letter was two pages long and though he scanned the beginning quickly, it took a while for him to read it all.

Maura could only stand there, controlling her impatience as he kept exclaiming in shock.

When he'd finished, he passed it to her. 'It's from Jacques Durand. Read it.'

She pulled a wry face. 'It's in French.'

'Oh, sorry. I'm not thinking straight. I'm so . . . shocked.'

He took a minute to calm down then started to explain. 'Jacques says Sylvie doesn't know he's writing. He's doing it because he doesn't want to ruin my life. He says — I can't believe this — they were married ten years ago, secretly and against their families' wishes. This was to ensure she couldn't be forced to marry anyone else while he was away.'

She was shocked too. 'So Sylvie committed bigamy.'

'Yes, but actually unknowingly. She believed herself widowed. After their marriage, Jacques left to make his fortune in Algeria, which is a French colony. She was to wait for him to return and then they planned to tell their families they had married. But she received news almost immediately that he'd been killed. It wasn't true. It was a mistake. It was another Frenchman who was killed in Algeria. But meanwhile she thought she was pregnant and that her family would never accept her as a widow, so when I asked her to marry me, she said yes, to escape shame, for the child's sake and because I had plenty of money.'

He shook his head, thinking it all through. 'Typical of Sylvie, that. She insists on living in comfort. She found out she wasn't pregnant, and Adèle was born much later, so she is definitely my child.'

'There's no doubting it. She looks like you.'

'Anyway, it turns out that Jacques wasn't dead, but it was a while before he came back and Sylvie's family destroyed all his letters. He found she'd married me and why in spite of that.'

'So she was never your wife?'

'No.' Hugh's smile was radiant. 'Anyway, to finish the tale, when Jacques let her know he was still alive and had made his fortune, she decided to go to him — her real husband and the man she loved. But she didn't want me to know we weren't married, for Adèle's sake, as the child would be considered a bastard. She did at least care that much for her daughter.'

'And she didn't tell you the truth in Galle for the same reason.'

'Yes. But Jacques thinks that unfair and I

425

should know I'm truly free.' Hugh's eyes were bright as he pulled Maura into his arms. 'I can't believe it. I really can marry you.'

She sighed and nestled against him. 'I would have considered myself married to you anyway.'

'I know, and I'll always be grateful for your trust in me. But this way is far better. Let's go and tell them all.'

'Just a minute. What about Adèle? I can't bear her to be scorned as bastard born.'

Hugh sighed. 'I know.' They both stood thinking, then he asked quietly, 'Do you think . . . would it matter if I told a lie about her mother?'

Maura finished for him. 'You could say her mother is dead, not that you were never married.'

'Yes.' He waved the letter. 'And I have the document to prove it, only I'll pretend it came in the letter and I'll say that's why we can now be married.'

'I think it's the right thing to do morally. It may be a lie, but it's one which won't hurt anyone and we're not trying to profit from it. I couldn't bear to ruin that child's life. You know how cruel people can be about people who're not born within wedlock.'

There was silence, then he took her hand and raised it to his lips. 'You're a wonderful woman.'

'I love Adèle.'

'And she loves you. As I do, so very deeply, my darling. I really am the happiest man on earth today.'

'I'm happy too.' She sobbed and fumbled for

426

her handkerchief, failing to find it.

He passed her his. 'Then why are you crying?'

'Because I'm so very happy.'

'Women!' But it was said fondly.

★ ★ ★

When they got back to Bram's house, the children were in bed. Bram and Isabella were sitting together.

'Now, what's made you look so happy, Maura?' Bram wondered aloud.

She looked at Hugh, waiting for him to give them the news.

'Your aunt has just done me the honour of agreeing to become my wife.'

There was silence, then Bram let out a yell of delight, jumped up and waltzed his aunt round the room. 'And about time, too. I don't know what's been stopping you.'

'I had a wife. Or I thought I did. Only I've just heard she died. A letter was waiting for me care of Dougal.'

'I don't like to be happy about someone dying, but I never knew the woman and I do care about my dear aunt's happiness.' Bram gave Maura a smacking kiss on the cheek and Isabella came to hug her too.

'We want to tell the children,' Maura said.

Isabella looked at her in surprise. 'They're asleep.'

'Then we'll wake them,' Hugh said. 'They've been nagging us to marry for a while now, but we didn't think we could. They're desperate for us all to live together, you see.'

'Oh.' Maura looked at her nephew. 'Maybe you feel your brother and sister should live with you, Bram?'

He spread his arms wide. 'If you two are married, I'm happy for you to have them. After all, you've been mothering them for months now, and your loving care shows. They love you, Maura, and as long as they're happy, I'll be happy. But I want to see them very often so make sure you live nearby.'

'You're right. I love them dearly, all of them.'

'So do I,' Hugh said. 'We've become a family.'

Hand in hand, he and Maura led the way upstairs, where they found Ryan still awake.

'Get up and help us wake the others! We have something exciting to tell you all,' Maura said.

'Don't look so worried. It's something good,' Hugh added.

Ryan looked at their joined hands and a smile crept across his face. 'Is it — '

'Shh! We want to tell you together.'

They went into the girls' room, leaving Bram and Isabella standing in the doorway.

When all four children were awake, Hugh put his arm round Maura's shoulders. 'Children, we've taken your advice. We've decided to get married.'

'But only on condition you all live with us,' Maura said.

There was a yell of joy from Brenna, a cry of triumph from Ryan and Adèle burst into tears.

'Darling, what's wrong?' Hugh asked, kneeling beside the bed she was sharing with Brenna.

428

'There's nothing wrong. I'm just . . . happy.'

He chuckled. 'Well, it's a good thing Maura is going to be your mother, then, because she'll understand perfectly if you cry when you're happy. She just did the same thing exactly.'

Epilogue

Bram was up early, even before the maid. It was going to be such a special day, he couldn't bear to lie in bed, wanted to enjoy every single second of it. He whistled softly as he got the stove going and pushed the kettle over the heat.

Hearing a noise, he turned round, to see his brother Ryan standing in the doorway, stretching and yawning. For a moment they stared at one another. Bram was still treading carefully with his brother and sister, knowing it would take time to build up any real closeness. 'You're up early.'

'It's my favourite time of day.'

'Mine, too. Come and sit down. We'll wait for the kettle to boil and share a cup of tea.'

Ryan nodded, coming across to sit beside him at the kitchen table. 'It'll feel strange not to live here.'

'You're not moving for a few days yet. We have to give the newly-weds time to get used to living together.'

Ryan nodded. A peacefully happy expression settled on his face, something that was happening more often these days, as he stopped worrying about whether his new life would continue to go well.

'I'm hoping you'll come back to visit us whenever you want. You must always think of this as your second home.'

'Sometimes I can't believe it.'

'I know exactly what you mean. We Deagans are lucky to have found a life as good as this.'

'Auntie Maura says it's hard work that does it, not luck.'

'She's a one for hard work. I never saw anyone get as much done during a day. But you need a bit of luck too, I'm thinking.' He was hoping his luck would hold and Chilton would finish the bigger ice-making machinery now he had the new parts, so that it could make money for Bram, not drain it out of him.

He pushed that thought aside. Today was his aunt's wedding day, a time for happy thoughts and hopes. 'Are you looking forward to living with Hugh and Adèle?'

The lad considered it for a moment, head on one side. 'I think so. Most of all, I'm looking forward to leaving school and coming to work in the Bazaar with you.'

'I'm looking forward to that too. But we have an agreement. You'll get yourself some education first.'

Ryan sighed. 'I know. And I'll keep my promise. I'll always keep my promises. But I don't like sitting still all day.'

Bram didn't smile. Ryan wasn't even sitting still now. He'd got up a couple of times, to put another piece of wood on the fire, or to stare out of the window. A proper fidget, his little brother.

Hearing a sound on the stairs, Bram turned round to watch his wife come in, her glorious hair cascading over her shoulders. Soon, one by one, the others joined them.

431

Maura was looking serenely happy.

'Didn't you want to have a lie-in?' he asked her. 'It *is* your wedding day, after all.'

She shook her head. 'Why would I stay in bed on a lovely morning like this?'

They'd had a little chat the night before. She wasn't worried about this marriage, and Bram wasn't, either, or he'd have spoken out. No, Hugh was a lovely fellow, who adored Maura. To hear the two of them sing a duet together was a real treat.

They all shared a cup of tea, sitting peacefully around the table. *His family*, whether they were Deagans or not.

Tears rose in his eyes, but men didn't cry, so he blew his nose hard.

Isabella smiled at him from across the table. She knew how emotional he was feeling. When he looked, Maura had the same understanding expression on her face.

Noreen, sitting beside him, patted his arm. Ryan grinned at him from across the table, and the other children were smiling at him as well. Ach, how could a man hide his feelings from his family? And why should he have to?

In a few minutes it'd be all rush and bustle to get ready for the wedding, but he could sit and enjoy the moment for a little longer.

Oh, dear. The tears were rising again. He was so very happy. One of his dreams had come true. An important dream. Not in the way he'd expected, but still, they were here, weren't they? His family, come to join him in Australia.

What more could a man ask than that?

Books by Anna Jacobs
Published by Ulverscroft:

FAMILY CONNECTIONS
KIRSTY'S VINEYARD
CHESTNUT LANE
SAVING WILLOWBROOK
FREEDOM'S LAND
IN FOCUS

GREYLADIES:
HEIR TO GREYLADIES

LADY BINGRAM'S AIDES:
TOMORROW'S PROMISES
YESTERDAY'S GIRL

THE KERSHAW SISTERS:
OUR LIZZIE
OUR POLLY
OUR EVA

THE MUSIC HALL
PRIDE OF LANCASHIRE
STAR OF THE NORTH
BRIGHT DAY DAWNING
HEART OF THE TOWN

THE STALEY FAMILY
CALICO ROAD

We do hope that you have enjoyed reading this large print book.

Did you know that all of our titles are available for purchase?

We publish a wide range of high quality large print books including:
Romances, Mysteries, Classics General Fiction Non Fiction and Westerns

Special interest titles available in large print are:
The Little Oxford Dictionary Music Book Song Book Hymn Book Service Book

Also available from us courtesy of Oxford University Press:
Young Readers' Dictionary (large print edition) Young Readers' Thesaurus (large print edition)

For further information or a free brochure, please contact us at:
Ulverscroft Large Print Books Ltd., The Green, Bradgate Road, Anstey, Leicester, LE7 7FU, England. Tel: (00 44) 0116 236 4325
Fax: (00 44) 0116 234 0205

Other titles published by Ulverscroft:

THE TRADER'S WIFE

Anna Jacobs

1865. Singapore is exotic and yet terrifying for a penniless Englishwoman, alone and vulnerable after her mother's death. Too pretty to obtain a governess's job, Isabella Saunders accepts an offer from Singapore merchant Mr Lee — to teach him English and live with his family. Two years later Bram Deagan arrives in Singapore, determined to make his fortune as a trader. Mr Lee, wanting to expand his business connections, persuades Isabella to marry Bram. She sets sail for a new land and life. But the past casts a long shadow and she and Bram face unexpected dangers. Can they achieve their dreams of a successful trading business? And will their marriage turn out to be more of a love match than they could have ever dreamed?

THE TRADER'S SISTER

Anna Jacobs

Ismay Deagan wants to leave Ireland and join her brother, Bram, in Australia. However, her father wants her to marry their vicious neighbour, the loathsome Rory Flynn. But after Rory brutally attacks her, Ismay realises she must escape. And, disguised as an impoverished young widow, she sets sail for Australia, hoping to be reunited with her brother. When she meets Adam Treagar on the ship, she believes her dreams of future happiness may come true. But before reaching their destination they are flung into adventures in Suez, Ceylon and Singapore . . . Can Ismay tell Adam the truth about who she really is? What secrets does Adam hide? And will Ismay's past catch up with her and threaten her new life in Australia, before it's even begun?

HEIR TO GREYLADIES

Anna Jacobs

1900: The death of her father forces Harriet out of her home to escape the advances of her stepbrother and the rule of her stepmother, and into service at Dalton House. Over time, Harriet develops a friendship with the Daltons' crippled son Joseph — but her life is changed completely when she inherits Greyladies, an old and possibly haunted house. Greyladies could be the answer to Harriet's dreams; but will it be enough to protect her from her family — and can she forge a new life?